PRAISE FOR ELLEN J. GREEN
TWIST OF FAITH

"This well-crafted tale builds to an unexpected, chilling ending."

—*Publishers Weekly*

"There are so many twists and surprises . . . The plot is great as well as the depth of the characters."

—Tulsa Book Review

"A steady build of intrigue and tension shrouded in a dark mystery that began decades before."

—Novelgossip

D1248378

ABSOLUTION

ALSO BY ELLEN J. GREEN

Twist of Faith

The Book of James

ABSOLUTION

ELLEN J. GREEN

 THOMAS & MERCER

Text copyright © 2019 by Ellen J. Green
All rights reserved.

Published by Thomas & Mercer, Seattle

www.apub.com

Amazon, the Amazon logo, and Thomas & Mercer are trademarks of Amazon.com, Inc., or its affiliates.

ISBN-13: 9781503904125
ISBN-10: 1503904121

Cover design by Rex Bonomelli

Printed in the United States of America

For my grandmother, Emily Heal

PROLOGUE

The water was warm, lapping against her shoulders as she struggled for balance on the shifting sand. She scanned the shore, looking for signs of life. Nothing. She'd been careful before coming here. A deliberately chosen spot on a deserted beach. It had taken weeks of planning, finding this place. Quiet, empty. Only the occasional fisherman popping up to cast a rod. She'd waited until the sun set, then moved steadily toward the water, wearing an abaya stolen from a woman at a nearby refugee camp. Made of black polyester, it was modest, cascading, forgiving. And with the cloth draped just right, she was sure no one had seen the skeletal remains she'd dragged behind her to the water's edge.

Now she dipped beneath the waves, naked, waiting and watching. Leaving the scene was even more important, because she knew the skeleton would be found in the days to come and an investigation would begin. She'd pulled the remains as far from the coast as she could manage, until her arms ached and water filled her nose and mouth. The bones—no skin, no hair, no nails, no teeth—seemed to glow in the moonlight. She treaded water, watching them float for a distance and then sink. Had she swum far enough for the remains to drift to Turkey? That was what she needed. An investigation of bones washing up on a Turkish shore would complicate things enough for her to get away.

The girl—well, young woman, really—had been sized up, stalked, watched for months before she'd been sacrificed. Her death had been quick. The throat slashed just deep enough so there was no struggle, but not so deep that it marred the bones beneath. Everything had to be right. And that took preparation and planning. It was difficult and painstaking to extract reliable DNA from bones, especially if some were missing. Thus the soaking of the body, the removal of hair, skin, organs, even fingernails. Only a skeleton could remain. The dead girl had floated in the tub in a dank apartment for months. Reeking. And rotting until the flesh bloated and separated from the muscle beneath. Perfect for carving.

The dead girl had been exactly twenty-three, dark hair, fair skin. Five five. Thin. Their similarities were remarkable. Same height, same weight. Same healed broken thighbone—that had been fortunate. After searching for the perfect victim for months, she'd stumbled upon this simple Greek girl in the market. Ava had heard her chattering that her thighbone always hurt when it was going to rain because she'd broken it in a fall when she was twelve. She was rubbing her left leg as she spoke. A perfect match to Ava's own broken bone from a fall off a swing set when she was a child. The only discernible difference between them was that the dead girl's eyes had been brown, but it didn't matter. No one would see them when she'd finished preparing the body.

Now the worst of the deed was done. The last part was inconspicuously getting from the water back to the clothes she'd left near a rock on the shore. She dipped down in the water again, realizing her nakedness was a problem. She gauged the distance from the edge of the water to the rock to be about fifty feet. The blackness, the absolute lack of light, save from what shone down from the heavens, was a comfort.

"Ti einai afto?" A young male voice came through the darkness. Greek. The best she could put together from the fragments was *What is it?*

"Kapoios einai ekei exo," came the reply. Another male. She sank farther down into the water so that only her eyes were exposed. She saw the people's outlines in the distance. Looking across the water. *Someone is out there,* he'd replied. They had a dog. She knew this only because it began to whimper and bark.

"Shit," she muttered, just above a whisper. "Go away. You're ruining everything." They were just boys. Not more than ten.

"Mia gynaika," one said.

A woman. He'd seen her well enough to know it was a woman bouncing in the waves not even fifty feet from where they stood.

"Mia gorgona," the other replied. He began to throw stones into the water. *"As tin piasoume."* She didn't know the word *gorgona.* But the last part was that these two boys were going to try and catch her. She turned and considered her options. There were none. Not unless she was willing to swim out into open ocean. And then what?

The boys were still there. *"Thelo na tin piaso kai na kopso tin oura tis."*

They were going to catch her and cut off her tail. *Gorgona* must be the word for *mermaid.* They thought she was a mermaid.

In one swift, fury-filled motion she pushed upward from the waves and walked toward them, water dripping from her limbs. Her nakedness there for them to see. She kept walking, aware of the balmy air, the droplets clinging to her breasts and thighs. She went right to where they stood, unmoving, staring. The dog bounced around their feet, growling.

She put her fingertip to her lips. "Shhh. You never saw this." Her Greek was quick and precise. "My name is Thalassa." She knew it was the Greek word for *sea.* But it was also the name of an ancient sea goddess. "Find me some clothes. Over there." She pointed.

Their eyes were large as they retrieved her abaya. She flung it over her head.

"Enas Mousoulmanos?" the smaller one ventured. *A Muslim?* "You're not a goddess. Just a naked lady swimming in the ocean."

"Is that true? Are you sure?" she asked. "Because if you tell anyone you saw me, your family may disappear one day." She leaned in to face them. "Dead. And when that happens, you will remember me. Thalassa."

Ava walked away without looking back. If they spoke of seeing her, no one would connect it with the body that would wash ashore in another country in the days to come. She was fairly certain of that. And she had more-important things to worry about. Settling the score with her family—her grandmother, Anais Lavoisier; and her aunt, Marie— was at the top of that list.

CHAPTER 1

MARIE

Marie opened her eyes to complete darkness. She knew without moving that her wrists were tied down to her sides, the leather cuffs digging into tender skin with every slight shift of her body. Straps attached her ankles to the bed frame, pulling her legs apart so that she couldn't bend her knees. The panic was starting again, like a rising tide, consuming her. She tried to sit up, yanking her arms and pulling her legs until she gave up and lay still, feeling hot tears roll onto her face. She had been in this bed for almost two days—the waxing and waning of light through the window giving a cadence to her misery.

She turned her head toward the white tiled wall and tried to ignore the fact that he was somewhere in the room. She could smell him—the unmistakable stench of cologne and aftershave that clung to his skin and announced his presence. She wondered how long he'd been there, watching her pull on the ropes that held her in place.

He stepped out of the shadows.

"Marie. I'm glad to see you're awake."

She closed her eyes and shook her head. But she felt movement near her and knew that soon his hands would be on her. She had no control over her body, who touched her, who moved her. The woman with the brown hair would be with him, behind him, watching quietly and following orders.

He touched the cuffs around her wrists, checking the skin underneath. "Bandage her arms. The skin is broken again," he said to the woman. "Can you tell me what happened last night?" He was talking to Marie.

She opened her eyes and looked down long enough to see the smattering of blond hairs protruding from the edge of his shirtsleeve, the veins on the hand, the thick fingers with short, manicured nails.

"We have to talk about this, Marie, before I can let you up. You know that." He pushed her gown up, oblivious to the fact that she was naked beneath, and pointed to the cuts that crisscrossed her thighs. Most were superficial, barely breaking through the layers of skin, but two were deep, now covered in bandages. "You needed stitches this time." He pushed the gown up farther, exposing her abdomen. "At least you left your stomach alone. You were doing so well, Marie. What happened?" He covered her with the blanket and took a seat near her bed. He nodded at the woman and she left the room.

Silence.

"You've been sleeping for several hours. Do you need to use the toilet? Are you hungry?"

She nodded. Tears wet both sides of her face, but she couldn't wipe them away.

"I know we keep going over this, but you've been less than cooperative, and I want to make sure you're still grounded in reality, so humor me and answer my questions again?" He leaned in, and the smell of his Armani cologne hit her nostrils full force. "Tell me your full name and age."

"Marie Lavoisier-Saunders. Fifteen," she whispered.

"Good. Do you know what this place is? Where you are?"

"Clinic. Switzerland. Very expensive clinic. Anais should have saved her money."

He cleared his throat. "Do you know who the president is?"

"The president of where? Switzerland? The United States? Please let me up now. Tell my mother I'm sorry. I don't want to stay here. I'm sorry."

He leaned over her. The thick, unruly eyebrows dominated his face. "Your mother will be back this afternoon. I called to tell her about this latest setback. Hiding the razor in your mouth. Why? The nurse said you had a good visit with your family yesterday." His voice was patient, calm, but filled with disappointment. "Marie. I want to understand."

She stared at the ceiling, looking for something to distract her from this conversation. But it was plain white, no cracks, no lines. "My mother isn't what you think she is. No one seems to understand that." She didn't want to talk about what had happened during that family meeting, how Anais had teased and taunted her. Called her pathetic. A whore. Ugly. Stupid. And then said she was never going to take her home, never going to sign the papers so she could be released. Marie had tolerated it for as long as she could before pushing away from the table and running back to her room. Then she'd dropped to the floor and carved up her legs, creating lines that went from her knees all the way up her thighs.

He stood. "Well, then, tell me what she is. You were looking forward to this family visit with your mother and sister. We talked about it at length during your last session." He was so close to her, she pushed down into the bed to put distance between them. "What happened with your mother? Why are you so angry with her that you're taking it out on your body? With a razor blade?"

She said nothing. This bushy-haired man didn't really care about her relationship with Anais. He didn't care about who Marie's mother was, her lies. About the games of pretend. He only cared about marking his chart and moving on to the next room.

"If I don't understand why you cut yourself last night, I can't let you up. You'll need to stay in restraints. I'll be back in an hour; maybe you'll feel more like talking then." He hesitated, then stood. "The nurse'll be back to bandage your arms and let you use the toilet." The door shut behind him, taking the light with it.

She started to sit up. "No. I'm sorry. I'll talk. I'll talk." But he was gone and the room was dark again, save for the sliver of light through the crack at the bottom of the door. She felt the sobs starting in her chest, the heaviness working its way through her body causing her teeth to clench, tears to stream down her face. There was ringing in her ears. Fogginess—

Marie jerked up in bed, sweat covering her forehead and neck. She rubbed her arms without thinking, to make sure it had been a dream. The same one now three times in a row. Ever since she'd gotten the news that Anais had died, this memory from years before, when she'd been confined to a psychiatric hospital in Switzerland, had plagued her sleep. Each dream filled with details she'd forgotten.

The phone on the bedside table was ringing. She rubbed her head and looked at the clock. It was almost four in the afternoon. She had to pull herself together, stop this constant napping.

She gave her brain a minute to leave the dream behind before grabbing the receiver. "Hello?"

"Marie? It's Sandrine. I'm so glad I finally got you. I've been calling all day. Do you have flight arrangements yet?"

Sandrine had been a fixture in her mother's life since the day they moved to Cherbourg. She lived three houses down and had saved Anais's life the night she had her stroke. Now she was here for her death.

"I just received final approval from the courts. I couldn't leave the country without permission. My flight is tomorrow morning." Marie swung her legs over the side of the bed and sat up.

"Keeping you in New Jersey for the past year and a half should be punishment enough for any crime, I'd think." Sandrine chuckled.

She was going to start digging again. Trying to get Marie to discuss her crimes, her incarceration, her parole. Next she'd be asking about her cellmates.

"New Jersey is lovely this time of year," Marie said. "Is everything set for the funeral? Just the way Anais would have wanted it?"

"Yes, yes. I took care of everything. She was cremated, as per her instructions, and her remains are going into the plot next to your sister, as planned." Sandrine hesitated. "Are you okay, Marie? You've lost so much over the past year. Your sister, now Anais. Not to mention Ava—"

"Let's not talk about Ava. If everything goes as planned, I'm flying into Paris tomorrow and renting a car for the drive to Cherbourg. If anything changes, I'll call you." Marie hung up before Sandrine could respond.

Ava. Ava Saunders, the little girl who'd joined their family at the tender age of three. A terrible tragedy had left her motherless, and so she spent the remainder of her childhood with Claire. The girl with the dark hair and innocent green eyes grew up and went on a rampage, killing six people at last count, including Claire and Marie's father—and maybe Claire too. Then she mysteriously jumped to her death from a luxury cruise ship into the Mediterranean. Poof. Gone. Dead.

Marie's eyes landed on her bare thighs. The scars from cutting years before were now mostly white lines, almost invisible against her pale skin. She ran her nails down her legs, digging in slightly. The scars represented a past she never wanted to think about again, not even in her sleep.

"Anais," she whispered. "What really happened to you?"

The circumstances of her mother's death were ordinary for a woman her age. A mild stroke, hospitalization, followed by a massive stroke. It was all so unexceptional, except that it wasn't. Anais's death had come only six months after Ava had jettisoned herself over the railing of their cruise ship a few miles off the coast of Marseille. Was it possible Ava had survived? And was out there killing? The date Anais drew her last breath was exactly two years to the day after Marie's father had been found dead in his little house in Harrisburg, Pennsylvania. Naked in the bathroom with a nasty gash on the side of his head. A coincidence, Marie wasn't so sure.

The irony didn't escape her either. That Anais's funeral might be a perfect trap—the final opportunity for Ava to end Marie. There was no one else left. Claire was dead, and now Anais. Marie felt moisture on her fingertips and looked down to see blood smeared across her leg. Her fingernails had broken through the old scars, creating fresh wounds. She watched the red beads form teeny pools against her white skin.

"If you're out there, Ava, I'm going to kill you for real this time," she whispered.

CHAPTER 2

RUSSELL

Six murders. He ticked them off on his fingers one by one. The priest, Connelly, followed by average, middle-aged Loyal Owens and his wife, Destiny. Then came Ava's grandfather, Ross Saunders. Next was the loner about town, Jack Quinn, and finally the man found in the bathroom in the house in Haddonfield with a knife in his abdomen— Michael Ritter. All but the last one—because Ritter's murder was a spur-of-the-moment anomaly—were each followed by a Polaroid shot of the victim's front door taken after the killing, mailed to the next intended victim. An ominous greeting card of sorts.

The case had consumed Russell Bowers for the past year, and he couldn't let it go. He knew the murderer, and that made it worse and more intriguing at the same time. His eyes darted across his desk, scanning the photos, taking in each grainy black-and-white detail again. Eerie, because as these doors were being photographed, there was a body or two behind each one. Stabbed, or poisoned, or bludgeoned, then left to die.

One Polaroid sat separate from the others. The shot of this front door was different. It was in color. A nice-looking green cottage door with some pink climbing roses clinging to the rustic stone wall nearby. He picked it up and pulled it closer to his eyes. The owner of this door was as dead as the others. Victim number seven, he was certain, though her cause of death had been reported as "complications from a stroke." But the murderer was still out there taunting him. New camera, new victim, same MO.

Russell stared at the dates printed in black ink at the bottom of the photo. One was the date the owner of the green door, Anais Lavoisier, had died. The other was his own wedding day, now only weeks away.

He'd rushed home when he'd received the photograph, afraid Ava had taken out her vengeance on his fiancée, only to collapse in relief when he found Juliette snuggled under the covers, drowsy and comfortable. But as what should be the happiest day in their lives drew closer, his anxiety kept ticking up a notch. Ava was alive. She'd killed at least once since he'd last seen her, and now she'd issued a direct threat to him in the form of a picture speaking a million words, and spawning a million worries.

"Hey, Russ?" Juliette stood in the doorway. She was wearing a black dress cut just above her knee; a satin coat lay across her arm. Her dark-blonde hair was swept up off her face. "This is it. I'm off to the final fitting." She clutched her bag with both hands. "I'm sorta nervous. I don't know why."

He smiled. "It's just a dress. Remember?"

She walked up and kissed the top of his head. "The most important dress of my life. I hope I haven't been eating too much." She ran a hand over her stomach. "Or we may have to push the date back a month or so."

He caught her eye and felt a tug of anxiety come over him. He didn't know how to start a conversation about Ava with her. It would just pull Juliette apart with worry and ruin everything that was left between them. He kept thinking if he maintained a close eye on things, if he could figure out where Ava was, where she was hiding, if he could just talk to her, it would all be fine. But time was running out.

Juliette glanced down at the Polaroids scattered across the desk. "You on this again? Because Anais died? She had a stroke, Russell. Nothing more. Ava, that psycho killer, has been dead for six months. Let it go."

How could he tell her that Ava wasn't dead? A body—just bare bones, really, no hair, no teeth—had washed up on a Turkish shore wearing tattered clothing that matched the description of the outfit Ava was last seen in. Not enough DNA could be extracted to make a positive match. Russell never accepted that she'd died when she jumped from the cruise ship. He *felt* her presence. And his suspicions had been confirmed when the Polaroid arrived in a plain white envelope mailed from, of all places, New York. He knew she was too smart to give away her whereabouts and had probably used a mail service of some sort to do the actual posting.

"Hmmm," he responded, tucking the color Polaroid under a file. "You might be right. But I'm not happy about Marie leaving the country for the funeral. Something about it bothers me."

Juliette put her hand on his back and leaned in for a closer look at the pictures. "Marie's the only living relative left. The courts will let her go to France to bury her mother, and she'll be back. But this"—she picked up one photo and then dropped it—"is depressing. Let it go, Russ. Ava Saunders is never going to bother us again."

He tilted back in his chair to really see his soon-to-be wife. She was nearly thirty-two but looked a few years older, thanks to endless nights on call during her surgical residency and fellowship. The past year of stress hadn't helped either. Ava Saunders had once been an ordinary translator for the courts, the same courts where Russell spent nights and days as a homicide detective assigned to the Prosecutor's Office. She had taken advantage of that proximity to firmly wedge herself between him and Juliette, leaving havoc and mayhem in her wake. Deception, disruption, seduction, sex, lies, murder. He'd spent the past six months trying to put his life back together. He wanted Juliette to be the most important piece of that.

He reached for her hand. "I'm sorry about Ava. I'm sorry—"

She pulled back. "I don't want to talk about her again. You lied about her, about your relationship with her. I think you slept with her, even if you won't admit it. I think you had this almost irresistible attraction to her. I think if you were on that ship and she'd asked you to jump with her, you would've. You sacrificed your career. Me. Everything for her." She took a half step back. "And I may never understand why. But she's dead. That's all I care about."

He nodded. "I'll—"

Her head was moving back and forth. "No. I'm not going over this again. Let's move forward." She pointed to the desk. "Put those away, please. I've gotta go. All the bridesmaids are going out with me afterward for drinks and dinner, so don't wait up. Bye." With that she twirled around and disappeared out the door.

He slid the color picture from under the file and held it up to eye level. The door was pleasant, innocent, inviting. There was no dead body hiding behind it. This murder had been committed more carefully, mimicking an ordinary death for a seventy-four-year-old woman.

"But you're not dead, are you, Ava? You're somewhere close. I can feel it."

He shut his eyes and saw her dark-brown hair. The eyes. The day she'd come to him, tears glistening. Asking for his help in solving the mystery behind her abandonment when she was a baby. Juliette was right: he had slept with her. The bits and pieces coming back to him through the drunken haze of that one night together. Her long legs. Taking off his shirt. Kissing him. The taste of wine on her mouth. Her small breast in his hand.

He heard a loud bang from downstairs and jumped, drawing his gun without thinking. The bang was followed by another. Then pounding. He holstered his weapon and descended the stairs. He peered through the glass in the front door and flung it open.

Joanne Watkins strode into the living room and dropped her purse on the floor before collapsing onto the sofa. "I waited for Juliette to leave, because it was just easier. What are we going to do, Russell? Tell me the plan."

"Want a beer?"

Joanne, Ava's one-time coworker and the closest thing he had to an investigative partner in this whole bit of nastiness, was the only other person who knew everything. She was the person Ava had chosen to mail the Polaroid to, to announce she was still alive.

"Why not?" Joanne said. She stood and followed him into the kitchen. "My son is gone, so I don't have to run out to taxi him anywhere."

Russell handed her the beer. "I'm sorry." He couldn't think of a better response, because there wasn't one. The custody battle between Joanne and her ex-husband had occupied most of their conversations for months.

"Hmmm, don't be. Tim might have won this round. But you know what pisses me off? That Steven chose to live with him. Because we all know fourteen-year-olds know what's best for them, right?" Russell raised his eyebrows but said nothing. She saw the look and stopped talking. "Okay, enough of that topic. If Steven were with me, I wouldn't be here to drink this beer." She took a sip. She was smiling, but her eyes were threatening tears.

"So." Russell clapped his hands together. "You asked about a plan. The only plan I have is to watch Marie go off to Cherbourg for the funeral, and see if she dies."

"And if she does?" Joanne's eyebrows disappeared under her bangs. "Are you planning on chasing Ava across France?"

Russell touched her arm. "If she does, then you know we have no choice but to hunt Ava down and end this before she shows up here on my wedding day."

"End this? What do you mean? Like kill her? Or are you just going to sit her down and talk to her in your really stern voice this time?"

He shot her a withering look. "Drink your beer."

CHAPTER 3

Ava

I pulled my hair back from my face. I was teetering on the brink of gaunt; my body was steadily digesting itself with every day I refused to bend to the gnawing in my stomach. I turned sideways, laying my hand against the concave area under my ribs. Today I would give in, put something in my mouth. My eyes were huge, almost popping from my face, a strange haunting green hue; I was convinced they gave away my secrets to the world. Those eyes stared back at me from the mirror, watching as I lifted sections of my hair and curled them with an iron, making waves around my face.

"I had no choice." I spoke to the reflection, a habit I'd developed during the isolation of my months on the run. "You know I had no choice in any of this. They killed the woman who gave birth to me." I smeared balm across my dried lips and then followed it with a bright reddish-pink shade that I thought brightened my skin. "And then they tried to cover it up. Every last one of them." I rested one hand on the edge of the sink and leaned in toward the mirror to apply mascara and eyeliner. "Anais. I'm sorry. I'm so sorry." I couldn't say her name without feeling a jolt in my stomach. "In all of this, you were the one I loved the most." When I looked up there was moisture in my eyes. "But you didn't love me back."

I turned on the water, shoved my toothbrush under the spray, and ran it across my teeth. "I didn't want to do this to you," I managed, though toothpaste dribbled from the corners of my mouth. "So the only thing I can do now is be there to say good-bye to you tomorrow. Deal with Marie, if I have to. And then find what's left of my birth family."

Distant lights twinkled through the window behind me and danced in the mirror. Paris was beautiful at night. I watched for a few minutes until the colors became fuzzy and started to fuse together.

Mailing the Polaroid of Anais's cottage door to Joanne after her death had been an impulse move. It was the only way I could think of to communicate with Russell after I'd jumped from the ship six months ago. The body of the young girl I'd gutted and skinned had been accepted as mine, as far as I knew. For all intents and purposes Ava Saunders was dead. Washed up onshore, just a skeleton, flesh eaten by sea life. Any DNA tests done so far had been inconclusive, from what I'd read.

That's what I'd wanted—to be dead to everyone. So I could start over without the baggage of multiple bodies, multiple murders following me. Clean slate. But Russell needed to know the truth. To know I was out here, somewhere, thinking of him.

Had he turned me in yet? Run to the authorities with the Polaroid in hand, little Juliette urging him on? Was he looking for me? For months after I'd left, I couldn't conjure his face in my mind, no matter how hard I tried. Something was always off. The eyes too small, the nose too long. The hair too dark or too short. But then one day, it was there. The curls. The brown eyes with creases at the corners when he made certain expressions. The mole on his temple. The one slightly crooked tooth on the bottom row that was only visible when he smiled. It was like he was in front of me. And I felt a sudden pull that couldn't be ignored. Mailing the picture was the next logical thing to do. I needed that connection with him again. Even if he hated me.

I walked to the windowsill and watched the people below. Eating, drinking, laughing. Like life wasn't a precarious balancing act, with happiness more often than not crashing around your feet. They were sitting with friends on a cool night, in a café with the heat lamps glowing, drinking a glass of wine, having a bite. My stomach rumbled at the thought and I pulled out my pack of Marlboro Lights. My fingers trembled when I held up the match. The dull ache in the back of my head became more pronounced, but I drew in fully anyway and felt the smoke deep in my lungs.

The nicotine killed my appetite, my taste buds, my desires. It filled my mind so I didn't think about death. The eyes of Father Connelly as he clutched his throat, trying to force air into his swollen esophagus. Loyal Owens as I made him kneel in front of me and then smashed his head open with the claw hammer. Jack Quinn, collapsed on the floor, clutching his heart—I'd watched every agonizing minute until he sucked the last bit of air into his wretched little mouth. Or Ross Saunders, my grandfather—the look on his face when he realized he was going to die at the hands of the child he'd spared from death years earlier. The irony of it all.

Those men had killed my mother. While I watched, pressed against the wall of the church, clutching my dirty stuffed rabbit in my arms. Screaming as her blood splashed on me. Now, I grabbed my hair with both hands as the memories came to me, marching one after another. I pulled, trying to get the thoughts from my head, but they kept coming. Loyal Owens had stripped my mother of her clothes, dragged her toward that priest, already dead, and tried to fashion them like dolls, like playthings, in some pose of bloody intimacy. My mother's eyes were open the whole time, staring straight through me, as they desecrated her.

I stood up and walked across the living room to the table in the corner and pulled out the bottle of whiskey. I didn't want to drink tonight. I'd promised myself that I wouldn't, but I needed it. Not only to fill my stomach with something it could digest, but also to fill my mind so that the thoughts would stop. I poured until the glass was nearly full, and took a huge swallow. For the first time ever, I felt completely alone. I'd always had Claire, a sometimes surrogate mother, to fall back on, a touchstone, and Aunt Marie, who, when things had been difficult, had always been in the background with a wistful expression, willing to reach out if necessary. I'd also had Grand-Maman, Anais. She would call and chat about nothing on Sunday nights when I was curled up in bed, warm, comfortable, and sleepy. Asking questions and listening to the answers, forcing me to speak French because she feared I'd forget the language, living in New Jersey. I'd been part of a family, even if that family wasn't truly mine. Now I was part of nothing. It was my own doing. I had pulled the loose threads myself and watched them unravel.

The living room of the suite was small and cramped with heavy, dark furniture. A nothing little flat—a third-floor walk-up with an iffy view of the far-off Eiffel Tower if you put the top part of your body out of the window and leaned precariously to the left. But the apartment was convenient and inconspicuous. Ironic that Anais had wanted to move me to an upscale flat in the fifteenth arrondissement, right here in Paris, less than a year ago. Now I was running for my life with only the money I could hustle up on the streets doing odd jobs, cleaning offices and hotels, waiting tables when they were willing to pay me in cash. And when truly desperate I did some things I'd never speak of.

I pulled the flash drive from my bag and looked at it again—a daily ritual and my biggest challenge. There were accounts and financial information on this chip. Money Anais had set aside for me in various banks that would carry me for years. But not only had the drive been in my pocket when I jumped from the ship, so it was thoroughly soaked and corrupted—putting it in rice, removing it from the plastic case, and drying the components by hand hadn't worked. Even if I could access the account information, though, I had no way to get at the money itself. I'd gone to huge lengths to be dead. I'd killed to be dead.

I couldn't march up to a bank in Hong Kong as Ava Saunders and start emptying out accounts. It was my nightly ponder.

Now that Anais was dead, she didn't have a beady-eyed watch on those accounts, but no doubt Marie did—if she knew about them, that was. I stood up and paced. Would Anais have told Marie about our arrangement? That she'd planned to give me money to leave the family, go away forever? Was Marie waiting for me to mess up? I took another gulp of whiskey and wandered to the window.

On the street outside my flat, there was the clanging of dinnerware and glasses, bits of laughter that floated upward from below; even a Sunday night in Paris was lively. My head was feeling detached from my body, just the way I wanted it. I knew I had only minutes to change my clothes, but I wanted those minutes to last an eternity, to listen to the sounds and pretend I was a part of it. I heard the buzzer on my phone go off, and I jumped slightly. "Shit," I muttered. "It's time."

I hurried into the bedroom and stripped down to nothing. I stepped into the thin, way-too-short black dress and zipped up the back, then slid on boots that lifted me up three and a half inches and forced me to walk with my rear end slightly protruding. The dress swished around my upper thighs, and I realized that if the wind blew just right, I'd be naked for the world to see. I'd make it work. Assuming that the sloppy Bulgarian businessmen who'd ordered an escort wanted a skinny girl with a pretty face and big green eyes. I swilled a mouthful of whiskey from the bottle and stuffed the flash drive safely in my clutch bag. I took a breath, pulled the apartment door open, and stepped into the hallway.

"Nine hundred and eighty euros for three hours with these idiots. Enough to get a cheap ticket back to the United States," I whispered, then thought about the computer-hardware convention the business-men were in town for. "And maybe much more than that if I can get into this flash drive."

CHAPTER 4

MARIE

Marie toddled down the hallway to the bathroom and stopped short. Only a little over six months ago, a dead man had been right here, on the floor. A knife in his abdomen, thanks to Ava. His head had apparently smashed against the toilet on the fall down, and though Marie hadn't been there to see it, the hollow thumping sound appeared in her sleep. Yes, it was true that Marie had stabbed him first. In a petrified moment filled with the worst paranoia, she'd been convinced Ava had sent him to kill her. So she'd protected herself. But the knife wound hadn't killed him, and he'd been able to summon Ava to get him to this house. Right here. Where, mired in her own confusion and typical sociopathic rage, Ava had thrust the knife deep enough to finish him off and then had fled, leaving Marie to take the fall.

She searched the white tiled floor for any signs of what had been. Everything had been scrubbed clean with bleach long ago, but there had to be some little detail unnoticed, left behind. Her head throbbed as she searched, sometimes on her hands and knees, feeling for a lost button or a splash of blood not cleaned. A single short strand of brownish-blond hair from Michael Ritter's head. She hadn't even known his name until they were hauling the body out in a black bag.

Ava was everywhere. Marie's eyes darted around the room, bouncing off the porcelain sink to the white tiles and back to the floor. Why she had decided to stay in this house wasn't a mystery. She'd been obligated to remain in Camden County and found no reason to incur more expense by renting an apartment.

Though her mother had shuffled her off to a convent after those turbulent years in the Swiss clinic, and she'd remained in the holy life until her arrest, she was never sure if she'd found God or if she'd simply relished the place of calm without Anais's interference and meddling. But now her religious life was over. Heading back to Christ the King with her little satchel in hand, begging for a third chance at redemption, was out of the question. So Claire's it was, the house her sister had bought when Ava was just sixteen. Or maybe seventeen. When she was just learning to kill but no one suspected. Marie often wondered if there were bodies buried in the backyard, Ava's first attempts at perfecting her craft. But the truth was, she really didn't want to know.

The papers she'd received from the court lay haphazardly on the windowsill. Those papers were her life, her lifeline to getting out of here. It didn't matter if she was sitting in the squalid cell in the Camden County Jail or in Claire's house. Both places were prisons. Ava had stolen her freedom.

She looked at the black letters jumping off the page. Permission granted to leave the country for a period of five days. She was to present herself to her parole officer by the end of business on day six, or she would be in violation.

Violation. That meant, unless she had a really good reason for not complying with the court order, her case would be reviewed by the parole board. She might escape punishment, or she might be forced back to the jail to serve out the rest of her sentence. She tried to calculate how many days that might be, until she shook it off. "I have to go," she muttered. "Stick to the plan and just do it."

The house had been cleared of most clutter in anticipation of selling it after Claire died, but it still held personal things, especially in Claire's room. Marie lingered in the doorway, taking it all in. Claire had moved to Haddonfield shortly after Marie took residence at the convent. She'd helped Claire find this house. They'd gone through it together several times, discussing whether Claire finally felt comfortable enough to put down roots after so many years of running away from what their father had done that terrible night that brought Ava into their lives. Marie ran her hand over the pale blue-gray walls. They could never have guessed things would take this turn. That Claire would be dead and Marie would be accountable for numerous criminal charges.

She opened the closet door. Empty. Sterile, just waiting for a new occupant. Marie wandered to the dresser and pulled out a drawer. Claire had been dead not quite a year and her things were still here, like she was going to walk right in and need them. Marie's fingers dug through the sweaters until they reached the familiar leather grain hidden underneath. She gingerly pulled the bag from its hiding place and put it on the bed.

The purse was old, twenty years or so, the leather cracked in places. A handcrafted Italian piece, but years of being shoved underneath things, stowed away, had left the leather dried and misshapen. Spattered blood graced the back and one side, there from the moment its owner was bludgeoned to death. Marie pulled the bag open and dumped the contents onto the bedspread. She'd done this many times before, scanning the belongings of a life cut short—Ava's mother's life cut short to be precise. Adrianna DeFeo (had Ava learned her name before she jumped from the ship? Marie didn't think so) had been carrying only a wallet with fifteen dollars, her passport, a Coffee Kiss lipstick, and a little blue book filled with numbers jotted down haphazardly, some with a notation attached, some not.

Marie found the book the most interesting. She sat down and began thumbing through it again, trying to read the same thing for at least the hundredth time and draw a different conclusion, but she couldn't. It was there, in black pen, clear as day. *Sanders*, the name spelled with a missing *u*, and a French phone number written in pencil, faded so that it was disappearing from the page. From what she could make out, it matched the only telephone number Anais had ever had. So the question that rumbled through her brain was, Was it possible that Adrianna had had some contact with Anais, knew her somehow? That her death wasn't random? Marie had been too frightened to even breathe that question to her mother when Anais was still alive. Petrified. But now that she was dead, it was time for the truth.

Marie was pulled from the pages by the sound of the front door chime—Beethoven's fifth. *Damn it.* She threw the things back in the purse and pushed it underneath the sweaters. Through the bedroom window, which faced the driveway, she could see the dark outline of a car. Its owner too was unmistakable, even in the dim light—Russell Bowers. *Shit.* He'd been hovering ever since Ava disappeared. Stopping by when Marie was meeting with her parole officer, just coincidentally, to see how things were going. His eyes had never really left her, though this was the first time he'd been bold enough to actually come to the house.

She sighed and hesitated before opening the door. She'd give him five minutes. Nothing more. When she opened the door he was standing there alone. Hands in pockets. He seemed casual, off duty. His face held an expression that was hard to read. Marie spread her arms, placing her hands on the doorframe to keep him where he was, not let him in.

"Yes?"

He tilted his head to the side. "Do you have a minute, Marie? I just want to have a chat, what with you leaving to go to France. My condolences, by the way, on the death of your mother."

She shifted slightly and dropped one arm, gesturing to the three packed suitcases sitting just inside the door. "My taxi to the airport will be here in a minute. I really can't—"

He took advantage of the space she'd allowed between him and the door, and slipped into the entryway. "We both know you're not leaving until tomorrow morning. I'm worried about you. You lost Claire not even a year ago, and now your mother. Not to mention Ava." His words echoed Sandrine's, spoken on the phone only that morning.

He was watching her face, trying to catch a fleeting moment when her guard was down. But she wasn't going to let him have that. She willed her expression to remain as flat as possible, but she couldn't be sure she hadn't flushed. She bit the inside of her mouth and drew blood, tasting the coppery saltiness slide over her tongue.

"Has Parole sent you to see me off? In some sort of official capacity? Because otherwise, I'd like you to leave." She opened the door wider. "They just gave you your badge back, Russell. Don't mess it up."

His head was still but his eyes were darting around, taking in every detail of the room from his vantage point. "Aren't you worried, Marie?" He wasn't leaving.

She folded her arms in front of her. "About what?"

He touched the top of one of her suitcases with his fingertips. "That you may not make it back alive."

Marie hated him at that moment. And she hated Ava more for bringing him into her life. She looked him in the eye and smiled. "Are you worried about a plane crash or—"

"I'd be more worried about Ava if I were you."

"Ava's dead . . . ," she started, but he'd moved. He'd taken the liberty of walking over to the sofa and sitting down.

"Have a seat, Marie. I need to have a two-minute conversation." He held his palms up to her. "And then I'll leave. Please."

She sat in the chair across from him without saying a word. Her right leg started to bounce. "Ava is dead. She jumped and hit the water and went under." It was an image that sometimes kept her up at night. That face, which once belonged to a little girl she'd both resented and loved, disappearing beneath the churning waves.

"The timing of Anais's death doesn't sit well with me," Russell said.

Marie's heart rate picked up, but she didn't move. Did he suspect the same thing she did? "Meaning what?"

He shook his head and stood. "What if she didn't die? What if she's out there somewhere? What if she circled back and killed Anais in revenge for whatever happened on that ship that made her jump in the first place? What if she's lying in wait for you to show up at the funeral? Your niece is smart, Marie. You know that."

Marie's fists were clenched. "Do you know something more than what you're saying, Russell? Has she contacted you?" She could feel the vein in her forehead throbbing. "I need to know, I deserve to know if this is just a hunch or something more."

He seemed to be hesitating, choosing his words carefully, maybe undecided about what he was going to say. "Let's say she did contact me. Hypothetically, of course. What do you think she'd be up to at this point?"

"Revenge. Against Anais." She ticked them off on her fingers. "Against me. Possibly you? Though I'm not sure about that one. And money. Of course money."

Russell's head cocked slightly. "Curious you'd say that. What about money?"

"If she's been out there, what's she been living off of? How's she been supporting herself?"

"If she's going to be circling back for money, maybe you should rethink attending the funeral at all. Pay some private respects here. Go to Mass or something."

Marie stood. "Nobody should have to make that kind of choice. Is this just some sort of a game to you?"

He shrugged. "It's not a game. At least not to me." He walked to the front door. "Assume Ava's out there, and you can't go wrong."

He left. From the window, Marie watched his car lights go on and his Jeep slowly pull away from the curb. After most of the trembling had left her limbs, she went from room to room, switching off the lights before heading up the stairs to bed. If Russell thought Ava was alive, he'd be searching for her. Marie had to find her first; Ava had the money or access to the money, and Marie couldn't sit back and watch Russell ruin things for her again. She was going to be careful. And, she thought, glancing at the suitcases near the front door, if things went as anticipated, she was never coming back.

CHAPTER 5

RUSSELL

The bulb was bright, burning his eyes, so he pushed his chair a few inches back and pulled the lampshade down. He'd read the same page three times and had to start all over from the beginning again. A new case. A shooting at Ninth and Ferry in Camden. One dead. Two wounded. Russell was sifting through the reports, rereading witness statements and trying to forget about Ava, about Marie, when he heard the front door open. He looked at the clock. One twenty-three a.m.

The lights went on downstairs, and he heard rumbling in the kitchen. He stopped and listened. Next, Juliette would be stumbling up the steps. The final fitting and subsequent dinner had gone on way too long for her not to be marinated in tequila. He heard her feet on the stairs, and when she finally appeared in the doorway, the evening showed clearly on her face. Eyeliner was smeared down nearly to her cheekbones, and her face was flushed. Her carefully combed hair was loose and tangled around her face. She was missing an earring.

He smiled. "I take it the fitting went well?"

She blinked. "Have you been sitting there all night, looking at those pictures?"

He shook his head. "Actually, Joanne came over—"

She turned abruptly and almost fell. "Oh, Joanne? Investigating the Ava mystery together again, are we?"

He got up and followed her into the bedroom. She plopped down onto the edge of the bed and flipped her shoes off one by one, letting them drop heavily to the floor, then fell back and tried to pull the covers over herself but failed. "Why'd you screw that stupid girl anyway, Russell? Why'd you do that to us?" She was drunk. She'd always been too afraid to bring this up when she was sober.

"Do you want some water? Ibuprofen?" he asked. She shook her head and pressed her face into the pillow. He could see black mascara smear onto the white case, and it took a moment for him to realize she was crying. "Juliette?" He sat down on the edge of the bed. He didn't know what to say. He was hoping if he sat there long enough she'd just fall asleep.

"What'd she have? Was it her hair? Her long legs? Her itty-bitty French accent? What?" She was sitting up now. Her face was a mess of makeup and tears. "Or was it that she was a nut, that she would just kill people like it was nothing? Was that what was so intriguing? That she was dangerous?" She stood up and started for the bathroom. "Or maybe it was because she was twenty-two? With a twenty-two-year-old's p—" Her words ended when the bathroom door slammed. But a second later it flung open again. "I'm so glad she's dead!" she screamed. "I hope she suffered when she drowned! I hope the sharks ate her—" The door shut again.

"Shit," he muttered after several minutes of silence. "Thank God that's over."

He wandered back into his office and closed the door. Eventually Juliette would exhaust herself and fall asleep. He slid the only picture he had of Ava out from the bottom drawer of his desk. Joanne had given it to him. They'd been at an after-work gathering at the Victor not long before Ava disappeared. She was leaning into the shot, her white shirt and blue Hermès blazer visible. Her dark hair was down, and she was smiling. Joanne's head was just behind Ava's shoulder. At the edge of the photo was Ava's hand holding a drink. The always-present drink.

Most of what was happening now was his fault. He'd let her go. He couldn't admit that to anyone. No one knew except Joanne and his partner, Doug. Doug had suffered enough because of Russell's actions— suspension, and then relocation back to duty at the Cherry Hill Police Department, while Russell somehow held on to his assignment at the Prosecutor's Office, still somehow part of a homicide unit that had jurisdiction over the entire county.

Everyone who knew he'd stood at the airport and watched Ava walk away had paid a price. It kept Russell up at night. He'd known Ava killed all those men because they had murdered her mother. Was that an excuse? A justification? She'd also killed Loyal Owens's wife because she happened to be there. And she'd killed Michael Ritter, the man Marie had stabbed in self-defense. Ava had rescued him from the street in Philadelphia, taken him back to the house in Haddonfield. Nursed him all night and then inexplicably killed him, leaving him on the bathroom floor for Marie to take the blame.

Russell stared into her eyes in the photo. Was Ava capable of killing Anais? What the hell had happened on that cruise ship that had caused her to jump? He needed to know.

He heard the bedroom door shut and the lock snap into place. Juliette was locking him out. He'd have to sleep in the guest room while she nursed her anger and, soon, her hangover. Great.

He flipped on the television and turned it to the BBC. This was a new habit, watching the international news. It started some months ago, maybe in an attempt to understand the world at large a little better, or maybe it was because he'd known Ava was out there even before the Polaroid had arrived, and he wanted a sense of her surroundings. The news anchor was talking about events in Korea. He half listened as pictures of Kim Jong Un flashed across the screen. Then the story switched to a bombing in Malmö, Sweden. Russell rubbed his eyes. He was half-tempted to knock on the bedroom door and make up with Juliette. He hated these fights, because there was no resolution. The past couldn't be changed, no matter how sorry he was.

Suddenly, the headlines on the screen were all about Paris. There was an image of a black car pulled over to the side of the road, surrounded by flashing police lights. A man was being interviewed, English subtitles flashing underneath. His friend had been found dead in the car a few hours ago, after a night of drinks on the town. The details the authorities were releasing were sketchy, but the victim was a prominent executive from Bulgaria, in town to attend an annual computer-hardware convention.

Russell reached for the remote to turn off the television, then stopped. The dead man had been out with friends, drinking in the company of women from an escort service. A policeman was now describing one of the escorts as a person of interest. Russell dropped the remote into his lap. "She had dark hair," the officer was saying. "Thin, approximately five feet five inches tall. Fair skin, green eyes."

The screen switched back to the witness. "We were all drinking in the club, and they left together. That's the last I saw him." The anchor began to speak again, asking that anyone who knew someone matching the description of the escort call the number on the screen.

"Paris." Russell said the word out loud, though he was having trouble putting his fragmented thoughts together. He felt sick. Ava had gotten her revenge on the men who'd killed her mother, maybe gotten her revenge on Claire and Anais too, for never telling her the truth, no matter how she begged. And now this man in Paris. And he was certain there was going to soon be another body added to the list. Marie Lavoisier-Saunders was walking right into a trap.

CHAPTER 6

Ava

The sharp elbow in my side, below my rib cage, threw me a few inches to my left. I turned to see a couple pushing past me to get to the check-in kiosk at Charles de Gaulle. I'd been up as early this morning as I could manage to lift my heavy head from the pillow, pulled on black jeans and a turtleneck, trying to appear inconspicuous. With an over-sized trench coat and hat, nobody would look twice. I'd sorted through my collection of passports. Gabrielle Rotton was done. No good. The police would be looking for an escort going by that name. The only one left to me was Jessica Roberts. A United States passport in the plainest of names. I studied the picture. This would do.

I rubbed the spot where I'd been elbowed. My ribs ached, but not just my ribs, my entire body. When I'd finally made it back to my apartment last night, under the darkest skies I could ever remember in Paris, I'd pulled that rag of a dress from my body and inspected every inch of me. I knew there'd be bruising, but I didn't expect so much blood. It congealed on my thighs, the area between my legs so painful I could barely sit on the bidet. The warm water washed over me, producing tears. Then I slid on cotton pajamas and examined my face in the mirror. He'd hit me pretty hard, the Bulgarian, his thick hammy knuckles missing my nose by centimeters. I touched my cheek, feeling the swelling no amount of L'Oreal foundation could conceal.

The men had been five drinks in when they'd picked me up, my nerves raw when I'd gotten in the car. I'd been promised there would be three other women along—a group date with drinks, and whatever came after was up to us. They'd wanted a fun night on the town with attractive French-speaking women who had a solid knowledge of Paris. Where to go—dinner, clubs. After-hours drinking and dancing. I'd jumped on the opportunity because there was no better place to solve my thumb-drive issue than at a computer-hardware convention. And these escort affairs, in my experience, usually ended either with the man passed out drunk in the back of a cab or with a feeble attempt at sex, which was nothing more than a pinch and a grab. But I knew the moment I stepped into the car this was going to be different.

He was the tallest of the group. Light-brown hair, stocky, with a crude, bulky face. He was well dressed, edgy, smart, funny, with a biting sarcasm he didn't think I could understand. He assumed my grasp of Bulgarian was limited to *hello*, *yes*, *please*. And *suck my dick*. After we got our drinks in the bar, I kept my head down, sipping at the vodka nestled in the ice, absorbing every word. I knew only a smattering of the language, but from what I gathered, he'd nicknamed me "the bird," for my tiny frame, and made stupid jokes to his friends all night about plucking my feathers and hearing me chirp. I smiled into my drink and waited for the right time.

I edged so close to him in the booth that I could see the small blackheads that dotted his nose, then leaned farther, making sure that our arms were touching. In basic French, I asked him about his hometown until the music slowed so I could hear myself talk. When I glanced up, the other men in his group had cleared out. Now or never.

I pulled the flash drive from my purse and put it on the table. I only wanted his opinion—what my options were. Could he help or direct me? "This is your hobby, right? Hardware? I need the information on this drive. It's been corrupted." My hair brushed his shoulder, strands lingering there while I waited for a response.

He took a large swallow of beer, a disgustingly mediocre brew, and picked it up. He had no idea how much money he was holding in his hands. His lips were curled at the edges. Mocking me, like I was asking Einstein to help me with algebra. "What's on here? Secret government documents? Are you a spy?" He winked at me, thinking he was clever.

"Some notes important only to me."

He snapped the case apart and I realized this had been a mistake. "This is rusted. Did you wash it or something?" I started to reach for it, but he pushed my hand away. "Did you try recovery software?"

I nodded. "I took the case apart and dried it out already. I bought the software, but nothing. I even took it to a computer shop, here in Paris. They said it was impossible. It was in water for quite some time. Salt water. And unfortunately I didn't have time to dry it immediately."

He snapped the case back together and smirked. "Nothing is impossible. You need only the right equipment. To replace the connectors." He scowled in concentration. "Or to extract the memory chip. And some patience." He put it in his pocket.

I sipped the vodka, feeling it burn my empty stomach. "Can you do it?" I eyed his pocket. "Do you have the equipment?"

He put his hands on my knees and slid them up my thighs. "When we're done, I'll take it and see what I can do. If there's anything on there, I'll get it. But first, let me—" His hands had reached my hips, looking for a string of polyester, some sliver of underthings. There was nothing but flesh. His fingers reached farther.

"No . . . ," I started.

He clasped his hands over mine and squeezed. "Change of plans. Let's go." He pulled me from the chair and wrapped his arm around my waist, nearly lifting me from the ground. "My car."

I felt the back of my dress blowing as he moved me down the street. Incredibly stupid, this dress. I'd always prided myself on being smart, two steps ahead of everyone else. It was how I'd stayed alive and kept from getting caught. I could see life like a chessboard, three steps forward. I wasn't sure if it was the alcohol, my despair over the flash drive, or the assumption that the Bulgarian would be stupid that had muddled my thinking, but I'd stepped into a pile of shit in my three-and-a-half-inch platform boots. He wasn't going to let me out of this without satisfying his every need. And I couldn't run; he had my life in his jacket pocket.

The shove into the passenger's seat was quick and rough. The black BMW maneuvered out of the city quickly, headed in the direction of the airport. My mind was in a panic—there was no way out. When he finally pulled over to the side of the road on a quiet stretch near Goussainville, I was out of choices. When it was over, I was bruised, my left cheekbone and lip swollen. He'd gotten his way with a hand over my mouth, pinning me to the seat, crushing me with his weight, the smell of dirty clothes, body odor, cigarettes, and beer mixing together and washing over me. He'd forced my legs apart, whispering *"Pute"* in my ear. The French word for *whore*.

But in the end, I had gotten my way too—when he'd finally shifted off of me enough for me to reach my boot, I'd stabbed him in the throat, seeing the hilt of the knife against his skin, feeling his blood drip down onto me. I held his eyes with mine and whispered back, "You forgot. Whores usually carry knives." I grabbed my flash drive and the wad of cash in his wallet—which turned out to be substantial—and left him there, dead in the driver's seat, with his pants down around his knees and his flaccid penis out for all the world to see. I hadn't wanted another dead body in my wake, but I'd had no choice.

Now I boarded the plane, took my seat near the back, and pulled the hat down over my face. I needed to sleep. I wanted to forget everything that had happened on that quiet stretch of road in that BMW. I wanted to forget, though my body was going to be reminding me for months to come, what he'd done to me. I knew now that the information on the drive was recoverable if I could find the right person to change the connectors or extract the memory chip. That was enough to have made it somewhat worthwhile.

The wheels moved along the tarmac and then lifted off the ground, leaving Paris behind. I had the row to myself, so I stretched out and closed my eyes. I needed all the strength I could muster for what lay ahead.

CHAPTER 7

MARIE

The rush-hour traffic was heavy as the car headed the eighty miles north to Newark Liberty International Airport. The bargain ticket to Paris had been purchased in haste, made cheaper by flying out of a major hub. All Marie wanted to do was get on the plane, get the hell out of here and away from Russell, the courts, and the never-ending curse brought about by that girl with the dark hair and green eyes.

As far as Marie was concerned, Russell Bowers was but a filthy remnant of Ava's life that Ava had left behind when she disappeared; like scabies, he'd crawled under Marie's skin, causing constant irritation. On the first morning after her release from jail, she'd stopped into Starbucks for a cappuccino—something she'd craved the entire time behind bars—and there he was, two people behind her in line. He'd just smiled, watching her, and said nothing. Then it happened again at the small grocery store in Haddonfield—miles from Cherry Hill, where he lived, and Camden, where he worked. His cart nearly careened into hers as she rounded the aisle, his face filled with innocence and feigned surprise to see her. But she could feel his eyes on her as she grabbed the rest of her groceries and checked out. There were more "accidental" meetings when she went to report to her parole officer, when there was no apparent reason for him to be skulking about. Parole was nowhere near the Prosecutor's Office or the courthouse. But each time, there Russell was. Watching, always watching.

She'd kept her head down, refused to acknowledge that anything was amiss or complain to any superiors, but inside, her emotions were roiling. Until it dawned on her that his obsession wasn't about her—not really. He wasn't hell bent on catching her in some minor parole violation and sending her to prison; no, he wasn't tracking *her* at all. He just wanted to be closer to Ava, and Marie was his thin thread of connection to her niece. It was about Ava and always had been. Russell Bowers was just one more reminder of the horror they'd endured since they'd brought that child into their family.

Marie watched the lights of the airport drawing closer. She was leaving Haddonfield, leaving her life with Claire and Ava behind once and for all. She was going to Cherbourg to say good-bye to her mother, see her buried and pay her respects, and then she was going to get her inheritance. How, exactly, she didn't know yet.

The Lavoisiers and money were odd companions. There was plenty of it, inherited down through the generations, that was true. But how that money trickled down to the individual family members was idiosyncratic and outlined by a misogynistic great-grandfather's will. It essentially left holdings to his direct male descendants only.

Anais had received an allowance from her father that permitted her a lavish lifestyle after she'd moved to Cherbourg. Privilege with no responsibility but plenty of resentment from others. Her cousins had fought bitterly to cut Anais off when she returned home with two young children in tow. Divorce was unacceptable. A bad marriage to a poor American was worse. And procreating several times during the course of that bad marriage was the most unforgivable.

Marie often thought of their early days in France. She'd been maybe four years old. Almost the same age as Ava when her mother was murdered, so Marie understood the texture of memories hazed by time. There had been the unmistakable undertone of not being accepted into the fold when they'd first arrived, of being shuffled between relatives. Arguments, tears. Angry voices from behind closed doors. Marie and Claire had huddled in corners, trying to remain invisible, praying they'd return to America and Papa. But it didn't happen.

They eventually landed in a hotel in Cherbourg after they'd worn out the patience of sympathetic relatives. It was a gray stone building with no elevator. The three of them, Anais, Claire, and Marie, would climb the steps to their room on the third floor. One bed had to suffice; their kitchen consisted of a teakettle, a hot plate, and an old metal pan. There Anais would prepare pasta and sometimes hot chocolate for them. The worst for Marie was watching her mother deteriorate from someone always put together with jewelry and a coordinated handbag to a frayed, haphazard mess.

Anais's father appeared one morning at the top of those steps to the room. When he entered, in his hand-tailored suit and leather gloves, trying not to show his distaste, his brow furrowed and his nose curled at the sight of their plastic cereal bowls perched on the edge of the bathroom sink. Anais's cousin, Armand, followed him in, his arms folded tightly across his body as if he was afraid to touch anything.

"You need to go home to your husband, Anais. This is enough," her father had said.

"Don't come here, Papa, if you don't like it." Anais stood straight and tall in the middle of the room, watching their eyes crawl over the shabbiness. "But I don't want to go back."

"We told you not to marry him. I told you at least three times. But you did anyway, and this is what you get." Armand spat his words at her like he was tossing coins at a homeless person.

Anais turned her attention to her father. "I'm not asking to live with you and Maman. I'm not. I'll even get a job—"

"Doing what?" Armand again.

Anais looked around. "As a secretary, or maybe a clerk, I don't know. I just need help with a house. Please, Papa. Even a small house, to raise the girls."

"You're not trained for anything," her father said. His voice was soft but stern at the same time. "You need to go back." He hesitated. "Was it so bad, Annie?" His nickname for her. "Was he cheating on you? Beating you? Tell me." He leaned in and caught her eye.

Marie could see from where she was, seated in the corner, that her mother was crying. She'd never seen her cry before.

"It doesn't matter, Uncle," Armand insisted. "It doesn't matter how bad it was for her. She got pregnant, she chose to go. And you said there was no coming back. She's not going to suck off the family for the rest of her life. No. Anais—"

Papa shot Armand a look that shut him up. "I will buy your tickets to Philadelphia. I have no problem with that."

Marie heard the words and her heart sang. The row home on North Fourth Street would be a dream come true compared to this. To play in the small backyard, walk to the deli around the corner with her mother a few times a week. The thought of the smells from Kaplan's Bakery, where they went early on Sunday mornings for bread, nearly made her mouth water.

"I'm not going. This room is only paid for the week. That's it. I don't have any money left. After that, I'm leaving with the girls, but I'm not going back to the United States . . ."

At that moment Claire came out of the bathroom. A thin white towel was wrapped around her small body, held closed in the back with one hand. She didn't say anything. She stopped outside the bathroom door and held the doorknob with her free hand; water dripped from her hair down her neck, onto the towel and floor.

In that one moment everything changed. "Armand, go wait in the car." Anais's father's voice was raised, and Armand didn't protest. Her father then agreed to buy the cottage in Querqueville. A small stone cottage, maybe meant to be a middle-class slap in the face, but rustic and beautiful. He also granted Anais a generous allowance for the rest of her life. It was all written out, legally binding, whether Armand wanted to comply or not.

The problem was, now that Anais was dead, the allowance stopped too. Marie's only hope was that her mother had stashed some money somewhere. But so far, nothing had turned up. No accountant or business manager, no accounts. No records. No money.

All that was left was the cottage in Cherbourg; that was something, yes, but even the house in Haddonfield that was worth nearly half a million dollars wasn't hers. Claire had mortgaged it to the hilt to maintain her lifestyle and had borrowed from Anais to keep it all going. Taxes were due, and the bank was going to seize it in a matter of time. She'd learned during a conversation with Anais—probably a slip on the old woman's part—that she'd given Ava some financial files before Ava jumped ship. Now all that information was either at the bottom of the Mediterranean Sea or in that serial killer's pocket. Marie wasn't sure which was worse. She only knew she had to get to the cottage, scavenge for whatever duplicate information was there. Or find Ava, if she was still alive. Whichever came first.

The driver pulled up in front of the Delta terminal and Marie quickly gathered her bags, feeling a sense of urgency to get through security and be on her way. She clasped her passport and court documents as she wound her way through the check-in line. Hundreds of people seemed to be taking the same flight, and she was bumped from behind and pushed forward while sweat began to form around her neck and trickled down her back.

Sometimes if you thought about something long and hard, through either love or hate, it seemed to draw that thing closer—that was what Marie had always believed. And now it was what she knew, because when she felt an elbow in her side, a careless man pushing through the line with two bags, not paying attention, that moment changed everything. She twisted her head to see who was there, and she caught sight of a woman through the window maybe a thousand yards away. A thin woman in a hat, nothing but a black line in the distance that Marie knew without hesitation was Ava. It was the way she moved, the way her shoulders were straight, not bent forward, when she walked, how she carried her single bag effortlessly, a coat flung over her arm.

Marie stepped out of line, her space quickly swallowed up by the people behind her. Her mind began twisting. *Ava.* The supposedly dead murderess, back in the United States. Marie had been afraid she'd see her at the funeral, hiding in the back, or at the edge of the cemetery, but it didn't take even that long. She'd opted out of paying respects to Anais and instead chosen to come back to New Jersey. Marie rushed out of the terminal in time to see the woman jump on a shuttle bus. The doors shut and the bus began to move away. She read the rolling LED lights on the side. *Grand Central Station*, it read. New York? That couldn't be right. She dropped her bags and watched the bus go.

A porter walked past. "Where does that bus stop?" She pointed at the back as exhaust poured from the tailpipe.

He glanced up. "Three stops. New Jersey Transit in Newark, then Penn Station, and then Grand Central. Just go inside to ground transportation and get a ticket."

Ava was headed to catch the train south. Back to Haddonfield. That made sense. "Think, Marie, think." She considered her options, then flagged down a cab.

"Newark train station."

"I'm not losing you, Ava, not this time," Marie whispered as the cab wove through the dense tangle of traffic.

CHAPTER 8

RUSSELL

The package was thick, mailed in a white bubble envelope that required a knife to open. He carried it under one arm as he climbed the steps to Joanne's front door. When he'd spotted it on his porch that morning, he'd decided it was best they look at it early, before work. Joanne opened only after peering through the curtains first, then unlatching two locks and the chain.

"Expecting an ambush?" he asked, walking past her into the living room.

She followed him to the couch. "Kind of. From either Ava or the vandals around here. I think I'm having surveillance cameras and an alarm system put in on Friday. The next-door neighbor's car was broken into last night. I blame it on those apartments." She pointed through the window to the complex just visible across the street. "I knew it was going to be trouble when they put them up. There's like a billion units, and they built them practically on the sidewalk."

"Ah, suburban problems, they never end, do they? But when you consider that a sixteen-year-old kid was killed last night in downtown Camden, two wounded, I think you can live with those apartments."

"Did you come here for something or did you just want to lecture me about my pettiness?" She headed to the kitchen.

"I need something sharp to open this," he called after her.

She returned with scissors in her hand. "Driving down Haddon Avenue is like being in a goddamned canyon with those apartments there. Six stories high—"

He fumbled with the wrapping on the envelope. "Hey." He shook it in front of her. "I have something interesting in here. Focus?"

She watched him pull the pages from the envelope, then wandered back toward the kitchen, calling, "Do tell."

"Okay, I got more-detailed background information on Ava's birth mother, more than just her name."

"Where'd it come from?"

"Philadelphia police did a dossier on her after she was identified. With my help." He smiled. "But they did the hard work. Look at this." He fanned through the pages.

"I'm dying to hear all about the woman who gave birth to her. Though I probably shouldn't say 'dying.'"

"Okay, so, as we know, her name was Adrianna DeFeo. She was born on August twentieth, 1974, in Italy, birth certificate says Tuscany, but she grew up in Vicenza, about an hour's drive from Venice or two and a half hours from the Swiss border. Only child of Philomena and Victor DeFeo. Her childhood was seemingly uneventful until she got pregnant at the age of sixteen. Her parents, devout Catholics, were appalled. They offered to send her away to have the baby, and then have the child placed for adoption. Adrianna refused."

"So she ran away after she had the baby?"

"Well, she dropped out of school to raise the baby, and everything seems to have fallen apart after that. She ran away with her boyfriend, Davide Tosi, and their then almost-three-year-old daughter, Giada— our Ava. But Davide returned home less than a week later. He said he left Adrianna in Tuscany but had no idea where she went after that. There's a record of her applying for passports for herself and her daughter. The DeFeo family had no information as to the whereabouts of their daughter or granddaughter for another eighteen years. They learned a few months ago, when I started digging into this, that their daughter was murdered in a church in Philadelphia a year after her disappearance."

Russell shuffled the pages. "It was the shoes Adrianna was wearing when she was murdered. Maritan shoes—not made or sold outside of Italy. Remember I talked to Adrianna's sister? Or close relative. Lia was her name, I think. She was with her when Adrianna bought those shoes."

"I remember the whole shoe thing. But that's the first her parents knew of her murder, because of you?"

Russell nodded. "It seems so."

"I have to ask, are you going out on a hunt for this David now? Ava's father? To get more information?" Joanne asked, returning. "Is that the next obsession?" She took a seat in the corner of the sofa with a glass of lemonade in her hand.

Russell glanced over. "It's Davide, not David. No, I'm not. It's just interesting, right? Ava's father is still living in Italy, probably near Vicenza. And she doesn't know. As far as I can tell, she never even learned her mother's name—at least not from me. And don't you want to use a coaster?"

Joanne purposefully set the glass down directly onto the wooden end table. "Well, let's hope she didn't get her murdering gene from him. That would be so awkward if they met for the first time in jail."

Russell gazed out the window, pondering. "Ava has grandparents, cousins, a father, all in northern Italy, and she doesn't know." He pulled at the pages. "Without interviewing the family, it's hard to say why Adrianna came to this country, where she got the money for tickets and passports. It's not exactly on the top of the list for the Italian police either."

"Loose ends." Joanne pulled at the pendant on her necklace, sliding it back and forth along the chain. "She was killed in '96. The Internet wasn't as comprehensive and organized as it is now, but it doesn't seem like her family tried very hard to find her. Like later on Facebook or Pinterest or anything? They never wanted to see their grandchild?"

He smirked. "Pinterest? You think she'd be pinning things, like crafting ideas?"

She chuckled. "You never know. And you're never gonna know the answers to this weird story without reopening an investigation." She caught his eye. "And without getting all consumed with Ava again."

"Not Ava—Giada DeFeo, that's her birth name. But I think she's going by the name Gabrielle Rotton now. Not sure."

"How do you know that? You know where she is?"

Russell pulled up the story about the dead Bulgarian on his phone and handed it to her. "Read the description of the escort he was with right before he was stabbed."

Joanne's eyes flitted back and forth across the screen. "Dark hair, thin. Green eyes. Fuck." She whipped her head toward him. "That could be a lot of people. Don't do this, Russell."

"Do what? Assume every dark-haired, green-eyed woman is Ava?" He shuffled the papers. "I've been up all night just thinking about it. Should I call the police in Paris? Tell them I suspect Ava Saunders, a.k.a. Gabrielle Rotton, is in the city? Tell them she killed the guy in the BMW by the airport? Tell them the Turkish authorities found a body after she jumped from the cruise ship but it's not hers?"

Joanne's face was slack as she handed him the phone. "Why won't this just go away?"

He looked at her, felt the soreness in his eyes, knew they looked bloodshot. "Because *she* won't go away. The police believe some sort of struggle occurred in that car. Maybe he deserved to be stabbed—"

Her hand went to her hip. "Do you hear yourself? Making excuses for her? Maybe she can tell you what happened in a few weeks—she'll be at your wedding, lurking in the back with a knife in her hand.

Speaking of which, what's going on with the soon-to-be Mrs. Bowers? Or will she be Dr. Bowers after the wedding?"

Russell checked the time on his phone. "She'll be home in about an hour, I think."

"Then you'd better go." Joanne finished the lemonade in one gulp. "Fun times ahead for you in your household, that I know for sure. And I'm not even a detective."

He tapped the pages with his fingers. "What are we going to do about this?"

She hesitated for a few moments before speaking. "Ava doesn't look like a Giada. That was a terrible name for her."

"Really, Joanne?" He stood and started for the door. "That's what you think?"

"No. I think you should call the police on the off chance Ava stabbed that man, but you won't. Instead you'll distract yourself with things that don't matter. Like Ava's father, David, who is completely irrelevant at this point." She'd followed him, and now she patted his back. "But of course I'll do what I can to help."

He opened the front door. "It's Davide," he muttered.

"Find the person who's breaking into cars here, Russell. Start with those apartments," she yelled after him.

He was down the steps and halfway to the street. He only raised his hand carrying the papers to let her know he'd heard her.

CHAPTER 9

AVA

Airports usually have a way of making me feel calm. When you live in a world where you never really feel connected, then wandering in a sea of people who are suspended in time, in transition, unattached for the moment, can be surprisingly comforting. A collection of nobodies going nowhere. Though Newark wasn't the best at bringing forth cozy, warm feelings of peaceful, unattached limbo. It was large, crowded, dirty. The eight-hour flight spent squeezed into an economy seat had left me exhausted and irritated as the line twisted toward customs.

The passport I had was good, and not easy or cheap to obtain, but it had gotten me across European borders and out of France. It was amazing to me that it was only a little more than six months ago that I'd washed ashore on a rocky beach slightly south of Marseille, with nothing but bare feet, wet clothes, and, of course, my flash drive. I'd huddled on those cold rocks, watching the last glimpse of the cruise ship disappearing into the fog. Jumping from the ship hadn't been a well-conceived plan—more an impulsive one. But when the Mediterranean didn't swallow me up, I saw it as a sign that I was meant to survive, to go on. That perhaps I'd been forgiven for my sins and now had a chance to start over.

A local woman spotted me in the darkness near the water, mistook my age for much younger, and brought me home, fed me, gave me dry clothes and a pair of rubber boots that belonged to her daughter. She asked questions in French, then Spanish, and finally some broken Italian, all of which I pretended not to understand as I babbled a few phrases in Greek, which wasn't in her repertoire. I took advantage of her kindness for a week, then emptied the cash jar she kept on the back shelf of the pantry and disappeared.

During the time I was making my way by bus through France into Switzerland, then Greece, my mind was always on Anais. The thought of returning to Cherbourg to finish things with her consumed me, but it wasn't time yet. So often I imagined catching a cab and heading to her door, as I'd done a million times before. To see her standing there, waiting and smiling, the climbing roses to the right of her front door either cascading against the whitewashed wall in full bloom or waiting for the first thaw, just barren stalks in the cold air. With its bare stone walls, old fireplace, and sagging roof, the cottage was rustic at best. But Anais had taken what her father gave her and polished it so that it became more French country chic, with a view of fields and a five-minute walk to the ocean.

I wanted to go there to her, but I couldn't. I knew she needed space. And I needed the attention on me to settle down first. When I finally did visit her, how could I know things would turn out the way they did? That I'd be setting into motion a series of events that would end in tragedy. Anais had always been my touchstone, my refuge, and my greatest champion when I was growing up. I couldn't fathom she wouldn't help me once she knew I'd survived—take me in, give me food, shelter. Surely when she saw how thin I'd become, she'd find it in her heart to sit me by the fireplace with a glass of wine and let me tell her my side of the story one more time.

When I couldn't take our separation any longer, I took the last train into Cherbourg that night to avoid being seen, and walked partway out of the city toward Querqueville, then caught a ride to the end of her street. It was a terrible twenty minutes, standing there after I'd been dropped off, the drizzle coming down steadily, while I watched the lights in the windows of her house at the end of the lane but was too frightened to move. When I'd finally made my way around to the back patio and let myself in through the always-unlocked back door, she was there, the fire going. It was everything I imagined it would be. Except it wasn't.

She was bent over, reaching for a book on a lower shelf, her back to me. "Grand-Maman." My voice was a whisper. *"Je t'aime."* I love you.

The cottage door was still ajar, my body filling the opening. Anais whipped her head around toward me, but her body didn't move. Not for what seemed an eternity. Her eyes became larger, her lips parted, but she remained in a curved position, one arm reaching for the shelf as if frozen in that moment.

"I'm not a ghost. I'm here. I needed to see you. To let you know I'm okay." The French tripped off my tongue, though I was afraid to take a step forward.

She finally stood and backed away, trying to put as much distance between us as possible. Her arms straight by her sides, she pressed her back into the wall. Her eyes never left mine. But they weren't the soft eyes I'd thought of while traipsing down dusty roads across the Balkans into Greece. They were filled with fear.

"I'm not here to hurt you. I just wanted to see you. So you'd know . . ." My fingers went to my face to wipe away the rainwater from my lashes. "I need you." I put my hands out toward her. "I have no money. The flash drive was destroyed by the salt water."

"You came here for money?" she asked. I wasn't sure, but I thought her lips might have been trembling.

I could see my reflection in the window behind her. I shook my head. "No, see, I've made it all this time, all this way, without your money."

Her eyes scanned me up and down, but her body was still. "You shouldn't have come back, Ava. There's nothing here for you."

I slipped out of my wet coat and took a seat near the fire. The log was spitting out sparks. I picked up the poker and prodded it a few times. "I came here because I have no family left. And I'm lost in this world, Grand-Maman. Look." I lifted up the back of my shirt far enough for her to see my ribs. "I can barely eat. I need to be here with you."

The shadows from the flames moved across her. "I didn't know it at the time, but you killed two of my daughters. Not one." It was a hiss. A stream of wet syllables spewed at me. But they didn't make sense.

I half laughed but I didn't know why. I felt an odd lump in my throat. "I didn't kill Claire. I thought we covered that already. And I didn't do anything to Marie that she didn't deserve, but she's still alive and kicking." I gave her a minute, but she was quiet. There was just the sound of rain against the roof and the spitting of the fire.

"Since the day you were born . . ." Her voice was low.

"You haven't known me since I was born. I was three. Remember, Grand-Maman?"

"You've brought nothing but anguish to everyone around you."

Her words were choking me, and I turned away. "Fine, then, if that's how you feel. Just give me the bank-account numbers again. I can't get anything from the flash drive." I turned to face her, but she wasn't there. I stood up and went into the kitchen, then the bedrooms. The front door was cracked open. She'd slipped out while my back was turned and raced down the path to the street. I saw her outline disappearing into darkness. "Where do you think you're going, Anais?" I muttered.

If I'd known what was going to happen, I would have chased her down, hugged her, brought her back to the house, poured her some bourbon or another strong drink. But the only thing I could think at the time was that if she wasn't going to welcome me back, I needed to find money. Money made everything easier. But after a half hour alone in the cottage, rifling through drawers, pulling her desk apart, looking for those account numbers, I'd found nothing. *Shit.*

It was the flashing blue lights through the window that sent me grabbing my wet coat and skittering to hide in the shadows outside the back of the cottage. Those lights, I was sure, had come for me. I didn't know the lights were for Anais, that something had happened to her out there in the darkness, until I saw the stretcher being loaded into the back of an ambulance and then disappearing down the lane. I discovered later she'd had a stroke—she had fallen by the side of the road while running away from me. Sandrine, a self-proclaimed one-woman neighborhood watch, saw her lying there and called for help. Anais never recovered her faculties enough to give away my presence at the cottage.

The funeral was this week, and I wished I could go, but I'd already said my good-byes. And I had more-pressing matters at hand.

My passport was stamped, giving me ninety days in the United States, though I figured I only needed seven, tops, and I moved past the luggage-collection area and out onto the sidewalk. The United States was a dangerous place for me to be right now, but I had urgent business to take care of. I felt the flash drive in my pocket—the lifeline to my future. Maybe as a bonus I'd find someone who could solve my memory-chip issue. I glanced around at the ground transportation signs. A shuttle, then a train, would take me south—toward Haddonfield. And toward Russell and Juliette.

CHAPTER 10

RUSSELL

Russell sat at his desk in the Prosecutor's Office. He shifted in his chair to relieve the crick in his back from sleeping on the hard guest-room mattress. He was developing a gritty headache to boot. He tried to chase away the pain with a few Motrin chugged down with coffee. Mornings always started with a review of open cases, a file filled with police reports, mug shots, notes, photographs. He flipped through the file, hoping there was nothing new on the Haddon Township car break-in scene. He'd never hear the end of it from Joanne.

He glanced up and saw a female form at the end of the office but didn't pay attention until she was leaning over his desk.

"A second of your time?"

It was Marie's parole officer. He swallowed what was left of his coffee and straightened his wrinkled shirt. "What's up?" he asked.

Bridgette sat on the edge of his desk, pulling her long legs to the side. She clasped her hands in her lap. "Nothing to be alarmed about, exactly. But Marie's plane took off this morning."

"And?"

"And I called the airport to make sure all went well, her documents were all in order—"

"I'm feeling this story isn't going to have a happy ending."

"I can't say that—the story hasn't ended yet, but it's not starting out good. Marie never got on the plane."

"Maybe she changed her mind? Maybe she's still at her house?" He was sitting upright now. "Have you checked?"

"I just got back. No answer. I, umm"—she hesitated—"didn't break in, because it's not at that stage yet, but I came to you because I know you were against letting her go. I need to know why." She moved back on the desk and her skirt slid up an inch.

"I wasn't against it—"

She smiled. Bridgette was young, only three years in, optimistic and seemingly devastated when she got a person wrong. "You were. You know it. What did I miss?"

"No." He touched her arm lightly and kept his hand there. "You didn't get anything wrong. I've just been involved in this from the beginning." He cocked his head to the side. "Maybe too involved. I know these people."

"So I've heard." Her lips curled into a smirk.

"Yeah, anyway, what worried me was that Marie had nothing left here. Other than parole. Her sister died, now her mother. She knows France. She grew up there." He thought about the stack of suitcases by her door. "I was afraid she wasn't coming back. It never occurred to me she wouldn't go at all."

Bridgette brushed her light-brown hair back from her face. "Technically she hasn't violated anything. It was her prerogative to stay or go." Her hands went out to her sides. "It just seemed like so much red tape to go through for nothing."

"So what are you thinking, exactly?"

"Something happened that kept her from getting on that plane. She was packed and ready."

"She was. I went to talk to her. She had suitcases piled up—too many suitcases for a five-day trip. But what do you think happened?" He was starting to squirm in his seat. There was no good reason for Marie to miss that flight.

"I'm not a detective. I'm a parole officer. And I'm in big trouble. My name is all over Marie's paperwork if she just disappears. If this funeral thing was a ploy of some kind."

He wanted to say something encouraging, but he had nothing. "You want my help in finding her, is that it?"

She nodded. "At least help me get an idea of what's going on before I bring it to the courts? If it comes to that, I mean. We're not there yet."

"You mean unofficially? Oh, Bridgette, I . . ." Then he saw the petrified look on her face. If Marie was gone, this was going to be a political mess. He just nodded slowly.

"Thank you," she said before he could manage to protest. She slid off the desk and wrapped an arm around his back. "Though all this is for nothing. I know she's curled up in that bed of hers, ignoring the world." She tapped his desk two times, then scuttled down the hallway and disappeared.

"Where are you, Marie?" he muttered under his breath. He picked up the phone and dialed a flurry of numbers. "Joanne, Marie is AWOL. Meet me outside in ten minutes."

They stood in line at the food truck so Joanne could grab an egg sandwich and coffee. "You were right about this Marie thing blowing up, and I was making fun of you, I know, so you can stop yelling at me," she said. "So what do you want to do?" She had her sweater buttoned up to her neck and her arms crossed to keep out the cold. She turned to face him. "Think really hard about your career and what we went through last year before answering that."

"I mean, first things first. I want to see if she missed the flight and is maybe sleeping in. But I know she isn't, so we start by going out there just to look around, see if she's planning on returning. She was ready to go, Joanne, three bags packed. What's she up to? Did she catch a different flight?"

Joanne grabbed her coffee and sandwich and walked to a sitting area. "You mean breaking into Claire's house? Again?" She blew at the coffee and then took a sip. She eyed Russell, who was in just a shirt and tie, the sleeves rolled up to his forearms. "Aren't you freezing?"

"I'm fine. Yes, breaking in, but no. We've been there before. I just want to see . . ."

Joanne raised her eyebrows. "And then?"

He shrugged. "Go wherever this leads me, I'd say."

"Russell, you're getting married in two weeks—"

"I'm—"

"Don't say a word, let me finish. If you jump into this like you did before, your relationship with Juliette is over. No going back, no fixing it. If you're only half-there for this wedding, just going through the motions, or missing in action, Juliette is done. At the very least, your life will be hell." She took a sip of coffee. "And she's not my favorite person in the world, but she deserves better."

His hands were in his pockets. "Are you looking out for Juliette now? Listen, I never said anything about letting it interfere with the wedding. I'm just checking a few things out." He took a step back. "How do you expect me to ever let this go? Aren't you curious where Marie is? Did Ava get her? Did she run off? What?" He grabbed her arm. "And you loved it, I know you did. The breaking and entering, sneaking around, piecing things together. Except this time we're going to be one step ahead of Ava. So are you in or not?"

She crumpled the sandwich wrapper in her hand and picked up her coffee. "Don't kid yourself, Russell. Ava's already a mile down the road in front of us. But all right, you know I'm in. Call me if you hear anything from Parole today, and I'll meet you at Claire's house after work."

He smiled. "Lunch. Meet me right here. We'll go over to the house together."

"No, Russell. Let's wait until it gets dark so no one will see us."

"Twelve thirty. Right here," he responded. He turned and headed back up Fifth Street to his office.

"I always hated that frickin' nun," she yelled after him.

CHAPTER 11

Ava

I hate to think of death, though death thinks of me often. It's found me in every crack and crevice of my life, lurking and waiting for me around the corner when I wasn't expecting it. I didn't plan to kill anyone. I didn't wake up the morning I showed up at Father Connelly's rectory with the thought that I wanted to end his life. I was bitter, angry. I felt the world pressing on my back, every day that passed more unfulfilled than the one before it. I had reached a point of no return.

The circumstances of my adoption never made for a comfortable existence. I wasn't the child bounced proudly on a longing parent's knee, loved, nurtured. I lived a constant reality of vague memories born out of blood and horror. And as I grew, the texture of what had been changed and faded slightly. I started losing what was maybe the only real thing about me, the identity that had defined me before my life with Claire. I wanted to hold on to my old self, blow new life into fading memories by learning about my past. But when that was blocked by the very people who had stolen that life, that family, from me, I lost all sense of right or wrong.

Claire was a rock. Strong, unyielding, enduring. She showed me love, not in the usual sense, but with her presence. She didn't leave me even when she should have. It all seemed ridiculously, unnecessarily complicated; when she could have and should have turned me over to the authorities, reported my existence, she didn't. When she suspected my crimes, though horrified, she did her best in that moment to protect me, to protect this situation that had been foisted upon her, upending her life. It might have been because of me that she never married or had a family of her own.

I could see her face so clearly now. She was standing in front of me. Her brown hair falling just to her chin, curling slightly at the ends, her sapphire earrings dangling from her earlobes, casting a weird blue shadow across her lower face. Everything about Claire was tasteful, understated, and expensive.

"This has to stop, Ava," she'd said. "It's over. Now."

I'd been dragged back from college for this confrontation. Fresh faced, dressed in an oversized McGill hoodie and jeans, I squared off against her. "It's not over until I get my mother's name, Claire. Just her name. If you'd given it to me, none of this would have happened."

"Ava—"

"Connelly wouldn't tell me her name. I watched him butcher her in the church. They smashed her head in with the candlestick—"

"It's funny you remember the murder with such clarity. You were what, three at the time? Barely. But you don't remember anything else. Like, what was *your* name? Your first name?"

I'd fidgeted. Crossing my arms, uncrossing them, pulling at the sleeves of my sweatshirt with my fingers. "I don't remember."

Her face changed in that moment, and I saw something angry and hard take over. "I can understand you not knowing your mother's proper name, because you probably called her Mama or something like that. But your own name? A child knows the sound of their own name at a very early age. So, what was your name, Ava?"

What was she doing, pushing and challenging me? "I don't know. I don't know, Claire. You don't think I've gone over all this in my head a million times?"

"How is that possible? Because you did know it, when you first came to us. You never wanted the name Ava, you'd scream from the first light until you fell asleep." I was starting to feel uncomfortable. Those first years with Claire were murky. Like I was viewing them through a veil of heavy muslin. "'No, that's not my name,' you'd say. Then you'd call for your mother. Do you even remember what language you spoke? Was it English? French? Spanish? Something else?"

I backed away from her. "I don't know," I spat. I didn't. It was all so confusing. I'd been three. Maybe this was where my search for languages had started—trying to find my roots.

"Well, I'm going to tell you it wasn't English, so you can cross that off your list." I kept retreating until my back was against the wall. "How about Spanish? Does *'Mamá, quiero a mi madre'* sound familiar?" she continued.

"No. Stop." I hadn't seen her so angry in a long time. I'd learned to avoid her when she was like this, but I couldn't—she was in my face.

"Or maybe Dutch? I don't know Dutch well enough to put those words together for you, Ava, but I'm sure you do."

"Claire—"

Her face was only inches from mine and I flinched, waiting for her to hit me, but she didn't. "Whatever you've been doing has to stop. I didn't know, when Father Connelly died, that it was you. I thought it was an accident." Her eyes narrowed and became glassy with moisture. "But then Loyal? And his wife? I can't protect you from this, Ava."

"I don't need your protection. I just need the truth."

She was in my face now. "The one truth I know is that this subject is done. This killing is done. You got your revenge. But you still have a place with me, with Marie. With Anais. That's all that matters . . ."

The memory of Claire's voice trailed off. I was sitting on the train, feeling my bag bounce against my leg as we moved along the rails toward South Jersey. I wish I could say the killing had stopped that day, but it hadn't. I picked at the skin around my cuticle. The man in the BMW who had raped me in Paris—that was the end of it, I was sure.

Or maybe just one more. Juliette didn't know what she had coming.

CHAPTER 12

RUSSELL

The Victorian on West End Avenue in Haddonfield was still the same. Charming, but showing the very first signs of neglect. Russell surveyed the front of the house from his car, noticing the same things he'd noticed when he'd visited Marie yesterday. Leaves collected in piles around bushes, dotting the yard where the wind had blown them months ago. Cracks and holes were appearing in the driveway where the asphalt had crumbled away. Though the house was still pretty enough, with its big porch and large windows, he found it odd and depressing that Marie had chosen to come back here to serve out her parole, given that her sister died in the upstairs hallway and a man had lain dead in the bathroom with a knife in his gut. The house had to be a constant reminder that her family, namely Ava, had sorely betrayed her by framing her for the murder. Yet Marie listed the house as her place of residence without hesitation, minutes before she dodged out the back gates of the jail.

Joanne had been quiet in the seat next to him on the drive over. Whatever she was thinking, whatever smart remarks were coming to mind, she wasn't letting them escape her lips. "It seems everything always comes back to this house, doesn't it?" she finally said. "Everyone who's lived here is either dead or gone, something bad has happened to them, and we still keep coming back here looking for something."

She shot a glance at him. "This house is cursed, if you ask me. Filled with bad luck."

"I think so too." He eyed the screen door, unlatched, opening and shutting with every burst of air. "But if I'm going to follow Marie's trail, this is the beginning. Come on."

Joanne slid out of the Jeep and followed him around the side of the house to the back. The doors were all locked up tight. "So what now, Detective?" she asked.

He smiled and knelt in front of the basement window. The frame wiggled under the lock. Russell continued to work at it until the wood broke free and the window pushed open.

Joanne stood behind him, staring at the opening. "Five years ago one of my legs might have fit through there. There's no way now, Russell, and I'm in a dress."

"Don't worry," he murmured before disappearing through the hole. Two minutes later he was pulling open the sliding-glass doors. Joanne lingered outside, not seeming to want to enter, until Russell yanked her in and closed the door behind her. "Cut it out. Let's get this over with."

The house was still, save for the low hum from the refrigerator. Marie had left the kitchen pristine. Not a cup in the sink or bit of clutter anywhere.

Joanne put her index finger to her lips. "Don't make too much noise until we know she's not here," she whispered.

He rolled his eyes. "Marie," he yelled. "Are you here?" Nothing. He moved into the living room and called again. Joanne was right on his heels. "Marie, Parole is looking for you." He climbed the stairs without hesitation.

The office door was directly across the hall from the staircase. He stopped short, remembering the night he'd spent here digging through boxes of photographs. The night he'd slept with Ava in a drunken stupor. The last night he'd seen her before she'd disappeared and he'd feared she'd been killed. He stared at the door. This was really where it had all begun—the downward spiral in his relationship with Juliette, the reprimand from his superiors for withholding information in an investigation, the endless chasing of Ava, who was always just out of reach.

He moved on to the bedroom. Claire's old bedroom. Marie had to be using this room. He couldn't imagine her sleeping in Ava's bed or the guest room. He knew he was right when he opened the door and saw the remnants of occupation scattered about. A scarf hung over the closet doorknob; a lipstick was on the dresser, cap askew. A hand towel next to it, thrown down as if she'd been in a hurry.

Joanne was uncharacteristically quiet, almost seeming respectful of a sacred place, or scared. It was hard to tell which. She turned her attention to the dresser and began opening drawers.

He went into the walk-in closet. An assortment of clothing hung from the rod, most of which probably belonged to Claire. There were several small suitcases stowed in the rack above, but the ones Marie had stacked by the door were not there.

Joanne's loud, slightly nasal voice came through the wall. "Come here. Look at this!"

She was sitting on the bed, a purse in her hand. Her head was down and she was intently pulling objects out and dropping them next to her. "I think you might like this."

He knew the face that stared back from the small passport she held in her hand. It had haunted his dreams. Ava's birth mother's dark eyes, the same eyes that stared from the artists' renditions after her death, were there, staring straight ahead. He grabbed the book from her hand. "Marie just had this lying around? Sitting in this room?"

Joanne lifted the purse. "Yes and no. I think this is actually the purse Ava's mother had on her when she was killed." She turned the small satchel around; the brown leather was cracked and spotted with dark stains. "Is that blood, do you—"

"Unbelievable!" he seethed. "Just grabbed after the woman was killed, leaving her nameless." Russell's head swiveled around, taking in the room. "Where was it?"

Joanne pointed. "Bottom drawer of the dresser, under a pile of sweaters. But there's more." She held up an envelope. "A letter."

Russell sat next to her on the bed. "Claire and Marie knew who Ava's mother was the entire time. They knew everything. Yet they let her beg and plead for the information and eventually kill for it, and all the while they had the purse?" He ran his hand through his hair. "Why was it so difficult to just tell her who her mother was? The kid witnessed the murder. It's not like she didn't know what happened. Why not help her find her family? It's so . . ."

Joanne was studying the letter, engrossed. "Claire moved constantly." She looked up at Russell. "We assumed she was running from Quinn, and maybe she was, but that never made real sense, to have so much fear of that one man. But maybe there's more."

"Like?" He was impatient, wanting to rip the purse from her hand and go through the items himself, but he sat instead with his hands folded in his lap, letting her finish.

"Like maybe Claire had some information. Adrianna had this letter stamped, addressed, and ready to send to someone in Italy. I wish I could read it, but it's in Italian." The envelope had been ripped open and thoroughly digested by someone—probably by Ross, Marie, or Claire.

"Google Translate?" He turned on his phone.

"That's so time consuming." The ink was light and smeared in places, written in scrawling cursive across the page. "It'll take hours to decipher this. I wish Ava was here, she'd unravel this letter in a second."

"Funny," he responded.

"Was Adrianna running from something and then ran right into more danger? This thing is an onion. The more we peel, the more layers we find underneath, and it all stinks."

Russell pulled the letter from her hand. "Let me see." He took the purse and dumped the rest of the contents onto the bed. Then he stuffed his hands in all the pockets.

Nothing. He threw the things back into the purse.

"Let's go." It came out slowly because his thoughts were jumbled.

"Where?" she asked.

"Back to work. But first stop is the post office to get a passport application for you." Her eyebrows rose. "Just in case we need to go to Italy. Because I have this undying urge to ask Adrianna's family a few questions myself."

"There's a thing called telephones, Russell. Call them. Wedding. Less than two weeks."

"I will. I will. But sometimes people are much more forthcoming in person."

They descended the stairs. "Just two things about all of this," she said. "One, we came here looking for Marie and what she's up to, and found nothing. Where is she?"

He shot a glance backward. "And two?"

"Why do you think Marie or Claire kept that purse? That's a terrible memento."

They stood near the front door. Russell had the bag tucked under his arm. "I don't think it was always in the house. Ava did a pretty exhaustive search."

"You think Marie had it all this time?"

Russell nodded and started to open the front door when he saw the police car parked out front. "Shit. Haddonfield." He was bound to know their faces. "And Bridgette's with them." He slammed the door and leaned against it. "Take the bag, go out the back door, hurry up. I'll stay to greet them."

"But—"

"Go. Out the back and don't let anyone see you or that purse," he whispered, but it came out like a hiss. "Climb the fence if you have to." He saw her expression. "I'll talk my way out of this—tell them I stopped by after my conversation this morning with Bridgette. Go."

The last thing he saw before opening the door to greet them was Joanne rounding the corner, purse under her arm, the back and side of it splashed with twenty-year-old blood.

CHAPTER 13

JOANNE

The letter was so faded it was hard to tell if it was written in pencil or pen. In places the writing smeared off the page. It was clear from the tatters at the edge of the page that it had been open and devoured numerous times before. The envelope was worn and slightly bent.

Joanne sat at her desk outside Judge Simmons's office at the courthouse. She was smoothing the paper out in front of her. Cursive writing, very choppy, ran to the edge. She turned on her computer and poured a cup of coffee. Russell hadn't called, and she assumed he'd been detained by the police at Marie's house. No matter how fast he talked, it was going to appear odd that he was there at the house. He'd been overly involved with the family before and been given a six-month suspension for withholding information. Now there he was again.

She was reaching for her phone to call him when it rang. She grabbed the receiver. "Joanne. I talked my way out of being at Marie's—thank God for Bridgette. But I got pulled away on a case. Sorry." Russell was speaking fast.

"Pulled away on what case? What's more important than this?" she asked.

"A homicide. Start trying to translate that letter and I'll call you later."

There was silence and some crackling from the other end of the phone. "Camden again?" she asked.

"No, actually, this time it's in Haddon Township. Akron Avenue. Gotta go. I'll call you." He clicked off.

"Oh God," she muttered. Akron was only a ten-minute walk from her house.

She pulled up Google Translate and stared at the paper in front of her. The first word was easy. A name—Philomena. Adrianna was writing a letter to her mother, Philomena. The next part became a guessing game, because the letters were mangled. *Ho solo abbastanza soldi per un altro paio di giorni.* After multiple tries, the sentence made enough sense that the translation engine spit out a sentence in English. *I only have enough money to last for a couple more days.*

"So you're running out of money, Adrianna? I pretty much figured that. Tell me something I don't know."

She plugged in the next sentence, but it produced nothing. In frustration she pounded her fist on the desk. "Maybe she's writing in some sort of Italian the computer doesn't recognize," she murmured. She squinted at the note and moved some letters around. *Ci proverò di nuovo stasera. Se non funziona, non so cosa farò.* She sounded it out as she typed it in. *I'm going to try again tonight. If this doesn't work, I don't know what I'll do.*

She put her hands under her chin and stared at the screen. "Try again? By going to the church that night? Try what? To talk to the priest? Why?"

The rest of the letter was just mangled swirls and lines of ink across the page. The only thing that jumped out at her was a name. Leo Martinelli. And an address: 2909 Cross Street, Philadelphia. "Was that where you were staying?" She'd run out of patience to try and decipher the rest.

It occurred to her that other people had read this letter. Certainly Marie and Claire. Maybe Ross. But who else? Had they tried to find Leo Martinelli? "Why would they?"

"Why would they what?"

She'd thought she was talking to herself, but she looked up to see Bridgette in front of her, leaning against her desk.

Their paths had crossed numerous times in the courthouse—Bridgette as the parole officer, Joanne as the court secretary taking notes—but Joanne didn't know her well. "I didn't see you standing there. What's up?"

Bridgette folded her arms. Her hair was pulled back in a bun, making her look harsh and angry. "Russell was at Marie's house when I got there. I guess you know that, right?"

This moment was tricky and Joanne knew it. Admit nothing. "I'm in the middle of something and I haven't seen Russell."

"I told the police I'd asked him to visit. But you know I was surprised. He said the front door was open, but I doubt that. You know I never asked him to break in."

Joanne raised her eyebrows. "And?"

"And I saw you there too. Running down the sidewalk to your car. The street's not that big."

"I—"

Bridgette put her hand up. "I didn't say anything to them, but I'm asking you. I get why Russell went, but why'd you go there? And what'd you find? Anything about where Marie might be? Or if she intends to come back?"

"I have no idea what Marie intends to do. And neither do you, obviously, but you assume she violated anyway?"

Bridgette's eyes narrowed. "Either way I was screwed in this. I vouched for her in front of the court—bad decision number one. And I realized going to Russell this morning was bad decision number two—it was going to create a bigger mess."

"So?"

"So, I haven't officially violated her yet. I just asked the police to go with me on a welfare check. They wouldn't have broken in, but since the door was already open—thank you, Russell—I did look around."

"And?"

"I found a small datebook on the counter in the kitchen near the phone." She fanned the pages in Joanne's face. "Nothing in it, really. Dates of travel, flight number. Numbers in France, of relatives, I assume. And then this." She handed Joanne a square of paper. "Stuck right on the side."

The plain yellow sticky note just had an address on it. Joanne peered up at Bridgette. "I don't get it. I'm not sure this means anything."

"It's an address in Vicenza, Italy. She only had permission to go to the funeral. It was all mapped out. Not Italy."

"Maybe she knows someone there and was going to mail a letter? Maybe it doesn't even have anything to do with this trip." Joanne was speaking fast; she wanted Bridgette to leave and was only hoping her face didn't show what she was thinking. The address on this note was the same as the one on the front of the envelope Adrianna had intended to mail the day she was killed. "Look, Bridgette. I need to run. Russell will call you, I'm sure."

Joanne stuffed the half-translated letter into her purse and turned off her computer. Vicenza could wait. She had an address right here in the United States to check out: 2909 Cross Street. She'd GPS it as soon as she got to her car. She considered waiting for Russell, but then she thought of the homicide in Haddon Township. He wouldn't be around for hours.

CHAPTER 14

RUSSELL

He pushed the door open and slid off his shoes. The living room was flooded with afternoon light. Juliette's black satin coat lay in a bundle on the couch, where she'd discarded it the night before in her drunken stupor. He picked it up, smoothing out the wrinkles that had formed overnight, and hung it in the closet. He'd noticed her car was still in the driveway when he'd pulled in. She must be nursing one hell of a hangover, he thought. This wasn't like her. She'd been distant, moody, and tearful lately, but he'd assumed it was just pre-wedding jitters. The closer it got, the more they seemed to pull away from one another.

"Jules," he called to her. "Are you up?" He was met with dead silence.

He just wanted to grab some coffee, go to his little office upstairs, finish his report about the homicide. He needed some time out of the Prosecutor's Office, away from the noise, distraction, and constant interruptions. His head still hurt. He hadn't heard anything from Joanne since she'd run from Marie's house with the purse, but he'd put his phone on mute to take a break.

The kitchen was devoid of natural light. He flipped on the overhead and pulled the coffee canister from the cupboard. He'd make Juliette a cup and bring it to her with some ibuprofen as a make-up gift. And maybe a glass of water if she was nice. The coffee started to drip, hissing as it fell into the hot carafe.

"I'm making coffee for you," he yelled. He wondered now if she was ignoring him on purpose. "I'm only home for an hour. I wanted to check on you."

He climbed the steps and could see before he even reached the top that the bedroom door was shut. He turned the knob, but it was still locked. He rapped lightly with his middle knuckle. "Jules, are you still sleeping?"

There was no answer, no noise of stirring from the other side. He knocked again, louder. "Juliette. Open the door."

He looked at his watch: 2:10. She couldn't still be passed out.

"Look, Jules, I'm sorry about last night. I don't want to fight."

He looked at the knob, at the small hole in the center of the knob. Then he went to his office and opened the desk drawer, sorting through odds and ends, looking for anything he could use to pick the lock. He slammed the drawer in frustration and darted out of the office and down the steps. "I need an awl. Toolbox, toolbox."

As he descended the steps into the basement, it grew colder by degrees. He reached the bottom, looking around. "Damn." He felt a draft coming right at him. There was a rhythmic tinging sound, metal striking metal. After a few minutes he realized the small window in the corner was unlatched, moving slightly with the wind. He'd just broken into Marie's house through a window almost exactly like this. The thought made him slightly uncomfortable. He secured it, then headed to the storage area and found his red toolbox.

He raced back up the steps and knelt before the bedroom door. "Juliette, I'm coming in."

He inserted the awl and jiggled it. The lock sprang loose and the door opened. The smell hit his nose before he even entered. Stale alcohol. Sweat. Stagnant air. Juliette was in bed, on her side, facing the window. The blanket was down to her waist, and he could see she was still in the dress she'd worn out the night before. Her phone was on the end table, the screen lit up with texts and missed calls.

He walked to the window, raised the blinds, and slid open the window, letting the cold air in. Juliette's eyes were slits, but she didn't move when the light hit her.

"Jules. You okay?" He leaned over the bed and put a hand on her shoulder. He shook her gently. Her body was stiff, her skin waxy. "Wake up." He leaned in and shook her harder. "Juliette! Get up!"

The first sign of life came when her tongue emerged and licked her lips. "I'm so thirsty." The words were garbled.

He noticed the trash can next to the bed was filled with vomit, and some of it had splashed onto the bed frame and the floor. "Great." He pushed to a standing position and moved away. "No shit. Stay here. I'm going to get you some water." He returned several minutes later with his hands full. He placed a cold bottle of water on the end table and unscrewed the cap. "Look at this." He pointed to the garbage can. "Disgusting. You're too old for this."

"Give." She motioned to the bottle.

She pushed to a sitting position. Her hair was twisted around her face. The skin under her eyes was dark, bruised looking. She seemed sick and fragile. Her eyes were glassy and bloodshot. The image reminded him of those heroin-chic models from the '90s. Russell glanced down at the phone. Steve Thomas, an orthopedic surgeon she worked for, had called fifteen times and texted five. Numbers that matched the hospital had called seven.

"Did you call out today? Because it looks like they've been trying to reach you all morning."

She guzzled the water and then glared at him. "Just go, Russell. I don't need a lecture right now." She put her hand up to her mouth like she might vomit again.

He kicked the garbage can closer to the bed. "There are things we need to talk about, Juliette. And you know what they are."

She shot him a look. "Is now the time, do you think?"

"Now's the perfect time. You went to the doctor's last week." Russell picked up her phone. "You started to tell me something three days ago. Was it about that? Does it have something to do with him?" He shook the phone.

Juliette's face crumpled. "Really? You think these past few weeks have been about an affair with my boss? Like that's the key thing here? Oh my God, Russell. It's so much worse than that. And if you weren't such a crappy detective, you might have figured it out." She shifted around to face him. Her mouth was dry and cracked; speckles of vomit clung to her lips. "You're pathetic."

He stood by the doorway, saying nothing, letting her spew words at him, each one worse than the one before it. He felt his blood pressure rising and, at the same time, the future he'd imagined with this woman disappearing as she told him the truth. She was right, it was worse than he'd imagined.

Ten minutes later, as he was darting down the stairs, he felt more livid with each step. He stopped at one point and almost went back up, but changed his mind. Juliette had been helpful, a true partner, toward the end of the Polaroid-murder investigation, but when she found out he'd let Ava go that day in the airport, everything changed. Not so much an all-at-once change, but a slow, steady journey toward indifference, sometimes punctuated by angry outbursts or below-the-belt insults, but never addressing the skinny woman with the green eyes who had taken up residence in the middle of their relationship.

Granted, the Ava affair had been his fault—not even an affair, just a one-time deal—but he'd done everything to make it up to her, like a servant, a puppy, to appease her over the following months, but nothing seemed to work. Juliette seemed to want to go ahead with the wedding and punish him at the same time. And he wasn't up for punishment in perpetuity. There was an end to everything.

He slammed the front door of the house behind him and marched toward his Jeep. "Fuck her. She gets what she deserves."

"What's up, Russ? Something the matter?" His neighbor Gordon was standing on his lawn near the driveway, his eyebrows up in a quizzical expression.

"No." Russell opened his car door. "Sorry. I'm just having a day."

Gordon waved as Russell pulled out in the Jeep. He heard his phone buzzing in his jacket pocket. He pulled it out. Joanne had tried to reach him four times.

"What's up?"

"I'm in Philly, Russ. You need to come here. Cross Street, the South Philly Cross Street, near Passyunk."

He plugged it into his GPS. The sun was hovering in the sky, dipping to the west. "I'm supposed to be at work and so are you."

"Yeah. I left a little early. I'm too busy tracking Ava's mother's last movements before she was killed in the church. I'd love to have your help. I'm parked in front of this house now. I'll wait for you. It's 2909. It was an address in the letter in Adrianna's purse."

He sighed. "I'll be there in thirty minutes. I could use a cheesesteak."

"I already bought you one. Hurry up."

Russell glanced at his house. His eyes were on the upstairs bedroom window. "Sleep tight, Juliette," he whispered.

CHAPTER 15

MARIE

Her thinness was astounding. Already at the brink of emaciated the last Marie had seen her, Ava looked to have lost another ten pounds. Dressed in black, she was like a whip of licorice walking down the residential street in Cherry Hill, the dark clothing hanging from her bones. Marie remembered that day in the Pine Barrens with Quinn, when they dragged Ava from the back of her car. Her hair had been hanging in wet clumps around her face. She'd been wearing black that day too. Confused, stumbling, weak. Light.

It was in those moments, watching Quinn take more than fifteen years of rage out on the skinny little creature, that Marie first knew Ava was a killer. It just came to her. The answer to the puzzle of that old Polaroid camera Marie'd found tucked in Claire's office drawer. Just sitting there. An implement of murder, or at the least a prop connected to the entire staged series of brutal events. Marie's hands had been shaking when she'd grabbed the camera up and stashed it in a bag and taken it to the convent for safekeeping. She'd tossed and turned in bed that night, trying to figure out if Claire, her sister, was capable of killing all those people. Ava'd been away at college during most of the violence. Could Claire have killed the priest, and Loyal and his wife? And had she killed their father, Ross? It made no sense. Had they had a fight?

But in that moment of finding the metal box camera, it'd changed the way she'd looked at her sister up until the day Claire died. Marie had never been certain.

She confronted Claire once, while she lay in bed, drinking tea and nibbling on dry toast weeks before her passing.

"Feeling any better, Claire?" Marie peered around the doorway, testing the waters.

Claire's eyes were large and shrunken at the same time, the bones of her face more prominent than ever. "Come in, Marie. I just got off the phone with Maman. She said she wants to come and visit next month."

"That would be nice. I only have a minute. I just wanted to ask you a question. Because I've been thinking a lot about Papa." Marie watched her sister's face for a moment before continuing. There was little change in her expression. "And I was wondering if you might have talked to him before he died. That last week?"

Claire sat up in bed. Her face tightened. "No. Not for a few months at least. Why?"

Marie shrugged. "Because it bothers me he knew he was next. He was the next one on the list to die. And I was wondering if he'd discussed that with you."

Claire pulled a tissue apart with her fingers. She didn't look at her sister. "He never called me in a panic, if that's what you mean."

Marie cleared her throat. "Where's that old camera, Claire? Have you seen it, by any chance?"

"Is this a game of charades, Marie? Are you suggesting I killed them all? Mailed them Polaroids?" She didn't seem so fragile and ill anymore. "Why would I?" Marie didn't say anything. "I didn't. Maybe you've been the one, Marie. Maybe it's been you all along."

That conversation had riled Claire to the point of exhaustion. Marie left the house knowing only two things. That Polaroid camera had been in Claire's desk drawer. And Claire had been withdrawing from everything and everyone for months.

The suspicions had consumed Marie until that moment in the woods. The truth slowly descending upon her, the clarity of it all shocking. Watching Ava on the ground, trying to reason with Quinn. Begging him. Playing innocent. Then getting angry. Everything with Ava was a well-choreographed affair. Always she had an agenda tucked neatly away, at the ready. The murderer had been Ava, and Claire had known it was Ava—that was what all Claire's secrecy had been about. Protecting the vile little creature until the end. Until—as Marie still believed—Ava killed her. And with that truth came the desire to see Ava dead. And Quinn was willing to do it.

Ava was on her back on a bed of pine needles. Her black turtleneck almost fused with the skin of her neck as Quinn strangled her. For the first time Marie could remember, that look in Ava's eyes was gone, that all-knowing, cunning, screw-you look. It had been replaced with rage and terror. The kind of terror you saw in small cornered animals, frenzied, unpredictable. Marie had stared down at her, and in that split second decided to spare her. She grabbed a handful of Quinn's shirt and yanked him hard enough that he stumbled backward, away from Ava, and fell.

Why had she let her live? Very simple. Anais. The old woman had some connection to Ava. And in the balance between telling Anais that Ava was dead or telling her Ava had gone on a murderous rampage, killing everyone, including Anais's ex-husband, Ross, and her daughter Claire, the second choice won by just one swing of a fist. Though the decision had been a flawed one, for the knowledge of Ava's activities left the old woman shaken to the core in a way that was devastating. She left the cruise ship at the next stop, in Toulon, after Ava jumped into the sea, appearing on the ramp, shriveled, in a wheelchair, barely able to breathe when she debarked.

Now Anais was dead, and Marie could see the ends of Ava's loose hair moving against the back of her black shirt as she headed up the street. Her long legs pumping fast. Marie stopped every few seconds and watched from a safe distance. Ava had a purpose for being in this suburban neighborhood, was going somewhere for a reason, and that reason had to be Russell.

This should be interesting. But it wasn't. Nobody appeared at the door of the house Ava approached. That was when Ava disappeared around the side of the house. Confident, like she owned the place. Her knit hat only partially covered her face. Her shoulders were back, straight. Marie was curious. If Russell didn't answer the door, he wasn't home. His Jeep wasn't in the driveway. What was Ava doing? Marie walked closer to the house, aware there was very little in the way of cover should Ava circle back around to the front of the property, but it didn't matter. This girl was up to something and it was too intriguing to ignore.

Time passed. Twenty minutes, maybe, and still Ava didn't reappear. Marie heard more than she saw from where she'd taken up position, leaning against the tree across the street. A faint scream of surprise, barely audible. Time went on and there was nothing more. No Ava, no sounds. No conversation. No movement. Marie was perplexed. Until she saw the girl shooting out from the other side of the house, her bag under her arm, running almost to the other end of the block and around the corner, before Marie even had time to push off the tree and follow her. *Shit.* She stared at the house, unsure if she should investigate or leave it alone.

She pounded her fist against the tree. What the hell had happened? She approached the house slowly, the same way Ava had, and let herself in through the unlocked patio doors in the rear, careful not to touch anything with her fingers. The house was still. Someone had to be home—probably Russell's girlfriend, but there was no movement. Marie needed to know what Ava had been after.

"Hello?" she called. If the woman came down the steps, she didn't want to seem like she was breaking and entering. She walked to the front door and opened it, as if she'd come in that way. "Is anyone home?" She shut it loudly behind her.

Marie stared at the steps. This had a déjà vu feel to it. She had flashbacks to the day she went back to Claire's house, only to find a bloody trail like breadcrumbs leading up the stairs to the bathroom and Michael Ritter's body. The police had blamed Marie, and her legal battles had begun. Was there another body up there? Was she once again walking into a trap? The house had an eerie, sticky feel to it. Marie hesitated, her hand on the banister. She had to see what Ava had done.

The hallway was empty. The doors were all shut. Marie tried a knob and the door opened slowly into an office. Russell's office. She shut it and moved to the next. A nicely prepared guest room. There were only two more doors. One was a bathroom, she could see because the door wasn't completely latched and the light from the window bounced off tile. The other must be their bedroom.

Marie pressed her ear against the door and listened. Nothing. Her breaths were coming hard. Her hand went to the knob when she heard rattling from somewhere close by. Her heart jumped and she froze. She was stuck in the hallway, afraid to move. She had to make a decision, so she twisted the knob and rushed into the bedroom.

What she saw made her stop dead. She pulled at her hair with her hands. Then she raced down the stairs and out through the back, not even bothering to close the patio doors behind her.

CHAPTER 16

JOANNE

Joanne was sitting in her car, fiddling with her phone, when Russell pulled up beside her. She took a few moments to look up and then waved frantically for him to park and join her in her car. As soon as he opened the door she thrust the cheesesteak into his lap.

"I've been staking this out for over an hour now. I almost ate your cheesesteak too."

"You think Adrianna was living here when she was in Philadelphia? Is that it?" he asked.

"No clue. It was just an address in the letter. One of the only things that was clear. It's gotta mean something, right?"

He started to peel back the wrapper on his sandwich. "This is South Philly. What are the chances that the people living in this house are the same people who lived here in '96? It's a long shot. What else did you get from the letter?"

"It was hard to get it to mean anything with that translation engine, but she was out of money and was going to try something again one more time, that night she was killed. I don't know what. Or how the church played into it. Or the priest. But this address was clear on the page."

"Interesting and definitely worth a look."

"I can't believe you got me back into Ava's mother's murder thing again." She glanced at him—he was chewing on his cheesesteak, a bit of sautéed onion hanging from the corner of his mouth. "Finish that, wipe your mouth, and let's get going."

Joanne pushed the car door open and went to the top step of two leading to the front door. It was a simple row home in the middle of the block. Brick front, one window facing the street. The neighborhood looked much the way she imagined it had in the '50s. She could see people coming and going from their homes all along the block. This was one chunk of South Philadelphia that had resisted the constant influx of new inhabitants. Solid Italian, as far as she could tell from the delicatessen at the end of the block and the Italian flags in a few of the windows, and probably had been since they'd swarmed off the boats in the early 1900s.

She knocked a few times and waited. Her stomach was doing flip-flops, though she wasn't sure why. If anyone answered, she was only going to ask a simple question. She waited for a few minutes and then the door cracked open. An older woman in a housedress stood there. *Thank God.* She was all of four feet eleven. Her hair was gray and curled like it had been done in a salon every week and kept in a hairnet at night in between visits. She looked like she'd always lived here. That was a good thing.

"Hello," Joanne started. Russell had backed up all the way to the car. "My name is Joanne, and I'm sorry to bother you. I was wondering if you know who lived here maybe twenty years ago or so? I'm trying to track down someone I used to know."

The woman eyed Joanne for a long moment before answering. "Weird question. I got a call not that long ago, someone asking the same thing."

"Really? Someone who?"

The woman's body was in the doorway, not moving. "Don't know who. But to answer your question, my father owned this house since the forties. Who is it that you're looking for?"

Joanne put her hand on the doorframe. "Do you remember anyone named Adrianna staying here? Young? Late teens, maybe a little older? This would be in the midnineties. Italian girl."

"Person on the phone asked the same thing."

"Did this person on the phone say why they were asking?"

"It was a woman, and no, I didn't ask. But I'll tell you what I told her. Just my family lived here then. Me, my parents, and one brother. We didn't take anybody in. I don't know anything about it."

"Is your father still around?"

She shook her head. "He died. In ninety-seven."

"Died? Died how?" Joanne got just a peek through the door and saw someone lying in what looked to be a hospital bed in the middle of the living room. The woman's eyes followed Joanne's gaze.

Her face lit with anger, and for the first time since the door opened Joanne thought their chat might be over. "That's my mother, and no, you cannot come in and talk to her. She can hardly breathe. We've been through enough. My father died and I don't know this Adrianna DeFeo. Now go away."

Joanne put her hand on the door to keep it from closing. "Wait, wait, wait. I never said her last name. DeFeo. How'd you know that?"

"I musta heard it somewhere. Maybe the other person asking." She pushed at the door to close it and then changed her mind. "Look, the woman's been dead for how many years? When is this going to end? I had nothing to do with what happened to her."

"But if you knew her, and I think you did—and that's okay, I don't care—when she died, you must have recognized it was her. In the pictures, in the newspaper. Why didn't you identify her?"

"My father wouldn't let me. We didn't want any part of it. That's all I can say."

Joanne took a deep breath. She was so close. "I don't want to know for any reason other than she had a daughter. With her that night she died. I'm doing this for her daughter."

"Giada."

Joanne was dumbfounded. "Yes. Yes. Yes. But after Adrianna died, did you wonder what happened to the child? Were you worried or concerned?"

The woman leaned in to speak, as if the information she was imparting were sacred. "They didn't stay here. And the child? The child ended up in the right place, I think. That's what my father said, anyway, before he was killed. Now go."

She shut the door, but Joanne didn't move. "Wait. Killed? What was his name?" Joanne started banging on the door with the flat of her hand until Russell came up and pulled her away.

"He was killed. Russell. Oh my God, he was killed."

"Get in and follow me." He pushed Joanne into the driver's seat of her car. "You're going to have her calling the police, and that's the last thing we need."

"What was Adrianna involved in? That this man was killed? And someone else is tracking this lead, calling this woman?"

"Don't get out of that seat again." He shut her door and got into his Jeep.

Joanne was very aware that the woman in the house was watching their every move through the one living-room window that faced the street.

CHAPTER 17

AVA

The evergreens at the back of Claire's house were amazing. I used to watch the wind blow through them from the kitchen window. They'd stay strong and true through the worst of winter storms, occasionally losing a branch, but never really changing. I remember when we first moved to this house, I was sixteen. Too old to be climbing trees or creating a play world in the branches, but I was driven out back anyway, away from everything inside. Stringing fairy lights, arranging a chair and blanket in the perfect spot. Hidden, but with a vantage point from which I could see everything clearly. Now, as I watched the branches sway for a few moments, I wished I could be a squirrel and just disappear amid the foliage.

It was a useless thought. I was here, alive and in trouble again. I'd washed my hands three times with soap and water, then gently probed the half-inch-deep cut on my index finger. Deep enough that a Band-Aid wouldn't hold, but maybe not deep enough for stitches. And stitches weren't an option anyway, not unless I put them in myself. I wrapped the cut tightly in a wash cloth and pressed to stanch the flow of blood. The hypodermic needle had sliced into my flesh when I was pushing off the bed. I thought of HIV, the alphabet of hepatitis viruses.

There was nothing I could do. I was more concerned that the contents of the needle had possibly entered my bloodstream.

And so I'd rushed back here to this house on West End Avenue to recuperate. It was my first instinct after fleeing Russell's house. Like a womb, this house was always warm, familiar, and hospitable. Good Marie would be away at her mother's funeral, I was sure. The house was empty but, at the same time, filled with enough to be comfortable. I ran my hands along the granite counters. The cupboards had enough of Marie's morsels—canned goods, peanut butter, chips—to make a meal. One pear in the crisper and a bag of carrots in the bin. She'd even left behind a few pieces of white bread. A smorgasbord to me.

My stomach had long since stopped calling for sustenance. It was used to being sunken and denied. I no longer got hunger pains or yearnings in the middle of the night. In fact, the sight of food often made me ill, but I knew I needed to eat. And now might be my only chance.

I took the pear and cut it into slices. Then smeared peanut butter on one slice of bread and arranged it on a plate. I looked at it, trying to ignore that the smells were enough to induce nausea. I needed energy. I'd come back to the States to retrieve something. But that in and of itself wasn't enough of an excuse for the trip. If I had to come up with an answer, I was here for Russell. To see him. To watch him get married. Or not. To stake some claim. But I'd put something into motion unintentionally today by going to Russell's, and I couldn't undo it.

And now I needed to find my way out of this trouble I'd created. The only thing I had in my favor was the fact that I was legally dead. But I had no home, no allies, no money, and I was leaving a trail of bodies behind me. My time was certainly running out. I forced the bread into my mouth and took a bite. The peanut butter was heavy and greasy, and I wanted to reject it, but I forced myself to swallow. Then I did it again until my plate was empty. My stomach felt so bloated, I had to unbutton my pants to breathe. That would certainly hold me for a while.

I noticed the cloth around my finger was saturated with blood and was threatening to drip onto my plate. I pulled a paper towel from the roll and wrapped my wound again, watching the fingertip turn white and then scarlet with the pressure. I took the steps to the second floor and went into the bathroom. The sight of myself in the mirror sent shock waves through me. I was skeletal, and I looked too old for my age. Lines were starting to form around my mouth and eyes. My skin had taken on a yellowish haunted hue.

I'd developed an odd relationship with food over the years, and it was taking a toll. I never looked at my body and thought I was fat—that wasn't the source of my anorexia. Denying myself a meal had more to do with creating the suffering and punishment I knew I deserved. A lasting, visible punishment I could see every day and feel in every part of my body. My joints ached, my head pounded, my skin was dry, my hair lifeless. Malnutrition was worse for my being than alcoholism and I knew it. I owned it. Once I was able to make peace with the things I'd done, I'd have a hearty meal.

"Enough. Change your clothes. And let's get on with it. Do the next thing." I said those words and thought of Claire. *Do the next thing* was her expression. Whenever I was stuck, feeling anxious or uncertain, she'd unravel it with that one phrase. *Do the next thing, Ava. What is that? The rest will come.* The next thing was to shower and change clothes. Get a few supplies and hit the road. I'd already accomplished my primary goal for coming here—to get Russell's attention.

Do the next thing, Ava. I turned on the spigot and waited for the water to get warm. I was going to soak my body in this tub until all the weariness within me was gone. My bones still ached from the assault yesterday, and the bruising that dotted my body had turned a vicious shade of purple black. I poured a glass of red wine from Marie's liquor stores and swallowed half the glass in one gulp. These were the next things. I had come to the United States, saving my money so that I could travel to Philadelphia, to follow the thread of information that had plagued me since the last day I'd seen Anais alive.

After she ran from me out into the rain, I'd searched the house for her financial information. A copy of the information on the flash drive. But in that frenzy, while ripping apart her desk, I saw the name Giada on the upper corner of a bundle of papers. At the bottom were telephone numbers in France and Italy, and one for a man in Philadelphia who seemed central to the whole affair. Leo Martinelli. And his address. The possibility that he knew my mother took hold and wouldn't let go. It was worth everything I had to do to get here and to find him. The one phone call I'd made had produced nothing. Now I was here to look him in the eye.

I slid into the tub and let the water settle around my body, feeling the luxury of a warm bath I hadn't experienced in a long time. The plumbing in the Paris walk-up had been sporadic, spewing cold brown water or a trickle of hot. Nothing in between. I poured in some lavender oil from a bottle on the ledge of the tub, put my head back, and closed my eyes.

When I got out of the bath, I was going to forget about Juliette and what happened at the house, I was going to get rid of the evidence and erase it from my mind. Once I'd gathered my things, I was heading to 2909 Cross Street to get the information I needed to find my mother. And maybe my father too.

CHAPTER 18

RUSSELL

"I think we need to back up. Start from the beginning." Joanne was rambling. Russell put the key in the lock of his front door and went to turn it, but it was already open. Joanne, oblivious, pushed the door open and walked into the foyer, still talking. "We can get that woman's father's name. That's easy. Figuring out how he was connected with Adrianna—are you listening?"

Russell walked into the kitchen. "For the past half hour, I've been listening. I agree with you. Let's start by getting his name. Background. Find out how he died. But"—he motioned to her—"understand that just because he was killed doesn't mean it has anything to do with Adrianna's death. Water?" He handed her a bottle from the refrigerator.

She took it and unscrewed the cap. "A coincidence? A year after she dies, he's killed. And that woman did say 'killed' before she shut the door in my face. As in murder."

"One step at a time. But unless we find someone else who lived there, we may never know where Adrianna was going that night, or why. And we really need to talk to her family. She was writing to one of them. Was it the first time they'd heard from her?"

"Interesting—"

"Hold on. Don't say anything." He put his fingers to his lips and walked into the living room, standing at the bottom of the stairs.

Joanne followed behind him. "Is that your phone ringing?"

He shook his head. "Juliette's. She can't still be hungover. Unless she's sick from something else too." He took two steps at a time and flung open the bedroom door. The phone continued to chime.

He glanced down at where it sat on the end table. Another call from Steve Thomas. Fifteen past attempts were visible on the screen. "Juliette." He leaned over her and grasped her shoulder. "What the hell is going on with you?" Her body was lax and pliable. She didn't resist his touch, but she didn't move on her own either. "You need to get up now or I'm taking you to the hospital. You've been in here all day."

She didn't respond.

He rolled her over gently and saw the blood on her upper arm. A thin line that ran from what looked like a needle mark. Her face was white, her lips bordering on purple. Her eyes were slightly open and he could see the pupils fixed on him through slitted lids. Russell had seen hundreds of death scenes. There were days he'd lived and breathed them. They'd become routine to him, if not mundane. He knew everything he was supposed to do—on autopilot. But this was different. This was Juliette.

"Joanne!" he yelled. "Call 911. Don't touch anything on the way up. Not even the wall."

He heard her feet scamper until she was next to him. Her hand went to her mouth. No sound came out, but tears poured from her eyes. "What's wrong with her, Russell? What happened? Is she breathing?"

"Stay with me, Joanne. I don't know what's wrong yet. Make the call."

"I never thought she'd do it. Ava. I didn't believe she'd kill her. Oh my God." Then she started to scream.

He rolled Juliette over and started doing CPR, though he felt the coolness of her mouth against his when he breathed in. It was way too late to save her. "Joanne?"

But she was no longer beside him. He heard her voice from the hallway, on the phone. "Now. Send an ambulance now. And the police, yes. She might be fucking dead. Hurry."

The room looked the same as when he'd been here a few hours ago. The water bottle she'd drunk from was on the end table. The ibuprofen bottle was there too. Juliette had been facing the window when he'd left her. The same as when he'd entered the room just now.

He stood very still and took a breath. He wanted to grab her and cradle her in his arms. The argument they'd had when he was here earlier was replaying. Those last horrible words. The things he'd said and done. He looked down at her graying skin. She'd been dead for over an hour. He was held in place. Shock. His mind twisting in twenty different directions at once. The room started to spin.

Ava had tricked him, played her cards well, lulling him into the assumption that she wasn't coming to the area until his wedding date. That he had a few weeks to find her or wait for her. Then he saw the murder in Paris on the television. A man stabbed in his car on the side of the road near the airport. The witnesses described Ava down to her skin tone and eye color and the mole on the back of her hand. Still he didn't turn her in. He hadn't called the police in Paris, or told his superior, or made a report. Nothing. And now Juliette was dead. And she was staring at him through half-closed eyes like it was his fault. He knew it was.

"Detective Bowers." The room was suddenly exploding with people. "We need you to leave this room. If this is marked off as a potential crime scene, we don't want any contamination. We have forensics coming in, we need to get photographs—you know the deal. It might be better if you left the house with your friend right now. Let us do our job."

"To go where? I need to be here. It's Juliette." He heard his own voice but didn't even know he was talking.

"We're going to have someone take your statement." The officer put his hand on Russell's arm to lead him away.

He saw another detective coming up the stairs toward him. He knew him, worked with him at the Prosecutor's Office, but his brain couldn't pull out a name. "Russell, man, come with me. Let's get out of here."

"Where're we going? Where's Joanne?"

"She's out in the patrol car. We decided we're taking you to her house to interview you, rather than down at the station," he said. "Not me, personally. We have Connors coming in to interview you because—"

Russell heard the word *station* and he felt his heart drumming against his rib cage. "I want to help here. This was my fault."

The detective, whose name started with a *P*, put his arm around Russell's shoulders. "Shhh. Don't say that again. Not here. Not now. We need to take this one step at a time. That means you only answer what they ask you." The detective looked at him almost like he was putting the pieces together for the first time. "Do you need a lawyer? Do I need to get you one? Or call your family to get you one?"

Russell was confused for a second. What was he asking? There were six cars out front. Three had their lights on, making a blue-and-red light show for all the neighbors to witness. And one of his neighbors, Gordon, was watching from his front door; his face held an expression of concern and horror.

Russell was surprised when they put him in a separate car from Joanne. They didn't want them talking, comparing notes. That was the first inkling they were treating him as a suspect, as if there was something in that scene that had aroused suspicion. How could he tell them the killer was Ava? A dead woman?

"So, let's start this from the beginning. Just one more time."

Russell pushed back and stood up. Joanne's living room was feeling claustrophobic. She'd been in her bedroom with an officer for over an hour. God only knew what she was saying.

"Look, Mike—"

"Detective Connors to you tonight. Sorry, Russell, I know this is hard, but we need to go over this one more time."

"Fine. Ask. But I'm really feeling like I should be over there, helping them. Oh my God, Juliette's family? Her mother? I need to be the one to tell them—"

"They've been notified. Sorry again. You can go be with them soon. We just need to make sure we have everything. And that the timeline makes sense." Russell put his head down and pulled air in sharply through his nose. It made him dizzy. "So you last saw Juliette?"

"I went home in the afternoon. She'd been out last night. Last fitting for her dress. Then a party. She drank a lot and came home drunk. I wanted to check on her."

"And?"

"And the bedroom door was locked. I had to jimmy it open, and she was in her bed. A mess. Vomit all over. I gave her water. The bottle was still there on the end table. I gave her some Motrin. She was sitting up. Talking. I opened the window to give her some air because the room reeked."

"And the blood on her upper arm. You noticed that?" Russell nodded. "A possible injection site."

"I didn't see any needles when I was there."

"There was no used hypodermic needle found at the scene. Or anywhere in the house so far. No vial either."

"I don't know how that's possible." He saw Juliette's dead eyes looking at him. "How is that possible?"

"Why was she behind a locked door when you went home this afternoon?"

Russell put his hands on the back of the chair and leaned in. This looked really bad. "We had a fight last night when she came home. Words. She was drunk and she locked me out of the bedroom."

"A fight about what?"

"About nothing, really. Pre-wedding stuff." It was the first moment he realized he wasn't getting married. His marriage, his life with Juliette, was over. He felt his eyes water. "She was angry." A tear rolled past his nose and he wiped it away.

"And today? When you went home the first time? Was she still angry?"

His head was moving back and forth. "No. No. Not really. She was sick."

"So you mention that you opened the window. And that's interesting because your neighbor was able to hear some of what was happening in your house through that window. He says you were arguing. Your voices were loud."

"She may have been loud because she didn't feel good. Do you think I brought her water and then injected her with sedatives? Or something?" He knew he shouldn't have said it once it was through his lips. He'd heard it a million times from suspects. Never give the police ideas. Or make connections for them. It looks like guilt. "I'm done for tonight. Done. I'll get a lawyer if I have to. I need to go back to the house."

"You can't. It's cordoned off. Do you have somewhere else you can stay?"

Russell nodded his head, then shook it. At least ten places came to mind, but he didn't want to stay at any of them. He wanted to be in the house he'd shared with Juliette.

Ava had left Paris and was now keeping her promise. She'd said it in her little quote on the Polaroid she'd sent him after Anais's death. *Dans chaque fin, il y a un début. Ce n'est pas fini.* In each end there is a new start. It's not over.

Yes, you are right, Ava. This is just the beginning.

CHAPTER 19

MARIE

When Marie got back to her car, her limbs were trembling. She had trouble breathing and needed to take a few minutes to try and calm down, but then it would start again. Russell's girlfriend was dead. Or not moving. Her eyes stared blankly, and her limbs were limp. She didn't stir even when Marie pushed her with a sheet-wrapped hand. Her skin was still warm, but maybe not warm enough to indicate life. The end table held a partially empty bottle of Poland Spring water and some ibuprofen. That's all there was.

But the woman had a small trickle of blood running down the crook of her arm like she'd donated blood or something. *What the hell?* Marie would be blamed for this, just like she'd been blamed for Michael Ritter lying dead in the bathroom. *So stupid. Not again, Ava.*

She jabbed at the buttons on her cell phone, then changed her mind and clicked it off. She held still, just surveying the whole scene, taking it in from every angle. Then she saw it. It had fallen between the edge of the bed and the end table near the window. A glass vial. She went to the bathroom and grabbed some toilet paper and gently unwedged the small bottle from where it had landed. *Potassium Chloride, 40 mEq.* She pulled at the blankets to see if the needle had fallen, but it wasn't there. Marie stopped, thinking she heard something in the distance, a car pulling up in front of the house. She peered through the open window. Nothing. She wasn't getting involved in this. Not now. She had to get out of here.

She had sudden flashes of standing in the shower, naked, in front of two female officers right after her arrest. The hands on her body, being treated as an object—it brought back memories of her time in the psychiatric hospital. It didn't escape her notice that Claire had been filled with needle holes when she died. Maybe Anais too, if anybody had bothered to look. Ava was an infection that needed to be wiped out. Juliette must have been ambushed, held down, injected. She shook away the thought, slid the vial back where she'd found it, and tiptoed down the steps, leaving the way she'd come.

Now, Marie sat in her car parked around the corner from Russell's house. "Why, Maman? Why did you have to make this so difficult for me? Why'd you give that girl everything?" She bumped her head several times against the steering wheel. No matter how hard she tried to get away from this creature, she was just drawn right back in.

Marie glanced around, almost expecting to hear sirens in the distance, but there was nothing. Not yet. Her mind whirled and her breath came heavy again. This was a crossroads. The decision she made now would affect the course of her life forever. She closed her eyes, and the damp cell at the correctional facility flashed before her eyes. Metal bunk bed encrusted with grime. The hard cement floor. The metal toilet bowl that was cold and dirty. The sounds of retching in the next cell over and then the smells that followed.

She started the engine and made her way back to Claire's house, surprised at how her body was reacting to what had just happened. She felt hot and then cold. Her hands still shook, and she had trouble holding a thought. Her mind was in a rage. And she was well aware that on top of everything else, she'd missed Anais's funeral because of this woman. If she hadn't seen that wisp dressed in black at the airport,

Marie would be in Europe, clutching to the hope that it really was Ava's bones that had washed up in Turkey.

As she rounded the corner, not even a few hundred feet down the street, this devil that had been consuming her thoughts—now dressed in jeans and a blue coat, maybe one of Claire's, she couldn't be sure—was walking toward her. She had her head down, a bag in one hand, engrossed in her own thoughts, but it was definitely her. Marie wanted to run up the curb and end this now, but she ducked down in the seat and held her breath. Ava passed by without noticing her. She had gone to the house and now she was headed in the direction of the PATCO Speedline, probably going into Philadelphia.

Getting on the same train without being seen wasn't easy. It was a stroke of luck she'd been able to jump off at Eighth and Market when she saw Ava had exited from a car ahead of her. During the walk from the PATCO station to the Broad Street line, Marie's anxiety transformed into curiosity. Wherever Ava was going, it had to be important. Reappearing from the dead was risky. Apparently first on her list had been to kill Russell's girlfriend. The second item most likely involved money or the never-ending quest for information about her mother.

The street in South Philadelphia was like many others. Very narrow, made even more so by the cars parked along one side. Brick row homes lined both sides. This area was still as solid Italian as it had been a century ago. Generations had occupied these homes. None of it meant anything to Marie. She'd never been to this particular street before, but she knew the address. And the fact that Ava knew the address was worrisome.

She leaned against a brick wall and watched Ava drop onto a stoop, hesitating, thinking or just trying to gather her courage for what she was about to do, Marie assumed. But it was all so interesting. She looked lost, forlorn, an orphan. Her head was down, her hands in her lap pressed together, almost as if she were saying a prayer. There was a half-second twinge during which Marie was inclined to feel sorry for her. Then Ava stood up and started walking.

She went right to the middle of the block and knocked on a door. After several minutes she was let inside. Marie reached the end of the block, pulled out her cell phone, and plugged in the address, 2909 Cross Street, something she'd never had reason to do before. After searching for a few minutes, a name popped up. The house was owned by a Dolores Martinelli.

She knew that name, Martinelli. She'd heard it when she was a little girl. Anais went to see a family with that name once, somewhere far from Cherbourg, not long after they'd moved to France. The trip was notable because it was the only time she'd left Marie and Claire with a neighbor. Marie was sure Martinelli was the name. And so she knew instantly that there had been some thread of connection between Anais and Adrianna, the dead woman in the Philadelphia church. What that connection might be would keep Marie up at night and instigate horrible dreams.

CHAPTER 20

AVA

The stoop was cold against my rear end. The temperature was dropping, and I'd been sitting long enough that the frigid air was moving through my body. I was afraid to get up and walk down the block, and the longer I sat, the more hesitant I became. This was just a random street of brick row homes like so many others in this area of town, but it sparked an odd feeling of familiarity. I knew it, but I had no memories of it at the same time.

When I finally pushed myself up and started walking, I stopped in front of 2909 without looking at the numbers. I stopped automatically and reached for the iron railing, pulling the bottom, knowing full well it was set unevenly in the cement. I turned in circles. I had been here before. That was the only explanation that made sense. Twenty years ago I had walked down this very street, holding my mother's hand. And I had to have been here long enough that I knew the oddities of the house—the uneven railing, the way the sidewalk sloped in front of a basement window. I put a finger on the concrete step and wondered whether I'd been told to sit there and not move.

I closed my eyes and tried to bring something out. Some detail that would lend meaning to this experience. Nothing. The house was dark, no visible sign of life, but I stood in front of it anyway and knocked.

There was shuffling behind the door. I could hear it, but the door didn't open. I knocked again, harder. I had traveled three thousand miles to come to this house based on nothing but a couple of scribbles on a piece of paper found within Anais's cupboards.

I pulled the sheet from my bag and looked at it again. The name that had caught my eye was in the upper-right-hand corner. *Giada.* It was written no bigger or smaller than any of the other writing on the page. It was followed by a random series of notes. As if jotted down while Anais was talking on the phone. *Vicenza. Philadelphia.* A notation that looked like flight numbers. *AA*, which maybe stood for American Airlines. There wasn't enough on the page to create a story. Just choppy interrupted snippets of information.

I banged on the door again and was surprised when it opened. A figure hesitated, almost hiding, out of view. When she peeked her head around, I stared into her face, wanting so much to know her, but I didn't. And from the puzzled look on her face, she didn't know me either. She said nothing but she gave me a questioning stare.

"I'm looking for Leo Martinelli," I started.

"Again?"

I was startled. "But I've never been here before." Or had I? I had called hoping for information only days ago. But maybe I knew the house from years gone by.

"Maybe you haven't, but there seems to be a mad rush around here all of a sudden. What's this all about?"

She thought I had answers. I had none. "I don't know who else has come, but I didn't send them. Is he around?"

Her eyes traveled up and down me, landing finally on the bruising on my face. "You've been in a fight?" She motioned toward me.

"Attacked the other night. Nowhere near here, though." It was starting to rain, a hard, cold, bone-aching deluge.

She seemed to take pity and motioned me in. "How old are you? You could pass for ten or fifty. When's the last time you ate?"

I tried to smile but my face hurt. "Today, actually." I had just passed through the door when I saw the woman in the bed in the corner of the living room. She was hooked up to oxygen and didn't seem to have any awareness of her surroundings, not even turning her head toward the noise of voices.

"My mother. I usually don't let anyone in." The woman seemed embarrassed by the mess—the newspapers stacked in piles, clutter everywhere. "I take care of her now."

I tried not to look at the bedridden figure, out of respect. "So who else has come here? Looking for Mr. Martinelli?"

"Pffft. I got a call about him, then earlier today, you only missed them by a few hours, a couple was here banging on the door, asking the same question."

"A couple? What'd they look like?"

"Average. Man was tall, curly hair—"

"Russell."

"You know him, then? You're all in this together? So I'll tell you what I told them. Leo Martinelli died. Twenty years ago."

"That can't be right. You have no idea what I had to do to get here." The reality of this wasted trip was sinking in. "How'd he die?"

She walked to the front door and opened it. I thought she was showing me out, so I followed, disappointed but ready to leave. "He came home one night and someone was waiting for him. Right there." She pointed to a slight recess between this house and the next. "Cut his throat. Took his wallet."

I scanned the sidewalk in front of the house, trying to picture it. "What about you and your family? Nobody saw anything?"

"My mother said she heard noise out front but didn't think nothing of it. Young people having an argument wasn't strange. I was asleep. I just remember someone banging on the door in the middle of the night. Woke us all up to tell us my father was lying dead right there on the sidewalk."

"They never caught the person?"

She shook her head. "No. It's why I get shaken up when someone bangs on the door. Even after all these years it rattles me." She was quiet for a minute. "There was this woman that my father knew. Well, he knew her father, maybe is more like it. A cousin of his from Italy. She was staying here a few months before he died."

The hairs were standing up on my neck. "What was she doing here, from Italy?"

The woman flicked her hand at me. "Who knows. She was bad news. Running from something or looking for somebody or both. She had a little girl with her. My father told her she had to go. We didn't have the room to keep them, and some things in the house were missing. I always thought she had something to do with his being killed." She shook her head.

"What was her name? What was the little girl's name?"

The woman's old dark eyes flitted toward me and I saw a spark of something in them. She was putting the pieces together. "You're her, Giada, aren't you?"

I nodded and felt my nose tingle and the tears forming in my eyes. This was the first person I'd ever known who had some connection to my birth family. "I think I am."

"Your mother was killed. The woman that was staying with us." She looked genuinely upset. "I'm sorry. I don't know that your mother was stealing anything from the house. My father might've just said that as an excuse to get rid of her. And I don't really know she caused my father's death either."

"It's okay. What was her name? My mother?"

She cocked her head to the side. "What happened to you? Where'd you go? I never heard anything about it after she was killed."

"I was adopted by a woman. And her family. They raised me . . . all over the country. France too."

She dropped down onto a chair. "But how'd she get you? The papers never said anything about a child being left behind when they found her body. Nothing. I've wondered every day what happened to you. It bothered me."

I had no desire to tell this woman that my grandfather and his friends were murderers. I was starting to feel angry. "You knew the whole time who she was, when they were trying to identify her. You knew and you never came forward? Why?"

"My father wouldn't have it. And then, not even a year later, he was killed on the steps. We thought it was connected. We were hoping and praying they didn't know she'd been here."

"So you left her sitting in the morgue? Did you think her family might want to know? So they could look for me? Take her body?" The woman's head was moving back and forth but she didn't answer. Suddenly, my rage deflated. There was nothing I could do to change the past now. "So, I'm trying to put the pieces together myself. Just tell me about my mother. Please?"

The woman showed her teeth for the first time since I'd arrived. They were crooked, and it set something off inside my brain. It was familiar. "She wasn't here long. Three or four days, maybe a week at the most. She had dark hair, dark eyes. Thin girl. Her English wasn't good, so my father talked to her in Italian. He told us she came here looking for something."

"What? What was she looking for?"

"She was a lot like you. Asking questions. Picking at my father the way you're picking at me."

"Her name?" I took a breath and waited.

"Adrianna DeFeo."

I let the syllables run through my brain, trying to make something of them. They had to resonate somehow. But it was just a name. It meant nothing. All this searching and I could've just pulled out an old phone book and run my fingers down the page for all the significance it had. I put my head down and sighed. "Why'd she take me to the church that night? Do you know? I remember she was in a hurry."

"You remember that day?" The woman looked startled and curious.

I shook my head. "Just pieces."

She put her hand to her chest. "Terrible night. She had words with my father. She grabbed you and ran out the door. I remember you were wearing this little dress—"

"I know. I know about the dress."

"She was going to meet someone. Someone she thought was going to help her in this country because my father couldn't anymore. We always thought whoever she met was the one who killed her."

I studied her for a second. "I came here looking for answers and all I have are more questions. Do you have any idea who she was meeting?"

The older woman in the corner turned her head toward us. She pulled the oxygen tube from her nose and tried to sit up.

"Mama. No. Do you need to use the bathroom?"

She nodded. "In a minute. She wasn't going to the church." Her voice was raspy but deep. She coughed several times to clear her throat. "That's a fact. How she ended up there is a mystery. She might have deserved it, but Leo didn't deserve to die on the front step. Now it's time for you to go."

Those moments outside the church came to me. The streetlights had come on, I remember that. I was distracted by the lights. My mother was pulling my arm. Was there anyone in front of us?

"How can you not help me find out who she was meeting when you think the same person killed Leo?"

"The only thing I know . . ." The older woman hesitated for a moment as if she wasn't sure she wanted to say anything more. "Leo told me, after she left, that if things went as planned that night, she was coming back and getting the rest of her things and would be staying with someone near Center City. She told him the address, but I don't remember it. It didn't mean anything. I thought she was full of it. Lying to buy more time."

"Nothing? You remember nothing?" I felt like shaking her skinny shoulders until she gave me an answer I liked better.

"Ralph's Bar. On North Third Street. Start there. See if Joe is still working there. He might know more than I do. Leo got her a job cleaning, washing up at night. He paid her fifty bucks cash at the end of her shift. She only went in a few times before she died, but maybe they know something. If Joe's not there, ask for his daughter."

I opened the door and went out into the rain, the cold seeping straight through my windbreaker to my bones. I glanced briefly at the spot on the sidewalk where Leo Martinelli had died. Ross and his three friends had probably not attacked this man and left him to die on the sidewalk as they had my mother. My gut told me Mr. Martinelli died for a different reason entirely, but I didn't have the energy to investigate two things at once. Ralph's Bar was waiting for my visit tomorrow morning.

CHAPTER 21

JOANNE

Joanne huddled over her kitchen table with a cup of tea. It'd grown cold, and she'd dumped it and refilled it with hot water two times. This third cup was now tepid. She stared at her whiteboard filled with scribbles from last year, when they were searching for Ava after she'd vanished. They'd cared about her. Now Juliette was dead at her hands.

She smacked the board with her fist and it clattered to the floor. Russell came out of the bedroom, looking disheveled and pale. "Sorry. I didn't mean to wake you up," she said.

"I was sick all night. Not sleeping anyway."

After the police had left the day before, he'd completely unraveled. He could barely string words together. He'd wept, and then been silent until Joanne had finally given him a couple of Benadryl—it was all she had in the way of sleep aids—and insisted he lie down. An hour later she'd heard him retching and fetched a trash can with a liner and some towels. She'd thought he'd want to go to his brother's or his parents' house for the night, but he'd refused.

"Tea or toast?" she asked.

He shook his head and sat across from her at the table. "I hated her sometimes, you know. I made so many mistakes. This was my fault."

"Don't even. Nobody wished her dead, Russell."

"Sometimes I did. You have no idea." He wrapped his hands around the back of his head. "I wonder if she suffered. If Ava tormented her before she killed her. Or if it was quick, if she even knew what was happening."

Joanne searched for words to calm him down. "Ava has good aim. She got her with the needle right in the vein, probably first try. So either Juliette wasn't resisting or—" She stopped, realizing it was too soon for that kind of speculation.

"You know, it was weird she didn't go to work." He looked up at her. "It's not like she had a nine-to-five job with sick time. She never missed work. Never. And they were calling her. Her phone was filled with missed calls. It doesn't make sense, Joanne."

"Okay." She was trying not to add anything more to his burden. "We'll get to that, I promise."

"We were together for what, five years? The last thing she said to me was 'get the fuck out.' That's it. That's everything." He leaned his head forward and she knew he was crying.

"She didn't know what was going to happen, Russell. She was just sick from drinking too much and miserable—"

"They want me downtown for more questions. I think they have some preliminary forensics back. If they arrest me"—she closed her eyes when he said this—"and I think they will eventually—"

"You're getting ahead of yourself. They don't even know how she died yet." She rested her fingers on his arm. "Let them finish the autopsy."

That was the wrong thing to say. She saw him cringe and he shook his head. The hair on one side of his head was completed matted. "They didn't find any kind of hypodermic needle in the bedroom. Or the vial, for that matter. The worst part is I went back to the house to have peace and quiet and finish a report. God, I wish I hadn't. I wish I'd gone back to the office like I was supposed to. But she was alive, Joanne. She sat up, drank some water, told me not to lecture her. I opened the window to let some air in because it stunk in there like booze and vomit." She nodded but didn't say anything. "The deed to my house is in my office. Look in the bottom-right desk drawer. It's filed there. Use it to bail me out if you have to."

"They aren't going to arrest you. But if, and I say if, it comes to that, you'll be in until you see a judge. Get a risk assessment. One, maybe two days. And they'll probably send you out of county." She didn't know why she was rambling, but it was making things worse.

He pulled out his wallet. "That makes me feel so much better. Here's my bank cards. I'll write down my PIN. I have about four thousand in my checking, but there's a savings account linked to this card too. Use it for a retainer for a lawyer. Get me Baldwin if you can. He's the absolute best."

"We need to get busy and figure out how to pin this back on Ava where it belongs, Russell."

He stood up. "I need to shower and change, but all my clothes are in my house."

"The Polaroid she sent? We'll show them that."

His eyes were ringed with red, and she thought he might start to cry again. "It's in the office at my house in a file with the whole case. I can't go there now. They won't let me. But they have to know she's alive. I ruined my life for this woman. Why didn't we turn the picture in when it came?"

She had begged him to turn it in multiple times, but she wasn't going to bring that up now. "Ava is smart, but she's not smarter than the two of us together. We'll find her."

The two were silent for a minute, and Joanne got up and picked up her whiteboard from the floor. She took a paper towel and erased all the columns of information she'd written on it, the meticulous notes, the research that had revealed that Ava had murdered Ross Saunders and his friends. Then she drew a vertical line down the middle.

"We have a few things going on now."

Russell's mind seemed to be functioning a little clearer. "I need you to talk to Juliette's family. And friends that saw her last."

"I will. And after that, I'll find Ava. It can't be hard. We just need to start scouring all the local bars and liquor stores. She's bound to show up."

Joanne saw the hint of a weary smile on his lips, but it disappeared when there was a knock on the door. Joanne opened it to see two officers standing there. They saw Russell sitting at the table. "Russell Bowers? They want you down at the Prosecutor's Office now."

He stood up and put on his coat. "Joanne. Remember everything I said." He pushed his bank cards to her. "Don't leave me."

She'd never heard him sound so abandoned and dejected. She nodded, but her hands were shaking and she had a hard time watching the officers lead Russell out the door. "My God, Ava. How could you do this to us? We were your friends," she whispered.

She wandered into her son's room, filled with all the things he'd left behind—clothes too small, Lego sets he no longer cared about. His old baseball glove that had been tossed into a box in the corner. School pictures lined the walls in black frames, each year showing new signs of growth. She'd wanted to pull the sheets and clean up Russell's mess, but her body was racked with sobs and she fell on her knees, unable to get up.

CHAPTER 22

MARIE

She was squeezed into the middle seat of a fully booked flight headed to Heathrow in London. The seat was narrow, and her knees were pressed into the seat-back in front of her. Marie clasped her hands in her lap and prepared for the seven-hour journey. At $430 for a one-way ticket, the cost had exhausted most of her resources. Seeing Ava scamper away from the Martinelli house and choosing to let her go had been difficult, but the first step in getting revenge on Ava rested in France, in her mother's cottage. Marie'd always tended to attack head on—something the little creature would see from a mile away if she were looking. This time was going to be different. This time she was going after the two things Ava cared about: money and her birth mother. The keys to those two things were in Europe.

She closed her eyes and thought of the cottage in Cherbourg, of the day they'd moved in, Anais, Claire, and Marie, with only their few belongings carried from the dingy hotel room. The space had been so empty. Anais had sat in the middle of the living room and wept. When the girls had asked why she was crying, she'd said they were tears of joy because she'd never thought she'd have a home of her own again.

"We'll fill this with furniture and it'll be good," she'd said.

But for the first week, they slept on their coats on the hard floor, using their bags as pillows, and were still using their plastic bowls, eating nothing but pasta and drinking only water. It wasn't long after that—how long, Marie didn't know—that Anais came to them and told them she was going on a trip to visit friends. By then things were better. They had furniture, money. Claire and Marie had started school. They'd made some friends, though they still pined for their father and their house on Fourth Street in Philadelphia.

Anais talked on the phone at night often in the days before she left on her trip. Marie heard her voice through the wall when she was trying to sleep. Whatever the reason for the visit, it seemed urgent. Someone was sick and needed care. Anais was going to take care of them. It was a Mr. Martinelli. Marie remembered that because the name was funny to her three-year-old mind.

"Maman, please don't go," Marie begged that morning as Anais was gathering her things. If she was going on a trip, why couldn't they return to Philadelphia?

"Je reviens vite," Anais responded. *I'll be back soon.*

"Je déteste Mister Martinelli. J'espère qu'il mourra," she spat back at her mother.

Anais didn't like her wishing this man dead, though Marie didn't know who he was. "You have no idea what he means to me. None. And if you did, you'd shut your mouth." It was one of only a few times that Anais had smacked her. This time it was soundly across the mouth. Marie could never forget that name. Martinelli. Whatever their connection, he meant a great deal to her.

The way the days turned into one and then another, Marie couldn't be sure now if it had been days or weeks or even longer that Anais was gone. But she was different when she returned. Angrier. Sadder. Eventually the memories faded and Marie didn't remember ever hearing Martinelli's name from her mother again.

But the name had been there in Adrianna's letter the whole time. It hadn't seemed significant to Marie all these years since Ava had first appeared in their lives. Her and Claire's only concern until recently had been concealing the little girl's past, not probing it. But Marie needed to be a step ahead of Ava, not a step behind.

Revenge was good, but any leverage Marie could use to extract Anais's money from Ava's grasp was even better.

The funeral was long over and the cottage was empty when the taxi dropped Marie off in Querqueville. It was raining, a freezing mixture that stung her face. The emptiness of the cottage surprised her when she opened the door. It was cold and drafty, and it hardly looked like it had held a social gathering just hours ago. But when Marie looked further, the signs were everywhere. A table pushed to the wall in the living room had probably served as a buffet. Some plastic cups littered the garbage cans. Not going to the funeral was perhaps a mixed blessing. There was so much emotion here, it would have been overwhelming. Losing Claire and then Anais within the year was a tangle of sorrow best kept at bay.

Marie threw another log with some kindling onto still-warm embers and lit a match. She could feel the wind coming off the ocean even while standing within the warmth of the fireplace. The house was chilly and the winters here were harsh. She hesitated to move, because moving would mean looking at things, and all those things reminded her of Anais. It was easier to just stare into the flames.

Anais had secrets. She always had. Her life with her daughters had been simple and easy, and the conversations had usually involved current practical things. She never discussed why she'd left Philadelphia and their father so abruptly and refused to go back. She would never talk about those few horrible months in the hotel when they were living out of the bathroom sink, waiting for Anais's father to resume his support.

And as the sisters grew up, they developed lives of their own. Marie's was a wild one filled with teenaged drinking, boys, sex, running away to Paris for days at a time until Anais nabbed her and put her away in the hospital. Claire was more serious, calm, centered, tortured, and elitist, above it all. What exactly Anais had occupied herself with during her later years was a guess. She'd acted the loving grandmother when Claire brought Ava to visit. There were no men after Papa that they knew of. Men flirted and Anais would show them courtesy and attention, but nothing permanent. Nothing outside of an occasional outing.

Martinelli. Martinelli. Martinelli. If he had been another man seeking her attentions, it had been short-lived and had ended badly. In Marie's memory, Anais didn't seem excited before leaving on the trip and was even less so when she returned. Marie could still see the serious, sad look on her mother's face; the vertical line between her eyes when she scowled became more permanent after that trip.

Marie adjusted the thermostat in the hallway and then moved to the kitchen and started the kettle. It was going to be a long, cold night, and she had work to do. She'd already looked through Anais's personal documents, but she'd been looking for something different then—money, accounts, financial documents. If there was anything to find, she was going to have to wrangle it from Ava. That would come later. For now, she was going to search through all the papers she'd ignored. The desk was large, dark mahogany, purchased from a craftsman when the girls were little. Anais had stashed stampers and ink pads in the top middle drawer to occupy the girls while she worked.

Marie pulled the drawer open. Postage stamps, paper clips held in plastic cups, loose change, keys to the house, notepads. Nothing of particular interest. The second drawer held files. The deed to the cottage, repairs done over the years.

Her paper checks were all kept organized in file boxes, dozens of them stuffed into the back of the large lower drawer. Marie pulled one from the bottom that looked the oldest and took it to the sofa. Anais's life could be tracked through her checks, how she was spending her money. Where she was going. Maybe if Marie studied it long enough, she'd figure out where the rest of the money was even without Ava. It was a trail. Marie just had to take the time to follow it.

She flipped open the top of the file box and saw immediately it wasn't what she expected. Instead of checks, there was a stack of letters, folded and pressed down to fill the container. The fire created enough light so she could read. She pulled an envelope from the very bottom and opened it, the paper slightly yellowed with time.

Annie, it began. It was her father, Ross, writing shortly after they'd arrived in France. *The truth, Annie. I need the truth or I'll find you and force it out of you.* Marie sucked in her breath. The trail she had in front of her was not a financial one at all. It was the trail of Anais's life, the one she'd never talked about—the relationship with Ross, the abrupt abandonment of her marriage, the trip away when they were little—all of it. It was the answer to the million questions Marie had had for as long as she could remember.

CHAPTER 23

Russell

It was uncomfortable, to say the least. Being on the other side of the table. They'd brought in an investigator he didn't know personally, and that made it better and worse at the same time. Better because it eased some of the embarrassment of being questioned by colleagues. Worse because this was no longer just preliminary fact gathering. They'd moved on to the next level and they didn't want the complications of his work relationships to throw a snag into things. Smooth, by the book. For the first time he was starting to panic.

Maybe he was guilty of being a bad boyfriend, inattentive, immature; maybe he took his relationship with Juliette for granted. And that probably would have evolved into him being a lacking, dismissive husband, with years of unhappiness in front of them, and the anxiety of children added to the mix. That was true. But he hadn't hurt her. He hadn't given her pills, or injected her with anything. He didn't even have access to needles, and if she did, it hadn't ever occurred to him to find them—he was rehearsing, mouthing the words to get them right. That's what he was going to tell this detective.

The house had been cleared, they'd told him. They were done collecting fingerprints, DNA evidence. He'd be allowed to go home now and clean up their mess, and change the sheets in the bed where his almost-wife had died, releasing her bladder and bowels at some time during the process. He'd be allowed to go home, but they just had a few more questions.

"Have you ever seen Juliette's medical bag in the house?" the lead detective started. He was middle aged, short, his stomach bulging over his pants and straining the fabric of his shirt. He was tired and gritty looking, like he'd handled this sort of case every day of his life. The other detective was playing second fiddle, quiet, taking notes.

Russell frowned. This was a tricky question. "Yes, I've seen it. But it's a case, I guess you'd say. She's a surgeon, not a family doctor. Not a country doctor who went to people's houses."

"When is the last time you saw it?"

"I don't know. Honestly. I'd say months. I didn't pay attention."

"And when you did see it, did you ever examine the contents? Open it up?" He looked up from the papers in front of him, staring into Russell's eyes.

Russell shook his head and then thought about it. He nodded. "Maybe. I don't know. She had a stethoscope, some surgical tools that had her initials on them. I think it's a thing with them, getting their own tools." He knew it sounded stupid. "But I didn't really pay attention."

"Were there hypodermic needles in this bag, that you know of?"

"I never noticed. I never looked. I knew about the tools because she told me. It sort of meant she was official. I never rummaged through it."

"But do you think she would have needles?"

"I never thought about it." Russell had heard, from another detective in the office, that they had Juliette's bag and it had contained nine hypodermic needles in a ten-pack. One was missing. *Ask for a lawyer,* he was thinking. *Now, before they discover prints on the needle pack. No, don't ask for a lawyer. If you do, they're going to think you're guilty and go hard. Just tell them the truth.*

"Are you diabetic?"

He crossed his legs. "No, I'm not."

113

"Do you take any medication in injection form? For any reason?"

"No." He uncrossed them.

"Did Juliette?"

"No. Not that I'm aware of."

"So, it's interesting she had a pack of fifty-milliliter large-gauge needles in her bag when she had no use for them. And one was missing. But it looks like the needle that caused the bruising and the blood came from that bag. Though it's a guess, because we don't have the needle. Do you know where it might be?"

Russell sat upright and placed his hands flat on the table. "I do not know. I never took the needle out of the bag. Did you get prints from that empty wrapper? Because mine are not on there. I had nothing to do with this. What is it you think she was injected with?"

"We'll get to that soon. So, let's back up a little and talk about Ava Saunders."

"Yes, please, let's talk about her, because she caused all of this—"

"Ava Saunders was declared dead by the courts, Mr. Bowers. But you were involved with her last year, were you not?"

"I was helping her, or thought I was, to find out who her birth mother was. Her mother was killed—"

"We do know all about that from your disciplinary file. But the question was, Were you involved with her, in an intimate way? And did Juliette find that out?"

"I . . . I think I'm not going to answer that, because I don't like where this is going. You think I killed Juliette over a relationship with Ava, but it never happened. Juliette and I were getting married in a few weeks. We were fine."

"Did you fight with your fiancée when you went home yesterday afternoon?" The detective leaned in toward him and waited, like this tidbit was going to wrap this all up for him.

"She was sick. Vomiting. I know you saw it all over the side of the bed. She was miserable. She'd been out with her bridesmaids all night after getting the fitting for her dress. Talk to her family. Talk to her friends. Her maid of honor or whatever, her sister, Gail."

The detective moved back in his seat. "We did, of course, you know that. And it's a funny thing. There was no fitting scheduled for her dress. None of her family has seen her in the past few days."

Russell's eyes shot up and held the detective's. "That's not possible. That's wrong. She told me she was going out for her final fitting, and they were having dinner and drinks later. She didn't come home until around one in the morning. Really drunk."

"Hmmm. Well, her mother says the final fitting was this Friday at three in the afternoon. The bridal shower was scheduled for Friday night, at a restaurant. Maggiano's. In Cherry Hill. They'd reserved a banquet room."

"So where was she that night?" Russell stared at the desk in front of him, but his mind was elsewhere. He tried to think of everything Juliette had done that day, what she'd said. She'd lied to him. He had thought it was odd that a dress fitting would be held so late in the day, but he'd never really doubted it.

"Exactly the question."

"I don't know."

"Was she seeing someone else—as revenge, maybe? Or did she never really leave the house that night at all, Russell?"

The thought made him sick. He stood up. "Are you arresting me?"

The detective hesitated. "We're not done."

"We are done. I'm leaving. If you need to speak to me again, I'll be calling in with the name of my lawyer. Talk to him. Or her, maybe." He saw the look in the detective's eye. "I know it might make me look guiltier, but I'm not. I'm really not, and I'm not going down for this. You want a suspect? Her name is Ava Saunders. She's alive and I'm going to prove it to you."

CHAPTER 24

AVA

Adrianna DeFeo. I rolled that name around on my tongue, over and over, like a piece of hard candy, hoping it would jog something in my memory. But the past was all mired in fog so thick I couldn't see through it. Something that I'd pined for, that had consumed and ruined my soul, now seemed so empty. Just letters that added up to nothing. But there was something deeper than just my mother's name that I was seeking. I had a link to my birth family. They were somewhere in Italy, and I would make my way back there eventually, once I'd figured out my mother's movements in Philadelphia on the day she died. I needed to close this circle first.

The thin thread of a clue, nothing but the name of a bar, might lead nowhere, but it was all I had. The Martinellis didn't know I knew who'd killed my mother. I knew who and why, how, and even where. I'd seen it all up close. I just didn't know the intangibles, the bits of information needed to color a whole picture. And those gray parts, to me, were the parts that mattered. Why my mother was in the United States, why she'd left Italy, where she was going, and who she was meeting. And if the meeting took place, how did she end up in that bloody massacre in the church?

I had no recollection of visiting a bar as a three-year-old that night. Or of any stops along the way at all. The flashes of the streetlights outside the church, and then what happened after, were still etched in my brain, even if they'd eroded with time. But that house in South Philadelphia, the people in it, the other events that occurred that night—no, they just weren't there. I thought if I closed my eyes and relaxed, I could conjure it up, but I couldn't.

Ralph's was still in existence, strangely enough. I had no idea what it might have looked like twenty years ago, but now it was a hangout for the unapologetic alcoholics, the ones who crept in just after the door was unlocked in the morning and didn't leave all day. The sounds coming from a small television propped in the corner—game shows, network news, and sports—lulling them.

I peered in and hesitated. Everything was dated, probably untouched for years, right down to the grubby bar stools and the scuffed, wide-planked hardwood floor. There were three people sitting at the bar; one turned and glanced at me, the other two didn't have the interest or curiosity to move in their seats. A woman sat behind the bar, chunky, nondescript, dirty-blonde hair pulled back in a ponytail. Her eyes scanned me quickly and then returned to the television. As I slid into the seat, I pondered ordering a drink. I had no choice if I wanted answers; water or Coca-Cola wasn't going to do it.

"Whiskey on the rocks. Whatever you have is fine."

She pushed up and made a big show of filling the glass with ice and putting it in front of me. She poured from a bottle of Evan Williams and then pulled back, leaving me with a few fingers in the glass. I took a mouthful and swallowed before speaking. She stood in front of me, waiting to see if I wanted more before sitting back down. I drank the rest and then motioned for more. She obliged but scanned me up and down.

"You from around here? Or visiting?" she asked.

"A little of both," I answered. "But right now I'm passing through. My mother used to work here, years ago. She worked for a man named Joe, I think. Back in the midnineties."

"Ha. Old Joe. He did own the place then. What'd she do? Bartend?"

My heart sank. If he was gone, none of these people were going to be able to help me. "I think just some cleaning. So he sold it off, then?"

"Nah. He died and gave it to me. I'm his daughter, Linda." She held out her hand, so I shook it.

"I'm sorry to hear that. I heard he was nice to my mother." Linda looked to be maybe ten years older than me, putting her in her early thirties. So she would have been in her early teens back then. "He gave her a job at night, cleaning."

She shrugged. "We were busier then. He hired lots of people under the table, to clean, wash glasses. Things have kind of gone downhill. I'm not sure how long I'll stay open."

"Her name was Adrianna. I think Leo Martinelli sent her here." I sipped the whiskey and felt it burn down my throat into my chest. I wondered, *If my mother worked here, why didn't any of these people identify her after she was dead?* Something was off.

"Leo." She looked at the television, suddenly engrossed in *Deal or No Deal*.

"You know him, then?"

She pushed off the bar and went down to the other end of it and started talking to one of the patrons. When she came back, she continued where she'd left off. "Leo was involved in some shady shit. Someone stabbed him, cut his throat, and I'm surprised it didn't happen sooner. Family thought it was some random murder. Word was he got killed for cheating someone out of money. That simple." She stared at me for a few seconds and then filled my glass without me asking. "Adrianna? Little scared Italian girl? Maybe eighteen, nineteen years old? She only came in a couple times to clean."

"How can you remember that?"

"I remember because she was the only other young person in the place. My father used to make me come after school and help out in the kitchen, unloading liquor boxes, cleaning. Whatever. She was only a few years older than me." She pulled out a pack of cigarettes, unconcerned about federal smoking laws, and offered me one. I took it. She lit them both and then placed a plastic ashtray in front of me. "And I remember her because she was killed." Her eyes slid sideways toward me.

I drew on the cigarette and tapped it on the edge of the ashtray. "So why didn't anyone identify her?" It came out maybe harsher than I'd intended.

"I was a thirteen-year-old kid. My father said to shut up about it. Leo was into all kinds of crap. Petty drugs, running numbers, low-level Mafia stuff."

"The mob?"

She saw the surprised look on my face and laughed. "Not like the Corleone family. Nothing that glamorous. Dirty stuff. Nobody knew where this girl came from. Leo must've told my father to shut up, so he did. That's my guess. Martinelli was a scumbag."

"So, what about after? When you were older? You decided not to go to the police, to give her a name? Martinelli was dead by then."

She didn't look like she was in the mood to be cornered or blamed. "I don't have an answer. I'm sorry. I had no idea what she was involved in. Let sleeping dogs lie."

I sighed. "Did my mother say if she knew anyone in town? Or was looking for anyone?"

The ashes on the end of her cigarette were long. I was waiting for them to fall onto the bar, but then she tapped the end into the tray. "Her English was crappy. I only saw her a few times." My words seemed to suddenly weigh on her, and she understood the full meaning. "Oh my God, your mother? You're the girl she talked about?"

I frowned. "What'd she say?"

"That she left Italy because she wanted to get away and find the truth about her past. Something about her parents."

"And?"

"And she would've scrubbed the floor with her tongue to keep anything from happening to you."

I swallowed some more whiskey. "Are you making this up because you feel guilty about not identifying her after she died?"

She laughed, much deeper than seemed natural. "No. One of those days she was here, my father had us clean the back room. We were together all day."

"Hmmm."

"I'll tell you this. She was here because she knew someone in the area."

"Did she say who it was? Not Martinelli?"

She shook her head. "No. Somebody closer. Someone she thought would help her. Someone she'd heard her family talk about."

"But she didn't say a name?"

"A priest. He was a priest, I remember that."

I pulled money out of my pocket and threw it on the bar. I thought of those four men beating Father Callahan in retribution for years of sexual abuse. Smashing his face. Calling him names. They'd hit him so hard some of his teeth fell out. I was there, close up, watching his skin split open, his blood pour out onto the floor. Father Callahan died a difficult death alongside my mother, and I'd had a front-row seat. Now it seemed she'd gone to the church specifically looking for him, and died because of it.

Linda tossed the money back to me. "On the house. Sorry doesn't even cut it."

I had all the information I was going to get, but I still couldn't push the bar stool out to stand up and leave the bar. Father Callahan. The name kept swirling. Why was my mother going to the church to see him? It made no sense.

Linda glanced up with a quizzical look on her face. "You okay, sweetie?"

"She was going to see Father Callahan? The murdered priest?"

Her brow creased. "I don't remember the name. You said Callahan, I didn't." She shrugged.

I ran my hands through my hair. I could feel the liquor taking over bits of my brain. Something about this didn't make sense. It was right but it was wrong. Callahan would not have been giving her any money. Not even charity money, unless he knew her and she was a parishioner or she was related to him. And he was an American and she was Italian; the connection wasn't there. And she'd only been in town for a few days. If she'd just been looking for shelter or food, that might make more sense. But going to that church, in that part of town, was odd. She'd been staying in South Philly and the church was in Frankford. Almost ten miles away.

I stood up and started for the door. "Callahan," Linda said aloud. "Another Irish name, maybe. But not that one."

I zipped my coat and had put my hand on the door when it came to me. "Connelly?" I didn't even turn around. "Father William Connelly?" I asked.

I wanted her to scream and jump up and down, but when I finally looked over my shoulder, she stared at me blank faced, like she hadn't heard me. "Did they call him Father Bill? She said it like 'Beel.' *Beel.*" She stretched the name out in a high-pitched voice. "That might be it."

I didn't even respond, just pushed the door open and headed out into the cold. Bill Connelly was suddenly there, in front of me, clutching his throat, asking without words for his EpiPen. I'd held it up, away from him, only concerned that this man had been one in the pack of men who had killed my mother. He'd helped take off her clothes, move her body in order to frame Father Callahan, make it look as if they'd been having an affair. I'd glanced into his eyes then, but even as his airway was closing and he was dying, they bore no regret. Only panic.

CHAPTER 25

MARIE

Annie, I had a dream that someone was trying to kill me. I couldn't see who it was, but I thought it was your father because he always hated me so much for ruining your life. But when I finally saw the face, it wasn't your father, it was our daughter, but I couldn't tell which one. I woke feeling like I'd seen the future. I blame you for this. You've destroyed our family. You've destroyed our daughters. And you've destroyed me. I won't give you a divorce. I will fight you until the end.

Marie felt the moisture on her cheeks but didn't even realize she was crying. The years of knowing, but not knowing, that something had happened between her parents had taken a toll. One week Marie, Claire, and Anais were walking around the corner to the bakery to get rolls, taking the bus to the Franklin Institute, the Academy of Natural Sciences, and the art museum in Center City, rolling on the green grass in the backyard, and the next they were squeezed into an airplane, landing in France. At school, they were the odd ones out, the Americans with the funny accents. They learned French but didn't want to use it. They wanted North Fourth Street. They wanted their father.

Marie flipped to the next letter.

Annie—Don't do it! If you continue with this, you're going to pay for it.
     —Ross

Marie dropped the letter and slumped over. "No. *Arrêtez! Nous en avons parlé. Ca ne vas pas marcher pour moi!*" Marie had heard her mother speaking rapidly into the phone one afternoon around the time this letter had been sent. She knew it was to her father, because the baritone in his voice traveled through the telephone to where she was sitting.

"Stop speaking goddamned French. You know I don't understand it," he'd said.

"No, Ross. No. It's over. I'll think about how to let you see the girls. We'll work something out."

He said something Marie couldn't hear.

"No. If I send them to the States, I'll never get them back. You'll get the courts on your side." Then there was silence. "It was all for the best. You know all of this was for the best." There was loudness from Ross, then Anais's voice. "Don't threaten me." With that, she hung up.

Anais looked unusually haggard during that time period. Her hair had grown down past her shoulders and was unkempt. Her face was thin and drawn, puffy purplish circles under her eyes.

"What, Marie?" she asked her daughter when she saw the child staring at her.

Marie just shook her head. In that moment she realized she'd never see Philadelphia again until she was an adult. She was right. The bitterness between her parents didn't fade over the years. Instead it became a noiseless virus that permeated the roots of the family so that none of them even attended Ross's funeral.

Marie glanced down at the letter. Just then there was a light rap on the door. She opened it to see Sandrine in the foyer, huddled against the wind. Marie pulled her sweater tighter and led her in, closing the door to keep out the chill.

"I saw your light on," Sandrine said. "I hope you don't mind?"

"No. Come. Sit by the fire." She led the woman to a chair and handed her a blanket.

She pulled it over her knees. "I'm so glad you made it, even if you missed the ceremony—"

"Sorry I was detained."

"You can go out to the cemetery in the morning. It was sad. You know, filled with all her relatives' faces, and some friends, but nobody really close."

"Sandrine. I've sort of been digging through the wreckage of my parents' marriage. Letters . . ." She looked so much older than the last time Marie had seen her. Her hair had gone gray; the glasses she'd chosen overwhelmed her face.

"Your parents? Now?"

"Trying to figure out what happened between them. Do you remember when she went to visit someone named Martinelli? When Claire and I were little? Right after we moved here? Maman had Mrs. Volton stay with us. The one who lived at the end of the street?"

Ever since Marie could remember, Sandrine had been the lonely widow, the neighborhood busybody, the gossip, the catalyst for so many petty arguments between people on the street. If anyone would have this information, it would be her.

"Vaguely. But what does that have to do with anything, Marie?"

"There's a Martinelli family in Philadelphia. I'm wondering if Anais went to see them for some reason? If that's where she went?"

"To America? No. I can tell you she did not."

She stared Sandrine down. "Then where'd she go?"

"Where did she tell you she went?"

Marie stood up and went into the kitchen. There had to be wine somewhere, and this conversation was going downhill quickly. When she returned she carried two glasses of red. "It's all I found in the cupboard." She handed a glass to Sandrine.

"Is there a secret?" Marie said. "Something you're keeping from me? I'm just asking where my mother went. I'm assuming she told you." Sandrine was silent; she seemed to be considering things carefully. "I think the reason she went was connected to Ava. I'm right?" Marie said after several minutes had passed.

"Ava? How do you figure? She wasn't born until many years later."

"I'm starting to think Anais knew Ava's mother, or knew her mother's family. Before she was killed. And the fact that Adrianna showed up in that church was a weird bloody coincidence."

"Where is Ava now?" Sandrine said this in a whisper.

"She's dead."

"No, she isn't. Marie, when I saw Anais that night on the ground, when she'd had a stroke and I called the ambulance, your mother was going on about Ava being here, in the cottage. I thought she was confused, but now I think it's true. Tell me."

"You tell me first. Did Anais know Ava's family? Before her mother ended up in the church?"

Sandrine squeezed her eyes shut. "That's not a simple answer."

"It's either yes or no."

"She knew the family, in a way, she did. But I'll tell you, Anais didn't go to America. She went to Vicenza, Italy, to stay with a couple named Martinelli. Those Martinellis are probably related to the American family in some way."

"Why'd she go?"

"One question, one answer. It's a trade. Is Ava really alive?"

Marie drank her glass of wine in one gulp. "Yes. I was late because I saw her get off the plane in Newark and I followed her. She went to a house in South Philadelphia owned by a Martinelli."

"Oh my God. Then she knows? She knows what they did?"

"Knows what who did?"

"Is that another question?"

Marie hesitated. "Why didn't Maman tell us she knew Ava? After the church incident. Why didn't she reconnect Ava with her grandparents or whatever? If she knew them?"

"She didn't know Ava at all. In fact, she'd never seen that child in her life—"

"But she knew Ava's mother?"

"No. Not in a real sense. I'd say she knew the family."

"You're making me drag this out of you, Sandrine. Why didn't Anais reconnect Ava with her family? Why change the child's name?"

"You're out of questions, Marie. I've said all I'm going to." Sandrine stood up, and the blanket fell to the floor. "If Ava's gotten as far as the Martinellis, don't waste your time hanging around. Take whatever you need and disappear before this all falls on your head. Do you hear me?" She was standing by the door. "Oh, I almost forgot, Anais left an envelope for you. It's part of the reason I came over." She pulled it from her coat pocket and put it in Marie's hand. "She gave it to me last year and said you should have it after she died. It's sealed. I never opened it. But heed my warnings, Marie. Don't linger around here too long. Please."

Before Marie could respond, Sandrine opened the door and hurried down the sidewalk to the road.

CHAPTER 26

RUSSELL

The house was dark and, from what he could see from the doorway, dirty. The police hadn't bothered to even go through the motions of putting the room back in any sort of order. He needed to go in, turn on the lights, but found he couldn't move from that spot. He knew they'd used powder for fingerprints, but he didn't expect the black graphite to be smeared across all his surfaces.

The living-room furniture had been moved, pushed to the side. They'd rummaged through his belongings. He stood in the doorway, feeling robbed. Completely violated in almost every way. His fiancée was dead. His home had been ransacked. Nothing belonged to him anymore. When he flicked the switch, it was worse. Shoe prints, dirty carpet, papers dumped onto the tables. He'd bought this house when he was on his own. Twenty-six years old, out of the military, finishing school, hired by the Cherry Hill Police Department. The minute the real-estate agent had shown it to him, he'd known it was his. Not too big, not too small. Not too much maintenance, nice kitchen. Now he would be happy to go away and never come back.

The stairway was remarkably free of remnants of outside presence. He climbed slowly and stood in the doorway of the bedroom. Days ago, things had been normal. He'd come home and eaten a pasta dinner, taken a shower, chitchatted with Juliette. They'd climbed into bed and drifted off talking about something that had happened at the hospital that day. That seemed a million miles away now. The whole world had tilted on its axis since then and was spiraling toward the sun.

The bedcovers were gone, presumably taken as evidence. The mattress was bare, and he could see a wet spot where Juliette's bladder had released when she died. He backed up to the wall and put his head down. He hadn't heard from her family, probably because they thought he'd killed her. He needed to go see them, to tell them the truth, to mourn with them, but he wasn't ready yet. His eyes landed on the windowsill, now covered in dark, powdery smears. The heels she'd worn lay on the floor near the closet. Wherever she'd gone that night, she'd been dressed up for an evening out. And come back drunker than he'd ever seen her.

Gray-blue eyes, smeared with makeup. Dark rings that made her look angrier and more dangerous as she spewed words at him. That was his last real interaction with her. But what had happened to her between the time she left the house and the time she raged through the front door at one thirty a.m. was a mystery.

Those months after Ava disappeared had been tricky between them. A battle had been raging inside Juliette between wanting to forgive him and resenting him. She wanted to move on but couldn't, and so her feelings flip-flopped from day to day, and any attempts on his part to have an open conversation about it were met with resistance. As their wedding date approached, resentment was winning the battle. And the situation was only exacerbated by the fact that Ava was alive and he hadn't found a way to tell Juliette. It became a permanent wedge between them, without her ever knowing why.

He went to the nightstand and picked up the bottle of ibuprofen. His last attempt at caring and comfort. The bottle of water was still there too, half-empty. The police had taken her phone as evidence, but assured him they'd return it when they were finished. They had moved the furniture around in search of the needle. The needle.

He was telling the truth when he said that he hadn't opened her medical bag on a regular basis. But only two days before her death, Juliette had opened it on the dining-room table, looking for something. She'd pulled out the contents, and the package of needles had fallen out. He saw it. He noticed it. He asked her about it, because it was odd. She said she was giving them to another doctor, something like that. He never questioned it further, but he couldn't remember if he'd picked up the pack while they were talking or not. He'd spent hours going over that conversation in his mind. He just didn't know. Now not only had the pack been opened but one of the needles had been filled with something and jabbed into her arm, killing her within minutes. This was bad. Really bad.

The Polaroid. His attention shifted to the only proof he had that Ava was alive. His only way out of this mess. The photograph and the envelope it was mailed in were tucked away in the file in the other room. He hurried to his office and stood at the desk. It looked untouched by the police. All the furnishings were in place, and the black graphite powder wasn't visible on any of the surfaces. He closed the door, feeling he'd left the world outside. This room had always been his retreat.

He was wrong. There was no graphite smeared on the surfaces, but the police had definitely scoured the place. He slid open the top drawer and saw the scattered papers left behind, not deemed pertinent enough to this case. His mind began to whirl. *It's fine. If they have the file, they have the Polaroid. It's fine.* But despite the repetition of those words, his breaths were coming fast. He dropped into his chair. Unless Joanne had gotten here first and had taken it.

He lifted his phone from his pocket and texted her. *Did you come to the house and take the Polaroid? The file is gone. Call me.* He dropped the phone onto the desk and turned the file over, starting from the beginning. His phone buzzed.

Don't stay there. Come here if you want. They wouldn't let me into the house. So, no, I don't have the photograph. The police must have it. Call someone and ask? Talk soon.

Goddammit. He hesitated and then punched in the number of the unit secretary. The only person who was still a tad friendly, probably because she knew him from way back when he'd started in Cherry Hill. He typed a text message and pressed "Send." *The evidence they took from my house. A file about the Ava Saunders case. Do you have access to it?* The worst she could do was tell him to buzz off.

Five minutes later she replied: *Detective Trout has it.*

He hesitated. *I just need to know if there's a particular Polaroid in there. Green cottage door? With two dates on it. And some French written at the bottom? If they have it, that's great. I just need to know.*

Ten minutes went by and he heard nothing. Her version of telling him to forget it.

Then, *ding*. A message appeared. *No. No Polaroid in the file. I asked for it so I could list the items in evidence. Went through it twice.*

He dropped his head. Gone. Ava had come into his house, killed Juliette, and stolen the Polaroid—the only maybe-proof she was still alive.

"I'm going to kill you, Ava." He grabbed his keys and raced to the front door, ignoring the fact that the knob was covered in black powder.

CHAPTER 27

AVA

I rang the bell to the rectory, feeling slightly uncomfortable. I hadn't been here in three years, and it didn't escape my notice that the night of Connelly's murder I'd been standing very close to the spot where I was standing now, holding that big clunky camera, snapping a photograph of the partially opened door to send along to Owens as a warning. Returning now to the scene of his murder was disturbing. My hands began to tingle, and I was jolted when the door opened. A woman was there, short, slightly stout, with an expression that held laughter even when she wasn't laughing.

"Come in," she said without even questioning what I wanted.

I followed her into the small reception area. It was poorly lit, and some of the details I'd tried very hard not to think about from years before were there. "I don't know if you can help me. I know a Father Connelly lived here a few years back."

"He did, yes."

She wasn't offering any more details. "I'm wondering if he had siblings in the area, or if anyone might have information about family." Her head tilted a bit, but she didn't respond. "I did one of those DNA tests, you know, and he came up as a relative." Her eyes widened. "I know, right? I was really upset to hear he died. But I figured it was worth a visit to try and connect with family."

"After he passed, all his belongings and information were transferred to the Archdiocese of Philadelphia. You might start there."

"Okay." I glanced at the stairway, remembering my slow, silent descent so as not to raise alarm while Connelly lay just upstairs, clawing at his throat in an attempt to breathe. The shadowy foyer had helped me to slip out the door without being noticed that night. "Is there anyone here who might remember him? You know, just so I don't have to run around?"

"I remember him well enough. I was here at the time."

I suddenly felt paranoid she might know my face, remember me slinking through the halls years before. "Can you just tell me if he has family nearby? That would be so great." I tried to smile with my eyes but it felt forced and phony.

"A sister. He had a sister, Donna. She was at the funeral. Donna Moran, I think her married name is. I don't know if she lives in the area or not."

"Thank you. I'll start there, then."

She closed the door behind me and I heard her click the latch into place. I stood there for a second, having trouble taking another step. My mind managed the terrible things I'd done by putting them in a compartment, separate from everything else, from who I am. As long as they were tucked away, it was easy to move forward without thinking about them. Those things I did were really not me, not the real me. And in those moments that I was forced to confront what I'd done, it was painfully difficult, almost like it was happening for the first time.

I shouldn't have gone to the rectory. I should have found another way.

Donna Moran. Philadelphia and South Jersey people were weird. Unlike in other areas of the country, these people rarely relocated. They stayed for generations, adult children moving just down the block and raising their families within yelling distance. I remember graduating from high school—the number of my classmates headed for the Ivy Leagues was astounding, yet most talked about returning to Haddonfield when they were finished. If I had to guess, Donna Moran was living somewhere in Northeast Philadelphia with her husband, no more than twenty miles from where she grew up. The Frankford area of the city had changed, become more drug infested, crime ridden, so I had to guess she'd moved north where the blocks were still clean and family friendly.

I had no clear idea of what I was going to say to this woman, should I find her. After a few minutes of searching online, I found one Donna Moran who lived on Woodhaven Road in the northeast section of the city. Cold calling might put her off. If she hung up on me, I was worried a follow-up visit in person might even be worse. But the thought of traipsing through Philadelphia on public transportation to find her was too much.

I pulled the phone number from the record, held my breath, and dialed. A woman answered on the second ring. The usual greeting ensued, and I jumped right into it.

"My name is Jessica Roberts." Using my real name was too much of a gamble and I wasn't willing to risk it. "I'm sorry to bother you, but I was wondering if you are related to a Father William Connelly, by any chance?"

Her response was hesitant and slow. "And who are you, exactly?"

"I know he passed away a few years ago, and I was sorry to hear it. But I was looking for a relative of his that maybe could help me."

"Help you how?" She still hadn't confirmed she was related, but I was willing to assume I'd reached the right person.

"I am trying to track down information about my mother, Adrianna DeFeo, who also passed away some years ago." I hesitated. I didn't add that Connelly had helped kill her, but I wanted to. "I'm wondering if they knew each other? If you've ever heard her name before?"

"I don't know who Bill knew. We weren't that close toward the end. The parish sent over some boxes of his belongings, there wasn't much, but he did have an address book in there, I remember. To be honest, I might have thrown it out."

I blew air out in a whoosh. "Is it gone for sure, do you know? Because if you still have it, it would be a great help."

She sighed. "I can look. I'll call you if I find it?"

I chewed at the corner of my mouth. I should have just gone to the house. This woman had no intention of looking or calling me back. "It is so important to me to find out a connection between these two. Your brother might have seen her the night she died. And I just need to know." I sniffled into the phone. And then held my breath as if I were disguising tears.

"Okay. I'll go out in the garage and see what's left in Bill's boxes. But don't get your hopes up. Call me in an hour." She hung up.

I sat in Starbucks near Fourth and South, biding my time. Hinging everything on a less-than-interested sister of Bill Connelly in the hopes of making some nonconnection between my mother and this wayward priest was ludicrous, and I knew it. But I had no choice. The papers I found at Anais's meant she knew the Martinellis in Philadelphia. The Martinellis in Philadelphia knew my mother. At the very least, Anais was linked to my mother indirectly. And if she knew my mother, did she know me, before Ross delivered me to Claire's? The crisscrossed lines of possibility were making me dizzy.

I called Donna Moran's number and heard her weary voice answer. "I have his address book, but it's all mostly things related to the church. Sorry. No Adrianna."

"No DeFeos at all?"

"One. In Italy. I have a number." She recited a string of digits.

I jotted them all down. "Do you have a name to go with that?"

"Victor DeFeo. That's it."

"Thank—"

"I hope you find what you're looking for." She clicked off the line.

Another connection. Bill Connelly knew someone in my family. Yet Connelly helped kill my mother. I took a gulp of my coffee and punched in the number Donna Moran had given me. My stomach churned. I was possibly about to speak to a bona fide blood relative for the first time in my life.

CHAPTER 28

MARIE

She ripped open the envelope and pulled out a bundle of papers covered in Anais's loopy cursive. The French was proper and meticulous, as always.

Marie, there are things you need to know. Things I should have told you before, but I never found the correct time to do that, and then Claire died. And by then it was too late. And Ava became the focus of everything. I've convinced myself for many years that none of what I am about to tell you mattered. I had to convince myself of that because it was so horrible.

I was never perfect, Marie. I wasn't when I met your father, and I wasn't during the years we were married. I chose to marry him against my family's wishes. I thought I understood the world around me but I didn't. I had no idea what America would be like to live in and raise children. Stay with me and let me tell you this story in my own way. Don't flip to the end of these pages or you won't understand. It won't make sense.

This story has everything. It begins with lust, a tainted tortured love, hardship, disloyalty, and ends with me almost murdering someone, wanting to murder someone, and often wishing I had. I came close enough that you might consider I did. And then I covered it up. I spent so many years covering it up, filled with shame and terrible guilt. Ah, yes, guilt. So where do I begin this story? With your father. Ross was stationed in Saigon with a special Army advisory committee sent to Vietnam in 1958. My family had moved north after the French evacuation, though they chose not to leave due to business interests. My father was also a diplomat assigned to the northern part of Vietnam, so we stayed. But you probably know all this.

Marie remembered the blue photo album she'd often looked at as a child. It was kept high in the cabinet, and it took a stool and a very stretched arm to reach it. It was another world. The lush vegetation. Her mother, Anais, so young and pretty, dark hair swept high on her head. She was smiling in most of the photographs. Marie and Claire used to gaze at those books and play pretend. Claire always played their father, putting on a cap and a long green sweater. Marie would pull her hair back, like in the pictures, and they would play house, making it all up as they went along.

But what I never told you was that I adored your father when I met him and didn't exercise caution or discretion. We only went on two dates, and I let things go too far. I got pregnant with Claire the second time we met, and told only one soul other than Ross. That's why I was so upset when you were rebelling at fifteen, running out at night, having sex. I didn't want you to repeat my mistakes.

My father didn't want me to marry Ross, but I was stuck, I had no choice and I couldn't tell him why. He begged and threatened, but by then it was too late. Your father and I had to plan quickly for a life I could never have conceived—maybe that is a bad choice of words? I was uncertain, so young, afraid of my father, afraid to tell my mother. I had no one who knew this except my childhood friend, Philomena DeFeo. Her father had also come to Vietnam on business, and our families had been close for years. Odd, I know, an Italian. But we learned each other's languages when we were young and both had a smattering of English and Vietnamese to fall back on. Philomena cried with me over the news, but in the end, there was no real choice. I married Ross in a ceremony with just a few friends present. My father and mother would not come. My father cut me off after that.

We stayed in Saigon long enough for him to see my stomach swell, and he knew. He knew what had happened and why I'd married so quickly. The only word he had for me when he saw me was "whore." He said I wore the shame for all to see because everyone could count the months in front of me. He told me that I had destroyed the family's good name by rolling in the dirty streets with an American soldier. In front of relatives at a large gathering, he asked if I had taken money from Ross to sleep with him and asked how much he'd paid me.

We left Vietnam shortly after that and started our lives in Philadelphia. On Fourth Street in the row home with the little backyard. Those first few months were strange and filled with changes and adjustment.

The papers slipped from Marie's fingers and fell to the floor. That horrible man with the gray hair who had come to the hotel that day, looking down on all of them. He had finally given in and bought the cottage for Anais, but Marie was sure that it had come with a price. And that price would probably be revealed within the rest of these pages. She picked them up again.

> I gave birth to Claire at Pennsylvania Hospital and came home with a bundle I had no idea how to care for. My friends in Philadelphia were few. I'd grown up in a pampered world, Marie! I was raised to dress for dinner, mostly formal occasions with other state officials present. To be polite, gracious, charming. I was sent to a finishing school to learn all the things a girl needed to know. I lived a privileged life. Nothing could have prepared me for the isolation and strangeness I found in America. My parents refused to take even my phone calls. I was as alone as any human could be on this earth. I spent my days holding Claire and staring out the window, down onto the street. I would cry until your father came home.
>
> And to add more to this, I'd not experienced as much drinking as there was in America. My parents drank cocktails with dinner. Sometimes after dinner too. Or they'd go to the club. But I'd never seen either of them in a bar. Bars were low-class, dirty things, I was told. Your father wanted to spend his evenings around the corner at the W&K with his friends, for hours after work, and I never grew used to it. I didn't understand any of it.

The W&K bar was a hole in the wall on Poplar Street. Marie remembered walking past it with her mother many times on the way to the store, or to catch the bus, and entering it at least once so her mother could pull Ross from the stool and force him to come home. Marie closed her eyes. She had never seen her parents argue like that. Though it had started out calmly enough.

"Ross, it's time." Marie rarely heard her mother speak English, and it sounded funny rolling off her tongue. Mangled by a thick accent.

He had turned around and laughed. Anais had Claire by one hand and Marie by the other. "Time for what, Annie? Is it the complaining hour, again? Time to hear you bitch about how much you hate the good ol' US of A?"

"Dinner."

"Go eat, then."

The words flowed back and forth until Ross stood up and pushed them out the door. The argument continued on the street, where he felt more comfortable raising his voice, getting in her face without an audience. The episode ended with a quick smack to her mouth. There were days Marie hated him.

> *I planned to leave him, take Claire and go to Saigon or Cherbourg—my family was scattered by that point—but then I found out I was pregnant again. With you. This may be hard to hear, I don't know, but it kept me with him. Times were different then. A pregnant woman didn't leave her husband, go running off alone. It was unheard of, and I had no money. I was praying my father would forgive my mistake, but he'd never forgive two, I knew.*

Marie winced. Had her mother just called her a mistake? The cause of her continued relationship with Ross? She placed the papers down on the end table and went to the kitchen in search of more wine, brandy, or even bourbon. There was only a half bottle of red wine left. She poured it into a glass and went to the window. Anais's confession wasn't comforting. What was the point? To tell her she'd had a crappy marriage to Ross? That was common knowledge. Then Marie thought about the beginning of the letter. *Murder.* Who had Anais almost killed?

Marie held the papers in her hand, tempted to flip to the end. She didn't want to relive her childhood outlined in tight little paragraphs, but the story was bound to take a few turns along the way, and though Marie had been along for most of the ride, it felt like she'd been asleep in the back seat for the entire trip. She'd never known this side of her mother. Anais had been prim, put together, and always in control.

Marie had swallowed the rest of the wine in her glass and gathered the pages when the words *I tried to kill her, not once but twice* popped out at her. That definitely wasn't referring to Ross. She stared at it for a few minutes and then found her place.

The thought occurred to her that maybe Ava's inclination toward killing hadn't been an anomaly. She'd spent all that time as a child with Anais. Maybe she'd acquired her craft from her grandmother.

CHAPTER 29

JOANNE

The funeral home seemed to be closing in on her. She sat in the back, hesitating to walk up to the front of the room, to the casket, to Juliette's sisters and mother. They clung together in a clump near the flowers, hugging each other, whispering, and occasionally wiping away tears. Joanne could see Juliette's face to the right of where they stood. The casket was open, though she'd prayed nonstop in the car that it would be shut tight, nothing but grainy walnut or cherry. But no, she was there, her hair styled nicely, swept across her forehead. She was wearing blue. A dark-blue dress, her hands folded across her stomach.

Joanne pushed up from her seat and walked slowly to the front. The seats were filled with people, some wearing scrubs or hospital garb. The flow had been steady in the hour that Joanne had been there. She stopped at the casket and looked down on the woman Russell had intended to marry. During their handful of meetings at Russell's house, Juliette had been smart, eager to help, enthusiastic, even, trying to wedge into the Ava investigation before she knew what was happening. And when she did learn of the dreaded mistakes Russell had made that affected his career, of his relationship with Ava, Juliette had kept her head high, no drama.

She felt someone behind her and turned to see one of the sisters, though she didn't know her name. "I'm so sorry" was all Joanne could manage. She was angry she was here alone. That the family had barred Russell because they felt he had something to do with her death. Her parents refused to speak to him in person, but managed to leave a message telling him he'd destroyed their daughter's life. She felt a softening toward the family when she saw the grief on their faces.

"Are you a friend of hers?" the woman asked.

Joanne nodded. "You're her sister?"

"Gail." She gave a weary smile. "I was the matron of honor."

"Oh, Gail. She told me about you." Juliette hadn't said a word to Joanne about her family, but small talk was painful under these circumstances, so Joanne was making it up as she went along. "I saw her just about three weeks ago. This is so shocking."

"Then you know she was getting married soon."

Joanne nodded. "All excited about the dress."

"She should have canceled. None of this would have happened." Gail's voice rose, and someone who looked to be Juliette's mother moved in and put an arm around her back.

Joanne stepped away and ended up leaning against the edge of the casket. "I didn't know they were having problems. They both seemed so happy."

"Hmmm. Then you must not have known them well," the older woman said. "Jules was having jitters. Half the time crying. She was worried about her age, you know?"

"Worried why?"

"That she'd invested so much time in Russell," Gail chimed in, "that to let him go and try to start over was impossible. She didn't think she'd find anyone else, and she wanted a family."

"I believe what you're saying, but it's hard for me. I always saw them as perfect for each other. I had no idea—"

"My daughter was a surgeon. Smart, beautiful. She could have gotten whomever she wanted. Instead she attaches herself to a cop who gets suspended. Did you know it took him two years too long to propose? That was the first sign this was no good, and I think he cheated on her to boot."

"Wait, wait, wait." Joanne was starting to get angry but wanted to keep it under wraps. They were skewing the facts. "That might be a tad unfair to Russell. He was trying to do a favor for a friend. That's how he got suspended."

"Wonderful," the mother said. "A favor for a friend included an affair with her? Listen—"

Joanne pushed herself up to her full height. "No one knows what happened between them, but everything in this world is a two-way street. I liked Juliette, but she was less than truthful with him too. She told him she was at her last dress fitting the night before she died. She came home drunk, supposedly after being out drinking afterward with her bridesmaids. Not true?"

Gail and her mother looked at one another, and Joanne couldn't help but notice the surprise in the mother's expression. Gail looked down, trying to find a distraction. "She told him that?" Juliette's mother said. "But her fitting wasn't until Friday. I told the police that. Did you hear this, Gail?"

"Juliette told me she was going out that night. Yes. But I didn't know she'd given some cover story to Russell. I mean, how would I?" Gail responded.

"Where'd she tell you she was going?" Joanne asked.

"To let off steam. To sow some wild oats. To get her balance back. I think she said all of that. I told you things weren't good between them."

"When's the last time you saw your sister?" Joanne asked.

Gail shifted from side to side. "I saw her that morning. At the house. She borrowed my heels. I dropped them off and we talked." She seemed to suddenly realize her dead sister was lying only a few feet away. She dropped her head and appeared to be crying.

"What'd she say? If you don't mind me asking."

Gail looked at her mother and unhooked her mother's arm from around her back. She walked Joanne toward the door. "My mother doesn't need this on her mind. Juliette was upset. She'd had a fight with Russell the night before. It got nasty. She said he scared her. She said he'd changed into a different person and she didn't always feel safe—"

"No," Joanne interrupted. "Russell was never violent. Never."

"Maybe not in front of you, but when they were alone? When he was angry? She said when he was out of work it was the worst. He was depressed and sullen. And mean. She asked to borrow my heels because she said she wanted to go out with friends from work. Just have some fun. And get away from him." She walked farther out into the lobby of the funeral home. "She said she was going to make up her mind about the wedding that night. If she decided to call it off, she was going to tell him the next day. But she didn't live to do that, did she?"

Joanne took a deep breath, her eyes wandering to the parking lot. Her thoughts were jumbled. None of this made sense. Russell never told her about any ongoing arguments with Juliette. And he didn't have a reputation for losing his temper. "Do you know anyone she went out with? So I can talk to them? This is really disturbing."

"Steve Thomas. Doctor." Just then Joanne's phone chimed with a text. Russell.

I got a text—the prints came back. Some prints in the house didn't match mine or Juliette's. But they found my prints on the hypodermic needle pouch.

CHAPTER 30

AVA

The telephone line seemed to buzz and then click in the rhythmic way that was very European. I counted the sounds. Five. Six. Then I heard someone answer, and a flurry of Italian. My heart was thumping so hard it was in my ears. I stared at the street through the coffee-shop window.

"Excuse me," I said. The languages were flowing through my brain. I spent my childhood traveling back and forth to France to see Anais. Learning foreign tongues became a passion, a hobby. It fascinated me— the rhythm of the words, how they fell together, the idioms, how the language summarized the culture, all of it. I'd spun it into a job as a translator for the court system. But my translation skills were failing me now, the flow of words circling meaninglessly in my brain. *Get it right.* In Italian. *"Mi dispiace disturbarla,"* I started. *I'm sorry to bother you.* "I hope I have the right number." The language was flowing easily for me now.

There was hesitation on the line. "Who are you looking for?"

"Victor DeFeo?"

"Where did you get this number?" he asked. I knew his voice. I knew the timbre and the cadence. It was distant and familiar at the same time.

Silent tears rolled from my eyes. "From Father Bill Connelly's sister."

"I haven't heard from Father Connelly in over twenty years. Who did you say you were?"

"Ava Saunders." He'd know the name Giada, but there was a lump sitting in my throat and I was afraid that just saying it would make me cry.

He seemed to be tapping something in the background. "Saunders? You said Saunders?"

"Yes, Claire Lavoisier-Saunders was my mother. Anais Lavoisier died and I found this name—"

"Anais is dead?"

The phone was pressed against my face; my hand was becoming damp with sweat. I coughed to clear my throat. "Yes. She is. She died last week. Her funeral was yesterday."

"Don't tell me anything else. I don't need to know." His voice was booming through the phone, and I had to pull it from my ear. I was afraid he was going to hang up.

"She had a stroke, Nonno." After I said it, I realized that it was too soon to call him Grandpa. Too soon, but it was too late.

"She deserved worse—what did you say to me? Did you call me Nonno?"

"Yes, Nonno. It's Giada. It's Giada." I had no concrete memories of him. But I knew this man just the same. My hands were trembling, my whole body, actually. It was all I could do to hold the phone.

"Giada. Baby Giada? But you said Claire was your mother. What—"

"Claire adopted me after my mother died. After Adrianna died."

"I don't understand. All these years after your mother disappeared we thought you were with her. We thought you'd show up again. That she'd show up again. I didn't know she died. We didn't know. When we checked with the police they always said, *'Nessuna novità, nessuna novità.'* *No news.* I heard the sound of the phone dropping, and I waited. Several minutes later I heard him breathing into the receiver. "How did you end up with Claire? Tell me."

"*Nonno, Ross ha ucciso mia madre. Ross e alcuni altri uomini,*" I answered.

"Ross killed Adrianna? Ross?" he spat back. "Is this true?"

I felt tingles in my spine. I was talking to my grandfather, and though I hadn't seen him in so many years, I was reconstructing his face from lost memories as we spoke. "And some other men, yes. And he gave me to Claire. I've been with Claire this whole time. I didn't know where you were. Who my mother was, even. I didn't have her name."

"Is this a joke?" The word for joke in Italian, *scherzo*, was drawn out. Like he didn't want to let it go. I heard gasping on the other end of the line, or choking. He wasn't taking this well.

"No, *non è uno scherzo*. No," I answered.

"Listen, Giada." His breathing was heavy and labored. "This is very important. Did Ross know he was killing my daughter? Did he know who she was? Did Anais know who you were?"

"I don't know. I'm trying to piece it together myself. She never told me anything. I only know she had a Martinelli's name in with some papers. I found them after she died. I've been on a wild chase, searching for you . . ." I put my head to my hand. I was feeling dizzy.

"Enzo Martinelli? Here in Tuscany?"

"No. Leo Martinelli. In Philadelphia. I think they're related."

"So she knew Adrianna had made it to Philadelphia." He hesitated. "She knew." There was a moment of silence. "Anais knew more about our child than we did. Adrianna went to see Enzo in Tuscany first when she ran away. Do you remember a farm? Three barns. A large white house with a flat roof? Grapevines? Hills as far as you could see?"

I closed my eyes and tried to think. Nothing came to me. "No."

"You were too young, maybe. But Adrianna went to see him. Then she ran from there and we never saw her again. Enzo never said he was sending her to Philadelphia to stay with a relative. He never told us. He said he didn't know where she was."

I felt a rock in my stomach. "Why would Anais not send me back to you? Back home? Why would she keep me away?"

His voice was hesitant and dropped to where it was almost inaudible. "There is no answer that I can give you in minutes, Giada. It would take hours. You grew up with this woman, Anais. Are you surprised?"

I felt my heart rate pick up. "Yes, I am. And no, I'm not. I can't answer that in a minute. It would take hours. I need to come there. To see you, Nonno."

"No, no, no. Not now." The words came out fast, like bullets sprayed in my direction.

"When, then? What about Nonna?" Grandmother.

"Philomena died. She died. And I'll tell you this, Giada, she'd be heartbroken to know you were with Anais all this time. Heartbroken. It would kill her. You can't come here. Please."

"Did something happen between them? Philomena and Anais? Is that why Anais didn't let Nonna know I was alive?"

I could hear him breathing heavily again, and I was afraid this conversation was too much for him. "Adrianna may have died in that church, but Anais tried to kill her years before that. More than once."

I laughed without meaning to. What he was saying was absurd. "How? How'd she try and kill her?"

"I don't want to go through this!" I could hear the anger in his voice. "Please, Giada. This is so hard for me. Try and understand. Give us time—give me time."

"No, no. Don't hang up. This is upsetting for me too. I saw my mother being murdered. I was there."

"You were with Adrianna when she was killed?"

"Yes, it happened right in front of me."

"Dio mio," he whispered. "How did this happen to my family? I need—I need to think about this. Let me think. Where are you?"

"I'm still in the United States."

"*Bene, bene.* I will call you in a day? We can talk more then."

"No, I'll call you back. I have so much I want to tell you." It took me a few seconds of silence to realize he was weeping on the other end of the phone. *"Nonno. Mi dispiace." I'm sorry.*

The line clicked off. I sat there for a few moments, unsure what to do. That call had crushed him. Destroyed him. And it had shocked me. The possibility was dawning on me that Anais had used me as a pawn to hurt the very people I'd been looking for over the past five years.

The thought left me feeling utterly alone again, as I always had been. I chewed on the skin around my nails and tried to think of any possible way that Anais, the DeFeos, my grandfather—Ross Saunders—and Bill Connelly, of all people, could be connected to each other in some twisted way. It occurred to me that after jumping from the ship and wandering the world alone, I had finally found my family, only to be told I couldn't meet them. There was no place in this world for me.

I looked at my watch. It was nearly three. I had an appointment with a man, a computer geek who might be my best chance to extract Anais's bank-account information from the flash drive. It was time. Even if I had nothing else, I had that little piece of metal, and the potential for a good deal of money that would take me to Italy or anywhere else I wanted to go.

CHAPTER 31

MARIE

Marie awoke from where she'd fallen asleep on the couch, and looked around at the cottage; the flames were casting shadows on the stone wall surrounding the fireplace. The light of day had not yet begun to seep through the curtains into the room, and she'd never felt more out of sorts in this little house. The pages Anais had left her were scattered across the ottoman. She drew in her breath as she picked up the next section and started reading again. This rambling tale was not going to have a happy ending, she just knew.

> Philomena came to see me in Philadelphia the summer after you were born, and it was the first time I felt I had companionship. She brought news of my parents, what was happening in Saigon. Sadly, most posts there were abandoned, most businesses left by that time. My parents had moved to Brittany and then Cherbourg. They were settling, reconnecting with family and friends, but they apparently never asked about me. Not once. I was crushed. I was hoping that we could make amends now that I was a little older, had been married for three years and had two children. Their lack of interest destroyed me.

It made me lose all hope, because things with your father were deteriorating and I wanted to go back to France to be with them.

Philomena had her own troubles that summer. She had been married to Victor for two years by that time. They had moved to Vicenza and he'd opened a hardware store. They had a nice little house in town, and she was close to her family. I can't even tell you how much I envied her! I begged her that summer to let me come and live with her. I promised to help with the store, and would try to get a job to contribute to expenses until I could move out on my own, but she said no. Victor said no. Philomena was pregnant, two months along, and I think he thought we would be a burden. I understood but I was heartbroken. I mourned her when she returned home. I continued with your father the best I could, keeping myself busy with you girls. Do you remember when we walked all the way to the art museum to see the Degas exhibit?

Marie did. It was about a five-mile walk through the city. They'd stopped at every park along the way, gotten hot dogs from stands, and meandered through the streets until they'd reached the museum. It had taken the entire morning, but Anais hadn't seemed to mind. She'd seemed unusually happy. They'd even taken a cab back home, Anais scraping the bottom of her purse to pay the driver. Anais had been alive that day. If Marie had to put a word to how her mother had seemed, it'd be *free*. Something had shifted inside her.

I found a way to cope the best I could by seeing the city with you and Claire, going to plays and concerts. But the church was the only thing that was really familiar to me. It made me feel, for a few minutes even, that things were normal and when I walked outside I'd have my life back. My English had improved, and I would spend Saturday nights and sometimes Sundays too at Mass. Your father absolutely refused to attend and didn't want me to go either, but I did. We had drifted apart, though I think he loved you the best way he knew how. He was a broken man. Marie, when I tell you something had sucked the life from him, I mean it. He was angry, sullen, drunk whenever possible, and it seemed to get worse, not better, during the time I knew him. I didn't know then that he'd been abused. I had no idea why he despised the church, and he never confided in me, so there was no way I could have comforted him.

I went to his friend, Bill Connelly, for support. He was a priest in the parish I attended. They'd known each other since they were children. He was an odd man too, though. Bill—I called him Father at that point—listened to me and my worries about my marriage, but his only suggestion was to pray on it and go back and serve my husband. He said he would talk to Ross if I wanted him to, but whatever was said between the two of them didn't help. I started meeting with Father Connelly on Sunday mornings between Masses or sometimes later in the day. He became my counselor, but maybe he was too close to the situation? I didn't know how close until sometime later, when I learned that he had been abused too. But I'm getting ahead of myself. Let me back up.

That fall, Philomena lost her baby. She miscarried at almost five months. In the process she almost died, but she pulled through, though she was never the same after that. I wanted to leave Philadelphia to be with her, but Ross said we didn't have the money. Money. Everything came down to money. If I had gone to Vicenza to be with her while she convalesced, things would never have happened the way they did. I tried to reach my parents to get their help, but they still refused to speak to me. When I look back on things, that was the turning point. Everything that happened after that point seemed destined to destroy us all. Mistake after mistake.

Philomena lost her baby in October, Ross lost his job in early November. Claire came down with pneumonia in late November. Her treatment took all of our energy and resources. It also left me in Philadelphia. If I had gone to Italy it wouldn't have happened, she wouldn't have gotten sick, and though you'll think that doesn't make sense, it really does. We would have been safely stowed in Europe, but as it was, we were on North Fourth Street with your father, no job, no money, more drinking, living in hospital rooms with Claire. And still my parents ignored me.

Marie tried to think. She'd been too young to remember any of this, only three or four at the time. She vaguely remembered Philomena coming to visit them in Philadelphia, though she didn't know her name then. She was just a friendly woman with a heavy accent. And Claire being in the hospital was just not recorded in her memory bank. None of it.

Marie, I feel as I retell this story that I let you two girls down. I know that now and I knew it then, but there wasn't anything I could do to make it better. I prayed on the rosary for hours. Claire got better, so I prayed some more. I even kept my meetings with Father Connelly, because he was the connection between my husband and the Catholic Church. He healed the divide. We had him over for dinner from time to time, and his presence seemed to soothe things for a while. He made me laugh when things were at their worst. And they did get worse.

In the heat of an argument with your father, I lost my footing and fell and broke a few bones. I won't say any more, as he is your father, and what happened that night needs to stay between the two of us. I had such mixed feelings, God help me! The pain weighed heavily, but the release of my responsibility for this marriage, knowing I wasn't at fault, wasn't the cause of the problems, was a blessing.

Where is this story headed? How does this end in near murder? Who did I try and kill? Not once but twice? This is the place in the story where you may need to get a drink. Some wine, perhaps. Because things get difficult from here. I started this letter by telling you I am not perfect and never was. My flaws were never more apparent than during this part of my life. My marriage was over, you need to understand that. We'd had some bouts of fights and violence, but I could never forgive him for what happened that caused me to fall. I never will. And so I attached myself to another man in a way I never should have. I leaned on him. Ran to him emotionally. Became close to him in a way a woman should only be close to her husband. He was there for me and made me feel that I could manage my life. I loved him in a complicated way, but I never imagined it was going to change my life.

Marie squinted down at those words and reread them. Anais had an affair? Marie hesitated with the pages in her hand and contemplated throwing them into the fire. Anais's life was her own. She'd lived it with the mistakes and triumphs that everyone experiences along the way. Reading this now was making Marie edgy and sick. Her hand held the pages over the flames, lingering. As she was about to release them, the phone rang. It wasn't her cell phone but Anais's phone. Her old-fashioned no-caller-ID landline sitting on the little end table.

Marie picked up the receiver. "Hello?" she said softly.

"Marie, don't hang up."

Marie gripped the phone so hard her fingers went numb. The voice belonged to the devil, reaching out to her from the grave.

CHAPTER 32

RUSSELL

The circling would begin, he knew it. That was the way it worked. They'd interviewed him after Juliette was found. They'd interviewed him again, asking harder questions. Now concrete evidence seemed to link him to her murder. Next they'd be digging into his relationship with Juliette, every fight, questioning friends and family. He knew he had maybe two or three days tops to figure out where Ava was, to prove she'd been in his house that day. Or he was going to be arrested, and he might not be released. It would be up to Joanne, and he wasn't sure she could do it on her own. She'd need help—but there was no one left who could help.

Juliette's autopsy had come back. She had a slightly elevated level of potassium, which wasn't unusual, as the cells released potassium upon death. The alcohol in her blood at the time of death was negligible. Her liver had cleaned it all up. They did find an antidepressant, Lexapro, and traces of Xanax. Russell was flabbergasted. He'd essentially lived with this woman for almost two years, and though she'd retained her own apartment for much of that time, they'd been together almost every night. She'd never told him she was depressed. She'd never said she was taking antidepressants or antianxiety medication.

The needle mark on her arm was clear. She'd been injected with something on the day she died, but the findings were inconclusive. The coroner had determined no definitive cause of death. But Juliette was dead, and Russell's prints were on the hypodermic pouch. He stared at the reports, his energy drained. He was in his office with the door shut and had only ventured out twice, to use the bathroom. The room next door contained the remnants of Juliette's death, the soiled mattress, the bottle of water, and he didn't want to look at it or be anywhere near it, but there was nowhere else he could go.

His family had come around, his brothers, his parents. They were horrified, empathetic, concerned. They wanted to consume him, take him in, erase all of this for him, almost encapsulate him within the family fold, but he couldn't let them. He needed to keep everyone at a distance until he could reconcile this in his brain. His mother had stopped by with a container of food earlier, but he had kept her at the door and wouldn't let her in.

"We loved Juliette," she'd said, standing on the top step. "This is so hard for us. Leave this house, come and stay with us, please?" Her eyes were warm and watery, and she reached out to hug him, because she didn't know what else to do. There was going to be no closure for his family. "It isn't healthy to be here alone."

He shook his head. "My things are here. I'm going to just stay in my office. Not my bedroom, sleep on the sofa in there until I can sort this out." He caught sight of himself in the mirror as he shut the door on his mother. His skin was dusky gray, his hair dirty, stuck to his head. His eyes were sunken in, swollen dark-purple spots spread out underneath them, making him look sick and haunted. His family was calling multiple times a day, sometimes taking turns until he had no choice but to block all their numbers.

He heard a rap on his front door and wondered if his family was back or if this was it, if this was the day he was going to be arrested. He jogged down the steps and opened it to see Joanne standing there, a bag of groceries in her hand. Unlike his mother, she didn't wait for an invite. She pushed in and went to the kitchen and began putting things away.

"I got you some microwave meals. Easy. Just pop them in and heat. You need to eat." She pulled out cereal and milk, canned soups, crackers, cheese, sliced ham, bread, some paper plates and bowls, and plastic utensils. She held up the plates. "No cleaning right now. Just eat and throw away. I went to the viewing."

"You did what?" He looked wounded.

"I got an earful from Juliette's sister." Joanne started making coffee, rinsing the pot and filling it with water.

"Don't." He took the pot from her hands. "That's the last thing I did for Juliette. This is all wrong."

She took it back. "It's a coffeepot. I'm going to make us coffee. Then I'm going to clean this kitchen up and heat you up some soup. You're going to sit here and eat it from a paper bowl." She started looking for filters and coffee in the cupboards.

"The one to the right."

"Gail did some talking. The family is not happy right now—"

"No shit."

She turned to face him. "Okay, that was a stupid thing to say. But they are looking to blame someone and they've picked you."

He watched her carefully. "What'd they say?"

She pulled out a chair and sat down. "They said you were not the person I know you to be. They said you'd become lazy, mean, and sullen when you were out of work. Abusive and controlling to Juliette."

He shook his head. "That's not true. I wasn't home that much, you know that. I was working freelance security, around the clock. I was studying for the law-school admission test." He slapped the table. "Why would they say that? I need to talk to them." He put his head down and felt moisture on his cheeks again. "I loved her. I loved her family."

A minute later she put a cup of coffee in front of him. "No. You don't want to talk to them. It'll make it worse. Gail kept saying this stuff and I was getting angry, but I wanted to hear it. To hear what Juliette was telling them, because someone is lying."

He picked up the cup and took a sip. "So tell me the rest."

"She said things were so bad Juliette was thinking of calling off the wedding. She was going out with friends that night to vent and to make up her mind about getting married. She was supposed to be letting you know her thoughts the next day."

"The day she died."

"Did you have any hint of this, Russell, that she was unhappy?"

"Yes and no. This past year has been hard. I mean, after she found out I'd let Ava go, things went downhill a bit, but I had no idea she was thinking of breaking things off. No. We were just talking about the honeymoon. She was excited about Vietnam. Here." He jumped up and went into the living room. "Here's notes she made about Da Nang and where she wanted to go, what she wanted to do. She was looking at pictures of the hut we're staying in"—he caught himself—"*were* staying in, just a few days ago. None of what she's saying is true. It's like you're talking about someone else."

"I think Juliette was having an affair. And I think it's been going on for a while." Joanne pulled out a pot and opened a can of soup. "We don't have time for me to be kind. I just need honest answers from you."

"I'm not hungry."

"Oh, you're going to eat. It's chicken noodle. I need you energized. And then you're going to tell me everything."

"Juliette was taking Lexapro and Xanax. It was in her bloodstream when she died. So, I don't know what I can tell you. I never even knew she was depressed. Or anxious. I never knew she was unhappy."

Joanne studied his face. "How'd your prints get on the hypodermic pouch?"

"I must have touched it when she took it out of her case. She had the needles on the dining-room table a few days ago. She was rummaging through her case. I must have touched the pouch."

"Think. Did she hand it to you for any reason, like, 'Hold this'?"

He shook his head. "I don't remember. It was on the table. I don't know if I picked it up to look at it or not."

"She had a diary, you know." Joanne put the soup in front of him, along with a sleeve of saltines. "Eat. I didn't see it. Gail said they'd read it and turned it over to the police."

He dipped the spoon in and then put it down. "What's in the diary?"

Joanne shrugged. "Pages of what I just told you. You'd become a horrible rotten jerk. The deterioration of your relationship. That you were sleeping with Ava." She sat down at the table and nudged the soup toward him. "Finish that. And then go take a shower. We're going to pay a little visit to Juliette's boyfriend."

"Let me guess. Steve Thomas?" he asked. "He only called her a hundred times the day she died . . ." His voice trailed off as the implication hit him.

"Bingo," Joanne said. "You'd make a good detective."

CHAPTER 33

Ava

The burly man with the uncombed, greasy hair was taking my flash drive apart. I watched him carefully. The last person who had done that had lost his life, I wanted to say. I didn't, but my eyes were glued to the bits of plastic and metal so that my only hope for freedom didn't disappear.

"I need the right equipment. To extract the memory chip. Can you leave it with me? I need about a week." His eyes were flat, dull, a brown so dark they looked black.

I stood up. "No. I can't. But if you let me know when you have everything you need, I'll meet you and wait as long as you need me to wait."

"Must be important, huh? Let me get some things together and I'll call you. Give me two days. A thousand dollars." He pushed my flash drive at me.

"Seriously? A thousand? To extract the memory chip and get the data?" I was stalling. I didn't have it and wanted to bargain it down.

"A thousand and I'm not going any lower. It takes time to reconnect those wires and extract the data. It's not easy, or you would've done it already."

I picked up the flash drive and slipped it into my pocket. "Fine. Call me when you're ready." He was slimy; just the look in his eye told me he'd steal those account numbers and head to Asia as soon as I left the room. "I need the information from this drive in two days at the latest."

He nodded. "Then get me the money by tomorrow and I'll work all night once it's in my hand."

I was in a catch-22. I wanted to get to Italy, but I didn't have enough money. The bank-account numbers were on the flash drive, and even if I could get to them, I assumed the bank accounts were in Europe. And I'd need money to get there to get the money.

I looked at my phone. I considered calling the line at the cottage and seeing if Marie picked up, though I dreaded the thought. I dialed the number, my finger hovering over the "Call" button, the pros and cons racing through my brain. Marie probably wouldn't contact the police, because she wouldn't want to draw attention to herself. Violating parole would be that much harder if she were in the spotlight. I jabbed my finger down onto the "Call" button and held my breath.

"Hello?" The soft, subdued voice seemed filled with sadness.

"Marie, don't hang up." There was a silence but no click on the other end of the line. So far, so good. "I could spend the next twenty minutes saying I'm sorry for sticking you with Ritter's murder, but we don't have time. Just know that I am. Sorry, that is."

"No."

"No, what?"

"Ava, no. I saw what you did. I saw you. You're a monster."

"Saw me what?"

"You killed that girl. Russell's girlfriend. You killed her. I followed you there, saw you go into the house. I went in afterward and saw her lying in that bed. Why, Ava? Why? When is this going to end?"

"You were following me? Marie, I don't know what you think you saw, but I didn't kill her."

"You know damned well you did. Everyone around you ends up dead. Claire, Anais—"

"I did not kill Claire. I didn't. I didn't kill Anais either. Not like that. I'm calling you because we need each other. I'm sorry, but we do. I have the flash drive Anais gave me with her accounts—"

There was a laugh. "So why are you still hanging around? Why not just go, Ava? Is something stopping you?"

"The drive is compromised. The salt water destroyed it. I found a guy who can extract the information—but I need your help."

"Ah, and here it is. I knew you'd only reach out for a reason."

"We'll both benefit. Get the information from the drive, split the money."

"We'll get the money and you'll stick a knife in my chest and disappear. I'd rather be poor, Ava, than get tangled up in anything with you."

"I found my family. In Italy. Sort of. I think."

Marie cleared her throat. "Uh-huh. Lucky them. Send me a postcard when the first one mysteriously dies."

"Adrianna DeFeo was my mother's name. My grandfather is still alive in Vicenza."

"I know, Ava. I've always known."

My heart stopped pounding. I could feel the blood in my ears. These people had lied to me my entire life. "So, was this a game—keeping the information from me all this time?"

"I had her purse. Your mother's purse. The one she had on her when she was killed. Ross took it. So, yeah, I've always known." Marie hesitated. "And you want to know why, why we wouldn't tell you?"

"Why?"

"Anais didn't want that to happen. She didn't want you any closer to the truth. She didn't want you anywhere near those people."

I felt like I was choking. "So you left my mother unidentified? Like she wasn't a person? Your father died like a pig. Squealing on the floor, Marie. The man who killed my mother—"

It sounded like Marie was yawning. "The man who saved you. Yeah, yeah, yeah. You're not going to bait me, Ava. How many people have you killed since you fell off the boat? Let me guess. Three? Four? Am I close?"

"It might be five soon, Marie."

"Exactly."

"But you need the money and so do I, so let's call a truce. I'll get the account numbers and figure out the logistics, but I can't really access any of it because I'm dead. But you can, maybe. Proving you're Anais's only living next of kin. We split the money—"

"How much money are we talking about?" I heard the interest rising in her voice.

"I don't know. I jumped off the boat before I had a chance to look, but Anais said it was around twelve million dollars. Six each. Free and clear. And we'll put our differences aside for the moment—"

"Fine." Clipped, terse. "How?"

"Stay there, I'll be in touch."

"Don't take too long. Parole will be looking for me in a few days."

I hung up and stared at the phone, wondering if I could work together with Marie. Or if she'd double-cross me and make me kill her first.

CHAPTER 34

MARIE

Ava's voice was distinct, like no one else's. Just a tad gravelly, with a hint of an accent, precise and clipped when she was making a point. Listening to it was making Marie angrier with every second that ticked by. This girl just randomly attacked people and her crimes seemed to go unnoticed and undetected. Then she talked about it like it was nothing. But here was the chance to make everything right. To fix it all, once and for all. Ava had the flash drive; Marie could get the money, maybe. But she was never going to split it evenly, or at all. She was going to make Ava pay for everything she had done to the family. Screw her over, the same way she'd done to everyone else. Even kill her if it came to that, if she had to. Technically she was already dead, so it wouldn't matter.

She stared down at the pages in front of her. Ava may have found her family at long last, but it wouldn't bring her comfort, it was only going to make things worse, Marie could just feel it. There was something layered underneath all this and it was probably explained in the pages Anais had left. She had to finish, to stay one step ahead of this girl. Because Ava didn't know the backstory. And the backstory probably created the front story. Anais continued:

I put myself in a bad situation, but looking back, it wasn't the worst of the decisions I'd made. My connection to this man was short, intense, and memorable but forbidden. I couldn't let go. I can't say I'm sorry for it, but it contradicted everything in me that was right and clean, if that makes sense. I'd had the moral upper hand in my marriage until that point. I'd slept only with Ross, I'd given myself to the marriage, taking full responsibility for my mistakes. I tried to be a good wife—but enough of that.

Ross never knew the reason for my desperation and despair after this man left me. Ever. It wasn't the reason for our separation. I never used it to torture him. I will not tell you anything about the other person because it doesn't matter. Not in the real scheme of things. Ross did know him, so maybe that's why I felt so guilty in some respects. He called me one day, and I'll call him Adam for the sake of giving him a name in this letter, and said he was leaving town, leaving me. I was devastated but had known from the beginning it couldn't last. Adam seemed so torn, but he wasn't giving up his life for a married woman with two children. He was also married, which adds another rather large fold to this story.

He asked me to meet him to say good-bye. I left you girls sleeping and went to Penn Treaty Park at the crack of dawn. It was deserted, empty. I sat on the bench looking out over the Delaware River. He was late, and I was thinking he wasn't coming. Initially I was crushed, but it would have been better if he'd left without saying good-bye, because what happened changed everything.

Marie heard a knock on the front door and was pulled away from the pages in front of her. It was Sandrine. Marie tried to hide her annoyance, but some of it must have slipped through.

"I'm sorry to bother you, Marie. But I was thinking about what we were talking about earlier." Sandrine walked inside without being invited and sat down. "I don't know how far you've gotten in that letter. But please don't hate your mother. She wasn't the strongest or best person back then." There were tears in her eyes, and she coughed to try and cover them up. "The woman you know never would have done it. Never."

Marie was still standing by the door, watching her mother's old friend, seeing the worried creases on her face. "I haven't finished the letter yet, but she had an affair while she was living with my father in Philadelphia? Is that it? So she left him? Did she try and kill him, maybe in a fight, before she left? I'm just guessing."

Sandrine shook her head. "It's not the affair. It's who the affair was with and what happened afterward. I thought you'd be done by now and I was worried. You came here to pay respects to her. I couldn't have you leaving with hate in your heart."

Marie glanced at the unread pages. It was all in there, though Anais was taking her time weaving this tale. "Ava called me a little while ago. Yes, Ava, risen from the dead. She has a plan, apparently. I'm supposed to wait here for her."

"Wait here for what?"

"It was about money, really. And about working together."

"Don't . . ."

Marie stared at Sandrine. "I've lived with Ava since she was three years old. I know who she is, what she is. The killing, all of it. I have a plan, Sandrine. I'm going to lie in wait. Get the money from her and end this, or her. I promise."

Sandrine was shaking her head. "You can't."

"And why is that?"

"Finish reading and you'll see. It's all one big, terrible trap."

CHAPTER 35

RUSSELL

They stood at the entranceway of the office building, watching people come and go.

"So are you taking charge of this investigation?" he asked. "Is that the plan?"

Joanne gave him a sideways look. "This isn't a police interrogation, it's just a conversation. Just talking, that's all. Casual."

"That's how it always starts."

Joanne pulled open the door and they entered the foyer. She scanned the directory for the office number. "I hope he's in."

"I told you I called beforehand. You weren't listening."

She ignored him and found the door, frosted glass, with the lettering across it that read *Orthopedic Surgery Associates*, with seven names listed underneath. "Steve Thomas, we're coming for you."

Behind the counter, a short, dark-haired woman dressed in scrubs glanced up at her. "Sign in, please. Are you a new patient?"

"No. I'm not a patient. I need to speak to Dr. Thomas about a private matter."

She held Joanne's gaze. "Umm, he's scheduled straight through until one. Can you come back?"

Joanne placed her hand on the counter and leaned in. "No. Not possible. Tell him it's about Juliette. It's important."

Her eyes widened. "Oh, I am so sorry. So sorry. Let me see if he has a minute." She disappeared from behind the counter and hurried down the hallway.

Enough time passed that Russell had time to make himself a cup of Keurig coffee and settle in to watch *The Chew*, which was playing loudly on the wall-mounted television. A man appeared at the doorway to the inner office, and his eyes locked on Russell.

"Did you need to talk to me about Juliette?"

Russell looked up and remembered everything about him from the night the doctor had come to their house for a dinner party. The night Russell left Juliette to host by herself because Ava's abandoned car had been found in the Pine Barrens when they thought she was dead. Steve Thomas looked the same, maybe a tad more worn. He was tall, with dark curly hair and skin hardened by the sun, like he'd been tanning on the beaches of Miami his whole life.

Joanne jumped up. "I was hoping for some minutes of your time."

"And you are?"

"I was her friend," she started, but Steve seemed fixated on Russell.

"I am so sorry about Juliette, but the police already talked to me. I'm not sure there's anything I can add to this conversation at this point. But we are certainly going to miss her here, and if there's anything we can do—"

Joanne cocked her head to the side. "'We can do'? That's a bit formal, isn't it? I mean, you knew her quite well, right? In fact, you were with her the night before she died."

He frowned. "Like I said, I already told the police everything I know. A group went out that night. Yes, I was one of them, but I left early to go home. I had surgery scheduled at seven the next morning. That's the last time I saw Juliette."

"She talked to you a lot, about her life, marriage?" Joanne asked.

"Upcoming marriage, you mean?" he responded.

"Yes, that," Russell chimed in.

Joanne put her hand out, indicating Russell needed to back off. "Yes, about her wedding, honeymoon, hopes, dreams, problems, life in general?"

Steve glanced over his shoulder to gauge how closely the receptionist was listening. "Here isn't the place to go into all of that. I have patients to see. But I'll tell you this, and I didn't mention this to the police because it didn't really come up and I saw no reason for it yet. You made her miserable, Russell. I saw you suck the life out of her with your crap over the past year or so. Cheating on her, losing your job. I mean, what the hell? How'd you expect her to deal with all of that?"

"So—"

"And then"—he looked behind him again to see if anyone was within earshot—"the argument where you hit her? I wanted to tell the police that. I really did, and I still might. Who are you? I mean, Jesus Christ."

"I never hit her. She said I hit her?" Russell stood and walked right up to the doorway, nearly touching Steve's face. "I'd never hit her or any woman."

"Yeah, okay, fine. I saw the bruise on her upper arm. I told her to leave you then, but she wouldn't."

"Bruise? When?"

"You don't know when? How many times did you hit her, for God's sake? This was about three months ago."

Russell took a step forward. "I never hit her. I didn't kill her. She was lying." He was looking into this man's eyes, trying to make sense of what he was saying, digging for anything that might have been misconstrued, but there was nothing. He didn't remember a bruise. Had she hit her arm on something, fallen? Had Juliette been playing them against one another?

"What happened that night? That night you guys went out? Is there anything that stands out as different? Anything at all that can help us?" Joanne took over again.

Steve shrugged. "The group went to Tequilas. I met them there and only had one drink—I had to leave early, like I said. Juliette seemed fine to me when I left. They had a table and were drinking pitchers. She was laughing, a little tipsy."

"Do you know she told Russell she had a fitting for her dress that night, that's where she was going?"

His face was blank, unreadable. "If she said that, it's because she needed space and didn't want you following her or asking a bunch of questions. That's just a very educated guess."

"Who else was there?" Joanne asked.

"Carla, Stephanie, Danielle, and I think Tanya," he answered.

"All people from this office?" Joanne asked.

"Why'd you call her fifteen times the next day? I saw her phone," Russell said. He'd known guys like this all his life. They looked down their noses at everyone not within their socioeconomic class. Steve Thomas was full of himself and used to people kissing his ass. Russell wanted to hit him. The urge was increasing with every minute he stayed in this office.

"She never showed up for work. She had a lot of patients scheduled. I was worried. Is there something wrong with that? As it turns out, I had a reason to be worried."

"So just tell me, were you fucking my wife?" He wanted to put his fist in this guy's smug mouth, but he kept his hands balled up by his sides.

Steve Thomas backed up; the expression of shock, of being caught off guard, was fleeting, and then it turned into a harsh laugh. "She wasn't your wife. And no. But somebody else should have been. I told her you were a sorry sack of shit for a prospective husband." He put a hand to his chest. "But hey, that's just my opinion. I'm sure the cops have their own." He started to turn and then changed his mind. "I was glad to see you had the good sense to not show up for the funeral. I can tell you, everyone there was relieved." He disappeared into the inner office.

Russell started after him, but Joanne caught his arm. "Don't. Let him go."

She dragged him to a corner of the waiting room and forced him to sit down. "Calm, Russ."

The receptionist was watching from across the counter. She glanced down the hallway and then back again. "They had a fight," she said. "He left early because they had a fight, an argument. They went outside and had words. Juliette had had a few drinks by that time, so I thought it was just the drinks, but she was crying when she came back. She said he'd ruined everything, but I have no idea who she was talking about. You"—she looked at Russell—"or him." She flicked her thumb in the direction of the hallway.

"And you are?" Joanne asked.

"Danielle. I can't say anything else here." She put her head down and stared at the computer as if she were working. "Call my cell later. And please don't tell him I said anything." She pushed an appointment card to Joanne with her number written on it. "I'm doing this for Juliette."

Joanne mouthed the words *Thank you*, and they exited the office and went to the car.

"I never hit her, Joanne. I swear on everything I am, I never hit her."

Joanne stared straight through the front windshield. "That's not the question, Russell. The question is why she was setting you up. As an excuse to break up? Or something else?"

"Like?"

"Financial reasons? Legal reasons?" But when she looked over at him he had his head down, engrossed in his phone.

"They want me down at the station at two p.m. The final interview, which is going to end in my arrest. You need to get to the bottom of this for me, Joanne." He felt the tears building in his eyes, threatening to spill over onto his cheeks. "Don't let them blame her death on me."

CHAPTER 36

AVA

The clock was ticking and I was very much aware of it. The sound marked every second that was passing without a solution to this mess. I was waiting for the text from the burly man, confirming he had everything he needed for my flash drive and was ready to start. I'd gone back to Claire's house in Haddonfield out of sheer convenience and comfort, though I kept the blinds closed and stayed away from the windows.

The conversation with my supposed grandfather destroyed me on so many levels. It was like rain that hits the surface and then seeps in over days; I wasn't sure how far the pain had gotten, but it was moving through me, and I was going to lose clarity and judgment soon, that was for sure. I'd waited my whole life to find a blood relative, my roots, and instead I'd been cast off by a man who said Anais had destroyed his life. There was nowhere left to turn, so I was forced to trudge forward and do what I had to do, with no regrets.

I unscrewed the cap from the bottle of Evan Williams I'd bought and put it to my lips. It burned as it slid down my throat, but immediately made me feel normal. I sat on the couch, the lights off, staring at the shadows as they moved across the room with each passing car. An odd sadness was starting to overwhelm me. The only person I really had left in this world was Marie. And I was sitting here planning on destroying her. Then they'd all be gone. Everyone who had ever meant anything to me.

The timing had to be precise. The banks and account numbers retrieved, then I'd be off to Cherbourg. Marie was the key once again. I thought back to that day she and Quinn had beaten me in the woods. I'd woken up in the dark, how many hours later I didn't know. And when the pieces of what had happened came together, it was the look in Marie's eyes that was the clearest, more painful even than the injuries. The hatred I'd seen there would pop into my mind when I was trying to forget, and I knew that revenge was boiling inside of me whether I wanted it to or not.

I did get her back, by framing her for the man-in-the-bathroom murder. That gave me a chuckle. But she'd slapped me again in the ultimate way by turning Anais against me. By sending that letter outlining my transgressions, making the only woman I'd ever loved afraid of me. Seeing the grandmother I adored staring back at me with fear and hatred was a betrayal that could never be forgiven, even if I had been able to forgive Marie for refusing to give me my mother's name. For holding on to my mother's only possessions all those years, digging through them and inspecting them like it was her right. I hated Marie now more than ever. I was going to let her help me, though. I was going to let her get the money from the bank, withdraw it, and transfer it to an account we could both access. Then I was going to kill her. And that was going to be my very last murder.

The clock chimed on the half hour. That stupid antique walnut clock that Claire had bought from a private collector shortly after we moved here. She'd ruminated over it for days after she first saw it, then one day it was there, exactly where it hung now, like it had always belonged. After that we were forever listening to those bells that spoke of nothing more than a life passing by. I pulled the clock from the wall and inspected it. Solid wood, handcrafted, the back signed by Elias Ingraham. It had to be worth something. It had to be worth at least plane fare to Paris. I'd stop by a pawnshop on my way to get my flash drive and sell it for whatever I could get.

The text from the computer geek finally came. *I think I'm ready. Be here around seven tonight and if you are going to stay, be prepared to wait. It might take a while. I upped the price. 1500 cash.*

The clock was stuffed into a bag, along with most of my meager possessions. I'd pared down to two changes of clothes and a smattering of grooming items. I did one more tour of the house I'd spent my last teen years in, shut off the lights, and headed out the door. I needed to sell the clock for enough to pay off the computer geek and buy a ticket to Paris, and then on to other places in Europe, or wherever Anais's information led me. I patted the clock through the cloth. It was worth at least $35,000 according to Google, maybe twice as much as Claire had paid. The pawnshop needed to come up with at least ten. At least. I was going to push for fifteen.

The computer geek's room was as dirty as the last time I'd visited. And he didn't look like he'd cleaned himself either. Large filthy sweat stains spread out under each armpit. His hair was plastered to his scalp with days of grime. He had a big table in one corner where he'd assembled everything he'd need, and he'd been courteous enough to put a chair in the corner for me. It was hard and wooden, but it was something. He took the little piece of plastic and metal from me, my heart pounding as I handed it over. It was everything I had. I took a seat and kept my eyes on it. I couldn't afford to be distracted or sleepy now.

I sat. I stood. I paced. I hovered over his shoulder and watched until he told me I was bothering him. He'd applied clear goop all over the memory chip, and I felt like this was the last opportunity. No one would ever be able to put it back together again. All that money might be lost forever.

After what seemed like an eternity, he turned and motioned to the computer screen. I started to get up when he grabbed my arm. "This is worth a lot, I'd say. Maybe more than fifteen hundred."

I jerked my arm back. "That was the deal, and I don't have any more money to give you. But I'll tell you what, my brother put up the money, and if I don't come back with the info, he's going to find you and kick the living shit out of you." I looked at my phone. "In fact, if I don't text him in the next hour—"

"I think you're lying, but here. Here's what I got."

I stared at the screen, my eyes ready to burst from my skull. Five bank accounts in five different countries. Singapore, Hong Kong, Switzerland, France, and the United States. She'd spread her money out.

"There's a file attached too. Looks like a letter or personal files. I'll print it all?" It was a question.

I nodded, staring at my life blinking on the computer screen. He'd done it. Unbelievable. Pages in hand and the remnants of my drive in a baggie, I headed out into the night. I checked my watch. It was almost six a.m.

The coffee shop was buzzing with early risers, and it took twenty minutes before I had a cup in my hand and a comfortable seat in the corner. The financial information was self-explanatory, but Anais had included a letter outlining everything for me.

> *Ava—*
>
> *Here's the account information as promised. What I didn't tell you was that I added your name and Marie's name to all of them. There's enough money to carry both of you through for the rest of your lives, but you need to work together, and you'll both need to be present to sign to withdraw any money. So you see, Ava, this may be difficult, but it's the last act I'll do to bring this family together. Or to let you two destroy each other. Your choice.*

She never did give Marie a copy, and clearly she was setting us up to kill one another.

Your path has never been an easy one, starting with your mother's murder, and then your never-ending search for her identity. If only we, as your true family, could have helped you with that.

The coffee burned in my stomach. True family? She was lying. Not only had she known my mother, she knew my grandparents very well, maybe too well. She'd written this note not as a deathbed confession, but when she thought we were going to sail across the Mediterranean together and part ways in Barcelona. She intended to give me the money with one hand and cast me adrift in a dinghy with the other, all the while forcing me and Marie to hold hands while on some sort of perverse scavenger hunt. Diabolical. This was the same woman who'd been so horrified at what *I* had done that she'd threatened to turn me in, forcing me to plunge off that cruise ship.

Anais had had no idea when she set this up that I'd soon be declared legally dead, and she certainly didn't think her own time might be short. She'd intended to watch from the sidelines as Marie and I dashed across the world in hunt of the elusive stash.

I felt sick. I didn't want to play her game, but what choice did I have? I scanned the printout. The bank in the United States was located right here in Philadelphia, in Northern Liberties, not even three blocks from where Anais and Ross lived when they were newly married. I just needed to bide my time, drink more coffee, and wait. At the stroke of nine, I was going to walk into the branch and try and wrangle some money from them.

CHAPTER 37

MARIE

Marie glanced at the papers scattered across the ottoman. "Sandrine, I can sit here and read the rest of this, or you can just tell me what I need to know."

"I only knew your mother for the end of it. After she came here with you girls. I wasn't there for the beginning. For the important parts. She needs to tell you that herself."

Marie took the woman's hands, keeping her in her seat. "I don't care how the story is told, in vivid detail or sweet and simple, I just know Ava is on her way and I need to be armed with everything I can to face her. So, please, you knew my mother for the last part of her life. Just tell me."

"How far did you get?"

"To where she had an affair. She named him Adam in the letter. They met at Penn Treaty Park. On the morning he left."

"He did. He was late and she almost gave up. But he came out of the shadows and surprised her, she said."

Marie sighed. "She seemed to have a knack for picking them. I just hope he was nice."

"Your father had his good points too. And this man, Adam, as she called him, I mean, he was good to her, as she told it, for the time it lasted, but he was married. And what he did to his marriage in the long run—what they both did . . . They talked that morning about running away together. Anais was going to leave you girls with her parents."

"But her parents, the Lavoisiers, didn't want us."

Sandrine nodded. "She was caught up in the moment, in love. She thought her parents would never refuse their granddaughters and she could make it right somewhere down the road, but for her at that moment, it was now or never. So that was her plan."

Marie felt sick. Her mother had intended to abandon them after everything they'd been through. "And this Adam was going to leave his wife?"

"She thought so."

"Did he have children?"

"No, he didn't. So that morning they met, she begged him to make plans to meet again. But he had different ideas. He'd been playing both ends against the middle, and the middle was finally right in his face. He had to make a quick choice, and it was too much. He tried to explain it, but your mother was devastated. He left her that day, and she never had that relationship with him again."

"Hmmm."

"Anais was headstrong and spoiled; she wasn't a woman to be scorned and abandoned. So she blackmailed him for the money to leave Ross. That's how she got out of Philadelphia, away from Ross, and ended up in Cherbourg."

Marie thought about the morning they left: Anais rushing about, packing things after Ross had left for work, sneaking out like thieves in the night, or in this case, the light of day, probably without explanation or discussion. She just gently pushed the girls out the front door, making them carry their little bags themselves, and shut the door behind them, leaving that part of their lives behind forever.

"Go on," Marie encouraged her.

"She went to Cherbourg hoping Adam would follow her. She told him she was there, if he wanted to find her. If he wanted to be with her."

"But he never came?"

Sandrine shook her head. "Not really. And Anais played her father well, getting the cottage and his money. But she never got what she wanted. Her life was in never-ending limbo."

"Because of Adam?"

"He came to see her once, and that was a mistake. She hadn't moved on, and thought he'd reconsidered, but he hadn't. It was cruel on his part, I think. I saw him." She looked at Marie. "She didn't introduce us, but I saw him from a distance leaving her cottage. And I saw her afterward. There aren't words to describe how she hung on to hope that they would be together."

"And during this time, Adam's wife never knew?"

She shook her head and chuckled. "He never told her, if that's what you mean. If his wife had known, we surely would have heard about it."

Marie liked how she said "we," as if she had some ownership in this. "So who did Anais try to kill?"

"Adrianna. Philomena's daughter. But that's the end of the story. The very end."

"Ava's mother? But in the part I read, Philomena lost her baby."

"She did, but she had another. A girl, obviously."

"But why? Why would Anais want to kill her friend's child, I mean?"

"You're getting too far ahead of the story." Sandrine picked up the pages and scanned through them. "Here. Read it for yourself. Start here, then figure out what you want to do about Ava."

I gave myself to him one more time before he left me
that morning. I know a child never wants to hear any of
that from their parents, but it happened for the last time.
He waited until afterward to tell me that he was leaving

me. And the pain I felt, I've never experienced before or since. My world crashed around me. I'm ashamed of what I did—crying and begging. I put myself in a position I'd never resort to again.

Marie skipped several pages ahead, since Sandrine had already filled her in on some of these details.

Philomena came to see me at the cottage in Cherbourg months after that. I'd been through hell and she was shocked at the sight of me. I weighed all of a hundred pounds, shabby and depressed; the world had taken a toll on me. We cried together and I told her as much as I could. I told her about the affair, and she met it with kindness. No judgment. "At least you got away from your marriage, Anais," she said. "You got a fresh start." Which was true. I did. But at what cost? I didn't know it at the time, but Philomena had had yet another miscarriage. She never said a word. She looked almost worse than me, but she never told me about her life, and sadly I never thought to ask. I would go on to destroy her within a year's time in every way humanly possible, and for that I'll never forgive myself.

Marie stopped reading. It was the story of the Lavoisier clan. Keep your friends close, your enemies closer, and destroy them both.

CHAPTER 38

RUSSELL

"So, let's start this off by saying the autopsy reports came back." Russell had never seen this detective before. Trout, his name was. And he looked like one. He was so tall his legs slipped under the table and reached the other side. His hair was shaved to the scalp, eyes spaced so far apart they were almost on the sides of his head; his mouth was wide, lips curved like he'd chewed tobacco at one point in his life. "The cause of death was tentatively determined to be homicide by injection of potassium chloride."

Russell dropped his head and covered his face with his hand. "Oh, Juliette." He thought about her being held down and injected. She'd been so sick and weak.

"This may be as conclusive as it's going to get. So let's talk. Did you ever hit her, Russell?"

This. Steve Thomas must have told them his story after their visit to the office. The liar. "No. Never. And if she said I did, she was lying."

"Hmmm. Her employer, Dr. Thomas, states she came in with a large bruise on her upper arm after a fight with you. This was, to the best of his recollection, about three months ago." Trout placed a notebook on the table in front of him. "This is her diary. She kept detailed notes for the past—"

"Yes, the past what? Let me guess. Six months. Maybe six and a half at the most. Right?"

Trout flipped open the diary. "There are no dates in this book. Not even a notation of the year. But from matching her comments to things happening in her life, this is very recent."

Russell was scrambling. No dates could mean anything. He took a breath. Everything was fine. Juliette was meticulous. If these entries meant anything, they'd be dated. But why keep the diary at all? When had this started? What had she been after? "Can I see it?"

Trout pushed the diary over to Russell. "Read it if you want. It's all been photographed and documented, but I'm sure you know that."

Russell flipped through the pages and saw Juliette's familiar scribbles across the pages. None of this made sense. She was a computer person. If she'd kept a diary, it would have been a digital one, not in a notebook like this.

Russell has become more controlling. He didn't want me to go to the movies with some friends. We had a fight at the door before I left. He wouldn't let me go and had me pinned.

He felt sick. That had never happened. Juliette had her own apartment. She came and went as she wanted. He couldn't even keep track of her work schedule. He turned the pages. Different ink, slightly different writing, like it was real. He had this feeling he was going mad, like this had all happened in some sort of alternate universe that he couldn't remember.

We had another fight. He threatened to kill me if I spent any more time with Steve. I told him he's my boss and nothing more but he grabbed me by my upper arms and squeezed so hard I thought I was going to die.

Trout was staring him down. "You hit her, you tried to control her life. You were angry because she was done with her residency and was moving on, maybe had just a little bit more time on her hands. Was meeting different people. Making a lot, and I mean a lot, more money. You, on the other hand"—he waved in Russell's direction—"were recently suspended for six months. Your career was stalling. You were making some money, yes, but nothing compared to what your fiancée was. So tell me about that."

"That was never an issue between us. I was leaving the force to go to law school—that was the plan. She and I'd talked about it. I'd put money away myself for that. There was no tension."

"So, your prints were on the hypodermic needle pouch. Can you explain that?"

He shook his head. "Really, no. I don't remember touching it, but she had things all over the table. I might have picked it up to move it. I don't know."

"Where's the needle, Russell? The used hypodermic?"

"I don't have the needle, Detective. I never did."

"What about the vial?" Russell just shrugged. "We searched all the trash cans, though we know you're too smart for that. All the surrounding bins in the area. Your neighbor Gordon said he was working in his yard. He didn't see anyone else enter the house that afternoon but you. Then you just happened to come home later with Ms. Watkins—what is your relationship to her, anyway?"

"We're friends. That's it. Did Gordon leave at all during that time, or go inside? Was he watching constantly? Because I guarantee you Ava Saunders was there. Thin, dark-haired woman, twentyish? Maybe looks a little younger?"

"Russell, Ava Saunders was declared dead. They found her body. He didn't see anyone but you. The only person anyone saw is you."

Russell was getting angry and pushed up from the table. "She sent me a Polaroid—her little calling card—right after her grandmother died. She probably killed her too. She never died in that ocean. She didn't. She's out there watching all of this. Laughing. And what about the prints in my house? The ones that didn't match mine or Juliette's? Do they belong to her?"

Trout's eyes were laser sharp. "Those prints haven't been identified." He leaned in across the table. "And if they were matched to Ava Saunders, it proves nothing. She could have been in your house before."

"No."

"And we'd be happy to investigate that Polaroid you say she sent. Just give it to me."

"I don't have it anymore. But go to the house in Haddonfield on West End Avenue. Go there. You're going to either find her or you're going to find the remnants of her stay in town. Ava was here."

Trout looked at the table and seemed to be choosing his words wisely. "Marie Lavoisier-Saunders is living there. What remnants do you think we'd find of Ava? Very small clothing? Or a few booze bottles? Yes, I studied her case. She's dead, Russell."

"She's not. I'm telling you. Am I under arrest, here? Is that what we're getting at?"

Trout clasped his hands together, fingers interlaced. "No. The Prosecutor's Office is not ready for that. They just need one more thing. But I'm confident they're going to find that needle, so I wouldn't plan any vacations out of town anytime soon."

"Fine. If you aren't going to do your job, I'll do it for you. I'm going to find Ava."

Trout's eyebrows rose, and he stood up to his full six feet five inches and stared Russell down. "Your days are numbered. When they assigned me this case, I couldn't understand how you could be so stupid. This wasn't a crime of passion, heat of the moment. You planned it and took your time. Yet you left your prints on everything, a nice neat trail. But now I have my answer."

"And what's that?"

"You are just stupid. Plain and simple."

Russell walked out of the interview room and down the hallway. He was going to find Ava. Because he knew she was still in town, he could feel it.

CHAPTER 39

Ava

The street was quiet, the traffic down Fourth Street heading into Philadelphia surprisingly light. The bank had just opened its doors. A single-branch bank, the kind I didn't think existed anymore. Through the windows I saw an ATM nestled in the corner. Perfect.

I pulled open the glass doors and approached the teller. There was just one, a middle-aged blonde woman in a navy-blue suit. I sized her up as I edged closer. She seemed relaxed, friendly, eager to please, a cup of coffee in one hand, a pen in the other.

"Good morning. Can I help you?" she asked.

I put both my hands onto the raised counter. "I really am hoping you can. My name is Marie Lavoisier-Saunders. I have an account here." I pulled up the information on my phone. "The number is—are you ready?"

"Go ahead," she responded.

"It's 3796037770. What I need is to sign up for an ATM card, and I was hoping to get a temporary one today."

Her face was scrunched in concentration. "There are two names on this account. Ava Saunders and Marie Lavoisier-Saunders. Both need to be here to make any changes or do anything to the joint account." She looked up at me. "Even to get an ATM card."

"Sadly, Ava is dead. She died about six months ago. So it's just me, and I only want an ATM card. Nothing else. It can even be mailed if need be."

She shifted in her polyester suit and it made a scratching noise. "If Ava Saunders is dead, we'd need her death certificate. You can come here with it, we'll copy it and send it on up to administration, but it's going to be about six weeks, maybe more, for those changes to be made to this account. Sorry."

"But—" I started.

"Another thing? There's a passcode needed, for security reasons."

"A passcode? My mother never said anything about a passcode." My cheeks were burning. It was anger and frustration kept at bay inside me, trying to chew their way out.

"Your mother set this up? You might need to call her. The information is right here on my screen."

"Anais Lavoisier-Saunders died. Her funeral was yesterday, actually. She never said anything about a passcode."

The woman's eyes held mine, her sympathy apparent. "You've had so much death. I'm so sorry about that. But maybe look in the packet that was sent when she opened the account? It should be in there."

"Did she set this up in person? Or electronically? Can you tell me that?"

"It looks like she came in herself. Can I see your identification for a minute?" She held out her hand.

I shook my head and slung my purse up onto my shoulder. "I don't think so. Not if there's nothing else that can be done here." I turned and started walking toward the doors.

"Ms. Saunders, we'll be happy to help you if you come back with the death certificate and the passcode."

I was stomping my feet before I even hit the pavement outside. I wanted to throw my purse onto the ground, jump on it, kick the trash can, and then throw something else. It was quite possible Anais had had some sort of involvement in my mother's death, and now she was still making my life impossible from beyond the grave. I could only assume the rest of the accounts on this list were the same. Locked.

It suddenly dawned on me that Anais might have given Marie the passcodes—that she'd divided the information needed to access the accounts in half as another incentive for us to work together. I knew in my bones that was exactly what she'd done. I took a deep breath and started walking toward the PATCO station. I needed to gather my things in Haddonfield and get on the next flight to Paris. And then move on to Cherbourg and Marie.

That was what I'd intended, but life had other plans. As I was approaching Claire's house, I saw him—Russell—standing right there near the porch. He seemed to be scanning the horizon, maybe looking for me. I stopped short and backed up, trying to hide behind an oak tree. This was the first time I'd seen him since we'd parted ways at the airport months ago. I was at least half a football field away, but from what I could see he looked horrible. Juliette's death had taken a toll, and in desperation he was here, staking out Claire's house.

I'd been keeping an eye on the investigation, and I knew that by taking the needle with me I was leading the police to the obvious conclusion that Juliette had met with foul play. I also knew they'd be looking at Russell as the nearest suspect. And then Russell would come looking for me, and here he was. But even from a distance I knew I'd made a mistake. He was a bitter, broken man, thinner than I remembered, slouching. His spirit was gone.

Everything I needed was inside that house. The money I'd gotten for the clock, my bag, clothes. And the needle. In fact, the needle was lying on the coffee table, wrapped in a kitchen towel. Just sitting there, because I hadn't taken the time to put it away. All Russell had to do was go through that front door.

I backtracked and circled the block, my palms suddenly sweaty. I didn't know if it was the adrenaline or just seeing Russell again that set it off.

I'd dreamed of him sometimes, even when I was awake. The image that always came to mind, when I could conjure his face, was when I left him at the airport. He'd had his hands in his pockets and an expression on his face that I couldn't name. Sad, maybe, tinged with a longing, or regret. I only know that that bittersweet moment stayed with me. And as much as I wanted to run up to him and throw my arms around him now, I couldn't. I needed to break into the house, gather my things, and get out of town.

The sliding-glass doors were unlocked, and I was in luck because he wasn't surveying the perimeter, only the front. Bad policeman. I slipped off my shoes and darted through the living room to the staircase. I'd drawn the curtains earlier to shut out the world, and they were helpful now, as they blocked his entire view into the front of the house. I grabbed my bags and my money from upstairs and raced down the steps. The needle, wrapped neatly in the kitchen cloth, was still sitting in plain view, like it meant nothing. I shoved it in my bag and headed out the back door.

I heard my name being called, I heard Russell's heavy footsteps, but I'd had a good head start, and as much as I wanted to turn around and look at him, I couldn't. If I slowed down, he'd catch up to me, and my flight was leaving in less than two hours.

CHAPTER 40

MARIE

How much worse could this letter get? Much worse. She scavenged around for anything to take the edge off—beer, vodka, even orange liqueur, but the cupboards were bare. She was going to have to endure this story sober.

> *Philomena was a tall, dark-haired, exotic-looking, pretty girl. She caught the eye of men much more easily than I did, and I always harbored just a bit of jealousy over that. I loved her and envied her at the same time. I hate to admit I felt smug I'd had two healthy children and she was unable to bear even one. Two miscarriages had depressed her and she feared she would never be able to carry to term. She was in her late twenties by then, so was I. In those days a woman was expected to get pregnant within a year or two of marriage. If they didn't, there were whispers and stares from relatives and the community. Everyone knew there was something wrong, and of course the blame usually fell on the woman.*
>
> *The two of us needed each other. I helped calm her fears about starting a family and she put a salve on my*

sorrow over being a divorced woman in an undivorced world, and also losing the man I loved. She had tests done, or what they could do at that time, and was told she might never carry to term. Her body was attacking the fetus each time she got pregnant. What they would call now an autoimmune disorder. They said it would take a miracle for her to have a baby. She and Victor took some time apart after this news. They weren't separated or even divorced. There aren't words for how devastating this was for both of them. And I was in the middle.

Then she told me she was leaving Victor for a time to visit a family friend, Enzo Martinelli, for a bit. I suggested I come along too. We both needed it. She had just left Victor, I was settling in Cherbourg and needed a break from the pain. You remember it as weeks but it was months that I was gone. Not quite four, when I count them. Or maybe just over four. I'm trying to make it sound better because even to my ears as I write this, it sounds like a very long time to leave two little girls. But it was necessary.

Martinelli lived in Tuscany. It was calm, peaceful, and absolutely beautiful there. We helped his wife with the housework and the orchards. It was there I learned to make wine and the most delicious bread with olives and olive oil. I had no contact with Ross. I had no contact with my family. And I'm sorry to say I had no contact with you two girls. It was the first peace I'd had since I left Vietnam to marry your father. The first relaxing, completely selfish thing I'd done.

Marie doubted that. She heard a noise outside and dropped the papers onto the seat beside her. Her heart began to pound. She hadn't had time to finish the story; she wasn't prepared to face this girl now. The door handle turned and Marie knew it was unlocked. Before she could even get up from the sofa, Ava walked in as if she always belonged there. She was taller than Marie remembered. Her skin was smooth and pale; her hair had grown from the choppy cut and hung below her shoulders.

Her thinness was striking. Her face had once been chiseled, with high cheekbones that now looked skeletal. Her striking prettiness had been replaced with a haunted near-death pallor. She wasn't exactly ugly, but was close enough to touch it. Marie saw she was carrying an overnight bag in one hand and a paper bag in her other arm.

"Liquor?" Marie asked. It was the first word the two had spoken face to face in months.

Ava smiled. "Why, of course. I'm a good guest. What will you have?" She pulled out two bottles of red wine, whiskey, and vodka. "I wasn't sure what mixers you had on hand, so I came prepared."

Marie noticed it was very natural. Like nothing had happened. Like Marie had never beaten this girl and left her for dead in the woods. And Ava had never framed Marie for murder and left her with a maze of legal issues to work through. They were just two women having a drink together. Girls' night in. Ava uncorked one of the wine bottles, poured two glasses, and handed one to Marie.

"A toast. To . . . to family," Ava said.

Marie eyed Anais's letter a few feet away. "To family, indeed," she said. "You look just awful, Ava."

Ava seemed to be regarding the papers on the ottoman too. "Grand-Maman left you a letter? What about?"

Marie laughed sardonically and gathered them up. "You'd like to know, wouldn't you?"

"One last explosion?" Ava made a sound and spread her fingers like a bomb was going off.

"I actually think you finally understand Anais. She's not sweet little Grand-Maman anymore, is she?"

Ava's forehead wrinkled into a scowl. "You really think she was that terrible, do you?"

Marie swallowed the rest of her wine in one gulp. "She kept me confined to a psychiatric hospital from the time I was fifteen until . . . I guess almost nineteen. You have no idea what that was like."

"Because you were crazy, Marie. Cutting yourself." She pointed to Marie's legs. "Threatening to kill yourself, from what I heard."

Marie filled her glass again. "Is that what Anais told you? That's only part of it. It was more about her being a horrible, controlling person that caused my insanity. And my insanity made her more controlling. One big circle. I can't believe we're having this conversation, Ava."

"Why is that?"

"Because you have no idea what it feels like to be strapped to a table for hours. You have no idea . . . She's ruined your life too. You don't even know the half of it. Yet." She was starting to feel the wine moving to her brain. "But you will."

"We need each other in this. We can't fight now, Marie."

Marie laughed. "No, see, you're dead. I don't need you at all. I can get that money—"

"It's not so easy. No. Anais made a little game of it. 'Find the money.' She gave me the account numbers, but they're in both our names."

"What?" Marie tried to hide her shock.

Ava smiled. "Oh yes. And she only gave me part of the information I need to access the money."

"Cette chienne," Marie whispered. "I assume you've tried already? To access the money?"

Ava swallowed some wine. "Oh yes. She was a bitch. And I won't be drinking any more wine tonight. The bank info is encrypted in my phone. You'll never get it. And just in case, I'm sleeping with my phone down my pants. We're in this together. Just like Anais wanted. Even if I'm not legally alive."

Marie studied her for a second. Then she stood abruptly and set her glass down. "Suit yourself. I'm reading a good book, so I'm going to bed." She pulled the crumpled pages closer. "In the morning, then."

She disappeared into her childhood bedroom and shut the door, hooking the latch behind her.

Anais was reaching from the grave with her well-manicured fingers, manipulating both of them. What part of the banking information was missing, Marie didn't know. The skinny girl had conveniently left that part out. But Ava had come here for a reason, and it had to be that whatever she needed was here in this cottage. Or perhaps in this infinite letter.

> *Just a week and a half after getting there I realized Philomena was pregnant. Yes, it's true! She'd been told to rest and not try again for another year, but nature had her own plan and once Philomena found out, she left her husband without telling him. To try and nurture the pregnancy on her own without his blaming eyes watching her every move. Enzo Martinelli took good care of us. He was constantly attentive to her, and mindful of me. His graciousness in this situation was overwhelming. With each week that passed, Philomena relaxed just a little bit more. Each morning was met with a cheer that a night had passed without her miscarrying.*
>
> *Her stomach expanded as the weeks passed and I was overwhelmed that I'd been allowed to be a part of her journey. And also overwhelmed because I hadn't told anyone the depths of my depravity (which I will explain later). My father would have reneged on our financial agreement had he any inklings of those depths.*

Marie drifted off with Anais's words swirling around her head. She woke abruptly to the sound of glass breaking in the living room, but she didn't get up to inspect. Instead she clutched the kitchen knife she'd hidden under the mattress for protection, and waited. The girl who'd killed without hesitation or remorse was standing on the other side of the door, wiggling the knob.

CHAPTER 41

JOANNE

Coffee is only good hot or over ice; anything in the range of tepid is disgusting. That was what Joanne was thinking when the waitress dropped the cup in front of her and disappeared. Diluted enough that it could have passed as tea, it was only a tad warmer than room temperature, but it didn't matter. That wasn't why she was here.

Danielle from the doctor's office was dressed in scrubs with a logo on the corner pocket indicating she belonged to Orthopedic Surgery Associates. They were blue gray, same as she'd worn last time Joanne had seen her. The fact that this woman who didn't know anything at all about her, nor probably any truth about Russell, had ventured out when Joanne had called made her like her immediately.

Danielle's iced tea was sitting on the table, the ice melting. She'd been playing with the yellow Splenda packet, bending it between her fingers, and staring at the door since they'd sat down.

Joanne looked over her shoulder. "Are you afraid Steve Thomas is coming here? Is that why you keep looking at the door?"

Danielle shook her head. "No. I just probably shouldn't have given you my business card. I'm not sure this conversation is going to help Juliette any."

"We aren't having a conversation. We're having coffee and watching the door."

"So, you came to the office with Juliette's fiancé that she talked about?"

"Russell Bowers is his name. Yes. That was Juliette's fiancé, though I'm not sure they would have gotten married, given what I'm hearing, even if she hadn't died." Danielle scowled at those words. "You know what I mean," Joanne added.

"I've only been working there about six months. I don't have loyalty to anyone in this. Except maybe Juliette. I liked her."

Joanne leaned forward. "What was she saying about Russell, anyway?"

Danielle chewed her top lip. "You're friends with him?"

"I have been for a while, yes."

"He came to the office a few times. They were arguing, and it wasn't nice. In fact, the office manager had to ask them to take it outside. Russell has some anger issues."

Joanne shook her head. "No. It had to be someone else," she said, though something inside her was starting to get worried.

Danielle gave a quick, sarcastic laugh. "I was there, I can see. It was him. They were in the corner, near where the water cooler is? And he was whisper yelling, sort of. They went back and forth and he grabbed her by the top of her arm."

"Are you sure?"

She ignored the question. "And then after that she had to deal with Dr. Thomas. I'm surprised she kept it together."

"What about him? What was he doing?"

Her chin dropped to her chest as she studied the place mat. "He's pushy, I'd say. Used to getting what he wants, I guess."

"And what did he want?"

"Juliette, obviously. He was always around her, taking care of her, whispering to her, bringing her her favorite coffee and cheese Danish when he knew she'd be in the office. And he'd watch her when she didn't even notice. Like from a distance. I saw it all."

"But wait, wasn't he married?"

Danielle showed her first real facial expression since sitting down. She burst into laughter. "Like that mattered. Yes, he's married. His wife's name is Karen. She was around the office sometimes. I don't think he was looking to get a divorce."

Joanne took a sip of her coffee and forced it down her throat. "So, what was it that he wanted from Juliette? And don't give me that look, I know the answer is sex. But it's just a bad idea in an office like that. You'd think he'd know better."

"Actually, I think he wanted to control her. He's that kind. Everyone in the office is happy when he's not there. Juliette was nice, but it was more about molding her, making her do what he wanted. And yeah, probably sex too."

The waitress came by and Joanne flagged her down. "This coffee is terrible. Can I have some tea, maybe with lemon and something sweet? A donut or whatever you have?"

After she left, Joanne looked at Danielle. "I've never seen Russell even raise his voice. You say you saw him angry, grabbing her?"

"Everyone saw it. And it wasn't just once. We all talked about their wedding. Worried if it was a good idea. Look, I need to go. I liked Juliette, and when you showed up, when I saw her boyfriend, I felt like I had to say something to you. But this isn't right either." She started to stand.

"Wait, wait. We haven't even gotten to the real question. Give me just five minutes." Danielle rolled her eyes and took her seat. Joanne was starting to get irritated. This woman had approached her, not the other way around. "Tell me about the night you went out. That last night."

She dropped her purse to the floor and settled in. "Juliette said she wanted a night out before the wedding. She made a big deal of it when she was in the office that week before, inviting all the girls. She picked the place—"

"Tequilas?"

Danielle nodded. "Yeah. And it seemed really important to her. We all liked her, so we went. We met there at six thirtyish, I guess, maybe seven. Everyone came but Ella, because she had something going on with her kid, but everyone else came."

"And what happened with Steve?"

She shrugged. "He came too, though she said, 'girls' night out,' not 'office party.'"

"I'm sort of getting that you don't like him."

"I don't. He's a jerk—but anyway, he showed up at Tequilas with some sort of present for her in a nice little bag. He pulled her away from the table—"

"How far away from the rest of you?"

"I didn't measure, but not so far away that we couldn't see what was going on. They were talking. She pulled a box out of the bag and opened it. Then shut it and gave it back to him."

"What kind of box?"

"A jewelry box."

"Then what?"

"Then he realized we were all watching, and they went outside. When Juliette came back she was crying. You could tell because her eye makeup was all smeared. Her eyes were red. She brushed it off and poured a big margarita and kept drinking."

"Would anyone there that night know what happened? I mean, who she'd confide in later? Was anyone close to her like that? To know if they were having an affair?"

"Ella. Even though she wasn't there, they talked a lot."

"Ella who?"

"Ella, the nurse practitioner. Ella Field. She's in the office all week."

Danielle got up from her seat just as the waitress came with tea and a cream puff. "It's all we had left that was like a donut, I hope it's okay?"

"Fine, thanks," Joanne said.

"Dr. Thomas is an asshole, make no mistake—ask anyone—but he didn't kill her, if that's what you're thinking. He had to leave the office when he heard the news, he was so upset, almost crying. I'm sorry to say it, we all think it was her boyfriend. It always is." With that, Danielle turned and left the diner.

Joanne took a bite of the cream puff and wiped her face with the napkin. She had to agree, Steve Thomas probably hadn't killed Juliette. He'd called her multiple times that day. Before and after Russell had gone home. Joanne had seen all the missed calls when she went into the bedroom. But there was a part of her that was starting to doubt her friend Russell. Juliette had said he had a temper. Joanne hadn't believed it. Now here was an eyewitness to it. He had gone home that day. They'd had a fight. Russell's prints were on the hypodermic pouch. Russell? Joanne bit straight through half the cream puff and chewed. There was something in her gut twisting, and the only thing she knew to do right now was to eat it away.

CHAPTER 42

AVA

I had jet lag that wasn't helped with any amount of coffee. I had spent most of the night on the couch, staring at the ceiling, sporadically getting up and searching Anais's papers for anything that looked like a passcode. I was still on East Coast time, and though the sun was coming up, my body felt like it was time to go to bed. I couldn't afford to sleep, because Marie would kill me if she had the chance. So I pulled a chair from the dining-room table and lodged it under the knob of her bedroom door, wiggling it and adjusting it to make sure either she'd be trapped or I'd hear her. She had shown me the person she hid under her bullshit religious garb when she tried to kill me the last time, smacking me in the head with that heavy metal box camera. She'd be fine in her room for a few hours. She had a bathroom and water from the sink. Screw her.

Knowing she was secure and probably furious, I took a walk. I needed to see where Anais had been buried, to pay my last respects while I had the chance. The cemetery was only ten or fifteen minutes away if I walked fast. I slipped on a sweatshirt, pulling the hood up over my head to obscure my face. It occurred to me I should have stolen Marie's identification while I had the chance, altered my appearance somewhat—okay, maybe a lot—so that I looked more like her, and tried to get the money without her. Then just disappear. No harm. No killing. But it was a stretch, anyway, and I wasn't sure I could pull it off.

The cemetery was empty when I got there, freezing and out of breath. Her grave was easy to find, a fresh mound of dirt marking the spot. Some of the dirt had blown and scattered across Claire's grave, making it seem that they'd both just died and been buried at the same time. A bunch of slightly wilted flowers were lying at the base of the headstone. *Anais Lavoisier-Saunders*, it said. Then *Vivre, Rire, Aimer.* Live, laugh, love. I could only imagine Marie came up with that one. I stepped to the side, aware that what remained of my grandmother's body was somewhere just below and that I had killed her. One way or another, I had killed her.

I sat on the freezing ground and just stared. These two women had impacted my entire life, good and bad, made me who I was, shaped what was left of my childhood, managed my trauma. I took out my phone and pulled up Anais's last letter to me. *Work together or destroy each other.* I dropped my head.

I closed my eyes and remembered a day at the cottage in Cherbourg when I was a teenager. I'd overslept and woken up to the sounds of the ocean in the distance. It was summer; Claire had come to France too, as she had planned a side trip to Paris and was sleeping in Marie's old room. I had rolled over in bed and was studying the walls. There were some art prints, a painting, a shadow box with a vase and nothing else. There was no hint Claire had ever grown up in this room. I was pondering that when the voices started. They were low at first and then grew in intensity.

"Explain to me why."

"No. Just no. You're not staying here. Ava is here until August twenty-third. I'll put her on the plane myself, Claire."

"Maman, you know how hard this has been? You know that Quinn is looking for me? For her?" I only imagined Claire meant me. "Why won't you help us? Let us stay here? Let her stay here? Before we all end up dead."

"Because Ross made this mess when he took her from the church. That's why. And I swore I'd never clean up another one of his messes. She's almost fourteen. Another four years and she'll be grown. Quinn can find her on his own then, if he's still alive or has the energy. Her life will be her own. I'm not talking about this anymore."

"Yes, Maman, you are. This is what I'm going to do. I'm going to get an apartment and move here. I'm going to take the money I have right now and find something to rent."

"Then I won't give you another penny. Nothing. You're on your own."

"I'll get a job, then. I was an editor before all of this. I can make enough to keep us. I don't need you."

The words that came from Anais after that have stolen many hours of my sleep. I heard it wrong, I translated it wrong, something, I kept telling myself. *Elle mourra.* I knew what those words meant. *She'll die,* that was what it meant. I'd racked my brain trying to make it mean something else. But there it was. I wasn't sure who she was saying was going to die. I only knew that on August 23 I was back on the plane, sitting next to Claire. Claire never said a word about it, about the argument. She never knew I'd been awake on the other side of the wall, listening. It never occurred to me that Anais had forced Claire back to the US by threat of death. But why? Why would she not want Claire to move to France?

I heard the crunching of leaves and turned to see Marie standing behind me. She didn't look any worse for wear after breaking out of the bedroom. No scrapes or scratches. Her hair seemed in place. But she was angry.

"I was half expecting everything in the house to be gone. Steal my identity, what's left of my money and whatever else you could find. Shocking you didn't."

I peered up at her. "Take a seat." I patted the ground next to me.

"You forget I grew up in that room. If I had a euro for every time Anais tried to lock me in—" Marie spotted the phone sitting by me with the copy of Anais's letter on the screen. "Anais wrote you a letter too?" Marie took a seat next to me.

"It was in with the account information. Not really a letter, more of a note."

"What did it say?" Marie asked.

I snapped my head up quickly. "How'd you get yours?"

"She left it with nosy Sandrine, to give to me if she died. Maybe yours is about something different?"

I felt Marie's eyes boring into me. "Listen," I said. "Did Anais leave you any strange numbers? Or words that didn't make sense? Did she write them down anywhere? Maybe a series of them?"

"That's an odd question."

I turned in the dirt to face her and felt the cold ground against my leg. "Just wondering."

"Is that the missing information you were talking about? She gave you incomplete account numbers or something?"

I'd said too much. My head was heavy, my brain gritty. Now she knew. "No, no, the account numbers are complete."

"Anais was a horrible person. Making us dance like monkeys." Marie stood up and brushed the dirt from her pants. "Let's just get on with this. You give me what you have, I'll give you what I have, and we'll get our money?"

It was the first time I'd ever seen Marie be so practical. I started to nod when I felt the thump across the side of my head and everything went black.

CHAPTER 43

RUSSELL

The middle seat was uncomfortable, especially for a seven-hour trip, but it was the only option left when he arrived at the American Airlines terminal looking for the next flight to Europe. The cabin was hot, and no matter how many times he reached up and twisted the little overhead air nozzle, it didn't help. They'd rolled the drink cart by once and he'd opted only for water; now he regretted it. A scotch and soda would be nice, even if they did charge him twelve dollars for it. Anything to be able to close his eyes and sleep.

He'd seen Ava, he was sure of it. Running away from him, too far down West End Avenue to positively identify, but close enough that he could feel it was her. He'd been right, Ava had been in town, staying at Claire's house. Where would she go next? Where was Marie? His instincts told him they'd both be headed for Europe—that Anais's cottage was where their showdown was going to take place. His freedom was dependent upon finding her, anticipating her next move, and bringing her to justice, proving she was alive and had been in his house the day Juliette died. He'd already lost so much, his partner and future in Juliette; the impact was hitting him in different and deeper ways every day.

Twice he'd called Juliette's cell phone without thinking and started to leave a message before remembering she was gone. Once he'd gotten up from the sofa in his office in the middle of the night, and, disoriented, he'd gone into their bedroom, expecting her to be snoring in the middle of the bed. It only dawned on him when he'd sat down and pushed his elbow out to the side to move her over that the mattress was bare. She wasn't there and never would be again. Even sorting through the mail was a struggle. Daily bills and advertisements came in her name. It was all too much. He'd constantly think, *I need to tell Juliette that,* or *She'd like that,* or *We should go there,* and it would bring back to him that the *we* was gone. And he blamed it on Ava.

The plane landed in Orly, and he hurried through the airport, carefully considering his options. Renting a car and driving to Cherbourg would be the least complicated and fastest, also expensive at a time when he had to watch his money. He'd been put on suspension with pay during the investigation into Juliette's death, but once he was arrested that would end. Still, time was more important than money at this juncture. Ava had at least a six-hour head start.

Forty minutes later he was headed north in a little dark-blue Toyota Aygo, and not long after that he pulled down the lane that led to Anais's cottage. He parked several houses away. There was no one in view. When he knocked on the door there was no answer. He peered through the window and saw nothing but shadows and filtered light. No movement, no sign of life. The doorknob turned freely, so he went inside. The living room showed signs that somebody had been there recently. A purse was slung over the back of a dining-room chair. An overnight bag had been tossed into a corner. But the most interesting was a chair jammed underneath the doorknob of one of the bedrooms. His pulse rose. Someone was being held captive in the bedroom, but who?

He wiggled the chair a few times to wrench it free and pushed it to the side. When he flung the door open, the bedroom was empty, but the window screen had been ripped apart, and it appeared someone had made a hasty escape. He saw a shoe with a sharp heel lying on the floor near the window. He backtracked to the living room and dumped the contents of the overnight bag he'd seen there onto the floor. A passport landed on top. He flipped open the cover. Jennifer Roberts, a.k.a. Ava Saunders, stared back. As he scanned through the pages, a photograph fluttered to the floor.

"Oh, Ava," he muttered. It wasn't the Polaroid she'd mailed, the thing he assumed she'd gone to his house to get. But it was proof she'd been in his house. The photo had been stolen from a frame in his home office and he'd never noticed it missing. Ava had carefully ripped Juliette out, leaving only Russell, just the way she'd ripped Juliette from his life. As he tossed the photo to the side, he caught sight of a folded paper on the table near the lamp. *Anais Lavoisier-Saunders,* it said. Her funeral program.

The cemetery. He grabbed the program and jumped in the car. It was a first stop, then he'd figure out where to go from there. The two women, Ava and Marie, were chasing something, either each other or money. It was the only reason they'd both be here.

He pulled over to the edge of the street that fronted the cemetery and got out of the car. It was easy to spot the freshly dug grave on the other side of the lot, more than five hundred feet away. As he drew closer, he became alarmed. What at first seemed like a bundle placed at the grave—he assumed flowers—took on a different form as he grew closer. A female. The ends of her long dark hair fluttering with the breeze.

Ava. He leaned over her and felt her pulse. It was there, thready and faint, but it was there. He studied her face—he hadn't seen it since they'd stood together at Gate 33 at the Philadelphia International Airport and he'd watched her walk away from him, down the plank to the plane. He could kill her now. She was defenseless—but it wouldn't serve his purposes. He needed her alive. To take back to Philadelphia with all the things she'd stolen from his house. He touched her face with his fingertips, pushed a few hair strands from her eyes.

That was when he saw the blood congealed at the back of her head. She'd been hit hard enough to be knocked unconscious, hard enough to break skin, and been left bleeding across these two women's graves. He glanced up at Anais's headstone and thought of the Polaroid Ava had sent after her death, with the dates indicating she had killed Anais and was coming for him and Juliette next. And she had. She'd just arrived a little early. And now Juliette lay in a cemetery not too different from this, with shovels of dirt heaped over her body.

"Let's go, Ava." He supported her head, cradling her in his arms. "I'm taking you home."

CHAPTER 44

JOANNE

The phones in the office were ringing nonstop. She couldn't concentrate, checking her own phone every few minutes to see if Russell had texted her back. She hadn't heard from him since that morning, and she needed to talk to him about Danielle's revelations. She wasn't digesting it well. It was one thing for Juliette to make those claims because she was angry, wanting to get back at Russell, feeling betrayed or whatever, but this was different. Danielle was someone with no stake in the game. An eyewitness to the same behaviors Juliette had claimed to have been subjected to. Now her accounts couldn't be so easily dismissed.

Joanne had left the restaurant and gone to the courthouse, the tears flowing before she could get to her desk, forcing her to hide out in the bathroom with a wet tissue pressed against her eyes until the redness had gone down. She'd trusted Russell implicitly. There had been no part of her that had believed he'd been abusive to Juliette. But now there was a little voice in the back of her mind that she couldn't quiet with cream puffs or jelly donuts. Had Russell been capable of killing Juliette?

He'd had opportunity and motive, and his prints were on the means. Someone had to have hit Juliette's vein, maybe while she was moving, to inject the potassium chloride. Not easy without training. But Russell had training in the military. It was one thing she remembered him talking about, his training as a medic, stabilizing bones, first aid, phlebotomy. She closed her eyes and imagined him lying across Juliette to keep her still, holding the arm out. The needle ready.

Her desk phone rang again and she grabbed it off the receiver.

"Camden County Superior Court, Judge Simmons's office."

"Ms. Watkins, this is Detective Trout over at the Prosecutor's Office. Can you come over during your lunch hour? It won't take long. We just have a few questions, if you don't mind."

Joanne's heart fluttered. It had come to this. They were questioning her now. "Let me check the court schedule, but I don't think it'll be a problem," she responded.

"Good. If something comes up, give me a call. But we need to do this today, even if it means staying late. Okay?"

She hung up the phone and put her head down. Her eyes landed on the bottom-right side of the computer screen. It was almost twelve thirty. She grabbed her purse and headed out of the building. Everyone was out for lunch. The line to the food trucks was eight people deep. She'd desperately wanted to grab a little something to calm the nerves in her stomach, but there wasn't time to wait. Whatever the police wanted to know, she had no answers, she only had more questions of her own.

The reception area was empty when she walked into the station, but they were apparently waiting for her, because the woman behind the counter ushered her back right away and deposited her at a conference table. The size of the room was intimidating. She'd expected a small, intimate setting, not a massive interrogation room. Five minutes later, Detective Trout came in and sat across the table.

"Why this huge office?" Her palms were pressed together in her lap.

He smiled. "It was empty. Why not? Gives us room to spread out."

"So, what's this about?"

He placed a file in the middle of the desk. Dark green. She knew it by sight. The Ava file, she called it. Russell kept it in his desk drawer. "When's the last time you talked to Russell?" he asked.

She bit her top lip. "This morning. Just a nothing text. Why?"

"He's sort of . . . I wouldn't say *missing* yet, but we can't find him right now. His car is parked in his driveway, but he's not home."

She shrugged. "I've been at work. I don't know where he is." She was starting to get concerned. This wasn't like him.

"You know this file?" He pushed it to her. "Go ahead. Open it."

She flipped it open to see his notes, handwritten, not computer generated, pages and pages of them, regarding the Ava investigation from last year. He'd documented everything. She knew it all by heart. She hesitated. "Why are you showing me this?"

"We searched his office, confiscated his computer. This folder was in his top desk drawer in his home office. You were involved in this thing from last year?"

Joanne was starting to feel trapped, like it was trick question. "Do I need a lawyer or something? What are you looking for? Just ask."

"I wish it were that simple to just ask. This is just an interview. I'm not interrogating you." He pushed a pile of printed computer pages over to her. Some sort of diary or accounting entries and notes. "We got these from his computer. Some of our IT guys had to really look for it. I just wanted your thoughts."

She couldn't help but read. One page was a detailed account of the last night he'd spent with Ava the night before she disappeared. The night he had sex with her.

Trout caught her expression. "Something surprising in there?"

She looked up. Keeping this in his computer in a house he shared with Juliette was unfeeling, if nothing else. Some of the details were more graphic than she'd anticipated, notes that seemed to have been added later, memories that had come back to him, or maybe had been manufactured to fill in gaps. It was a clear accounting and description of her naked body in his lap. Joanne shut the folder, feeling like a voyeur.

"Oh, no, keep going."

She flipped the page to see a picture of another woman naked. Familiar somehow, yet Joanne wasn't certain who she was. She was on her back, her eyes closed, asleep or not caring that Russell was capturing her on film. Another photo of her on her side. And then another, each a little more graphic.

"What the hell, Russell." It came out involuntarily. Trout was staring at her.

"Surprising? He seemed to have a little fetish for this woman, I'd say. Moving her like she was a doll," he said. "Weird. It's hard to tell if she was even awake."

He pushed another pile of papers into the middle of the table. She pushed it back. "I'm not interested in looking at any more of Russell's porn. I need to go back to work."

"This is a little more interesting."

She started reading the first paragraph. They were notes about Juliette. No photographs but plenty of detail. Not about sex with her, but about his feelings.

I love her but it's not enough. It's not what I want for the rest of my life. And: *She's too plain. Too ordinary. We've become old already. If I wake up next to her for the rest of my life will I be sorry? And she's been up to something herself. Cheating? Lunch with Bridgette not as expected.*

Joanne stopped so she wouldn't see the rest of that paragraph. Then she reached for the photographs again and looked closer. Bridgette had been hanging around Russell's office for months, but Joanne thought he'd cultivated the relationship to keep tabs on Marie. She looked back at the pages and forced herself to read the next lines.

I was afraid she'd become clingy after I screwed her in the car but she's been okay. Maybe keep her in case I need it again?

It didn't leave much room for doubt. The woman in the photographs was Bridgette.

Joanne shoved the whole pile back at Trout. She felt tears coming and she stood up to leave, but he pushed a manual into the middle of the table. A yellowed military publication. She lifted it and flipped through the pages until a sticky note on one page caught her eye. There was nothing written on it, it was just there to mark the spot: *Potassium Chloride Poisoning*. She read the paragraph and threw the book back onto the table.

"Was there a Polaroid in there, by any chance? Of a green cottage door?"

He shook his head. "You sound like Russell now. No."

"I really just want to leave now."

"Two more things, Ms. Watkins. One." He leaned toward her. "We're watching you."

"And two?"

"We are putting a warrant out for Mr. Bowers's arrest. I called you here to gauge your reaction. Clearly, you didn't know about any of this. Let's keep it that way. If he shows up, call our office."

Joanne nodded, then turned and ran until she reached the street. "Fuck you, Russell. I hate you."

CHAPTER 45

AVA

My eyes opened slowly, though I wasn't really seeing anything around me. Piercing light came in through the window, blinding me, setting the back of my head on fire so that I couldn't think of anything else. I just wanted it to stop. Someone had stuffed a lit oil rag into my eye socket and was keeping it there, watching my brain burn. My eyelids were heavy. I gave in and let them flutter shut. Sleeping diminished the pain. But when I opened them again, uncertain how much time had passed, the light was gone but the deep aching throb was not. I thought I was still in the cemetery, the last place I could remember, but there was no cold against my skin, no hardness of earth under me. I just felt softness and warmth.

When I stretched out my arm, I felt a blanket. A heavy comforter draped over me, the mattress underneath me. The pillow cradling my head. I shot up in the darkness, blinked, and looked around. That was when I saw him. In the corner, watching me. Staring. He'd pulled up one of the living-room chairs and propped his feet onto the bed. I might have assumed he was asleep, but he wasn't. I could see the outline of his open eyes, and it chilled me. I lay back down and stared at the ceiling.

"Russell." It wasn't a question or a calling to evoke some sort of a response. Just a recognition of the fact that he was there. I saw his hand move, so I knew he was awake, but he didn't say anything for a long enough time that I thought I was hallucinating. "Are you going to kill me?" I asked.

"Should I?" he responded. It had been so long since I'd heard his voice. "You've destroyed my life."

I didn't want to look at him. "Juliette?" I mumbled, though my tongue felt thick and useless.

He jumped from the chair and was on the bed next to me. "I gave you one chance, Ava."

I pushed up, ignoring the thumping behind my eyes. "You gave me a chance and look at how much I've accomplished."

This seemed to make him angrier. "I think you oughta shut up, because the only thing keeping you alive is the fact that I need you. I need you to prove you're really alive, that you killed Juliette, so I don't do time for it."

I pushed off the bed, away from him, but my legs were wobbly. "You're talking like you did it yourself. I need ice. For my head. Marie hit me good." I looked around. "And probably took my phone with all the bank-account numbers in it." It was almost surreal, because when I hobbled into the living room, the table was set. Like we were on vacation at my grandmother's cottage and everything was normal.

"Sit down. I'll get you ice."

I sat down gently on the chair and saw the torn photograph he'd placed there. The one of Russell I'd ripped from the frame on my way out the door. I picked it up. He was handsome, with slight dimple-like creases in his cheeks, his eyes wide. His arm disappeared at the edges of the torn paper, but it had been around Juliette's shoulders. I'd shoved that half into my bag and shredded it with my fingers later, erasing her. "A memento," I said.

He didn't respond but placed a plate of baked ziti in front of me and rested a cold pack against the back of my head. "It's all Anais had in her freezer. Ice and ziti. I think it's heated through. You need to eat, because you look like hell."

I took one bite. It was freezer burned, but I cleaned the plate in five minutes. My body was craving it. "Now what? We sit here until the next flight out and just let Marie steal my money?"

"I am so sick of your insane family. I'm going to prison for a long time if I don't take you back."

I was confused. "Really, Russell. That's not going to happen. I . . ."

He raised his arms to the side and then dropped them. "What's not?"

I stood up and made a beeline for the kitchen and the booze stash, but it was gone. In its place were three empty bottles.

Russell was behind me. "I dumped it. We both need clear heads until we can get out of here. So sit. Start by telling me what happened when you went to my house."

I eyed him up and down. "I got to the house. Your car wasn't there. I broke in through the basement window and went upstairs. I found the Polaroid I sent. I wanted it back. It was so stupid." I moved the pack slightly and winced. "It was the only proof I'm alive. I wanted it, but I also wanted to see you." I thought he might be moved by this, but his eyes were ice cold. "So I went into the bedroom. Juliette was there. On her side. Eyes open. And—"

"What?"

"She was watching me while she was dying. Her eyes were moving around. It was horrible."

He seemed livid, his hands clenching and unclenching, and I was sure for a second he was going to assault me. "You're admitting you injected her with the potassium chloride, then?"

I said nothing. Potassium chloride was the same thing used to kill Claire, so they said, and they were blaming that on me as well. Officially, her death had been ruled natural causes, a heart attack, but it seemed like everyone who knew me remained suspicious. Admittedly, she'd had pinholes in her from possible injections. But how many times did I have to deny I'd had anything to do with that? "No, you don't know the whole story. Listen, let me tell you—"

"All I want is to get through tonight, Ava. Tomorrow we go back home. I turn you in. You tell the truth about what happened. They arrest you for, what, seven or eight murders, one of them being Juliette. And then there's the guy in Paris that they found in the car—"

"The Bulgarian? He raped me, Russell. Brutalized me."

"There's always a reason. Here's some sort of painkiller. I couldn't read the box but I think it's like Motrin. I found it in the medicine cabinet."

I took the box from his hand. "It's for arthritis, but it's good enough." I popped two in my mouth and swallowed. "And what about Marie?"

"What about her? When she doesn't go back they'll violate her parole."

"I'm sure she'll be petrified over that while she's running across the world with my twelve million dollars, that bitch. I need to find her." He seemed to be staring at me. "What?" I asked.

"Anais left you twelve million dollars?"

"Yeah, but the account information was incomplete. There were passcodes. But guess who's got those? I think." My only consolation was that Marie had seemed baffled when I mentioned the passcodes. Which meant Anais hadn't given them to her outright. But now that she knew what to look for, that wouldn't hold her back for long.

The line between Russell's eyes that appeared when he was concentrating was suddenly there. "Let me guess, Marie?" Then he started laughing.

"I'm glad it's amusing." I stood up and dug through my pockets, though I knew they were empty. "I lost everything my grandmother left me because for two seconds, Russell, two seconds, I took my eyes off of Marie." I felt sick all of a sudden and rushed to the bathroom. The ziti ended up in the toilet while Russell stood in the doorway and watched. "I don't feel good." I stumbled backward.

"Did she suffer?" he asked. It came out of nowhere. His hands were on the doorframe, keeping me from leaving the room.

"She didn't seem to be suffering, Russell." I leaned into him and put my arms around his waist. "When I went in, Juliette was just lying there. I feel dizzy."

"You might have a concussion from that bump on your head. You need to lie down. I'm going to make you some tea and see if I can scrounge up something else for you to put in your stomach in a bit. You need food."

He put me into bed, and I drifted in and out of consciousness, listening to the ocean in the distance and then the patter of rain against the windows. It picked up in intensity and turned into wind rattling the frames. I had strange dreams about being shackled in the lower part of a boat and the waves consuming me. When I woke up, I saw why. Russell had handcuffed me to one side of the bed frame. I'd been pulling against it in my sleep. It was still raining and dark, but I'd lost count of days and hours. "Russell," I yelled. Nothing. "He left me," I muttered. "He left me." I rattled the cuff as hard as I could, but it was attached firmly. "I need to use the bathroom, Russell." Nothing.

I had a partial view of the street from where I was, the driveway and the street, but I wasn't close enough to open the window and yell for help. I was stuck until the police came. It wasn't the worst predicament I'd ever been in. Then I heard tires against the stones—someone was pulling in. I expected to see a police car or officer approaching the door, but a little blue Toyota sat in the driveway. And Russell was getting out of it, carrying bags. Two minutes later he was in my room.

"Good. You didn't try and escape."

I snorted. "To do what? Go out in the rain? I don't have any money. It would have been nice to pee, though."

"I got a few supplies. We may have to stay longer than a day. You definitely have a concussion. I can't bring you back brain damaged. So I'm thinking I need to watch you for the next forty-eight hours. Then we leave." He lifted the bag in his hand. "Some food. I got some pain medication—no booze, though." He must have seen the look on my face. "Relax, Ava. It's a day or two, tops."

I kicked the blanket off of me and was surprised I was just in panties. I couldn't remember taking off my clothes.

"In case you got out of my cuffs, I took your clothes so you couldn't leave. I have them," he said.

"Anais knew my mother."

He hesitated in the doorway. The collar on his olive-green jacket had been pulled up around his neck to keep out the cold. His hair was longer and unkempt, and his eyes held something I'd seen that last night we were together. Intrigue. Excitement, maybe. He just stood there looking at me, then he came over and undid the cuff. "Say that again?"

I pulled the blanket up tighter around me. "She knew Adrianna. She knew her parents. I found the information in her desk—anyway, I called him, my grandfather. He was crying." I felt that lump in my throat again. "My grandmother died, so I lost every chance to get to know her, but my grandfather, Victor DeFeo, is in Vicenza, Italy. This circles back to Anais. She murdered my mother and kept me from my grandparents."

"And you want me to take you to Italy? Before we go back? Is that it?"

I scooted down the bed toward him. "It's my only chance. It's my whole life. Everything." I felt the drops slide down my cheek and I wiped them away with the back of my hand. "If I go with you to New Jersey, that's it. It's over."

"Ava. No. You're trying to make me feel sorry for you, but you killed Juliette. I was expecting you on my wedding day. I was going to be ready, but you showed up early. Why, Ava? She did nothing to you."

I shook my head. "No, Russell, you don't know—"

He whirled around and left the room. "Take a bath. I'm going to make you some tea."

Despite his posturing, it was clear he still cared about me. I knew in that moment I still had a sliver of a chance of seeing Vicenza in the next few days.

CHAPTER 46

RUSSELL

She was on her stomach, her face in the pillow, when he took off her clothes. He thought she was going to wake up, but she didn't. Her breathing didn't even change. He pulled the black shirt over her head, careful not to rub the growing knot on the back of her head. Marie had hit her hard. He felt the skeleton underneath her clothing; she was much thinner than he'd remembered. He rolled her over. She almost looked like a child, her collarbone jutting out, a harsh line against the softness of her skin. He ran his hand over each rib. She wasn't wearing a bra, but she didn't need one. When she lay on her back, the swells of her breasts were flattened to nothingness. The plum-colored rings of her nipples marking the spot where they'd existed.

He unzipped her pants and pulled them down gently. Greenish-yellow bruising trailed down her back and disappeared into her underwear, as if she'd been hit or dragged recently. Maybe she was telling the truth about having been assaulted. He pulled on the elastic at the back and saw the blotches continuing down one cheek of her buttocks. He held the elastic and stared. The bruising turned deeper, surrounded by abrasions and scabs covering barely healing wounds. He gently spread her butt cheeks and then stopped. She needed to see a doctor. Whatever had happened, she'd been viciously torn apart, and probably beaten. Some of his anger began to dissipate.

He sat on the edge of the bed and watched her sleep, the rise and fall of her chest. She reminded him of the images on TV of a horribly abused, starving dog covered in wounds. Only this dog would bite back if given the chance. He took his handcuffs and attached one to her wrist, hooking the other to the bed frame, forcing her arm out to the side.

He turned away and then back again. She was both a murderer and a victim, he told himself. Her face was gaunt but still attractive. High cheekbones, full mouth. He leaned over and ran his finger over her lips.

"No." He pulled the blanket up over her and threw on his jacket. She wasn't the same person she'd been before last year. And he wasn't here to get involved in Saunders-family drama again, to get sidetracked and go on a chase across Europe after Marie. He was here only as a bounty hunter of sorts, to bring Ava to justice.

He needed air. To clear his head. He'd find the nearest store and buy some supplies—coffee, water, food—and ponder the next step. He'd made the mistake of coming here and now he was stuck, torn between wanting to kill her and something else entirely. Sorrow? Responsibility? Attraction? Pity? He didn't know. But whatever it was, it had been there from the moment he saw her stretched across the graves with blood congealed on the back of her head.

She was vulnerable. Underneath all of it. Needy in a way Juliette had never been. He chewed on his lip and tried to think. He thought about those final bits of conversation with his fiancée the last time he'd seen her. She had tried to torment him, and he'd known from the moment he'd stared into those raging black-ringed eyes that their wedding was never going to take place. And it wasn't because of this girl, sleeping here now. It was because of Juliette. Her lies. Her secrets. If she had come to him earlier and told him the truth about what was happening with her, it might have brought them closer. But instead she had done the worst thing possible and thrown it in his face. Betrayal stacked upon betrayal. *What are you going to do about it, Russell? Nothing. That's what. Now get out.* He'd left the room then and returned moments later, taunting her. He shouldn't have. Would it have made a difference?

His phone dinged. *Where the fuck are you? They're putting a warrant out for your arrest.* Joanne. Shit. In that second he decided. They couldn't stay in the cottage. They'd leave in the morning and start driving south toward Paris. See how it went.

They had me down there today, questioning me.

They got your computer files. Naked pictures? Cheating with Bridgette? I'll tell them you're coming in but I'm done with you. Don't call me again.

Oh, and BTW: one of the office women saw you hit Juliette. WTF?

So they'd hacked into his computer. He'd half expected it but was hoping he could have talked to Joanne first so it didn't all come as a surprise. Bridgette had been a mistake. A nothing mistake. She was there, offering. No strings. She knew the deal. And she just caught him at a bad time. A day when he had had another bout of nastiness with Juliette and needed something. The pictures were just stupid. And even stupider not to get rid of them. *Shit.* And he had never hit Juliette, exactly. He just needed to talk to Joanne and explain what people thought they'd seen.

He found an open store with electronics in the window, in downtown Cherbourg, and pulled into the parking lot. He bought two burner phones and typed Joanne's number into one of them.

"It's Russell. Don't hang up. Tell the Prosecutor's Office I'll turn myself in the day after tomorrow," he said when she answered. She was still on the line but refused to speak. "I didn't kill Juliette. I'm going to prove it to them. And you. Give me a chance."

He heard a click in his ear. He walked past the inlet and threw his old phone into the water. Nothing to trace.

Now on to Ava.

CHAPTER 47

JOANNE

Joanne hung up the phone and pulled out the business card Detective Trout had given her. His line rang and his voicemail picked up.

"Ahem. Detective, I wanted to let you know I heard from Russell. He didn't say where he was, but he said he'll turn himself in to you the day after tomorrow. Also, I texted him and he called me back on a strange number. He must have a new phone. That's all I know." She hung up and then threw up into the bathroom sink.

She'd known Russell for almost four years. Well enough at first that they'd chat in the hallway or sometimes he'd come to her office. They ate together outside on numerous occasions. He was one of the good guys. He was with Juliette, everyone knew that. He didn't have a reputation for cheating or running around, or just being a general pig about things. He seemed smart and serious. He was funny. She was a good judge of character, and she'd liked him. But she'd liked Ava too, so her people radar must be on the fritz.

She wiped her mouth and went into the living room when her phone began to chime.

"Hello."

"It's Trout. Tell me everything." He sounded far away and groggy.

"I already did. I sent him a text. He called me back from a strange number. He said he'll turn himself in to you the day after tomorrow. That was it."

"He didn't tell you where he was, then?"

"No."

"I need to come over and get your phone."

Joanne hesitated. She didn't want her phone confiscated. There had been so many texts back and forth between her and Russell last year. Personal things. "Why would you need my phone?"

"To look at the number, figure out where he called from. I'll be there in ten minutes."

"Look, this isn't cool. I don't want anyone coming to my house. I'm not giving up my phone." She started to feel sick again. She was utterly alone in this now. It had always been her and Russell and sometimes Juliette. She hadn't had to maneuver through the system by herself.

"I can get a court order to get your phone. You know that. What's going on, Ms. Watkins? You were so cooperative earlier today. What changed? What did Russell say to you?"

She didn't have to be in this alone. "I'm getting a lawyer. I'll call you in fifteen minutes with the name. Until then, don't call me again." She put the phone down and burst into tears. "No, stop, Joanne. Get it together. You can do this. Call a lawyer. Think. Where would Russell go?" But she knew where he was. He was chasing Ava, who could be anywhere. If she'd wanted to be honest with Trout she would have told him to search for them in New Jersey, and then maybe France. But she didn't, because there was a small part of her that was still protecting Russell despite everything.

When did he change? When did he start chasing women and taking creepy pictures? When did he become the kind of asshole she'd always steered clear of in the courthouse? It was about six months ago, if she had to put a time frame on it. Though she didn't know, exactly, and certainly never knew about the computer files or the Bridgette affair. It was just small things. Language that slipped out that he'd never used before. A shift in attitude. More sarcasm. Nasty, biting humor that wasn't funny. Less tolerance of others. These things were all coming to her now, but the shift had been so subtle she hadn't noticed at the time.

She grabbed her purse and headed out the door. Russell's house was dark and quiet when she arrived. No squad of patrol cars, or unmarked cars staking it out. She used the key he'd given her and went in through the front door. At least she wasn't crawling through windows this time. She turned on the lights and went from room to room, not even afraid to be seen. The house was the same as it had been when she was here last. He hadn't taken much with him. And everything was still a mess. If she was going to get inside of his head, she'd need to live in his space. Eventually it would all come together.

She put on a pot of coffee and headed upstairs. His office looked like it had been torn apart and ransacked. The computer was gone; every drawer had been pulled out and dumped. The bookshelf was emptied down to the wood, books thrown all over the floor. She could barely move into the room without treading on something. She took a step and stopped. Why had Russell changed? What had changed? She pushed some books off the couch and sat down.

Dinner four months ago. One of the only times she'd gone out with both Russell and Juliette. Ava had just been declared dead. There was a buzz at the table that night between them. It had caught Joanne by surprise, and she took note of it but never thought about it again. People were the sum total of their actions, not just the aberrations.

A waitress had wandered by and Russell's eyes had wandered with her, staying on her for far too long. Juliette was talking and didn't seem to notice. Joanne kicked his leg as if to say *Cut it out*. He kicked her back right in the shin, hard enough that it brought tears to her eyes and left a bruise visible for weeks. Then he'd winked at her as if it had been a joke. But that was nothing, right?

Then there were all the times he'd hide or cover his phone when texting. Joanne had just thought it was business. He wasn't her boyfriend. There was no reason for him to hide his personal life from her. But he had been.

She glanced around the office, debating whether or not to clean it up, when her phone dinged. She dug through her bag, a feeling of dread coursing through her.

I know where the vial is.

The number was one she'd never seen before. Russell with yet a different phone, maybe. At first she just stared at the message, not believing he'd have the nerve to keep this up.

How? Where? Her fingers rapid fired back.

The response was quick. *I know because I found it. Someone's prints are probably all over it. Who can you trust? Watch the ones closest to you.*

Her hands were trembling and she wasn't sure what to do. She had no idea who had texted or where it was coming from. It had to be Ava or Marie. That was the only thing that made sense. Her phone kept dinging on her drive all the way to Cooper River, but she was too afraid to read any of the texts. She jumped out of her car and stood on the bridge. Without even looking at it, she threw her phone as far as she could into the water, realizing too late that Detective Trout had pulled up behind her and was watching her every move.

CHAPTER 48

Ava

The water was warm, but it burned parts of my body that were scabbed over and healing. Russell was watching me from the doorway. Always watching.

"Cuff me to the soap holder if you want, but don't just stand there. It's creepy."

"What happened, Ava?"

"With?"

"That bruising . . ."

I frowned. "You checked out my body? You had no right. I told you, that Bulgarian deserved to die. I'm fine, though. My bodily functions are just about back to normal."

"You're not. You should be in a hospital, at least for that bump on your head. Finish bathing. I got some food and then you need to sleep. We're leaving in the morning."

I pushed up to a sitting position. "To go where?"

"Not sure, but they've got a warrant out for my arrest, and once they realize I've left the country, this is the first place they'll send Interpol or the French police to look. We need to be on the move."

"But I thought we were going back. You were going to turn me in."

"I am. But not yet. Not until you're stronger. And since we have some time to kill, and you have a clean passport, Jennifer Roberts—"

"You're going to ditch the rental car and you want me to get another one? And then we drive to Italy?"

"Something like that."

I saw his face, the look in his eyes. He had something up his sleeve. Something not right. "What do you know about Philomena?"

He did a double take. "Your grandmother?"

"About her connection to Anais."

He shrugged. "I only know her name. I found that out after you disappeared. I didn't investigate after that. Why? What are you thinking?"

"I'm thinking there's something worse under all this. And maybe it might be better to just return to the States."

"Ava—"

The back of my head was throbbing where Marie had hit me. "What if my grandfather won't talk to me? They hated Anais for something. And probably have more reasons now since my mother is dead. What if he won't talk to me?" I started to get up, not caring what he saw.

Russell reached for a towel and wrapped it around me. "I found some things in the dresser, I think you can wear them. I'm making something for you to eat—"

"And what about Marie?"

A strange expression crossed his face. "Marie has to get into your phone first. Then she needs to get at the information. You said it was encrypted?" I nodded. "She's not going to be getting the money today unless she's really lucky," he continued. "And somehow I just feel like we're going to see her again. Come out when you're finished."

The pajamas hung off of me, but they were flannel and warm. I combed my wet hair and wrapped it in a towel. It was the first moment he'd left me alone, all by myself. I stared at the ripped window screen, not even ten feet from where I stood. I could go. I could make my way to Vicenza myself if the money from the clock and my passport were still in my bag. Not now. But after he fell asleep. I knew this area and language much better than he did. I could be halfway across France before he even woke up, and he was right, renting a car with my clean passport was the way to go.

I didn't need him. Especially if he planned to take me back and pin Juliette's murder on me. Why hadn't he let me explain? Did he already know the truth? Did Joanne? I wanted to text her, but Marie had taken my phone.

When I went into the living room, I saw Russell in the kitchen, his back to me. My bag was in the corner. Two burner phones sat on the table. I scooped one up and returned to the bedroom with my bag and closed the door. My passport was still there. Marie or Russell had lifted the five grand I'd stashed in the pocket. I opened the phone and texted quickly. I only had minutes. This phone was the only way I had to even the score. I got a response and sent back a note quickly.

Russell came into the room, and I shoved the phone under my leg. "Come on," he said.

There were soup and crusty bread smeared with butter on the table. I sat down and forced myself to eat. Russell watched me, pushing the food at me when I stopped, like he had a vested interest in my appetite.

Later he came into the bedroom with a tube of salve in his hand. "I need to put some on. You've got open wounds. I don't want them getting infected."

I reached for it. "I can do it."

"Do you need help?"

He was acting like he owned my body because he'd seen it before. "I'm good."

"Let me just check your head, then." He put his fingers near the wound, probing it gently. Then he checked my arms. He looked at me like he wanted to keep going, but he dropped my hands and stepped away. "Do you feel dizzy, nauseated?"

"Not right now."

"Good. Get some sleep. I need you rested."

He was confusing me. Taking care of me but determined to turn me in so I'd end up in prison. Willing to drive me to Vicenza, which was at least a fourteen-hour drive, if not more. Hating me and caring for me at the same time. This version of Russell was making me uncomfortable. I needed to get out of here tonight, as soon as I had a chance, even if I had no clothes and no money. I'd figure it out, I always did.

I put my head down on the pillow for a moment and lost all sense of consciousness. When I woke up, it was dark. I heard breathing and rolled over to see Russell next to me, snoring, with his arm flung out to the side. I moved my own arms and was relieved I hadn't been manacled to the bed frame again. I needed clothes and shoes. The room Claire had used as a child still held a dresser. There had to be something there.

Ten minutes later I was dressed in passable jeans and a sweater that swallowed me whole. I needed at least twenty euros to get a cab into Cherbourg. Russell's jacket was hanging over a chair. I reached in his pocket and felt crumpled papers. I pulled them out and counted five hundred euros. I glanced toward the room where he was sleeping, then walked slowly to the edge of the bed. I leaned down and kissed his lips. He didn't even move.

I wanted to stay. I needed to leave. After rummaging through the kitchen for supplies, I stuffed a few dinner rolls and a bottle of water in with my things. It was all a prisoner-to-be like me deserved. Then I left Russell there, cuffed to the bed frame, just like he'd cuffed me, with the keys dangling from a hook across the room. I knew he'd be angry, but I knew he'd be amused at the same time. It was our version of foreplay.

CHAPTER 49

JOANNE

She was falling apart. She felt it, like nerves pinging with pain, only it was in her brain. Trout had watched her throw the phone. He'd seen her destroying evidence. She expected cuffs on her wrists, but it didn't happen. Instead he just got out of the car and stood next to her, looking out at the water.

"Nice night," he'd said.

She nodded. "I suppose," she murmured and started to move away.

"Joanne, you're in over your head. Should I drag the river for your phone or just get a court order for all the information that was in it?"

"No." She couldn't think of anything else to say.

"Did Russell contact you again?" he asked.

"No," she said again.

"You're going to end up being arrested, you know. And I find it odd you'd go so far for him. He isn't worth it. Giving up your job, your life. Your son."

"Leave my son out of this!" It came out harshly. "Steven is living mostly with his father now. He's got nothing to do with any of this."

Trout turned around and started walking back to his car. "I'm going to get started on that court order. That river looks really dirty to be mucking around in it. I'll be in touch."

Joanne held in everything until his car pulled out, and then she burst into tears. He was right. She had a day, tops, to try and clear Russell, or she was going to be arrested. That meant talking to Ella Field.

Ella was in her forties, short and thin with a decent sense of style, but it was clear after two minutes that she was impatient and edgy, uncertain about meeting with Joanne. Joanne had approached her outside her office, picking her out from her photo on LinkedIn. It might not have been the best idea, but it was the only one she had.

Desperation had taken over during the past few hours after the texts came in, with Joanne vacillating between grief, disbelief, anger, and feeling absolutely betrayed. She settled at some point on letting it all go. She refused to believe Russell had killed anyone. He'd just become a jerk who needed some sorting out. The past year had been difficult on all of them. Their friendship would never be the same after this, but she didn't want to see him go to prison for something he didn't do.

"You were friends with Juliette, then? Pretty good friends?"

Ella folded her hands on the table. "We were. I told you, though, I didn't go out that night to Tequilas. My daughter had a dance recital. Ballet. I asked Juliette to reschedule, but she was firm on that date."

"Why then?"

"Can't tell you. What's this about, anyway? The police already interviewed me."

"What was going on in Juliette's head that week? Or the weeks before she died? Was she excited about the wedding? Did she say anything?"

"She and Russell were this couple that were probably great when they first got together. And they might have been great together if things had moved along the way they should have, but it seemed like the longer they were together, the more it all fell apart." Joanne frowned but said nothing. "Let's cut to the chase. His affair with that child pushed her over the edge." She opened her hands. "Imagine how you'd feel. Juliette was accomplished, worked hard, did everything she was supposed to do. She loved Russell. Then comes along this little twenty-two-year-old twit, Ava, and he was after her like a bloodhound."

"I was there and I didn't see it that way. But even so, Juliette didn't leave him. She was going forward with the wedding."

"Maybe. Maybe not. Look, I know she was hurt, humiliated, wondering if this was the man she wanted."

"Do you think Russell killed her?"

She seemed jolted by the question and took her time before answering. "I don't know. I think it's certainly possible."

"What about Steve Thomas? It looks like Juliette was having an affair of her own. And they had some sort of fight that night at the party. What did she tell you about him?"

She leaned so far forward, her necklace scraped along the middle of the table. "Juliette got tangled up with Steve, yes. But she wasn't looking to have an affair with a married man. She wanted to settle down, not be some sidepiece."

"When's the last time you talked to her?"

"That next day."

"The day she died?"

"The morning of the day she died, yes. She was crying on the phone. I have to say, I was worried."

"What'd she say?"

"She was rambling. I think she was still drunk. She told me about Steve showing up, pressuring her. He had some bracelet he wanted to give her. He wanted her to call off the wedding."

"And?"

"And she was waiting for Russell to come home from work. She was going to call things off with him, she thought."

Joanne put her head down. That didn't look good for Russell. "Did she tell you he was hitting her?"

"The police asked me that too. No, she never told me that, but I'm not sure she would."

"Danielle, the woman who works at the reception desk—"

She smirked. "Danielle is a gossip of the worst sort. What did she tell you?"

"She said that Russell came to the office, they had an argument, and he grabbed Juliette right there in the waiting room."

Ella seemed to be staring at something past Joanne's shoulder, out the window. "Danielle loves drama with a capital *D*, even if she has to concoct it herself. She was sleeping with Steve on and off and was stupid enough to think it meant something. I never saw anything violent with Russell, and believe me, if that happened in the office, everyone would have been talking about it. If it happened outside of the office . . . I wouldn't know."

"There's something you're not telling me."

She studied Joanne for a second. "Juliette was having some problems. I don't know if it all had to do with Russell, but she was depressed, moody, irritable. I finally gave her the name of a therapist. She tried to be so mature about things, but it chewed her up."

"Is there more?"

"She had, ummm, some gynecological issues. Endometriosis. Fibroids. After years of treatment, her doctor told her that getting pregnant might be an issue. She was only thirty-one. She wanted a family. We talked about options—you know, surrogate, adoption."

"When did she find this out? Did she tell Russell, do you know?"

"I'd guess it was about four months ago or so. I don't know whether she told Russell."

Four months ago? Ava'd been declared dead. Had Juliette told Russell she might not be able to have children? Was that when all the changes with Russell started? Joanne breathed out. "She was taking Lexapro and Xanax. Did you know that?"

"She didn't tell me she was on medication, but I'm not surprised."

"So how did your phone call end that day she died?"

"I told her to meet me after I got off of work. She said no. She didn't feel up to coming out. So I offered to come to her house. She said no. She wanted to talk to Russell when he came home, and obviously she didn't need an audience to do that. And that was it. The next thing I heard was that she was dead." Ella stood up. "This is all really upsetting. I have patients to see."

"I've only got one more question."

"Do it fast."

"Why would Juliette have hypodermic needles in her surgical bag? Is there a good reason?"

Ella's eyebrows rose. "Needles are counted. Accounted for. It's not something you can just walk in and take. Even if you work here. I don't believe Russell's story that she had them. I think he had them. And in case you're wondering, we don't use potassium chloride for anything in our office. It's not something ortho would have anything to do with. I'm not sure any outpatient office like ours would. It would need to be administered in a hospital setting."

Joanne hesitated. How many times had she seen inmates in court for possession of paraphernalia and substances they should have had no access to? If Juliette had wanted the needles and the potassium chloride, she would have found a way to get them. No doubt. The question really was not where she got them but why she wanted them.

Joanne thanked her for her help and left. Every time she turned around, she was smacked in the face with more of Russell's lies. She needed to stop, mind her own business. Go home, clean her house, go to work, keep her head down, and leave all this behind. But she knew she couldn't.

CHAPTER 50

AVA

The rental car Russell had driven from the airport was perfect. A small Toyota, automatic shift. Inconspicuous. The dark blue blended in with every other car on the road. The car was half-filled with fuel and I had the few hundred euros from Russell's pocket to fill the tank if necessary. I headed out into the night, on roads I knew very well, south toward Italy. I needed to put some miles between me and that cottage. I'd hobbled Russell, I hadn't completely crippled him. I'd left him twenty euros, the keys to release the cuffs, his wallet, and his passport. I knew it wouldn't be long before he'd be on my tail, but I actually looked forward to it.

With every mile I covered, I relaxed a little more. It was a straight run to Paris, and after that I had some choices to make. The direct high-way route or the back roads. It made sense to keep moving as fast as I could, but I wanted to head through Geneva and ditch the car there in the event that the police were looking for the tag. Geneva was a central point. I could easily catch the train to Vicenza from there if I had to.

The sun started to come up just as I began seeing signs for Paris. I needed a coffee break, so I took the exit for Le Chesnay and pulled over when I saw a Nespresso shop. Ten minutes and I'd be back on the road, feeling better. I sipped the coffee in the car, watching the people going into the mall. It brought back too many memories of when I was struggling here, trying to pay my bills. Working odd jobs. I was only thirty miles or so from the spot where the Bulgarian was killed. I hadn't altered my looks much since then, and it was keeping me on edge.

I put my head back and started thinking about Marie. I could still feel the throbbing knot on the back of my head, and I vowed I was going to see her again, if only to remind her she'd beaten me twice and left me for dead. Pain came in many forms. When I was done, Marie was going to spend the rest of her life in prison. I felt the slight smile on my lips, imagining her shuffling around in a brown uniform, confined to a small, dank cell for all her years to come.

I looked up. There was a police officer parked in the next space over. He glanced up at me just as I noticed him. He didn't smile; he just continued staring at me with a steady gaze. I felt the urge to back out and find my way to the highway or get out of my car and walk into the mall. I couldn't just sit here; he was making my skin crawl. His eyes followed me as I locked the door and made my way to the entrance. I didn't know he was actually following me until I heard his door shut and the heavy heels of his boots on the sidewalk behind me. I was starting to panic.

The burner phone in my pocket began to buzz. I hesitated, because no one could possibly know this number. Except Russell.

"Head feeling better?" Marie said.

"I just got this phone last night. How the hell did you get the number?"

"Your boyfriend wasn't too happy with you when I called the cottage. Look, I've got a problem." Her voice sounded far away. I heard traffic noise in the background.

"The passcodes?" I asked.

"You have them?" Her voice was urgent, angry, rising above the clamor behind her.

"Marie, I can't believe you're calling me. You hit me. Again. And now you want me to give you all the information so you can steal the money? What the fuck is wrong with you?"

"You know where they are, don't you?"

"Maybe I do have them. And maybe I have the account numbers too. Now all I need is to get you out of the way," I responded.

"Shhh. Stop talking. I need to think for a minute."

I said nothing more, but I was listening carefully to everything else going on behind her. The bits of a language—something familiar. After a few minutes it was clear this call was a waste of time. I couldn't stand here any longer in this parking lot. The *flic* was still watching my every move. "It's been interesting listening to you think. Gotta go, Marie. Since you're in Geneva, you might want to take a quick ride back to that hospital Anais put you in. Where was it? Zurich? Check back in, because you're losing your mind."

"How do you know I'm in Geneva?" she asked sharply.

"Because Geneva is on the list of accounts, and in the past two minutes I've heard four different European languages."

"I need those codes, Ava. I'm going to find you!" she screamed.

I clicked off the line. Marie was becoming unglued, but I was glad she'd called. I'd learned three important things from her. One was her whereabouts. Two: that she must have talked to Russell to get this number. Which meant he was loose. Up, walking around the cottage, able to reach the landline phone—and he was pissed enough at me that he'd told Marie how to reach me. Three: she'd gotten into my phone and had the account numbers, but she still had no idea where the passcodes were.

The latter both relieved and concerned me. I had another copy of the account numbers, of course. But if Anais hadn't given Marie the passcodes, where were they? Did they even exist? Without them, there was no way for either of us to access the money.

As I headed back to the car, I saw, out of the corner of my eye, the cop hurrying back to his car. I floored it out of the parking lot and didn't look back. Chances were he'd either recognized my face as matching the description of the suspect in the Bulgarian's murder or run the tag number of the Toyota and linked it to a fugitive named Russell Bowers. Both scenarios were bad. At that minute I regretted my decision to leave the cottage. It was only after I got onto A13 and was leaving Paris behind, no sign of the cop behind me, that I heaved a sigh of relief. I needed to ditch this car and get another rental, but it was impossible right now.

As the rhythm of the road lulled me, my thoughts returned to Marie and the passcodes. Where would Anais have put them? Then it dawned on me. They were probably in the letter she'd left for Marie. Fairly obvious if she knew to look for them, but perhaps easily overlooked if she didn't. That had to be it.

Marie had the only copy of the letter with her in Geneva, but I didn't need to go to her. She would try to find me, I knew, because after everything she'd done she still hadn't been bright enough to sort this out on her own.

For now, I would keep moving south to Vicenza. And when I saw Marie again, there was going to be major payback.

CHAPTER 51

JOANNE

Fibroids. Leiomyomas. She Googled it. Symptoms: pain, bleeding. Could be rectified with surgery and only in the most severe cases interfered with fertility. Something stank like rotten fish in this whole thing. Joanne wished Russell was sitting next to her, throwing ideas out—sort of. Every time she thought about him, she felt sick to her stomach. Lies, lies, and then twenty more lies.

She heard a knock at the front door and checked her computer's clock. It wasn't even six in the morning. The sun hadn't come up yet. She made her way from her home office to the door in her flannel pajamas, coffee cup in hand, and peered through the peephole. Sheriff's deputies. Two of them. She'd know that uniform anywhere. She put her back to the door and took a breath. A tear made its way down her face; she wiped it off with the back of her hand. The only reason they'd be here at this time would be to issue an arrest warrant. She grabbed her phone and dialed a lawyer whose number she knew by heart.

"Baldwin, it's Joanne Watkins. From Judge Simmons's office. I've got sheriff's deputies at my door and I think they're going to arrest me. Don't even ask. I'll need you for first appearance later this morning. Please? Or send someone from your office?" She threw the phone onto a chair and opened the door.

She knew this officer. His face, anyway. Young. Started maybe two years ago. "Ms. Joanne Watkins?" Then she saw Trout behind the two officers, a half smirk on his face. "We have a warrant for your arrest."

She backed up. "Can I get dressed? Finish my coffee?"

"Yes, and no," Trout answered. "But don't even think of running."

"Like I can run. Seriously."

She came out five minutes later dressed in sweats. She knew the deal, what to wear, what to bring with her, after years of seeing people arrested at court and hearing stories. Don't wear clothes you care about. You might not get them back. No jewelry. No cash. No underwire bra. She took off her earrings and put them on the counter. No purse.

She left everything behind, but they took her to the Prosecutor's Office, not the jail, and seated her in the conference room. "Why'd you throw your phone into the Cooper River, Ms. Watkins?" Trout started.

"Can I have a lawyer?" she asked.

"Certainly. Anyone we can call for you?"

"Andrew Baldwin," she responded, "is my lawyer. I already called him, but calling again would be good."

Trout motioned for one of the people in the hallway to make the call. "Since you don't want to talk, maybe you can just listen. Russell is in big trouble. You're not—yet. Like I said the other night, I think you're just caught up in this thing, trying to help a friend, do the right thing."

"Have you found the needle? Or vial?" she asked. "Any evidence to pin this on Russell?"

"I'm not going to answer that. I'm asking the questions." The words were drawn out as if he needed to think about it. "So, where did Russell Bowers go?"

"The needle bothers me," Joanne continued. "And the vial. Where's the vial?" She was fishing. "Russell is smart. He would never have killed someone in a way that was so obvious. Do you think?"

"I think he wanted her out of the way. Maybe something happened and he wasn't able to be as careful as he'd planned."

"But he was controlling the whole thing, right? He could have taken his time, cleaned up the blood on her arm. Staged the whole thing. Left the house, stayed away—busy at the office, came home very late. Found her, called the police. But he didn't. He took me home with him, a witness to the blood. Does that make sense?"

He shrugged. "Strange what people will do, huh? So where's your cell phone?"

"I'm not at liberty to discuss anything until my lawyer gets here. But I really could use some coffee. And I'd like to make a phone call. If that's within my constitutional rights."

"Certainly. In good time. So, how did your meeting with Ella Field go?"

It caught her off guard. They'd been watching her every move. "It was lovely. She made me coffee and let me use the phone. I wish you'd do the same."

He stood up. "Great."

Just then, Andrew Baldwin was escorted in. He was scrappy, tough. You could tell just from looking at him. Late fifties, six two, gray hair in a buzz cut, but long enough that he looked like he belonged in the 1950s. The only thing missing was his fedora. She'd always thought he'd make a good hard-boiled PI in an old black-and-white movie, and she'd seen him perform miracles in the courtroom. She'd said a hundred times that she wanted him if she ended up in hot water. And the water she was sitting in was boiling.

"This conversation between the two of you is over," he said.

"Fine," Trout said. "I am arresting your client for obstruction of justice, aiding and abetting a fugitive from justice, and conspiracy to commit murder."

"Murder?" Joanne protested. "I didn't kill anyone. And I'm not aiding Russell—in fact I'd like to kill him right now myself. The only thing I did was take a phone call from him. That's it."

Baldwin put his hand out to keep her from speaking. "Don't say anything else. I'd like a few minutes with my client, if you don't mind."

Trout left the room and shut the door behind him. Baldwin looked through the glass, out into the hallway, and then at Joanne. "What the hell, Joanne? I only had a minute to look over the case, but what the hell? Where's Russell?"

"I think he left the country. That's my best guess. I don't really know."

"What do you know?"

"I know that the needle used to administer the potassium chloride was taken from the scene. So was the vial, for that matter. Someone has it, though."

He crossed his legs and glanced around as if he wasn't sure the room was secure. "How do you know that?"

"I got a weird text on my phone before I threw it in the river—I don't know who it was, but they told me they had it. And that Russell was guilty."

He leaned across the table toward her and lowered his voice. "What'd you do?"

"I didn't do anything."

"You do know they can still get your texts even if your phone is gone. Right?"

She knew. Of course she knew. But she hadn't been thinking clearly. "What do I do? Help me."

"You shut up. That's number one. Stop being smart and cute with the comebacks. Let me handle it. Two, though you didn't ask, I'm not going to charge you for this. Chalk it up to the years between us. And because I never woulda guessed Russell'd get himself mixed up in something like this."

"Wait. If I'm going to be sidelined, I need you to do something for me." His eyebrows rose, but he didn't say anything. He seemed to be loving all of this. "Juliette, the dead woman?"

"Nice of you to refer to her that way, but go ahead."

"I need more information about her. Ella Field, the nurse practitioner in her office, said she had endometriosis or fibroids. I need to know more." His eyebrows were no longer raised. She'd lost him at *endometriosis*. "No, it's important. It has something to do with all of this, I just don't know what. I need her medical files."

"Which is against the law. I don't need to tell you that."

Joanne leaned forward, putting her elbows on the table. "I know. But this thing has layers. See what you can do?"

He stood up. "I'll see you at first appearance. Oh, and here's a hint. Tell them you're going to kill yourself. They might take your clothes, but they'll put you in a cell by yourself, away from the population." He patted her arm and left the room.

With everything happening so fast and her life apparently circling a drain, all she could think about was Juliette's leiomyomas. The key to her death was right there. Joanne didn't know how, but she knew it.

CHAPTER 52
AVA

Pretending to be a lost American, helpless, usually worked with police—in France, anyway. He took my license and disappeared. It was good and I'd paid quite a bit for it. Issued in California, matching my passport. None of that was going to help me if they were looking for the car.

"Vicenza." I said it slowly when he asked where I was going. It took three tries for me to understand his broken English. I wanted to just answer in French, but it was better this way.

"Did you rent this car?" he asked.

I shook my head. "A friend." He didn't understand. *"Ami." Friend* in French, but I said it almost like I was saying "Amy," and smiled. After a few minutes he understood.

He was looking at the plate, and then he asked, "Do you know Russell Bowers?"

They were looking for him. I had to think. "Is that his name? He is a friend of a friend. He stayed back with her. I'm just trying to get to Italy. I told him I'd turn it in to the rental place in Vicenza. Is there a problem?" I slowed my English to a crawl, enunciating every syllable.

He motioned for me to stay and went to his car. He was talking on a cell phone freely, thinking I wouldn't understand. *"La voiture est enregistrée sous le nom de Bowers. Mais il n'est pas avec elle."* He seemed to be listening and taking instructions.

He made his way back to the car. "Do you speak French?" he asked, leaning down to the window.

I shook my head. "I'm friends with Marie Lavoisier-Saunders. Well, my sister is. She was with the guy who rented this car. He told me it was okay to take it to Vicenza. Is he in trouble?"

"Sortez de la voiture." He wanted me out of the car, but I didn't make a move. I didn't speak French. "Out." He motioned.

I opened the door and obeyed, my hands clenched into fists. I was two steps away from serious trouble. "Yes?"

Two more police cars pulled up behind us. I saw *Police Nationale* across the side and I put my head down. This was where it was going to end. On the side of the road, not even ten miles south of Paris.

Four officers approached us. They all looked bored and eager at the same time.

"What's your name?" the short one asked. He was scanning my documents as he spoke. His English was perfect.

"Jennifer Roberts," I answered.

"How do you know Russell Bowers?"

"I don't. I came over to Cherbourg to see a friend, and he was there. He said I could drive this rental to Vicenza—I'm hooking up with some girlfriends there—as long as I turn it in to the rental company by Friday. He gave me cash"—I pulled the bills out of my pocket—"and I said I'd pay for the car at the rental agency. Is anything wrong?"

"He's wanted for murder in the United States."

I put a hand to my mouth. "Oh my God, I had no idea. Where in the United States? I'm from California. I can't believe he was standing next to me."

The cop gave me a look like he didn't believe I could be so stupid. "New Jersey."

"He knows my friend Marie Lavoisier. She might be going by the name of Marie Saunders. Or both names hyphenated. You might want to talk to her, she probably knows more about him."

"Did he say where he was going? Why would he give you the car?" The first one was taking over again, struggling with his English.

"He didn't say. I hardly spoke to him. He was quiet. A little off. I tried to talk to him—small talk, but he wasn't interested. I was leaving to go to the train station in Cherbourg and he offered me the car."

"That didn't seem strange? To offer you the car?"

I shook my head. "Those two were all hooked up, and she had a car. I wanted to head south, so we made the arrangement. Cash for the car. I pay when I turn it in. Made sense."

They kept me there and searched through all my belongings, chattering to each other the whole time. They were calling me "idiot American," that I could only speak one language. I wanted to tell him I could handle ten, but I played the part, staring off into the distance.

"What are we going to do with her?" one asked.

"Take her to the station. Run her name. Look for warrants. Check her against all wanted persons. If it comes up clear, find out everything she knows about Bowers and her friend and then drop her off. The sooner the better. I can't stand her voice."

My face must have turned bright red, because I noticed they had started watching me closely. I could kick myself for not disguising myself when I had the chance—cut and dye my hair, put in contacts. I looked exactly like that escort who'd stabbed the man in the BMW.

Somehow they missed it. Five minutes later they told me to gather my belongings; they were towing the car and taking me to the station. Twenty minutes after we'd arrived, I was standing in the middle of Versailles with my bag in my hand. They had taken all of Jennifer Roberts's personal information and let me go. My heart was still pounding as I hurried down the street. Luck had been on my side, but better not to tempt it.

I still had Russell's burner phone, but I needed a computer or a smartphone. An Internet café would be perfect. I turned in a circle. It was right in front of me. A vape bar called, of all things, Vapor Lounge.

I slid in and tried not to laugh. Men were huddled together at tables, inhaling from long metal tubes. It looked like something out of Amsterdam. There was a small bar to the side that served cold drinks and coffee.

"Is there a computer in here? Or something? I need to get on the Internet."

The bartender pointed me to the back, where a lone computer sat, presumably so vapers could custom order a product. I Googled *Victor DeFeo, Vicenza*. Ten names came up and I ran down them, eliminating them by age, until I knew I had the right address: 28 Via Lago Trasimeno, right smack-dab in the middle of Vicenza. From street view on Google Earth it was a nice-looking salmon-colored house with a terra-cotta roof, surrounded by cypress trees. Private but conveniently located. Perfect for a confrontation.

I grabbed my bag and headed down the street. I needed to get a new rental, and fast. I'd already lost over two hours, and Russell was right behind me, I was sure. And he had a problem. His passport had most likely been flagged. Getting on an airplane in France was going to be out of the question.

CHAPTER 53

JOANNE

The admissions department at the jail was crowded. It was the one thing she was hoping on the block-and-a-half ride over—that it would be empty, that this process of being strip-searched and showered would be done with a minimal number of people around to see it. It was a low point in her life, certainly. During all the hours she'd put in at the courthouse, other than the one visit to Marie here last year, she'd only made it as far as the tunnel that led to the jail—a passageway that allowed inmates to be brought directly to court without having to leave the building. She'd gone down the tunnel once to relay a message to an inmate's public defender, and she'd felt like she was entering another world. The space was closed in, one side filled with cages. It was a place she'd never wanted to see again, and now here she was, except on the less desirable side of the door.

A female officer stood near the wall, looking impatient and bored, as Joanne stripped down in the shower room.

"Squat and cough," the officer said. "Lift up your arms. Okay, lift up your breasts." Then, "Hmmm, okay, get in the shower. The nurse is going to see you next."

The water was barely warm. Joanne didn't look down to see what she was standing on in her bare feet, but every second that passed made her more sure that her friendship with Russell was over. She wouldn't have cared if she saw them drag him in and force him into the shower on the other side. She'd loved him like a brother, like the best friend she'd ever had. It wasn't romantic, it was better than that. And he'd left her holding the bag without a word.

She dried off quickly and slipped into rough orange scrubs. She was now the property of Camden County. The one saving grace was that she overheard some of the officers talking, saying, "That's Judge Simmons's secretary, she's got to be housed alone." Joanne said a silent thanks. She wouldn't have to be on suicide watch to be by herself.

She was escorted up an elevator and through the same doors she'd entered when she'd visited Marie. Déjà vu. Her cell was small and dirty, but she was alone. She had barely had time to put her mat down before she was called to an interview. Her hair was still wet, her stomach felt sick, and she didn't really want to see anyone. But she was flooded with gratitude when she saw the sharp-edged crew cut of Andrew Baldwin through the windows.

She rounded the corner and took a seat across the table. "Well, this is interesting. I only got up here ten minutes ago."

"This is bad, Joanne. I didn't know how bad. I'm rethinking doing this for free."

Her pulse ratcheted up. "Why? What's going on?"

"I shot a call over to the Prosecutor's Office, thinking we could wrap this up today. But they got your texts." He gave her a sideways look. "They saw the info someone sent about the vial. And they're wondering why you didn't give them this information."

"I didn't have anything to do with any of this, except that someone sent the text to me."

"And they think that someone is Russell. They think you were in on this together. You were together when you found Juliette."

Joanne put her hands flat on the table. "Why would I want to kill Juliette? What reason?"

"Oh, I don't know, Joanne, maybe the two of you are in love. Or you were hoping he'd be in love with you. Then you saw the naked pictures, the fact that he was having an affair with Bridgette, and you freaked."

"They're just making it up as they go along. I wasn't in love with him. I'm disgusted that he was doing all this creepy stuff and Juliette never knew. I never knew. How is that possible? That you can know someone and never know them?"

Baldwin sighed. "They're combing through the texts between you now. I'm pushing for release tomorrow, and I'm going to do the best I can, but given that Russell is still on the run, that may not be possible. So we're looking at bail. I don't know how high they're going to go, but how much can you raise to get out of here?"

Joanne put her head down. This was surreal. "I don't know, I've never been asked this before. My house? It's worth a few hundred thousand. I can't ask my parents for money for this, but if I had to, what kind of number are we looking at?"

"We'll see. This is your last chance, Joanne. Is there anything you haven't told me? Anything that's going to pop up that I need to know about?"

"There were tons of texts between me and Russell last year. I don't think there's anything horrible."

"Do you know where Russell is now? Are you helping him?"

"He's chasing Ava. If you find her, you'll find him."

Baldwin's eyes widened and she almost wanted to laugh. Almost. Then he said, "I found a way to get you what you wanted on Juliette. No matter what the name on it says, it's from Juliette and it's from the coroner's office." He pushed a manila envelope over to her. "See you in the morning."

She watched him get up and leave the room. She could see his back as he was standing at the elevator, and she'd never felt more alone in her life. It was all she could do not to run out and beg to leave with him.

After she was led back to her cell, Joanne spread out the thin green mattress on the bottom metal bunk. She made her bed the best she could with the thin sheet and blanket, but without a pillow it was going to be like sleeping on a slab of cardboard. The overhead fluorescent light was steady but didn't really fill the room. She sat on the edge of the bunk and opened the file.

Joanne Watkins. Female 31 years old. She knew he'd just substituted her name for Juliette's. She scanned down the page. *Uterus intact. Severe uterine leiomyomas. Evidence of recent surgery, possible pregnancy. Prolapsed uterus.* She thought back to her viewing at the funeral, Juliette's sister angry at Russell. *She'd invested so much time in Russell, that to let him go and try to start over was impossible. She didn't think she'd find anyone else, and she wanted a family.*

Three questions popped into her mind, one after the other. Possible pregnancy—what pregnancy? What happened to it? And whose child was it?

CHAPTER 54

AVA

The house looked exactly as it had on the computer screen. It was the color of a nicely grilled salmon, the roof made from terra-cotta tile. Cypress trees dotted the landscape, allowing only a partial view of the property. It was dark, and I found my limbs were heavy. I wanted to get out of the car and walk to the door, but I couldn't. I just sat there staring, once again trying to spark a memory about this place, wondering if this was where my life had begun, but there was nothing.

I saw movement out of the corner of my eye. Near the fence line. Then a woman came through the gate and latched it behind her. Older, thin, with hair that was no longer dark but was thick, falling in waves around her face. She was wearing dark clothing, so she almost blended in with the night. I had no idea of her age, but she seemed hearty enough.

She came to the window when she saw the car, and stared in at me. Her hand went to her mouth. "Oh my God, Giada, is that you?" she asked. Her Italian was thick, heavy with a dialect that was difficult to understand. "Is that you?" Then she turned and screamed toward the house. "Victor, come!"

I didn't respond. I didn't even roll down the window. The doors were locked and I felt comfortable in here. Everything outside of this car was frightening me. The woman put her hand on the door handle and tried to open it. There was an expression of surprise and then confusion. "Giada? Is it you? It is. I know your face. Let me see your left hand."

I looked down at the back of my hand. The mole was smack-dab in the middle; it had always been there. It was flat, approximating the shape of Australia, though it wasn't something most people noticed. Someone, I think Claire, once told me that perhaps little people lived there and I couldn't see them because they were so small. I raised my hand up to the car window now and watched tears well up in her eyes.

A minute later I was out the door and in her arms. "Where have you been, Giada? All this time I thought you were with Adrianna. When they said she was dead, I, well, we just didn't know if you'd been taken and killed too. We started to look, but didn't know your name. There were no records."

"Nonna," I said. "He told me you were dead. I didn't know you were here. I didn't know."

"Vieni con me," she said, willing me to follow her. Her hand was on my wrist, pulling me back toward the gate. I knew the house would swallow me up; the door was the mouth of a great whale, and when it spit me out again, I would be a different person. I didn't want to be a different person, but there was something unfamiliarly familiar about this woman who held my arm and so I didn't resist.

We climbed stone steps to a sitting room. The room smelled of a recent fire and some hints of citrus or wine. Philomena motioned for me to take a seat on the sofa near the fireplace and pulled up a chair across from me. She was taking me in with goldish hazel eyes filled with tears. "I can't believe you're here. You look so thin. So thin, Giada. Do you need to eat? Are you hungry?"

My tongue itched for liquor. I'd driven over ten hours, only stopping for gas. I hadn't had any alcohol in two days. "Wine. I don't even care what kind. Just wine."

"Of course. Wine with food." She stood up and rounded the corner but kept looking over her shoulder like I might disappear. Ten minutes later she motioned for me to come to her. She'd put out a place for me with red wine and a sandwich. I sat down and took a mouthful of the drink, ignoring the ham on thick bread. I felt better already.

"Where have you been all this time? Years?" she started. "Tell me what happened. Tell me all of it."

"You don't know? Victor didn't tell you?"

She looked toward the door down the hallway. "Tell me what? I don't understand."

I finished the wine and motioned for more. "I've been with Anais. Well, with her daughter Claire, actually."

She looked like someone had punched her in the stomach. Her mouth opened and she touched her abdomen. "Claire? Since when? For how long?" It was a whisper.

I pulled in as much wine as my mouth could hold and then I swallowed. "Since I was three. Since my mother was killed."

I saw her hand shaking, but I wasn't prepared for the scream that emerged from her mouth. No words, just noise. Victor heard it and came barreling down the hallway like a bull in a stall. He stood at the edge of the room, frowning.

"I told you not to come here. I told you she was dead so you wouldn't come. You're going to kill her." He went to the table and put an arm around Philomena. "Anais is going to kill us all. From the grave."

"She's dead? Victor, why didn't you tell me any of this? Why? Giada, how did you end up with that family? Explain. I need to know."

Victor jumped in. "Would it help? It's just more pain."

Philomena put her hand on mine. "No. Tell me."

I thought I was going to be sick. There was too much emotion here. I hadn't let myself cry or care or be close to anyone in so long. I didn't trust a soul in this world, but these two people seemed safe. "I need more wine." It was all I could think of to say.

Philomena put the bottle on the table. Her hands were trembling. "She stole you from me, Giada. She stole you from me. You need to hear it from me. She didn't want Adrianna to be born from the very beginning."

"No, Philomena." Victor's face was livid red.

Watching this play out between them, I felt like I was sitting on dynamite that was going to blow any minute. I desperately tried to put the pieces together. Ross had spirited me from the church, refused to let the others kill me too, but Adrianna's murder hadn't been the random crime of opportunity I'd always assumed. I thought I'd made those most culpable for her death pay, but had I? Anais knew these people intimately and had never said a word to me, even after she learned what I'd done in the name of justice. This woman—my real grandmother—had the answers to how the whole event was connected.

I thought back to an afternoon on Anais's patio when I'd been drinking soda, looking through photograph albums. The blue books kept high on a shelf in the cottage. Vietnam. There was a picture in there of this woman—Philomena, I knew it now, but then she was just a young, pretty woman in a photograph. Anais had become angry when she saw me looking at it, and ripped it from my fingers. She spewed a string of invectives and put the book back even higher so my tiny fingers couldn't reach it.

"What did Anais do to you?" I asked. My eyes went from Philomena's face to Victor's, knowing that despite how long I'd searched for the truth, I wasn't prepared for the answer.

CHAPTER 55

MARIE

The pages of the letter were scattered across the floor. Marie sat cross-legged in the middle of them, occasionally pulling at pieces of her hair. She stopped and smacked herself on the side of the head. "Think, Marie. Think. The codes. All I need are the passcodes."

She lay back onto the carpet and tried to think of anything important to Anais—words, phrases, sayings in French, birthdays, months, important dates, names of places she loved. None of them had worked. In a frantic moment she'd called Ava, hoping Ava would be more motivated to get the money than anything else, but she wasn't. She was holding on to her anger over being whacked in the head with a rock.

Marie looked at the calendar. Parole had certainly violated her by now, which made everything more complicated. She could see Bridgette running around filing papers with the judge, squawking and rambling about conditions of parole. Marie looked out over her balcony onto Lake Como. The Alps as a backdrop behind the lake were breathtaking. She wasn't going back to that dirty jail to serve out her sentence. No. Ava's phone was sitting on the table beside her. Getting the account information hadn't been nearly as hard as she'd imagined. A store that fixed broken phones, a made-up story about the information in the phone being her whole life. Begging, pleading, and money, most of the money she had left, convinced the man to try. And in trying he'd produced the five banks, locations and account numbers, everything she'd needed.

She was almost free. But she knew that freedom didn't exist, really. She'd come from a family of lies, destruction, and death. She could run from country to country, pulling money from accounts as she went, and she'd never find the peace she was looking for. She could never erase the memories of the moment she saw toddler Ava covered in blood in the back of the car, how Ross had lifted her out, her hand clinging to his sleeve, and everything that followed. Or the knowledge, recently learned, of what had happened between Anais and Philomena. That would haunt her. It just went on and on.

She grabbed one of the pages and studied it again. She'd been thinking about it—when Ava came to the cottage she had to have been looking for something. It was the only thing that made sense. And the only thing she could have been looking for were the passcodes. Anais had split the information, giving them each a piece. So Marie must have the passcodes somewhere and always had, she just didn't know where. Were they in her memory from a conversation she had with Anais? Were they in the cottage? Or maybe even hidden somewhere in this letter? She read:

> I watched her pregnancy advance and I was envious. She was having a baby with her husband and I was alone. Except for you and Claire, I was alone. But you were children and that's not the same. I knew about Philomena's condition. I knew she wasn't expected to carry to term. I thought I'd be there to console her, to nurse her back to health after this loss, to let her know it was a good decision that she hadn't told Victor, but instead she was flourishing. She looked healthy, was happy. Why wasn't I? Maybe because I had a secret. A terrible, terrible secret I'd

kept from absolutely everyone. I had left Ross, but I was concealing a pregnancy under layers of clothing.

Marie stared at the words. There was nothing going through her mind when she got up and went into the kitchen and poured whiskey into a glass. She'd become numb reading her mother's confession. If the two women were pregnant at the same time, only one of the babies survived. It meant yet another death in this family saga. Marie stared out over the balcony railing. The sun was setting behind the mountains and a mist hung over the lake, just above the water. It was calming, peaceful, as if nothing bad existed inside this place. No mother who hid bank codes or did terrible things. No niece who went on killing sprees when it suited her.

But the apartment was only hers for another three days, and then her money would run out. Three days to get the codes and get to the bank in Geneva—that one account held a payoff of over $600,000. Only a drop of the twelve million, but a good-enough start.

"You're reading for clues, not content, Marie," she muttered. "Get back to it." She flopped back onto the chair and picked up where she'd left off.

Now you see why I couldn't tell Papa. Every day in Tuscany was a ticking time bomb. And someone was going to leave dead. I knew it from the minute I arrived.

CHAPTER 56
AVA

Philomena had moved me and my glass of wine to a more comfortable chair in the living room. The lights were partially dimmed, and Victor, in disgust, had chosen to return to the back of the house. I was beginning to realize how different my life might have been if I'd grown up here. The colors in the room were soft, the people seemed warm and accommodating. I was starting to resent Adrianna for pulling me from this little haven.

Philomena's voice was soft as she recounted her early years with Anais in Vietnam. "We lived in West Lake in Hanoi. In a house with a pool out back. I remember it got so hot Anais would shuffle over from three doors down to go swimming. I barely spoke English. And only a little French. She spoke only French, so it was a funny friendship, but it got easier. By the time we were teenagers we were both fluent in English and French. I remember when she met Ross." I felt the inside of my head calling on me to sleep, but I kept my eyes open. "She tried to make it seem like she was dating him—she wasn't."

"No?"

She shook her head. "She said that after she got pregnant, but she was really just meeting him and having sex—though it didn't happen many times. She was pregnant after their second encounter. Shocking."

She started laughing. "Women didn't get pregnant like that in the fifties—not even the early sixties. If they did, they hid it. So she arranged a quick marriage. Not a joyful one. And then she was gone." She lifted her hands out to her sides. "Gone to Philadelphia, with her new husband, Ross. I went to see her a few years later. It was so bad, Giada."

"What do you mean?"

"Her life. She'd had another child. Ross had gone back to what he was doing before Vietnam—a warehouse worker. But Anais wanted more—she wanted her parents' life. It was too late for that. Her parents weren't even speaking to her anymore." Philomena leaned back and took the wine bottle and poured some in her glass. Her hair was framing her face, and in this light I thought she might look like me—same-shaped face, same eyes—because I wanted her to.

"So you were with Anais when my mother was born?"

She leaned forward and the back of her shirt lifted. I saw her thinness, just the hint of her ribs visible. The longer I sat here, the more I saw the connection between us. "Ah, jumping ahead, are we? Okay. Well, let me just tell you this—I had had two miscarriages during the years that Anais was in Philadelphia. I was married by that time, to Victor. Not that any miscarriage is good, but I was well into my second trimester both times. It devastated me. They told me I'd probably never carry to term."

"But you did."

She nodded slowly. "When I found out I was carrying again, I left Victor." She leaned in and put a hand on my knee. "Not because I didn't love him, but because I felt so much pressure. I wanted this baby more than anything in my life, and I wanted to carry surrounded by peace and harmony, not worry and pain. I saw the pain on Victor's face with each loss, so I went to stay with an old family friend who has a farm in Tuscany."

"Martinelli? Victor said I should remember the farm. That Adrianna took me there when she left home. But I don't."

Her face lit up. "It's such a beautiful place, and Martinelli—Enzo is his given name—was a gracious host. I told her I was going to Tuscany. I was surprised she wanted to come too. She said she needed some time away. But she had two little girls in Cherbourg. She'd left Philadelphia and was settling in Cherbourg. I was surprised, but I accepted her company."

My eyes fluttered shut for a moment and I started to drift. Philomena nudged my arm and I jolted awake. "I'm sorry." I sat upright with both feet on the floor.

"You must be exhausted, driving here from Cherbourg. It's late. Let me make a room for you and we can talk tomorrow."

I rubbed my face with my hand. I would have liked nothing more than to lie down on a cool bed and go to sleep. But I couldn't. I knew Russell was on his way and Marie was out there circling too. It was only a matter of time before they showed up on this doorstep. I had to get the information while I had the chance. "No, please, go on."

"Okay, just for a little bit." She stood up and stoked the fire. "I think Anais was surprised when she found out I was pregnant. And that things were going well. I think she thought she'd be there to fuss over me when I miscarried, or help get me back to Victor in one piece, but it didn't happen. All of this came to a boiling point one afternoon." Philomena put the poker down, but her hands began to twist together in a constant motion. This story was making her anxious. Or maybe it was that I was here.

"Came to a boiling point how?"

She sat down. "Anais might have managed to get out of Philadelphia to Cherbourg, but she wasn't back with her family. Her mother and father were harsh. But being out of the States was a good first step. She seemed preoccupied, like her mind was elsewhere, the whole time in Tuscany. But anyway, we sat together that morning having just water, enjoying a bit of sunshine after so many cloudy days, when she brought up Victor. She wanted to know if I intended to return to Vicenza after the baby was born. Giada, I was stunned. It hadn't occurred to me to leave Victor. Not at all. She said I should come and stay with her and her girls in Cherbourg. That she'd help me with the baby. I didn't know what to say. I didn't know where this was coming from. So I got up and started walking. I wanted to get away from it, from her." She waved her hand out to the side and I noticed tears in her eyes. "I was almost eight months pregnant. Almost." She pinched her nose and I saw the tears fall freely onto her cheeks.

"If this is too much . . ."

She took a breath. "No, no. I started walking toward the barn. To the yellow barn." She half laughed. "It wasn't even yellow then, but that's what they called it. A cow had calved three days before and I went to look after it. To see how it was doing. I didn't know Anais had followed me until she came in behind me and latched the door."

I was fully awake now, sitting upright. "Why? What'd she want?"

"She just started talking, like she'd done when we'd been sitting out back. That I should not go back to Victor. That I should start a new life, leave him. That he hadn't been supportive during my miscarriages. She said I was going to be a mother. That I had to think of the baby. She was getting riled up, and I didn't know what was wrong. I hadn't seen her like that before. Then she started saying that it was my fault I'd lost those other babies. That it was my fault she ended up in the States with Ross." Philomena wiped tears from her cheek with her finger. "I had been with her when she first met Ross, but I had nothing to do with anything that followed between them. She started circling me." She made a circle motion with her hand. "Cornering me. Telling me her life was ruined. Then she lifted her shirt."

"Lifted her shirt? For what?"

"To show me her stomach. She was pregnant too but carried very small. She'd carried small with her other two too. She said she'd never be accepted by her father with yet another child. He'd barely forgiven her for the two she already had. And that was true." She looked at me.

"That part of what she was saying was true. I told her to go back to Ross; she got angrier. She said I had no right to go on with my life when I'd destroyed hers. She told me Victor was no good for me. That he was worse than Ross, that she and I would be fine without men. And—"

"What?"

"At one point she shoved me against the stall. My back hit the wood hard. She was in my face. In a rage. I wanted to get to the door, to unlatch it, but she was in the way. She wouldn't let me pass, and every time I stepped away from the stall, she'd hit me again."

"What do you mean, hit you?"

"No, not hit. Pushing my shoulder. I felt moisture between my legs, and when I reached down it was blood. I felt a pain and I knew something was wrong. I felt labor pains, like when I'd miscarried before."

I stood up and started pacing in front of her. "So what happened? Did she help you?"

Philomena bent over and put her head to her knees. She told me the story slowly, stopping when tears prevented her from going on. "Now you know," she said finally, "why Victor didn't want you to come. It wasn't you." Her hand was on my cheek. "This story is just too terrible."

She was still grieving. After all this time. In pain after what Anais did to her. I felt uncomfortable. "Philomena, I need you to know I'm in trouble," I blurted.

She scowled. "What do you mean?"

"That's part of why I came here. To meet you. But someone is chasing me, following me. They may come at any time."

"Why?"

"Because I did something terrible. And all things considered, I should have gone somewhere else. But knowing I finally had family, I couldn't. I needed to see you. But I don't want to cause a problem—"

She shook her head, the frown holding on her face. "What kind of trouble? You can't leave now. Stay tonight. In the morning we'll figure it out. I have more to tell you—about your mother. And father."

I hadn't thought anything about my father. It just escaped me because my whole world had been about seeing my mother killed. I wanted to leave this woman in peace, but the thought of driving anywhere was too overwhelming. One night. I'd stay one night.

The clock struck three a.m. when we climbed the rounded staircase, which was strangely familiar, haunting. This place was in my brain and always had been. She showed me to a room and came in and sat on the bed.

"Do you remember Lia?" she asked.

The name meant nothing. "No."

"Lia is my niece. Victor's sister's daughter. She stayed here for a time with us. She and Adrianna were very close. Adrianna called her 'Sister.' She was five years older than Adrianna and left us to go work in Milan. In a seamstress shop. Adrianna went to visit at least once a month. You used to wait for her to come home, watching out that window." She pointed toward it.

I stared at the window but remembered nothing.

"Well, anyway, Lia is in her forties now. She lives in Rome. I need to tell her about you when the time is right." She stood up. "Get some rest now."

She shut the door behind her. I stood at the window for a while, watching the lights from automobiles move across the lawn as the cars drove past. I was sure Russell was going to be in one of them very soon.

CHAPTER 57

MARIE

Anais was running across a field at night. She had on a long dress that tangled at her knees as her legs moved through the grass. It was dark save for what moonlight filtered through the clouds. She glanced back over her shoulder at the barn behind her, the outline disappearing into darkness. Her arm was draped across her stomach, cradling it, protecting it. This was all a mistake, Philomena on the floor in the barn, the baby covered with blood and dirt, dying before her eyes.

She reached the side of the house, gasping for breath. They'd blame her for all of it, if Philomena was still alive to tell the story when they found her. Anais looked around the corner toward the door of the house. She'd already decided she was leaving. She'd gather her belongings, walk to town, catch the bus to France, that's what she was going to do. Philomena might die, she knew. She'd lost so much blood. It was everywhere. She'd cried and pleaded, her legs spread, the labor pains coming. And she'd pushed on her own. Begging for help. Begging not to die. Anais had watched her push that little form out, like a dog birthing a pup. The baby was small and a bluish color. But there was nothing that could be done. Nothing at all.

She'd shut the barn door, leaving them inside, and then latched it, making sure no one could escape. Her hand hesitating only briefly on the wood before patting it and then choosing self-preservation over everything else. And self-preservation was what carried her through the house and the miles of walking into town.

Anais's arms and legs ached. She'd been walking for hours in the dark. She was exhausted. She wanted to sleep, but she had to conserve her money. She had to put as much distance as possible between her and that terrible thing that happened. She needed to save her own baby now—her baby with Victor. Philomena had never known of the affair. When Anais had cried on the other woman's shoulder, she'd never told Philomena she'd been sleeping with her husband, conceiving the child Philomena yearned to have. It had all been so well planned. Anais would have the life she deserved with Victor, give him a child. He never could have turned her away. But Philomena had ruined everything by getting pregnant too. Not only pregnant, but able to carry. And she thought she was just going to return to Victor. Destroy everything? No. Anais rubbed her stomach in anger, justifying in her mind what she'd just done to her lifelong friend.

At first, when the truck pulled up beside her, dark red, covered in dirt, like it had driven off-road through muddy hills to reach her, she was relieved at the possibility of a ride. Then the man got out. She didn't recognize him at first in the dark; he called to her but Anais, frightened, ran from him. She knew his voice but sensed something in it—vengeance, retribution. And she was right. When it was over, Anais lay in a heap on the side of the road, near death.

Marie jolted awake in her bed. Ever since she'd read the letter, these dreams of Anais that night in Tuscany had replaced the ones of her own psychiatric confinement in Zurich. Anais's confession had followed and haunted her. Marie had reimagined the events, and in what order they happened, but the outcome was always the same. The blood. Sometimes there was a dead baby on the floor. Sometimes just blood.

She lit a cigarette with trembling fingers and walked to the balcony. It was too dark to see anything but the moon, a half moon just beyond the mountains. Clouds were moving in. She flicked the cigarette over the balcony and picked up the letter. She'd developed a theory that all the accounts might have the same passcode. One passcode hidden within the depths of the letter to ensure Marie, and maybe even Ava, would have to suffer through the detailed account of Anais's wrongdoings in order to get the prize.

One question Anais didn't address was why, after Philomena had survived, she had never turned Anais in or made her accountable for what had happened in that barn. Maybe it was because she thought Anais had paid a price too, lying on the side of the road for hours, her own child stillborn in blood and pain. But Marie felt like there was something more to it. Something deeper and darker. Another secret the two women shared, something that had connected them, that lay just beneath the surface and answered every question she still had.

Marie pulled up the banking website and logged in. The bank clerk in Geneva had set it up for her. Once she logged in, it asked for the account number and the passcode. The woman at the bank said she wouldn't be able to access the money until she provided legal proof Ava was dead, but that she could try a passcode and see if it worked. Marie had tested it repeatedly, hoping to get a hint, whether it was numbers or letters, how long a string. She'd even begged the clerk, told her the story of Anais dying, even providing her death certificate, but it didn't matter. The clerk couldn't give her any information.

Marie typed in the name *Philomena* and waited. *Access denied.* Then she tried *Tuscany*, then *Victor*. *Access denied.* She slammed the laptop shut and grabbed Anais's crumpled letter to search through it one more time.

Only a knock came at the door just then and she never had the chance.

CHAPTER 58

AVA

Philomena was there when I woke up, though I can't really say I slept much. I tossed and turned and watched out the window, but mostly my mind swirled with just how horrible Anais had been in her life, horrible and manipulative.

Philomena was just standing in the doorway, watching me. She was already dressed. It was almost like she was willing me to leave.

"What trouble are you in?" she asked before I had a chance to push myself upright in bed. "Is that why you came here, Giada?"

I shook my head. "I'd still be in trouble whether I came here or not. I'm not asking for your help. I only told you in case someone showed up at the door."

She sat on the edge of the bed. "Who might show up?"

"Marie, maybe."

"Little Marie. Why?"

"She's not so little anymore. She's almost five ten. And she's coming because she needs the passcodes to Anais's bank accounts. She thinks I know them but I don't." Philomena had a puzzled look on her face. "One of Anais's little parting shots, you know. Hidden passcodes to make us try and kill one another over her money."

"So what terrible thing did you do that you mentioned last night? I don't understand."

"That's part two. A cop from New Jersey may show up too. He's tracking me because he thinks I killed his girlfriend and he wants to take me back to the States. Can I have some coffee?" I asked. "Or tell me where I can get some?"

"Did you kill her?"

I kept my eyes on the window, not looking at her. "I was there when she died. Maybe that's enough? But—"

She stood up. "Get dressed. Come downstairs." When I got to the kitchen she handed me a cup of coffee and motioned for me to sit down. "We don't need trouble. And it seems that anything connected with Anais means trouble." She reached out and touched my hand. "I'm sorry you've had to go through all of this. I couldn't even sleep just thinking about it."

She was sitting in a kitchen chair near a window, and I couldn't help but glance over her shoulder at the street, watching and waiting. "What were you going to tell me about my mother?" I asked.

"I just wanted to say, Victor and I weren't happy when Adrianna got pregnant with you. We wanted her to finish school, you know, but we accepted it. We offered her all kinds of options—adoption, letting someone we know raise the baby—but she refused all of them. When you were about two we sent her to Tuscany for a month, to Martinelli's, just by herself. I thought the freedom might make her see things differently, but instead it set off an explosion. Six months later she ran away."

"Why? Why'd she run away?"

"I don't know. I don't know. He must have told her the story about when she was born. She was on a tear to find Anais after that. She asked us for the number, but we said we didn't have it. She got it somehow and must have contacted her. That's all I can think. Adrianna was my only child, you have to understand that. She made mistakes, but I loved her. What happened between me and Anais was a lifetime ago." Her face crumpled and I saw tears forming again.

I drank half the coffee in my cup and put it down on the table. "Is Enzo Martinelli still alive?"

She nodded. "He is. He still lives there with his wife." She was silent for a second. "I need to finish telling you about Anais, about what happened that night. To her."

"What?" She had ended her story with Anais trapping her in the barn. With Martinelli finding her later. About waking up in the hospital, the baby in the NICU, attached to tubes, barely alive. About her own blood loss. We never got to Anais, about what she did after that.

"I went through labor on that dirty floor. Anais watched. She watched me in pain, pushing. She didn't get help. She didn't help me—she just sat on the stool in the corner. I begged. I couldn't understand how she could do this. I'd never hurt her in my life."

My mouth opened but nothing came out.

"In fact, when I screamed in pain, she put a rag over my face so no one would hear. She watched me squeeze that baby out. It took so long and it was stifling hot in there. There was dirt and dust everywhere, in the air. The baby wasn't breathing when she came out. My baby was blue. The umbilical cord was still attached. I cried for Anais to get help. And then she left, just like that. I thought she'd come back—but she didn't. She latched the door behind her and left me." Philomena was reliving this like it was happening again. There were desperation and panic in her voice. "I was there for hours, in the dirt."

"But your baby lived, Nonna. Adrianna lived. And I'm here."

"Anais left me in that barn. And she fled the house that night. I think she was going to walk to town. But she never made it. Someone stopped her before she got there and beat her really badly." Philomena got up from the chair and poured more coffee. "They left her in a pile by the side of the road. Like garbage. Enzo found her, though. Brought her back to the farmhouse and took care of her."

"And her baby?"

She shook her head. "Her baby died. From what Enzo said, there wasn't much to bury. He said it was awful and we shouldn't mention it again to Anais or anyone else."

"So you never said a word? To anyone? How about to Anais? Did you two talk about it? Oh my God, you can't live through something like that and then never talk about it." The words were through my lips when I realized that wasn't true. You could experience so much and find a way to keep it to yourself. I realized I'd been shouting when I saw Victor coming into the room. He poured himself some coffee and then stayed, leaning his back against the counter.

"You weren't there. You should have seen her. Black and blue. Her face was so swollen you wouldn't have known her. What happened to her was terrible. It almost made up for everything. Almost. And I have to say, after what happened in the barn. What she did to me? There was part of me that was glad to see her like that. God sometimes works it out for us. We don't have to do anything."

I drank the rest of my coffee and stood up. "I'm going to Tuscany."

"For what?" Victor asked.

"I need to talk to Martinelli. To find out what started all of this."

"Leave the man alone," Victor responded.

"I'm going with her," Philomena said. "We'll take my car. It's about three hours from here, but we can do it faster maybe. Put your car in the garage. Get your things."

She took me by surprise. I liked this grandmother. I threw my few belongings into my bag, brushed my hair and twisted it up off my neck, washed my face, brushed my teeth, and met her by her car. Those few acts of hygiene changed everything. Then, as I started to open my car door to move it to the garage, I saw him.

He looked tired and worn, his bag slung over his shoulder. He was walking toward me, not even fifty feet away. I had been this close to complete escape.

"Ava. Don't even think of running. I've taken three buses and a taxi to get here."

Philomena looked at me and then at Russell. *"È questo il poliziotto?"* she asked.

"Yes. This is the cop."

He waved his hands back and forth. "English, please."

"I knew you'd come. I only wish it had been ten minutes later, you know. Get in the car," I said to him. "We're going to Tuscany. And don't even *think* of cuffing me to anything."

"Can I sit for a minute? Use the bathroom?" He dropped to the ground with exhaustion.

"Why'd you come, Russell? Why'd you give Marie my phone number?"

"You two deserve each other."

I smiled. "True enough. Marie is definitely going to get what she deserves."

"Che cosa stiamo facendo?" Philomena jumped in.

"We need to bring him to Tuscany, if that's okay," I answered. "Let him use the bathroom to freshen up?" Philomena nodded slowly. "Russell, hurry. Because if I see Marie coming down that road, I'm running her over."

CHAPTER 59

JOANNE

Joanne lay on her bunk with a balled-up undershirt stuffed under her head as a pillow. She'd been in the jail for one day. Twenty-four hours and she was already sick. The food had come and she'd left it untouched. The tan tray smelled of sour milk, and the compartments were filled with rice and beans and two pieces of bread. The cup of juice was untouchable—some sugary purple mix in a plastic cup. Joanne had grabbed the orange from the tray before they'd removed it from her cell. If nothing else, she was going to lose some weight in here.

She'd asked Baldwin to dig further into Juliette's medical files. The coroner's report had only autopsy information, not clinical notes from her gynecologist. Baldwin had come through, but he wasn't happy when he dropped the file off. She was almost out of favors from him. She scanned the first page.

Juliette Lewis. 31 yo cauc female. H/o leiomyomas, extensive fibroid occlusion of fallopian tubes. Prolonged menses, extensive bleeding. Surgery recommended. Past hysteroscopy not successful. Fertility compromised. Discussed myomectomy or hysterectomy.

That note was dated six months before her death. Her gynecologist was recommending possible hysterectomy. She couldn't get pregnant. What had happened? Joanne flipped to the next note.

Patient c/o tenderness of abdomen. No sign of worsening leiomyomas in previous CT scan. PP with tenderness, missed menses x 2 mos, sweating, dizziness, loss of appetite. Wt loss of 5 lbs. Upon examination, urine is dark, poss dehydration. No masses detected upon internal examination. Cervical smear done. CMT, CBC, chemistry, HCG quant and qual ordered.

HCG was a pregnancy test. Two days later there was another notation in the chart.

Positive pregnancy. Pt informed. Set up appointment with Dr. Steinmiller to discuss options. High risk.

Joanne dropped the folder. Juliette had been pregnant. By Russell? By Steve Thomas? Her one and possibly only chance to have the baby of her dreams, and it was not Russell's? Had she aborted? Miscarried? The stolen medical notes ended there. A story unfinished.

Joanne walked to the phones and dialed the number of Juliette's sister. Baldwin had given that to her too. The problem was all calls from the facility were collect. She had to pray Gail was in a forgiving mood and would entertain her for a few minutes.

The line clicked through. Joanne was stunned. "I don't know if this is Russell or Joanne, but you have some nerve to call my house after you killed my sister."

"No, no, no. I didn't kill her. Please, just give me two minutes. I have a question. One question. Please," Joanne said.

"Two seconds."

"Was Juliette pregnant? Do you know? In the past four months?" There was silence. "Nobody wants the person who killed Juliette to pay more than I do. Please. This is important."

"If she was, what does that have to do with anything?"

"It has everything to do with everything. Did Russell know? That's all I need to know."

"Joanne, what's this about? Seriously?"

"Russell took off and left me to hold the bag, Gail. I had nothing to do with your sister's death. But things are strange—she lied about the dress fitting. She had fibroids, maybe needed a hysterectomy. But she was pregnant. I just need an answer to my question. In the meantime I'm talking to you on a dirty pay phone. I'm in an orange jumpsuit, sleeping on a dirty bunk, and I hardly even knew your sister, let alone conspired to kill her."

"What do you want from me?"

"To know if Juliette told Russell about the pregnancy. If she miscarried or had an abortion."

"I'm paying for the privilege of this conversation. At like three dollars a minute. I must be crazy."

"I'll pay you back. Talk fast."

She sighed. "I don't know why I believe you, but I do. I hate Russell. Yes, Juliette called me about three weeks ago or so. She said she was pregnant. She was crying and I didn't understand. I thought it was perfect—I mean, she was getting married anyway. It wasn't a huge issue. But for some reason she was more upset than anything. She's had medical issues. No one knew about it in the family but me—not even my mother. She'd had surgery once and didn't think she was going to be able to get pregnant. So she was caught off guard. I thought she was upset because she was worried about her health."

"So what happened with the baby?"

"She miscarried two weeks before she died. Lost the baby. When she was only a few weeks along. I don't know exactly how many. It wasn't surprising, but it brought on a whole new bout of tears. She seemed inconsolable."

"But she did tell Russell?"

"Russell found out. That's how she worded it. 'He found out.' I don't know how. Maybe he found some doctor's discharge papers or a medical bill."

"So, what did he say about it?" This was just one more piece of information that incriminated Russell. She had no idea how many more times she'd have to stumble over these tidbits before she accepted that her friend might be guilty.

Gail was silent for a second. "Let's just say I worried about her. I worried about her marrying him. I worried, period. She was under so much stress."

"Was Juliette cheating on him, do you know? Is there a possibility?"

"Joanne. I need to go now. This is too much. I'm done."

Joanne heard the click.

Russell had never said a word about any of this to her. Not that he had to, but it was just one more odd thing in a whole list. She picked up the phone to call Baldwin, when a woman came up behind her. "Uh-uh. Your time is up. My turn now." She took the phone and pushed Joanne out of the way.

CHAPTER 60

AVA

The farm was located in the northern region of Tuscany, toward Cantagallo. The landscape became hillier. The houses quainter. I rolled down the window, leaned back, and tried to enjoy the cool air. I must have dozed off, because when I woke up we were pulling into a long driveway with stone walls on either side. The landscape was something out of a picture book. Rolling hills in every direction. Philomena parked near a house. Victor had told me about this, asking if I remembered it. Adrianna had brought me here when she ran away. I blinked and looked again. The flat-roofed white house, the grapevines in the distant field. The three barns. I tried to find something familiar.

We got out of the car and just stood in the driveway, taking it all in. Russell had been quiet since getting in the car.

"Why are you here?" he asked.

"Just be quiet and you'll see."

An older woman opened the door, took one look at Philomena. "Oh, my angel." She wrapped her arms around her and hugged her. "Enzo is out with the grapes. Is everything fine?" she asked.

"Yes, yes. We'll just go find him to say hello."

We started out into the fields. I looked down and laughed. Russell had on loafers. Loafers to walk across a cow pasture in the middle of

Italy. I wasn't going to say a word. After five minutes, we could see a man at a distance, standing next to a fence line. Philomena rushed forward.

"Enzo!" she called to him.

He looked up, rather startled, and walked to meet her. He was at least eighty, slightly bent over but still in good-enough shape to walk these fields and tend to his grapes. "Philomena. Why are you here? Did you hear something about Adrianna?"

No one had told him. "Adrianna is dead, Enzo, but her daughter is not. Giada, come," she said. I still wasn't used to being called that name.

"What happened to Adrianna? Why didn't you tell me?" he asked.

"Mr. Martinelli, I just need to have a few minutes in private with you. Private, and then we'll leave you be. I promise."

I took his arm and left Philomena and Russell standing together in the field. He was sturdy and saved me from falling several times. His face was weatherworn but friendly. He still seemed startled by our sudden arrival.

"You seem to be the key to this all," I started, trying to get the dialect just right so as not to throw him off.

"Me? How?" He took a seat on the edge of a low stone wall and motioned for me to follow.

"You were there that night. The night my mother was born. You saw it all."

"I found Philomena in the barn, if that's what you mean. I did."

"And when my mother came here with me, when I was two—she came here alone. What happened that she suddenly ran away?"

He shook his head. "I don't know. She was here for one month only. Just her. She was asking the same things you are. 'What happened when I was born? Why did my mother give birth in a barn?' I told her a very important woman once gave birth in a barn, a barn of sorts, and she should feel no shame."

"You mean the Virgin Mary?"

"Of course," he said indignantly.

"Look, I'm not going to go away. I'm sorry, I'm not. I need to know what happened to Anais that night. Who attacked her? And what about her baby? What are you holding back?"

"I don't like this," he grumbled. "I found her, yes. I found Philomena in the barn. She was bleeding profusely. I'm a doctor. I took care of her. The baby . . ."

"What about the baby?"

"I did CPR. I cut the cord. I kept it up until the ambulance got here."

I looked down at my sneakers, now covered, almost black, with dirt. "The nearest hospital capable of dealing with a premature infant is twenty miles away. That's at least thirty minutes of driving on these roads. You kept up CPR for thirty minutes?"

He scowled. "I did the best I could."

"And what about Anais?"

"What about her?"

"Nobody called the police after what she did? Nobody did anything?"

He stood up. He was angry. "I did!" He pointed at his chest. "I did. After the ambulance took Philomena and the baby, I went in my truck looking for Anais. That's when I found her."

It was true. "So, you did find her?"

"Yes. She was halfway to town on the side of the road. Near some trees. You just don't understand."

"Understand what?"

"You need to leave. You need to leave. Take Philomena with you. Leave this alone."

"You were looking for Anais by the side of the road? You expected her to be on the ground? How did you spot her? It must have been dark? Yes?"

"It was dark. But I've traveled that road my whole life. I know it—"

"Enzo." I pushed off the wall. "I think you're lying. I think Adrianna knew you were lying. I think Adrianna came here asking the same sort of questions. I think she found something out when she was here. And it made her not so much run away from her family. She wasn't running away from anything. She was running toward the truth. Just like I'm doing. Is that right?"

"No. Please go."

"Il luogo dei segreti," I said. *The place of secrets.* "That's what this is." I squinted up at the hills. "Anais said a man with a truck attacked her. Was that you?"

He almost leaped off the wall. "No. I did not attack her. Why would I do that? I saved her. I saved her and I saved the baby."

"You saved Philomena and the baby, you mean?"

His face clouded. "Yes, I did. That's what I said."

"Where is Philomena's baby? Tell me."

"Adrianna left the hospital with her parents. She grew up and gave birth to you."

I shook my head, the puzzle pieces clicking into place. "I think Philomena's baby was buried here. Somewhere that night. She said she was unconscious. She wouldn't have known her baby was dead, and then she wakes up with a baby in the NICU. Maybe we should get the police to start digging. Somewhere on this property? What do you think?"

His head was down and he wasn't responding.

I continued. "I think you found Anais and you—"

"I did not." He was in my face. "She was beaten by the road. I found her. I brought her back here and cared for her. Her baby died. I did my part that night."

"Tell me this and I will leave. Does Philomena know the true story? The whole story?"

He knew what I meant, and he shook his head. "She's been through enough. I told her what she needed to know."

A sound like a laugh came out of my mouth. "Did you think Adrianna might tell her? Seriously?"

"I did what I had to do." His face was bright red.

I backed down; antagonizing him wouldn't get me any more information. "I'm the daughter of that baby that survived that night. That was my mother." I looked at him. "So, thank you for saving her. Thank you." I touched his hand and walked to where Philomena and Russell were waiting.

He wasn't going to say the truth out loud. But I knew it in my heart and I felt sick. I felt sick in the car, all the way back to Vicenza. The family I'd been looking for my whole life might have been in my face the entire time. If Anais's baby had survived and Enzo had made the decision to give it to Philomena, as I suspected, that might have been the right decision, but it also meant Marie was really my aunt. It meant Claire was really my aunt. It meant Anais was really my grandmother.

And it left me wondering why my mother had run to Philadelphia. Linda at the bar had said Adrianna was looking for someone in Philadelphia. Someone close. Was she looking for Ross that night at the church and not Bill Connelly? Was Bill Connelly somehow just an easy conduit to Ross at Anais's urging? Had Adrianna been trying to find her father that night and ended up being killed by him?

I asked Philomena to stop the car, then I jumped out and threw up on the side of the road.

CHAPTER 61

RUSSELL

The drive back to Vicenza was torturous. Ava cried on and off, and no matter how many times Philomena asked her what Enzo had said to her, she wouldn't answer. Russell was quiet, because he had an agenda. This part of Ava's journey was her own. He only cared that she wasn't out of his sight. That she got on the plane with him. That she didn't escape or run away. The days of discussing the never-ending machinations of the Lavoisier clan were over. Though there was a tiny part of him that was curious. He'd never seen her so upset. But that was a conversation for the nine-hour plane ride in front of them.

She didn't resist, and that surprised him. She got in the cab, went through immigration in Milan with her fake passport, and was asleep within an hour of takeoff. He had called the authorities and let them know he was coming back. They'd be waiting for him when they landed. The fact that she could curl up in comfort on the hard airline seat and tune everything out stymied him. Her head was just resting on the seat-back—no travel pillow, no hoodie to block out the noise and light. During one of the most stressful times, when he needed to talk to her about everything that had happened, she'd just shut down. He watched her breathing. Three days and she already looked better, more filled out. Maybe just rest and a few good meals had helped.

She was different since the last time he'd seen her. Calm, almost reserved. He didn't know if the answers had brought her peace or had sent her to another level of hell. Only time would tell.

He leaned back in his seat and let his eyes flutter. In about five hours, both of their worlds were going to be shattered. The police would arrest him, and her. He'd tell them the whole story, everything from the beginning. At the very least the murder charges against him would be dismissed. He could deal with everything else.

When the wheels skidded across the tarmac in Philadelphia, he opened his eyes. Ava was still asleep, not even jostled awake by the rattling and the noise. He shook her shoulder, and her eyes sprang open.

"Let's talk, Ava," he said.

She shook her head and gathered her belongings. "I don't need to. I just want to get this over with."

"They should be meeting us here, so I don't know how much we'll be able to communicate later—"

"Look, I didn't kill Juliette. I didn't. I showed up at the house to get my picture, because I knew it was such a stupid thing I did, sending it. She was dead, or well on her way. Unsavable. But you want to shove me forward like the sacrificial lamb, so let's do it. Let's get you off the hook, by all means. I've certainly done a lot of other things I was never punished for, so this serves me right."

"You think I killed her, don't you? Why would I throw my life away to get rid of a woman I wasn't even married to? Why wouldn't I just leave?" he asked.

She looked at him long and steady. "I have my own sins to grapple with. I'll leave you yours." She gave a sad smile. "Whatever you did, I'm not in a position to judge." She stood up. "Let's go."

He hadn't expected this from her. She was making it all so easy. He got his suitcase from the overhead bin and moved so she could exit first. He was going to keep his eye on her. No escaping this time. He thought of Joanne. She'd been completely screwed over in all of this, and there was no way to make it right. He had no idea what was happening with her and didn't want to complicate her life by calling. He knew she'd never forgive him, and he was already feeling the loss.

The gate was crowded when they got off the plane. He grabbed the strap on her bag to keep her close. He was glancing around, looking for the police, immigration, some sort of official. There was no one, not even someone he could peg as plainclothes. He was on his own, with only a slight grasp of Ava's bag to keep her in sight.

Someone bumped him, and his hand slipped. It took only a second, but she wiggled her way through the crowd and vanished. Just like that. Her black jacket was no longer in sight, nor her dark hair, pulled back at the nape of her neck and tied with an elastic. She was nowhere around. Russell dropped his bag onto the floor and turned in circles. Scanning the gates, the walkway. Then he grabbed his things and ran forward. She could have slipped into the bathroom, a shop, another gate. He dropped into a chair, exhausted, wanting to weep. It was then that he saw the police circling the gate. He tried to get up, but they'd already spotted him. He squinted. Trout was there, out of jurisdiction, his eyes locked on Russell.

"You've roamed a little far today, Trout," Russell said.

"Stand up, Bowers. You're under arrest. You have the right to remain silent."

"Wait. Ava Saunders is here. In the airport. I doubt she had the chance to leave yet. You need to find her. She's traveling under the name Jennifer Roberts. Check the flight manifest. She sat next to me."

He didn't even seem to hear. "Anything you say can and will be used against you in a court of law."

They were putting his arms behind him. This couldn't be happening. "You aren't getting it. Ava is not only alive but she admits she went to my house that day to steal the Polaroid she sent of Anais's door."

"You have the right to an attorney. If you cannot afford one, one will be appointed to you."

"Fine. Arrest me. Keep me here. Send me to CFCF. I don't care. But have someone look for her. I'm telling you."

"You actually have a choice. They can book you here as a fugitive, and you can sit here and wait until the extradition paperwork from Camden County arrives. Or we can skip that, and I can put you in the wagon and take you across the bridge. I just have to fudge the reports a little."

Russell shrugged. "Always play by the book, Trout. Always."

"Fine." He turned to the officer behind him. "He's all yours."

The Philadelphia police officer took Russell and started to lead him away. Everyone was looking, watching, even if they were pretending not to. He saw Ava out of the corner of his eye. A glimpse. A shadow in black. She was at the edge of a group of people. She wasn't smiling. She was just there. And then she wasn't. He watched his only chance at freedom walk away, and nobody was listening.

CHAPTER 62

AVA

Though I was upset by the way Russell and I had parted, I had no idea how to fix it. How to make it right. I only knew I wasn't going to suffer for Juliette's death.

The next day, he was being arraigned on charges in the Camden County Superior Court, being dragged in with everyone watching—this was a high-profile case in the county, and all the local news channels were broadcasting it. The anchors were talking, showing pictures of Juliette. Showing pictures of Russell in his police uniform, graduating from the academy. I sat up in bed and turned on the volume. His head was down to avoid the cameras. He was cuffed, hands behind him. It almost seemed he was walking to his death, bent forward, resigned. The cameras followed him into the building. I watched the screen and wondered, How many times had we entered that building together, sat at those outside tables eating lunch? Life could change on a dime.

I felt a need to call Joanne, to see her again. Our relationship had never had closure, and it bothered me. She hated me, I was sure, but I didn't care. I loved her and was going to try and make all of this right before I disappeared forever. I didn't have her number anymore, so there was only one option—go to her house. Just walk up to her house and knock on the door. It was risky. She could call the police, but I had something for her that might change everything. If the timing was right, if I could speak before she shut me up, all of this just might work.

Center Street in Westmont was quiet. There didn't seem to be anyone around, but Joanne's car was in the driveway, parked at a slight angle, like she'd pulled up, jumped out, and run inside. She had probably been trying to escape reporters. They were like flies buzzing all over this story, but now that Russell was in custody, things had calmed down. I walked slowly up to her door, my heart pounding in my chest. I was afraid, and I was rarely afraid of anything. Joanne had been put through hell, and she could destroy me. But I found myself needing her forgiveness. I stood on the porch and held my breath and then rapped twice lightly. Then I pressed the bell.

A curtain parted, and the door opened slightly, the chain in place. Her face appeared in the crack, and she just stood there. Not speaking, not saying a word, like her body had gone into shock. She shut the door and I thought that was it. I started to turn around to leave when the door flew open and a hand latched onto my wrist, yanking me inside. She shut the door, bolted it, chained it, and turned to face me. I didn't see the smack coming. It was fast and hard, right across my mouth. My lip split and blood poured into my hand. My skin was stinging.

"Are you here to kill me, Ava? Let's go. I'm ready for you. When I toss your skinny carcass out onto the porch it'll be self-defense. Justifiable homicide." But she handed me some paper towels to clean myself even while saying these words.

"No. I wanted to see you. I've seen Russell—"

"I bet."

"And Marie. Though she cracked the back of my head open. But I needed to see you before I leave."

She crossed her arms. "Seriously? You think you're leaving? Russell is sitting in jail for a murder you committed. I haven't even had time to wash the stench of Camden County Jail off of me—I just got released, and you think you're going to prance in here and say 'Oh, I needed to see you' and then just waltz out? Are you fucking kidding me? I'm calling the cops." She started for her phone.

"No, Joanne. Don't. I have something that will clear Russell. I was in the house the day Juliette died."

"I know you were."

"No, I only went to get my Polaroid back. I was hoping to see him too, but that didn't work out. The Polaroid was the only proof I was alive. When I got there, Juliette was in her bed. She was dying. There was blood coming from her arm—"

"Don't. Don't do it, Ava, or I'll hit you again."

"It's the truth. I took some things from the scene. I don't know why now, looking back. Did I think I was protecting him? Did I want them to blame him? To force him to come looking for me? His attention? It's a game we play with each other. I don't know."

"What'd you take? Tell me."

I reached in my bag and produced a kitchen towel folded in threes. I opened it one flap at a time, revealing the hypodermic needle.

She looked at it, then me. "So you took the needle from the scene? It just proves you did it."

I shook my head. "My prints aren't on it."

"So you wiped them off. Wore gloves."

"But someone's prints are on it."

"How do you know this?"

"Because the person who killed Juliette didn't wear gloves. I have proof of that."

"Where's the vial?"

"It wasn't there. I don't know."

"The needle was there but the vial wasn't? That makes no sense."

"I didn't see it, okay? This is only half the evidence. I have something else, but I need something from you."

"No, see, Ava, I'll just call the cops. They'll confiscate everything you have on you and put you in jail and release Russell. You have nothing to bargain with."

We were still standing in her foyer and she was keeping me there, trapped between her and the locked door. "I didn't bring the rest of it with me. If I go to jail, no one will ever know the truth about what happened. It'll all make sense, I promise. But I need Anais's letter she wrote to Marie."

"What letter?"

"Anais wrote this long confession letter for Marie, to be read after she died. I need it."

Joanne seemed to loosen up a little bit and moved toward the couch. "Sit. For two minutes. Why do you want this letter?"

"Because it's got the passcodes to the money she left us—"

Joanne raised her hand. "I don't want to know. But you aren't going to be spending any money. It's not even just Juliette's murder. It's the four men that killed the priest, including one of their wives, who had nothing to do with any of it. Then there's the man in the bathroom that you stuck Marie with. And I'm thinking the man in the BMW in Paris—he was one of yours too—"

"Listen—"

"You made a mistake coming here, Ava. I'm not Russell. I'm not letting you go. I'm calling now."

"You aren't even curious who killed Russell's bride-to-be? Look. I'll stay here. Cuff me to something. Marie is going to be at the Parole Office. I know she is. Call Bridgette, find out when. Get her bag with the letter—it's gotta be in there. I'll figure out the code and give you half the money. Russell gets off, you end up not having to worry about money again. Pay off this house. Don't go back to the courthouse. And if you're not happy, then call the police."

"I'd play along, but I don't have handcuffs."

I laughed. There was something just a tad appealing to her in all of this, in punishing me. "I happen to have a set in my bag. I bought them just for this occasion. But can you cuff me in the bathroom, in case I have to pee?"

"I'll bite, Ava. This is only going to delay your arrest by a few hours, or maybe days, we'll see. And I'm only doing this because I'm curious."

She dialed a number into her phone and waited. "Listen, Bridgette. This is Joanne. I need to know if Marie called your office. If she's coming in anytime soon, if you've heard from her. It's important. I am out of jail. Call me at this number." She recited the digits and hung up. "Voicemail. So let's just sit here and wait."

CHAPTER 63

JOANNE

Joanne entered the Parole Office in Cherry Hill. Her heart was pounding. She'd left Ava cuffed to the radiator pipe in the bathroom. She'd searched her in case she'd stashed another set of keys somewhere on her person. She even made her strip and squat and cough like the officers had done to her in the jail. She didn't trust Ava and she wasn't taking any chances. But Ava seemed so keen on getting this letter, instinct told her she wasn't going to run anywhere.

Bridgette sat at her desk, and Joanne knew that the woman sitting in the chair next to her was Marie. She knew it from the shape of her head, from the color of her hair. How she hated this nun.

"Ah, Marie. I see you made your way back from Europe," she said.

Marie swiveled in her chair, her expression changing to one of disgust. She didn't look quite as severe as she had when she was wearing her nun's regalia. Her face was softer. Prettier. "Made my way? Is that what you call it? No. I was forced back." She looked at Bridgette. "I was coming back anyway, though."

"Forced back?" Joanne asked.

"Ava reported me. She found out where I was and reported me."

Both Joanne and Bridgette stared at her. "Really? Why would she do that?" Joanne said.

"It was her turn. It's what we do." Marie shrugged. "And now it's my turn. That's all I'm going to say."

"Marie—"

"What are you doing here, Joanne, looking for Russell?" Marie said sharply. "Always looking for Russell."

"No, I came to see Bridgette here, if you don't mind."

Bridgette's eyes were wide. She handed Marie a tube. "Marie, go give me a urine sample, please. And take your time, I need to talk to Joanne."

Marie left without another word, and Joanne dropped into the vacant seat. "What did you want, Joanne? You seemed to want to talk to Russell, from the message you left."

"I saw the pictures Russell took of you," she said.

Bridgette smiled. "Why do you care? So many hours of spinning it took to look that good. So what's it to you? Russell's a grown man."

"If you like sleeping with married men. Older married men."

Bridgette laughed. "He's about maybe six or seven years older and he wasn't married. It's not horseshoes—'almost' doesn't count. So stop, what's this really about? Are you jealous? By the way, the jail life looks good on you. You look like you've lost a few."

"Is Marie's parole going to be violated? Is she going back to jail?"

She pushed back in her chair. "I think she has some things to answer for, but we'll see. I don't know how this pertains to you."

"Never mind. Sorry I bothered." She picked up the purse sitting next to the chair and walked out.

She wasn't even breathing when she pulled out of the parking lot. All of this for a letter. Humiliating herself in front of Bridgette for a letter. It probably wasn't in there anyway. She was maybe stupider than Russell, letting herself be manipulated by Ava. Maybe she'd leave her in the bathroom forever, chained to the radiator. She had a toilet and water, and the girl didn't eat anyway.

She unlocked her front door, rushed in, and locked it behind her. Ava was in the bathroom, just as she'd left her, lying on the floor, staring at the ceiling. Joanne opened the door. "I got the bag." She tossed it onto the floor. "They may charge me for stealing now."

Ava rummaged through it, flinging things aside, and pulled out a ball of crumpled papers. "Ah, success." She turned onto her stomach and started reading the letter.

"Are you going to say anything, maybe show me the proof you supposedly had? Or should I just leave you here?"

Ava glanced up. "Bring me my bag."

"But I thought you only had the needle with you."

Her eyes met Joanne's briefly. "I lied. I'll give it to you now."

Ava sorted through things and finally pulled out an envelope, using some bathroom tissue so she didn't touch the paper. "Here. Don't put your prints on it. That would be bad."

Joanne took the envelope and went to the living room. Using a tissue, she pulled out a single sheet of paper, torn from a spiral-bound notebook, and flattened it on the coffee table.

> *Russell, please forgive me for everything. It's been a hard year. This is a no-win situation for both of us. I need to tell you I had an affair with Steve Thomas. It was short-lived and maybe payback for Ava. I knew it was a mistake. And I got pregnant by him. I had an abortion last week and you never knew. I had no choice, as I saw it. I've ruined my one chance at a family—and I lied to you about all of it. When you found out, I knew I'd lost everything. I lost you. My career, the thing that really mattered so much, that I've spent the past nine years building, feels like it's crashed at my feet. I can't marry you, Russell. I can't have children with you. This pregnancy was a fluke, and maybe my one chance to have*

a child. I've had fibroids all my life. I need a hysterectomy.
I know there are other ways to have children. I know
that, but given I've destroyed our life over my mistake I
can't even think beyond that. The depression has made it
impossible for me to know what's right or wrong anymore.
I'm sorry I'm ending things like this, but I can't face you.
I can't face my family. I've ruined everything.

> *Forgive me,*
> *Juliette*

Joanne looked up. She'd killed herself. After all of that, she'd killed herself. She'd brought home the needles and the vial of potassium chloride—got it from somewhere, the hospital, maybe. She'd waited for Russell to leave that day and in that moment of despair had taken her life. She'd planned it all. Maybe not for that day. Maybe it had been a backup plan and things all just lined up right that afternoon and she did it. And Ava, with her usual panache and luck, had stumbled onto the scene and had taken all the evidence. But the vial was still missing. Though the mysterious someone who had texted Joanne seemed to know where it was.

Joanne stumbled back to the bathroom and saw Ava on her stomach, the pages scattered across the floor. Tears were streaming down her face. "What, Ava?"

She flipped over in one swift move and sat up. "Are we even, Joanne? Russell can go free. You can go free."

"Did you get the passcode yet?"

Ava shook her head. "Give me an hour. Go do what you need to. I'm not going anywhere."

CHAPTER 64

AVA

I heard the front door close. Joanne was gone and I was cuffed to the radiator, only able to move far enough to sit on the edge of the toilet, but I could reach the sink easily. The thought occurred to me that Joanne might leave me here forever. But at that moment I didn't care. Anais's letter to Marie had contained everything. Everything I didn't want to know about what she had done. It had closed the gaps in all my questions. It had confirmed all my suspicions. I'd read those pages at least six times, and I couldn't stop.

> *I hated Philomena. I wanted her life. I was carrying a child I couldn't have, I couldn't keep. But the sad part of this is that we were both carrying children of the same father. Yes. It's here, in print. I'd had an affair with Victor when they came to Philadelphia. I was desperate. I was lonely. I needed something. I betrayed my friend to serve my own needs. Not only did I have an affair with him then, but I made him come back alone to see me later. I wanted him, period. I saw him as a means to end my misery in the United States. To start anew. Philomena was barren and in the way.*

But things went badly. After leaving Philomena in the barn, I started to walk to town, to catch the train or bus north. A truck pulled up beside me and he got out. I ran ahead, looking for something, a house, a light of some kind. But there was nothing, only fields all around me. I knew his voice, Marie. I knew who it was and I ran faster. He caught up to me and shoved his face right in mine. He hit me until everything went black. When I woke up in a bedroom in Enzo's farmhouse it was all vague, like it had happened to someone else. But my baby was gone. I'd lost it. And Philomena and her baby survived, and maybe that's the way it should have been.

For years that was what I believed. Until that little baby contacted me years later. I hadn't spoken to her mother since that night. Adrianna was searching. Maybe she was angry at the way she was born, but she reached out when she arrived in Philadelphia. She wanted to know the truth about what had happened between me and her mother. She also needed help starting a new life. So I did the most horrible thing I could think of. I sent her to Ross.

Why? Ross had called me only hours earlier. Timing is everything. He was with his friends at his class reunion. He was drunk. He said many things I won't go into now but he told me he was going to find the priest, Father Callahan. That they were going to make him pay for what he'd done, for the years of abuse. Ross could be violent. I knew that firsthand. I knew this situation wasn't going to end well. But the reason he was calling me was to say he was sorry. For everything that happened in our marriage, for every time he'd hit me, and for beating me and leaving me on the side of the road in Tuscany—yes, it was Ross who found me that night, Ross who beat me. He cried when he called me from the reunion. And I cried. And as the call wound down, I hung up knowing he was saying good-bye, that whatever he was going to do that night, things would never be the same.

So when Adrianna called me? The baby that seemed to have taken my life from me, my life with Victor. The life I was supposed to have from the very beginning. I told her to find Ross. I told her he was going to the church. I gave her specific directions. I told her he had business inside with the priest, so she should wait ten minutes or so and then go in. I said he had money to give her, and maybe a place to stay to help her out—though he knew nothing of her, of any of this. I sent her into a hornet's nest. I knew what I was doing. And so she died. Adrianna, Philomena's daughter, died because of me. I tried to kill her twice, and finally succeeded.

I only realized my hubris later. I didn't know at the time! I didn't. I swear on everything I am. I didn't know. Enzo called me late one night not long after. He was crying, upset about something. I hadn't heard from him in years. He told me Adrianna was going to be reaching out to me, not knowing it was too late, she already had. He told me the whole story about the night Philomena gave birth. He'd found her in the barn just like he'd said. He'd called an ambulance and brought her to the house, with the help of his wife. The ambulance seemed to be taking a long time. They'd treated her and she seemed to be stabilizing. The baby was dead. It had been a girl. He was so angry at me. He told his wife to stay with her and he went looking on the road for me. Ross had attacked me, left me by the side of the road. Enzo found me there and took me back to the house, where I gave birth to a child. A month and a half premature, but alive.

That's when he got the idea. When the ambulance finally arrived, he sent Philomena and the baby—my baby—off to the hospital together. Adrianna became hers from that day forward, and I blamed Ross, Philomena, Victor, Enzo, everyone except myself, for the death of my child. The irony of it is that I was the one who killed her all those years later.

Though I always had a special bond with her, I swear I never knew that Ava was my grandchild. I tortured you and Claire by not saving you from that horror of what your father did in the church. What I helped set in motion. I've thought about these events every day since, and I never forgave myself for destroying my family.

I don't expect you or Ava to forgive me now. Just remember something, Marie. In the end, family is everything. Everything is in a name. Good-bye, Marie. Take care of Ava.

I rolled over, the sobs racking my entire body. Anais really was my grandmother. She'd killed my mother and destroyed everyone around her. She—

Then it occurred to me. The passcode. There was just one, and it was right there in front of me. Anais had ensured we had to know her terrible secrets in order to get her money. I sat up, the cuffs straining against the radiator.

I needed to get to the bank. I hadn't figured out how to get the money, exactly. I had the account numbers. I thought I had the potential passcode. But I didn't have Marie. No matter, I'd figure it out.

I pulled at the metal, but it was tight. The pipe was thick. The cuffs were new. Stupid me. I should have bought some trick ones from a magic shop.

I could stand, though, and I could reach the closet. I peered in, past the towels and myriad bottles of shampoo, and found some hope. A toolbox.

I took the hammer and began pounding at the pipe.

CHAPTER 65

RUSSELL

He got the text. *Meet me at city hall. Southeast corner at four o'clock.* He'd been free for only three hours. Enough time to go home, take a shower, change his clothes, call his boss, schedule a hearing-slash-meeting to discuss his future with the department. Joanne had produced the hypodermic needle and the suicide note, presenting them to the prosecutors, just like that. She said they were in Marie's bag that she accidentally took from parole. All wrapped up. After they authenticated the signature on the letter, and all the medical information they needed, they'd released him on his own recognizance, pending a hearing to finalize it all. He wasn't home free. Neither was Joanne. They found it suspicious she happened to suddenly have this evidence in her possession. But Marie was being held on a parole violation. After some wrangling, she admitted she had been to the house that day, had witnessed Juliette's demise. But adamantly denied taking any evidence. Then they slapped her with obstruction of justice and tampering with evidence.

Russell hesitated. Every time he got involved in any way with Ava, it ended badly for both of them. She'd ducked him at the airport and let them take him in. He easily could have killed her in that minute she'd escaped his grasp, when they got off the plane. Now she wanted to meet him one last time?

He looked at his watch. It was 3:10. No time for a train to Philly. Uber it would have to be. He called for a car and sat out on the steps of his house and waited. When he got out at the appointed place and time, checking to make sure it was actually the southeast corner, there was no one there. He paced for ten minutes and considered calling it a day. And then she appeared. Running and smiling, like they were meeting for coffee, or for a date. Her dark hair had been cut shorter, evened out. She had on big sunglasses, though the sun was going down. She'd bought a dress, navy blue, with matching pumps, which he couldn't help but notice had red soles. Louboutin. The shoes were easily $600 a pair.

"I got us tickets. I need you to come with me," she said.

He looked around, thinking this was a joke of some sort. "To where?"

"Ah. That's the question. Flying into Florence."

"Italy again?"

"Of course. Driving to Vicenza. Just for a few days. Philomena said it was fine. Then the world's our oyster. Wherever you want."

"I can't run away, Ava. I have a meeting in two days to discuss my future in the department."

She dropped her bag. "Really? You were arrested for murder. It's not over. You really think they're going to reinstate you?"

"And if I leave now, I'll be on the run again. My charges haven't been officially dropped."

She took off her glasses. Her eyes were beautiful. She looked healthier. More vibrant. "But they have Juliette's letter. What more do they need? Hire a lawyer to take care of all that. Come with me."

"It doesn't work like that." He looked her over. "I assume you got the passcode?"

She smiled wide. "I did. It was in the letter, right there the whole time. Marie was just too stupid to see it. The almost-last line: *Family is everything. Everything is in a name.*"

He leaned his head back, trying to think. "A name?"

"Adrianna Lavoisier. A name. A puzzle you had to put together. You had to read the whole letter first."

"So you somehow managed to pretend you were Marie and took everything?"

She shook her head, the ends of her bob moving with her face. "No. You think so little of me. I got Marie to sign off. Got a letter of incarceration. Presented everything."

"You risked them discovering Ava Saunders is still alive and you took all the money?"

"I keep saying no. I left a quarter of what I got from that account for Marie. She'll get more later. I hired her a really good lawyer. I gave him a cashier's check. She'll be fine."

"How much did you give her, a hundred thousand?"

"A little more than that."

"So you have the rest? You can't get on a plane with that much cash. You know that, right?"

"Russell, you think I'm an idiot? I transferred it to Philomena's account. She's going to keep it for me until I get there. I have enough money, though. Enough for first-class tickets to Florence." She waved them in his face. "Leave all this behind."

He laughed. "You live a strange life. No. I can't. I have to go."

He started to walk away from her. "Russell," she called to him. "I want to have sex with you. Real sex. All-day sex. Not the drunken, passed-out kind. I want to spend a day with you, eating, maybe eating in bed, and making my body bigger. Drinking—only moderately, though. I want to show you the sunset on the isle of Lesbos. Greece, that is. It's fantastic. I want to—"

He stopped. Turned. "No. Ava. That's a fantasy. Life isn't like that. I can't trust you. You'd do something, knock me out, take my money. Try and kill me at some point. It's inevitable. So, let's just leave it at that. You're dead. I won't tell anyone you're not, though now that you've accessed the money from that account, the government will figure it out. You have a family now. In Vicenza. Whether they're a real family or not a real family, I don't know. But you have a family. Go enjoy your life. Send me a card from time to time. Maybe we'll see each other again."

She looked like a child ready to have a tantrum. "If I leave now, you'll never see me again, Russell. I promise you that. You're giving all of this up." She raised her arms and twirled around. "It's been so much fun."

He walked to her and wrapped his arms around her. He smelled whatever expensive perfume she'd applied while getting dressed. His face was in her hair. "It hasn't been fun. I can't be with you. I can't. But have a good life, Ava. Don't kill anyone. Promise?"

She nodded. "Philomena's waiting for me. I have to go. She said she wants to tell me all about my father when I get there. With everything else going on, I never even thought to ask. I'm sure that's a story." She hesitated. "I don't think she knows the real story—about who I am. Enzo kept it a secret for so long, I'm going to honor that."

He watched her walk away. Her blue dress swishing around her legs. Her little suitcase dragging behind her. He wanted to go with her. But he knew it would never work. Living off of her money. Playing by her broken rules. But he kept his eyes on her until she disappeared around the corner like a wisp of smoke, gone. She never even looked back.

CHAPTER 66

JOANNE

Joanne stared at the broken pipe. The bathroom was a mess when she got home, and, of course, Ava was gone. She looked around in disbelief. She had taken a hammer or another tool and smashed part of the metal plate apart, releasing the cuff. She was now running around with one cuff on her left wrist, the other one hanging free. Ava'd gotten what she wanted when she came here and she'd left, just like that. Just like she always did. Joanne dropped onto her couch and burst into tears. It had been one thing after another, never ending. Joanne would never see her again. Hopefully the suicide note would exonerate all of them on murder charges, but Joanne knew she could never go back to work at the courts. Not now. Not after all of this. She'd only put in seven years toward her pension. Not enough time to be vested. Not enough time for anything.

She stood up and started walking to the bedroom. She needed to close out the world, take a nap. Then she'd get up and clean the bathroom, that was the plan. But something caught her leg and sent her flat on her stomach in the middle of the floor. When she sat up she saw it was the strap to a bag that wasn't hers that had wrapped around her leg. Black, more a duffle bag than a purse. She pulled it to her and unzipped the top. She saw the letter before she saw the stacks of hundred-dollar bills.

I always keep a promise. Or try to. This isn't as much as I'd hoped it would be. But there's more to come from time to time. If you want to see me, contact Philomena in Vicenza. I never had any real friends in life, you may be the only one. You're good and always have been. Spend the money on Steven. Fourteen-year-olds need to be spoiled. And spend it on yourself too. The money is good, clean. Untraceable. I'm sorry for all the trouble I've caused you. I hope this makes up for some of it. Live, laugh, love.

—Ava

She riffled through the bills. There was at least $75,000 in there. Joanne stood up, dumbfounded, and started to drag it into a closet. Then she heard a light knock on her door.

"No," she said out loud. "I've had enough of visitors. Stoppers-by. Newspeople, the courts. No."

"Joanne, it's me. Open up."

She pulled at the door to see Russell there, dressed in jeans and a hoodie. He looked like he was twenty. She opened it all the way and started to walk away. The bathroom could wait. Russell could wait. She needed a drink. She pulled the cold bottle of pinot grigio from the refrigerator door and filled a wineglass to the top. "I should ask if you want some, but I don't care if you do. There's not enough for two."

"Joanne. It's over. It's all over. Ava left for Europe. I just saw her."

She raised the glass. "Hurray! I'm so happy."

"She's gone."

"My life is gone, too. How about that?"

Russell eyed the bag on the floor. "Cash?"

She nodded. "Look at the bathroom. She destroyed it. It was the least she could do, leave money to pay for it."

"Do we need to debrief?" he asked. "You know, talk about everything that's happened over the past two weeks?"

"Lord no. Please. I don't want to hear about the Lavoisiers, Saunderses. DeFeos. Ever again. I've had enough."

Russell looked at her. He hadn't paid any attention to her in so long. He had been so preoccupied with Juliette's death. She looked lighter but worn. She had bags under her eyes, dark circles. Her face was haggard. She was slumped over, like a broken doll. "I mean about jail?"

"It stunk. I lost five pounds. The water was brown. The end." She drank some more wine, then looked at him. "Do you need to debrief? Talk about Juliette? You were getting married, ummm, the day after tomorrow. That's rough, her killing herself."

"Who would have thought Juliette, strong Juliette, would do something like that?" he asked. "She was talking about our honeymoon the day before."

Joanne leaned against the counter and took another sip of wine. "Not me, not in a million years. You know, I turned in the needle, but the vial is still missing. It's weird. If she killed herself, would she jump up and hide the vial? Maybe Ava took that too? Or Marie?" She swallowed some wine and pointed in his direction. "My bets are on Marie."

"Ava didn't take it. She would have told me."

"Like I said, it was the psycho nun. But why?"

He shrugged. "I don't know. By next week, things might be sort of back to normal. The charges will be dropped, anyway."

Joanne pushed herself upright. "Let's hope. You need to go now. I'm going to finish this wine, count my money, and take a nap, in that order. And I'm still mad at you. For Bridgette. Of all people. Really?"

"Ah, Joanne. She was just there. That's all. It didn't mean anything. Things were really bad right around that time, and she wanted it."

"Things were always bad, Russell. You said that after the Ava one-night stand too. But the pictures? That's just creepy. Too much."

"It was . . . impulsive. Let's just say that. People do it, you know, photographs, sex tapes . . ."

Her eyes were large, her eyebrows raised. "Did you make a sex tape too? No, I don't want to know."

He laughed. "No, Joanne, I did not. Just those few pictures. That's all. And I need you to know I never hit Juliette. Not ever."

"So what was it that receptionist in the office saw? And the bruise?"

"She saw us having a little spat in the lobby. I never touched her, though. No clue where the bruise came from either. But the fact that she was blaming it on me? When I swear, I mean swear, I had nothing to do with it, means she was setting me up. Making me into the bad guy for her coworkers' benefit."

Joanne swallowed the wine in her mouth. "Hmmm. If you say so."

"Do you mind if I use your bathroom?"

"Go ahead. Use the one in my bedroom. The other one is indisposed."

Russell's phone, left on the counter, began to ding. She looked at it and then toward the bathroom door. She picked it up. It was a series of text messages.

I wanted to leave things nice.

But I can't.

I found the vial in your bag, stuffed inside the ripped lining—yeah I searched your things when you raided me in Cherbourg.

So, I kept asking myself why.

I somehow missed it when I was in your house. You must have found it when you found her body.

And then:

I know she killed herself. But did you suspect she was having thoughts when she brought home needles and potassium chloride? Did you research potassium chloride poisoning?

Did you bring them to her, put them in her face during some kind of terrible fight that day? And then leave her to it?

It's just my theory but I think also a fact.

Trust me, your guilt will fade. We belong together. You know we do.

Meet me in Florence. There's a flight at 11:40 pm, change in Rome. I'll pick you up.

Love you.

Joanne clicked the phone off and put it back where it had been. Her hand was clutching her wineglass so hard she thought it might break. She drank the whole thing in one gulp and poured the rest of the bottle into her glass. Russell came out and grabbed his phone and keys.

"Hey, see ya." He reached over and gave her a hug, but her body remained rigid, stiff. "I'll let you know about our court dates." She didn't answer. "You okay?" She nodded. "Okay, then." He opened the door and walked to his car. She watched him get in and drive away.

She picked up her bag and dialed a number. It went to voicemail. "Tim, I wanted to let you know I'm going out of town. You can reach me at this number if you need me. I'll call Steven and let him know too. Bye." Leaving her son would be hard. But it was just temporary.

She threw some things into a suitcase. Cold weather or warm? Warm. Then she grabbed the black bag and flung it over her shoulder. She shut off the lights and walked to her car. Seventy-five thousand dollars in cash. She could go anywhere. And if it ran out, she could just blackmail Ava for more. Wasn't that how the game was played? She turned on the engine and headed toward Philadelphia. I-95 South. That was what she wanted. To keep moving south, away from this place. To lie in the sun and drink fruity drinks. To sleep until noon and read mystery novels. To not take care of anyone or anything. Whatever came after that was yet to be determined.

"Live, laugh, love, Ava, isn't that your motto? I'm going to live, all right. And I'm going to laugh all the way to the bank with your money. And love? No. Live, laugh, and fuck someone over. That's what I'm going to do." She'd decided her relationship with Ava was just beginning.

ACKNOWLEDGMENTS

As always, many thanks to my children, Eva Elizabeth and Ian, for your patience and understanding, your ideas, editorial assistance, and excitement when you read a good review or see my books tucked on a shelf at the library. I couldn't do any of this without you.

To Caitlin Alexander, the developmental editor who has been with me for three books and counting, your ability to resolve my timeline and plot issues has saved me more than once. Thank you for the numerous phone calls, notes and advice, and sense of humor. Your restructuring and polishing of my writing so that it is coherent has saved me three times. I look forward to book number four.

To Liz Pearsons, you probably don't know that sometimes when I send off an email to you, I'm privately panicking that the task in front of me is beyond my skill set. More than once, your calm, directed responses have set me back on track. I appreciate your encouragement and never-ending patience with me more than you know.

To Dr. Jack Gibbons, thank you for the fabulous title for this book and for letting me pick your brain about growing up Catholic in Philadelphia. The many conversations we have had added tremendous depth and descriptiveness to my writing. I appreciate you as an advisor and a boss. And I'm forever indebted to you for teaching me how to make the perfect martini—rocks on the side.

To Lisa Field, many thanks for reading my work and brainstorming ideas in between seeing patients. And for not ignoring my texts when I'm in a quandary. Your help is always appreciated.

Many thanks to my coworkers who have tolerated my moods, my bouts of writing during work time, and my disorganization. You know who you are, Yolanda Hughes, Steve Respher, Mike Zanotti, Lance Stahl, Jacob Baiden, Christine Martinelli, Jack Gibbons, Patty James, Beth Mackley, and Coleen Serzan. The laughs we've had at work have kept me sane.

To my husband, Shawn Graham, many thanks for finding and sending me the lost file of *The Book of James* when I thought it was gone forever. If you hadn't discovered that file on the old computer, I'm not sure I would have had the fortitude to rewrite the entire book. It was that one file that started me on this journey and I am forever grateful.

And to my grandmother Emily Heal, I will never forget your encouragement when I finished the first draft of my first novel. Your words push me forward to keep working no matter how hard it gets or how long it takes. I think of you often and miss you. You were a woman way ahead of your time.

ABOUT THE AUTHOR

Photo © 2017 June Day Photography

Ellen J. Green was born and raised in Upstate New York. She moved to Philadelphia to attend Temple University, where she earned her degrees in psychology. She has worked in the psychiatric ward of a maximum security correctional facility for fifteen years. She also holds an MFA degree in creative writing from Fairleigh Dickinson University. The author of Amazon Charts bestseller *Twist of Faith* and *The Book of James*, Ms. Green lives in southern New Jersey with her two children.